THE
NIGHT
THEY STOLE
MANHATTAN

THE
NIGHT
THEY STOLE
MANHATTAN

by Lewis Orde and Bill Michaels

G.P. PUTNAM'S SONS
NEW YORK

Library of Congress Cataloging In Publication Data

Orde, Lewis.
    The night they stole Manhattan.

    I. Michaels, Bill.   Joint author.   II. Title.
PZ4.068Ni 1980   [PS3565.R38]   813'.5'4   79-25392
ISBN 0-399-12489-6

To Harvey Klinger

Contents

THE RETREAT   9

BOOK I—THE GENERAL   23

BOOK II—THE RECRUITING CAMPAIGN   67

BOOK III—THE INVASION   127

BOOK IV—OPERATION APPLEJACK   201

THE
RETREAT

THE WHOLE DAMNED MESS was Washington's fault; Peter Stiehl was certain of it. Since Vietnam, the Americans had been going out of their way to prove their days of meddling in the internal affairs of other nations were over. No more would they interfere, nor would they allow other states within their sphere of influence to launch military ventures which might eventually bring the world's accusing finger pointing back to Washington. There had been the Mayagüez incident, of course, when the United States gave a rare demonstration that it had not gone completely soft, but that was Indochina, a long way from the seething bush of Angola, where Peter Stiehl now found himself.

The plan had been beautiful in its simplicity. South African troops, reinforced by arms and supplies from Israel, would drive into Angola from the south and scatter the Cubans who were backing the communists. Trained for the conditions, the South Africans would overwhelm the Cubans. When that was accomplished, there would be nothing to stop the remaining communist forces from being routed. Until the White House stepped in,

11

pressuring the Israelis, telling them that their arms supply from Washington would be terminated if they supported the South African attack. The Israelis backed down, and South African units—already ten miles inside Angola, forcing the Cubans into panic-stricken flight—were left to pull out.

Stiehl sat awkwardly on top of a Land Rover, legs dangling down over the radiator grille, a Sterling submachine gun cradled gently in his arms. He was angry with the Americans. First, they had let down the South Africans, his own people. Secondly, they had let him down personally; even a mercenary was entitled to some support when he was opposing a communist takeover. Everyone knew about the domino principle; if Angola fell, which African nation would be next?

Christ! If ever a country needed to have its foreign policy straightened out, it was the United States.

The sound of footsteps made Stiehl look up. His untroubled blue eyes took in the small clearing and the three Americans who worked with him—clipped eagles, Vietnam veterans who had hired themselves out to mercenary recruiters because they could find no work at home. What did they think of their government? Stiehl was tempted to ask them but refrained since he knew they would defend it. Even after this betrayal, they would remain loyal and would support the decisions which made the Statue of Liberty look as if she were standing on her head. Jogging his memory for the source of the quote, he finally remembered it had been made by Ho Chi Minh at the height of the Vietnam War. Annoyed that he should use the same words as the Vietnamese leader to describe American policy, he pushed the thought from his mind. His reasons for criticism certainly were not the same.

After sliding down from the Land Rover, he walked across the clearing toward the three men. He could sense their nervousness as a predator smells fear in its quarry. Ten miles separated them from the border and safety; it would be a long ten miles, even in the Land Rover. They had heard rumors about Americans being captured by the communists, tried and executed immediately. Now the minds of the three Americans dwelled on the same

12

frightening possibility awaiting them. Better get started, Stiehl decided, before their nerve really cracks.

"Ready to roll?" he asked.

The three men gazed at him, sheep looking to their leader, .hope in their eyes that Stiehl would lead them to safety. God, what he wouldn't give for a company of crack South African regulars right now, not these three lost Americans, who had each put in a thirteen-month tour of duty in Vietnam and thought they knew it all. In this kind of situation the South Africans were like gold compared with American pewter. What couldn't he do with the company he used to command, before the role of mercenary had been thrust upon him? What magic couldn't he perform with those men? A battalion of Cubans between that company and the border would have been swept aside without breaking pace, annihilated, left to rot as fertilizer for the vegetation.

"Let's do it then. Once we get near the border, we should receive support from my own people." He hoisted his tall, rangy frame into the Land Rover and slid into the front seat, checking that he had a round in the chamber of the Sterling. Behind, he heard one man operate the bolt of the thirty-caliber machine gun mounted between the seats.

The Land Rover started off slowly, bumping across the clearing, growling in low gear as it entered the darkness of the trees and followed the rough trail toward the border. Stiehl had no doubt there would be an ambush. There had to be one, unless the Cubans were unbelievably naïve; they must be watching out for stragglers of the retreat.

"What about it?" the driver whispered after four miles had passed without incident.

"Another couple of miles," Stiehl guessed. "Where the trail narrows down to single-vehicle width. Where we can't turn around and run."

"You reckon they know about us?" The driver's voice contained a touch of the Midwest.

Stiehl laughed quietly, a grim chuckle which tickled the hair on the driver's neck. "What do you think?"

The man made no further comment, concentrating on his driving, unwilling to hear more.

A mile farther on, Stiehl ordered the driver to pull off to the side, to enter among the trees. He got out and began covering signs of their passage with branches and shrubs torn from other areas. Satisfied that a quick glance would not discern their movement, he grouped the three Americans around him. "If there is a setup, it'll be about a mile downtrail. Only they'll be waiting for vehicles, not men on foot."

"What about the thirty?" one man asked, glancing at the machine gun on the Land Rover. "That's our best weapon."

Stiehl shook his head. "Surprise is our best weapon. The thirty's useless in this kind of scrap." He slung the Sterling over his shoulder, checked the cluster of fragmentation hand grenades hanging from the straps of his pack, and set off, waving for the others to follow.

None of the Americans knew what to make of Stiehl. He looked like a soldier—tall, well built, crisp—but there the similarity ended. To their way of thinking, he did not act like a soldier. There were no set pieces in Stiehl's military repertoire. Plans were finalized only at the last moment; he was always ready to improvise. The Americans wondered how they would have fared in Vietnam with a commander like Stiehl, outguessing the Vietcong at their own game, always having an extra move in his pocket. They knew he had been a captain in the South African Army before resigning his commission. Rumor had it that he was forced to resign after leading a counterinsurgency force across the border into Mozambique in a retaliation raid on black guerrillas. His mistake had been that he was too successful, totally eliminating the guerrilla camp. The search-and-destroy mission—twisted by the international press into an unprovoked massacre of women and children—had been Stiehl's downfall. Regretfully the South African High Command had asked for his resignation to quell the rising tide of foreign criticism. Government officials admitted the error freely, but the country could not afford to have a man like Stiehl on its payroll. Without a job, Stiehl had taken the path of many before him,

14

that of hired soldier, seeing action in Biafra and now in Angola, with a less dangerous spell in Saudi Arabia training royalist troops. The assignments had paid well, buying him a home in Port Elizabeth, providing luxuries which would have been impossible on a captain's pay. He had even found the time to indulge a yearning to write, although the manuscript—on a mercenary's life—was now lying unfinished in the den of his Port Elizabeth home; perhaps the Angola exercise would provide the final touches.

Twenty minutes passed as the four men crept stealthily through the bush. Stiehl kept the lead, stopping every minute or two to survey what lay ahead, glancing quickly left and right, listening carefully. The Americans looked at one another in partial bewilderment. Was Stiehl really capable of detecting changes in the bush? Or was he just pretending, using psychology to fill them with confidence? None of them had the slightest idea where they had left the Land Rover, let alone where the border was. As never before, they had to trust Stiehl.

Stiehl stopped again, dropping to one knee, the Sterling off his shoulder and in his hands in one fluid movement. The Americans froze. Quietly Stiehl inched his way back, gesturing for them to lie flat on the dry, baked ground.

"Smell," he whispered.

The man who had operated the thirty caliber lifted his nose into the air and sniffed experimentally. He shook his head, unable to smell anything.

"Cigar smoke." Stiehl mouthed the words. He turned away and began slithering on his stomach, the submachine gun resting across the crook of his arms. The Americans watched the ridged rubber soles of his canvas jungle boots disappear into the bush, knowing they were being left alone, willing him to return.

Stiehl maintained the low crawl for thirty yards, stopping only when he heard voices. Spanish. But not the accent of Spain. He had heard it before, from Cuban soldiers captured during the short Angola affair. Inch by inch, he crawled forward, moving bushes with his hands as he strove for a better look.

There were eight of them, sitting on the ground around two

15

American-made jeeps with no markings, part of the loot from Vietnam which had somehow found its way to this corner of the earth. On one jeep was mounted a recoilless rifle; on the other was a Browning fifty-caliber machine gun. Off to one side, Stiehl noticed two more men and guessed them to be the officers. One was smoking a thick dark cigar the pungent aroma of which had revealed their position.

Stiehl waited five minutes more, his eyes continually flicking to the radio transmitter in the jeep with the Browning. That had to be the first target, destroyed before the Cubans could get out a message.

He began to crawl away, confident that his unit was facing only ten men, already working out the plan of action. "Two jeeps, ten men," he whispered, rejoining the Americans. "Fifty-caliber machine gun and a recoilless rifle are the main armaments. We've got to take out the jeep with the Browning immediately; it's got a transmitter." He pointed to the man who had driven the Land Rover. "As we open fire, you lob in a grenade. Don't miss."

Followed by the three men, Stiehl returned to the perimeter of the Cuban position. He stopped in the same place as before, pointing through gaps in the bush at the patrol, ten soldiers waiting for the unmistakable growl of a Land Rover coming down the trail. Stiehl smiled grimly; the Cubans were so confident they had not even posted a lookout.

The four men began to spread out, with the Land Rover driver ensuring that he was within easy range of the radio jeep. Stiehl and the two other men selected their areas of fire. To avoid casualties of their own, the firefight had to be over within seconds. If even one of the Cubans managed to reach either jeep, he would be able to return devastating fire.

Stiehl chose a group of four men, including the two officers. Lying prone, elbows on the ground, he sighted along the stubby barrel of the Sterling, gently taking up the slack of the trigger, knowing the others were waiting for the first round to shatter the eerie stillness of the bush.

The Sterling's savage chatter ripped the silence apart, smashing back off the trees to hammer at the eardrums. Scores of birds soared into erratic, terrified flight; dozens of small animals scampered through the undergrowth. The Cuban officer with the cigar jerked upright, a marionette yanked savagely by unseen hands. He lurched drunkenly, like a man suffering an epileptic fit, teeth biting through the cigar, shredding tobacco as his nervous system registered the two bullets which had slammed into his side. The officer with him spun around, mouth open in screaming agony, red stains spreading quickly across his chest as he crashed to the ground.

On the edge of his vision, Stiehl saw other figures catapulted into violent motion, spinning, sprawling, twitching grotesquely as the last of life's energy oozed away. Maybe the Americans had a lot to learn about fighting in the bush, just as they had to learn about jungle combat, Stiehl thought, but when it came down to the actual shoot-out, they held their own. He switched the Sterling's aim to the other two men in his selected group. The face of one disappeared in a haze of red as bullets stitched a rising pattern from his rib cage. The other man threw himself to the ground and began scurrying under the hail of bullets toward the jeep with the transmitter. As he reached the vehicle, a grenade arced lazily through the air and landed in the back, detonating almost immediately. The man's screams were loud enough to be heard above the cacophony of noise as he staggered to his feet, fingers clawing at his lacerated eyes, blood streaming down his face as he stumbled blindly in Stiehl's direction. The South African watched dispassionately for a moment, then lifted the Sterling and held down the trigger in a short burst which lifted the Cuban three yards through the air before dropping him to the ground in a ragged, bloody heap.

As suddenly as it had started, the firefight was over. Stiehl got to his feet, standing warily, the Sterling pointed at the blood-spattered bodies, a fresh magazine inserted. The three Americans also rose, scanning the area. Except for some wisps of smoke from the shattered jeep, nothing moved. Stiehl walked forward to turn over the body of the cigar-smoking officer with his boot. The man stared upward, eyes forever fixed wide open, tongue hanging out from the side of his mouth; flakes of wet tobacco clung obscenely to his lips and teeth.

"Well done," Stiehl said quietly, closing his eyes for an instant as if to blot out the scene. He felt drained, emotionless. Killing always left him the same way. It was a task that had to be done, but he could take no pleasure in it. "Let's get the hell out of here before their friends turn up."

The Land Rover driver made himself comfortable behind the wheel of the remaining jeep. Stiehl took up a position in the back, examining the recoilless rifle, loading it from the rack of shells fixed to the floor. He felt the jeep shudder into motion and sat back, wondering if they would make the border without further trouble.

"Reckon there's more, sir?" the driver asked.

Stiehl took careful note of the question. Although he held the rank of colonel in this ragtag and bobtail army, none of the Americans had ever called him "sir" before. Perhaps they were finally accepting his authority. "No idea," he replied truthfully. "I guess we'll have to wait and see."

By Stiehl's estimation, the border was only two miles away when his unit ran into the ambush—a second Cuban patrol, smaller than the first, but all the more dangerous because of its unexpectedness. The initial blast of gunfire shattered the windshield of the jeep. The driver clapped a hand to his face, feeling in numbed shock the four-inch gash made by flying glass.

"Get off the trail!" Stiehl yelled.

The shouted command was unnecessary. Using one hand, the driver slewed the jeep into the bush. More bullets caromed off the metalwork as the vehicle disappeared into the dense growth, bumping over obstacles, almost throwing out its passengers. The four men jumped to the ground and spread out, listening for the sound of further gunfire to betray their attackers' position.

Tranquillity settled slowly as the bush swallowed up the incident. Nature's sounds returned, the singing of birds, monkeys chattering. Chalk up one for Castro's inefficiency, Stiehl decided. We walk straight into an ambush, and our only casualty is a cut from flying glass. If there's one thing you never make a

18

mistake about, it's an ambush. Once you do, the roles become reversed; it's the attacker who goes on the defensive, his chance lost. Stiehl returned to the jeep, studying the recoilless rifle. His eyes rested on the sighting gun fixed to the top, which, with its small tracer round, paved the way for the high-explosive shell that followed the same trajectory. Dare he risk firing the tracer into the bush across the trail, hoping for the noise of it striking metal? Or a scream as it burned through flesh? He glanced sideways, indicating his intentions to the other men. They began crawling forward, closer to the trail.

Estimating the position from which he had last heard fire, Stiehl lined up the weapon and fired the sighting gun, watching the tracer flash through the trees, praying it was not deflected by a branch. He listened intently. There was nothing, not even the satisfaction of return fire. Reloading, he moved the weapon a few degrees to the right and fired again. This time there was a short burst of retaliatory fire, high, undirected. Stiehl moved the heavy gun even farther to the right, preparing to fire a third time. The whiplash crack of the tracer leaving the tube was lost in an almost instant shout of pain. Before the yell could die away, Stiehl sent the explosive shell screaming after the tracer. The deafening report of the main gun was echoed as the shell found its target. A sheet of flame roared upward as the gas tank of a jeep erupted. Simultaneously three Sterling submachine guns added their insane chattering to the noise as the Americans cut down two Cuban soldiers trying to escape from the inferno.

Stiehl offered up a silent plea that South African border patrols could hear the sounds of battle. They had to be close by, on the lookout for troops approaching the border. If they knew the force was friendly, they might even risk further international censure by crossing the border to help.

"Let's go!" Stiehl yelled, jumping into the driver's seat. "We're moving out!"

The Americans raced to the jeep and threw themselves aboard as it broke cover. Closer to the border, the trail began to spread out into open country, trees and scrub hewn down, stumps flat-

19

tened to create a no-man's-land. A shout from behind made Stiehl turn his head for an instant, long enough to see a second jeep in pursuit, its fifty-caliber machine gun spitting an erratic but nonetheless terrifying shower of bullets.

"Hang on!" Stiehl rammed the jeep into a lower gear and pressed hard on the gas. The little vehicle bucked violently, rocking back and forth as it struggled to cover the uneven ground. A scattering of Sterling fire came from behind as one of the Americans opened fire defiantly at the Cuban jeep.

A shadow loomed over Stiehl, cutting out the sun. A second passed before he recognized the clattering sound of helicopter blades beating against air. He glanced up to see the craft hovering overhead at four hundred feet, appearing out of nowhere, a conjurer's trick. The rondels on its fuselage told him all he needed to know. South African. A friend when he needed one most. Now he could relax; the helicopter would take care of their pursuers. He eased off the gas, feeling the jeep slow, riding more smoothly. His shoulders began to droop as the tension drained out of his body, replaced by a growing feeling of relief. Another few minutes and it would be all over; he would be home.

But wait! Why was the helicopter hovering over him? Why was it not about to launch a wave of death and destruction on the second jeep, still six hundred yards behind?

"Wave! For Christ's sake, wave!" he screamed as the terrifying truth suddenly became clear. They were in an unmarked jeep taken from the Cubans, and they were about to get blown off the face of the earth by the very people he had been counting on to save them. He took a hand off the steering wheel and waved frantically upward, shouting at the Americans to do the same. The jeep slowed even more as the helicopter descended for a closer look before opening fire. It veered off to the right and swung around, coming in low, the fifty-caliber gun in its side pointed directly at the jeep. Stiehl braked violently, no longer worried about the threat posed by the second jeep; the helicopter, piloted by his own countrymen, presented the greatest danger. He jumped to the ground and began signaling with both hands above his head. Then he pulled a dirty white handkerchief

20

from his pocket, waving it wildly. His relief was indescribable when the gunner finally waved back.

"There!" Stiehl yelled through cupped hands. "Back there!" He pointed excitedly at the second jeep, which had also stopped and was beginning to turn around. "Cubans!"

The gunner never heard the shouted words, but the movement of the second jeep was enough to make him understand. He relayed the information to the pilot. The helicopter swung around again, climbed another hundred feet, and hurled itself in swift pursuit of the fleeing jeep, slashing the distance in seconds. The man behind the jeep's machine gun tried to stage a final, defiant defense, firing long, useless bursts into the sky as the vehicle rocked crazily beneath him; he was swept aside as the helicopter's firepower transformed the jeep into scrap metal.

Stiehl waited for the helicopter to return before he got back into the jeep, feeling secure as the shadow remained over him during the rest of the journey. At the border, jubilant South African soldiers welcomed the four men as heroes, slapping them on the back, offering them food, cigarettes.

As they parted, Stiehl shook hands formally with the three young Americans, thanking them for their efforts. He was going home to Port Elizabeth; the others would get home as best they could to spend their money, grateful that they had escaped from Angola. "Look after yourselves," he said. "And stay in touch. You never know when we might bump into each other again."

The three men watched Stiehl being driven away in a South African Army staff car. He never looked back, as if he had already cast them from his mind. They picked up their weapons and began walking toward the army truck that was waiting for them. They sat back exhausted as it moved off.

Book One

THE
GENERAL

1

SIX BLUE-AND-WHITE police cars, emergency lights still flashing, were angled into the curb at Sixth Avenue and Forty-ninth Street in Manhattan. Police officers armed with revolvers and shotguns crouched behind the vehicles, peering furtively at the bank on the corner. Other uniformed men blocked off the streets and turned away traffic to keep the area clear.

The bank's silent alarm had been tripped ten minutes earlier. Police had responded immediately. Blockading the bank's entrances and isolating the building, they prepared to wait until the men inside decided to make the first move.

A police captain appeared with a bullhorn. He leaned across the hood of one car, directing his words at the glass doors of the bank. "You inside! The bank is surrounded. There is no chance of escape. Throw out your weapons, and come out with your hands raised." As the amplified echoes drifted away, the words were repeated in Spanish.

All eyes turned toward the bank doors. Weapons were shifted from one hand to the other, sweat wiped off palms as the period

25

of waiting played on the policemen's nerves. There was no telling what could happen in a situation like this. Would the guy—or was there more than one?—come out and give himself up? Would he come out shooting? Or would he try for a hostage situation, grab one of the bank's employees or a customer as a passport to safety? There was no knowing what could happen.

One of the glass doors opened slowly. Weapons became rock-steady, trained on the single figure of a slim middle-aged woman, blond hair looking as if she had just come from the beauty parlor, the knee-length cashmere coat obviously hand-tailored. The guns were lowered as the arm around the woman's neck and the handgun pressed into the side of her face became visible. It was a hostage situation, a time for patience. Wear the guy down; listen to his demands; humor him; keep him calm; always let him believe he can get away with it. Until it's time to strike.

"We got hostages!" a voice screamed.

"How many?" the police captain asked. He could barely make out the man behind the woman hostage—he seemed young, twenties maybe, white, could be Hispanic.

"Plenty. You try anything, and we'll blow them away."

"We're not trying anything." The captain turned to the patrolman beside him. "Check up on that emergency unit we asked for. Find out where the hell they've got to." He looked back at the bank. "Stay cool, man. We don't want anyone hurt today."

The man holding the hostage made no reply. He backed through the door into the bank, disappearing from sight. The captain reached into his car, picked up the mike, and asked to be patched through on the telephone circuit to the bank. The phone rang twice before it was snatched off the hook.

"Yeah!"

"This is Captain Mastro, NYPD. We wanna talk."

"What about?"

"How about letting a few of your hostages go? Show your good faith."

"Then what?"

"Then we'll know we're dealing with people we can trust."

26

"How do we know we can trust you?"

"Chance you gotta take. How many hostages you holding?"

"Over twenty. Bank staff and customers. And we ain't letting none of them go till we get what we want."

"What do you want?" Keep them talking, Mastro told himself. The longer they're in there, the less chance of someone stopping a bullet. Leave it long enough, and they'll be begging to surrender.

"We wanna car. And a plane," came the answer from inside the bank. "All gassed up. And a pilot."

"What kind of plane?" Mastro began to feel he had them now. This was his fifth hostage situation, and he'd never lost one yet.

"Any kind of fucking plane!" the voice screamed. "Just to get us outta here!"

"Where to?"

"Cuba! Algeria! We'll tell the pilot when we're good and ready."

And you think they want you, buddy? Mastro thought. You'd be better off in an American jail. "I'm working on it right now. Just take it easy, man." He looked sideways, relieved to see a man in a blue baseball cap and blue fatigues running toward him.

"Hanratty, Emergency Service Unit," the man said, crouching down alongside Mastro.

"You took your sweet time."

Hanratty ignored the gibe. "What's the situation in there?"

"Silent alarm was tripped. We think there are two of them at least. With a bankful of hostages."

"Anyone hurt?"

"No. We've kept them talking. They want a car to the airport and a plane with a pilot."

Hanratty clapped Mastro on the shoulder. "Good. We'll take it from here; have them out of there in a minute." He took the mike from Mastro. "This is Lieutenant Hanratty. You read me?"

"Yeah. Whaddya want?"

27

"How many of you are there in the bank?"

"What's it to you?"

"We need to know for the car and the plane."

There was a long pause from within the bank, then: "Two."

"I've got a proposition for you," Hanratty said. "Listen good, and think it over carefully. We're willing to trade two unarmed police officers for all your hostages. You got that?"

"Fuck you and the horse you rode in on."

Hanratty looked at Mastro. "They aren't that dumb. Pity. I'll try another angle." He picked up the mike again. "How about letting all your hostages go except two? You've got a bankful of people right now; you might get jumpy. We don't want to see anyone hurt. Keep two, one for each of you. Otherwise, how are you going to get everyone into the car?"

"That car ready?"

"Sure."

"We'll get back to you."

Hanratty and Mastro watched over the hood of the car. A minute passed; two; then the bank's glass doors opened. People streamed out, blinking in the sudden sunlight, staring uncomprehendingly at the wall of police cars. Some of the released hostages broke into a run toward the nearest police officers; others stood in a daze, unable to believe their ordeal was over. Figures in blue moved quickly toward them to lead them away, leaving the sidewalk between the bank and police cars clear.

"Get me the bank manager," Hanratty said. Mastro trotted toward the closest group of freed hostages. He returned moments later with a man wearing a light gray suit.

"What's it like in there?" Hanratty asked.

"They've kept back two people. Regular customers, woman and her daughter."

"The one they brought out before?" Mastro asked.

"That's the mother."

"How old?"

"Mother's maybe fifty. Daughter's about twenty-five."

"What about the two men?" Hanratty asked. "They getting nervous?"

"Yeah. You guys had better do something quick."

"Did they say anything when they hit your bank?"

"FALN," the manager replied.

Hanratty nodded. FALN—Fuerzas Armadas de Liberación Nacional, the Puerto Rican liberation movement. There was no way of predicting how those lunatics would react. He turned around and waved his arms. A plain black Oldsmobile Cutlass, driven by another man in blue fatigues, moved forward. Hanratty picked up the mike again.

"You in there! Your car's here. See it?"

"Yeah."

"You wanna driver. Or you wanna handle it yourself?"

"What about the plane?"

"Being made ready now at La Guardia," Hanratty lied. "TWA Seven-twenty-seven." Hell, he didn't even know if TWA had any 727s or if they even used La Guardia, and right now he didn't care. All he wanted was those crazies out of the bank before anyone got hurt.

"How do we know you're telling the truth?"

"You don't. But you're holding the hostages."

"Okay. We're coming out. No tricks."

Ten seconds passed; then the bank doors were opened. The middle-aged woman who had appeared earlier was pushed forward, a man's arm around her throat, gun still pressed into her face. Behind came a younger woman, attractive, long blond hair falling to her shoulders. There was a gun at her head as well. Moving slowly, the small group began to cross the sidewalk. Hanratty signaled, and the Cutlass's four doors were thrown wide open.

The leading gunman saw the flurry of movement and tightened his grip around the older woman's throat. "Don't do nothing! I'll blow her fucking brains out!"

Hanratty went to the bullhorn. "We're opening the car doors for you. We don't want any accidents."

Reassured, the group continued across the sidewalk. When they were only ten feet from the Cutlass, Hanratty lifted his right hand and touched the peak of his baseball cap, pushing it

29

back marginally. Sharp reports from two high-powered rifles rang out. The man holding the daughter leaped back through the air, a red-rimmed hole suddenly appearing in the center of his forehead, the back of his skull shattered. The other man twisted back, clutching at his shoulder, face contorted in pain and rage at being tricked. As the two women hostages screamed in terror, he brought up the handgun and fired twice. Both rifles barked again. The gun flew from the man's grasp, spinning away across the sidewalk.

Hanratty and Mastro rushed forward. Mastro clutched the younger woman, holding her face into his shoulder, trying to stifle her hysterical screams. Hanratty went to the other woman, and bent over her. One look was all he needed. The first bullet had torn into her right arm; the second had taken her in the center of the face as she spun around, smashing through the bridge of the nose, exiting in the center of the skull. Hanratty turned away, calling for a blanket; then he joined Mastro.

"She all right?"

"God knows," Mastro replied. "I'm not a shrink. How would you feel if you saw your mother blown to pieces in front of your eyes? What made you pull shit like that?"

"In my judgment, it was the only way. There was no plane, nothing. We were dealing with two politically activated terrorists. The longer we left them, the more desperate they would have become. This way we saved one."

"Try that justification on her," Mastro said disgustedly, nodding at the young woman in his arms. "It might look great on your report, but she won't buy it."

Hanratty seemed not to notice Mastro's anger. "Better check who she is, notify the next of kin."

"That's a job you can do." Mastro took the young woman's shoulder bag and passed it to Hanratty. The lieutenant opened it to check through till he found a driver's license. He looked at the name, then at a small color photograph of a family group he also found. Then at the name in the license again.

"We've got troubles," he finally said.

"Huh?" Mastro turned his attention from the woman. "What's that supposed to mean?"

"Check this out. Does that name ring a bell with that photograph?"

Mastro glanced at the license, then at the photograph Hanratty was holding. "Holy fuck," was all he could think of to say.

The Senate subcommittee session had dragged on for three hours, and nobody seemed to be paying attention anymore. Even the reporters in the press gallery were doodling idly while they waited for the witness to finish his testimony. Then they all could go home. Of the five senators on the panel, only one was showing any interest in the witness; all the others were looking elsewhere, at the spectators, at the ceilings, at the walls.

One of the reporters nudged the man next to him, indicating the witness. "You'd think by now Old Stoneass would have gone off this kick, wouldn't you? Found some other way to keep himself in the public eye. All he does is babble on and on about the same old invasion scare and how we're in no shape to defend ourselves."

"He makes some kind of sense, I guess," the other man acknowledged grudgingly. "Depends on whether or not you're in the arms business."

"I reckon he's being paid off. Start a scare and get the factories full of orders. His own included."

The object of their discussion sat ramrod-stiff behind the witness table. His steel gray hair was cropped short, brushed back. The blue, almost violet eyes seemed to contain a smoldering fire beneath the bushy white eyebrows. He was dressed simply, the accent on neatness rather than on elegance—a perfectly pressed navy blue suit, a crisp white shirt, and a red-and-blue-striped tie. The only piece of jewelry he wore was a tiny pin on the left lapel of his jacket; from close up it could be recognized as the white stars and blue background of the Congressional Medal of Honor.

"We think you've made your point, General Huckleby," one of the senators said, "and we promise to look into it and make the appropriate recommendations."

Major General Harlan Stone Huckleby, United States Army, retired, fixed the senator with a frosty glare. "Sir, I could never make this particular point strongly enough. As a patriot—that

31

means a man who loves his country above all else, for the benefit of those of you who have forgotten the word—I will do everything in my power to make certain the American public is fully aware of the perilous situation the United States faces. I will ensure that every citizen of this country knows how abysmally prepared our armed forces are to repel any kind of invasion. In Europe, for example, a handful of our tanks would be forced to hold off seventy communist armored divisions should the Soviets decide to attack the Federal Republic of Germany . . . as one day they will."

"Yes, yes, yes," the senator cut in wearily. "We've been through all this before." He raised a hand to stifle a yawn, hoping the old war-horse would not take offense. But Christ, how many times was he expected to listen to this claptrap about the state of unpreparedness of the armed forces? Everyone past grade ten knew we could wipe out the Russians a hundred times over, and they could do the same for us. Nobody would dare start a war anymore.

In the press gallery, a reporter from the Washington *Post* looked down at the biography on Major General Harlan Stone Huckleby he had taken from the newspaper's files. It read like something from a John Wayne movie script. Enlisted in the army at seventeen. Jumped in Normandy and during the Arnhem offensive. Received appointment to West Point after the war. As a major he won the Congressional Medal of Honor in Korea for leading a bayonet charge on a heavily fortified Red Chinese position. Served as an observer with the French in Vietnam, then as an adviser to the South Vietnamese during the early sixties. Finally went on to command a division over there when the pace began to pick up. The reporter smiled when he came to the next batch of facts. Huckleby had suffered one drawback: a big mouth that continually got him into trouble for advocating that the United States should invade North Vietnam. Passed over twice for promotion to lieutenant general because of his outspokenness, and finally retired from active duty in 1968 at the age of forty-five, with twenty-eight years of active duty behind him. As far as the army chiefs were concerned, they had not lost a good general officer; they had merely disposed of an embarrassing problem.

Huckleby had married well, the reporter read, to Alice Nelson, only child of a chemical magnate named Howard Nelson, when he returned from Korea after winning the Medal of Honor. His forced retirement from the army had coincided almost to the day with the death of his father-in-law, so he had stepped in as president of Howson Chemicals, exchanging his filigreed cap and the double black stripe down the sides of his uniform trousers for command of a multimillion-dollar chemical concern. And from that weighty platform—here, the reporter began to smile again—Huckleby had continued to slam the government for inactivity in its defense of the country. Freed of any military restrictions, Huckleby had been only too willing to appear as a witness before Senate subcommittees on national defense. If the army had thought that by putting him into mothballs, it could shut him up, it had been sorely mistaken; Huckleby had become more vociferous than ever.

Looking up from the biography, the reporter returned his attention to Major General Harlan Stone Huckleby, U.S. Army, retired, wondering who had blessed him with the nickname of Old Stoneass. It had certainly stuck, just as Blood and Guts had stayed with Patton. Vaguely the reporter recalled that Huckleby had been wounded while leading the bayonet charge in Korea, fired on from behind after he had broken through the Chinese line, a bullet embedded in his buttocks, refusing to call for a medic until the position had been secured.

As the reporter pondered the unusual nickname, a uniformed guard approached the retired general and passed him a white envelope. Huckleby glanced down, scanned the note, then abruptly got up from the table, excusing himself to the panel of senators. When he returned, less than a minute later, his face was ashen, his walk unsteady. He had to reach out for support as he moved to his seat. When he spoke, the clipped, assertive tone had disappeared.

"Gentlemen, you . . . you must excuse me. I . . . I have just received some tragic . . . tragic . . ." His voice faltered

33

and finally broke. He looked down helplessly at the tabletop, eyelids blinking in a regular rhythm. The five senators on the panel fidgeted uneasily, confused over what could have happened. Huckleby coughed twice into his hand, wiped his eyes with a handkerchief, and then called on all his resources to face the panel.

"Gentlemen"—the voice was firmer now, the man more in control of his emotions—"I have just received the tragic news that my wife, Alice, has been fatally wounded during a bank robbery by FALN terrorists in New York. My daughter, Linda, was with her at the time. As yet I am unaware of her condition."

A gasp of shock erupted around the committee room as, for the first time in almost an hour, all eyes were turned upon the witness. The chairman of the panel stood up, hands outspread in silent communication, uncertain what to say. Before he could think of anything, Huckleby squared his shoulders in a parade-ground stance.

"I am totally distraught by this news," he said. "But nothing on earth—particularly when it strikes so close to home—could illustrate more clearly what I have been saying. We are completely unprepared for a situation as simple as this, dealing with so-called liberation fighters on our own streets, scum with pistols. What chance do we have of defending ourselves against a concerted military operation against our own country? If nothing else can make you see this, please let my own tragedy bring it home."

As his words died away, Huckleby spun on his heel, shook off the helping hand of the guard, and strode toward the door. He flung it open, then turned around to face the committee room. "If you continue to do nothing, just sitting on your butts and believing everything's fine, you will all live to regret it. By God you will!"

Without another word he left the room, slamming the door on the stunned meeting.

2

THE SIX-BEDROOM house in the exclusive Upper Montclair section of New Jersey had always been too large for Major General Harlan Stone Huckleby's tastes, especially after the smaller homes to which he had been accustomed during his military career. Even when his daughter, Linda, had lived there, before moving to a condominium he had bought for her in Fort Lee—overlooking the Hudson River and upper Manhattan—the house had felt too large. It had been a present from his late father-in-law, however, and there was no gracious way Huckleby could refuse it. Now, three months after his wife's death, the house was like a mausoleum, filled with echoes and strange, haunting shadows.

The funeral had been a nightmare, and only his years of practice at withholding emotion had saved Huckleby from breaking down. Linda, however, had not been brought up in the same tradition. As they had walked away from the grave side, accepting sympathetic wishes from mourners, who had included three White House officials and a dozen general officers from all service branches—even the President had sent a letter of condolence—Linda had broken down and been carried, screaming, to one of the cars. She had started therapy immediately, and Huckleby gratefully acknowledged, she was pulling through, gradually washing from her mind the memory of her mother's slaughter.

Fortunately for Huckleby, the business he had inherited from his father-in-law, Howson Chemicals, kept him to a rigid schedule which did not permit him time to dwell on his grief. He rose promptly at six each morning, and left the house at exactly six-forty-five to be at the Newark headquarters of Howson Chemicals by seven-thirty, an hour before anyone else. It was the time of day he liked best, when he could work without fear of interruption; the early start reminded him of the army, a period in his life he liked to recall, the happy years before politics had taken over.

When he came downstairs, a blue silk dressing gown covering his shirt and trousers, the housekeeper had breakfast ready—a glass of freshly squeezed orange juice, two slices of toast, and a cup of black coffee. He ate quickly, listening with one ear to the continuous news report from WINS in New York. As he swallowed the last of the coffee, he slipped a tiny white pill into his mouth; he let it rest on the back of his tongue while the housekeeper removed the breakfast plates. The pill dissolved slowly, while Huckleby thought about the inconvenience of relying on pharmaceutical products for life support.

He had learned a year earlier about the atherosclerosis, the advanced and far more dangerous version of arteriosclerosis, a severe hardening of the coronary arteries which impaired the flow of blood to the heart. He had experienced a constricting pain in his shoulder and neck, usually after any kind of exercise, for several months. The doctor had listened to the symptoms before arranging an appointment for Huckleby with a heart specialist. The diagnosis had been simple: Look after yourself, eat carefully, and you could live for a few years yet; take chances, eat foolishly, smoke, and the next shareholder's letter from Howson Chemicals might be signed by someone else. Huckleby thought it somewhat inglorious that a national hero—albeit a dated one—was forced to rely on little white pills, even if his own company did manufacture them. During the commotion after his wife's death, he had taken three nitroglycerin pills within an hour since his chest threatened to burst. The third one, miraculously, had worked, finally lessening the pressure. He was proud that he had managed to keep the news of his own illness from his daughter, especially now, so soon after her mother's passing.

The sound of the housekeeper's voice asking what he wanted for dinner that night made Huckleby look up. The woman's friendly face made him force a smile onto his own. He had hired her shortly after the funeral, choosing her from dozens of other applicants sent by the agency because of her warm disposition. He told her he would be eating out and would be home late; if she wished, she could take off the entire day. Thanking him, the woman left the room to go about her chores.

Huckleby returned upstairs, threw his dressing gown onto the bed, and selected a tie. Over his suit, he put on a light topcoat, felt in his pocket to be certain he had a supply of pills, and returned downstairs. In the double garage, he got into his Cadillac Seville, settling himself comfortably into the driver's seat. Although he occasionally envied the sleek lines of the Mercedes his daughter drove, he considered it unpatriotic to own a foreign car; the Cadillac was his fifth in a row. Having pressed a button on the dashboard, he waited for the garage doors to open, then guided the car outside, where he let the engine warm up while he waited in the semicircular drive. The sky was clouding over, offering evidence of the early spring snow warning on the radio, and Huckleby shivered involuntarily. Satisfied that the engine was warm, he pushed the transmission into drive, turning on the wipers as the first snowflakes drifted lazily across the windshield.

The cobalt blue year-old Mercedes 450SLC coasted to a stop in the guest parking area of the luxury high-rise condominium building in Fort Lee. The driver's door swung open, and Linda Huckleby stepped out and reached back into the car for the two bags on which were printed the name Gucci. Straightening up, she read the notice about residents' being prohibited from parking in the guest area, and as always, she ignored it. The building management had not towed away her car yet, and she was fairly certain it would not start now.

Returning from her second visit of the week to the psychotherapist, Linda Huckleby felt that the treatment was working. Maybe it was the need to have someone to talk to, the pressure to spill out the memories that had plagued her since that terrible afternoon outside the bank. She had still not managed to discuss the event in any depth with her father, only mentioning it in passing terms, reflecting on it when she talked of her own progress. She had grown up in the shadow of a great man, and in many ways he still frightened her. No, she corrected herself; not frightened in the true sense of the word, as she had been during the bank robbery when the man had held a gun to her head. She simply remained in awe of her father. She loved him dearly and knew that his feelings for her were just as deep. But during any crisis he seemed to remain so aloof, so distant, like the times she had seen him on television or even that horrifying day when he had been relieved of his command and forced to resign from the army. No emotion had crossed his face, no trace of sorrow had impeded his speech as he talked to reporters after seeing the President. He had spoken about the situation in such a matter-of-fact manner that Linda was certain he possessed no feelings whatsoever. Yet she knew that this, too, was a wrong judgment. Her father did feel; he just kept his emotions bottled up inside, refusing to share them with the rest of the world.

At twenty-four, Linda displayed a degree of certainty and security which took other women half a lifetime to achieve, if they ever achieved it at all. Tall and slim, she possessed the style of a top fashion model, showing off to perfection the short ranch mink jacket and designer trousers she wore. Lustrous natural blond hair was swept back from a finely featured face, dropping down over her ears to lie casually on her shoulders. Violet eyes—inherited from her father—dominated her face, almost but not quite taking away attention from the high cheekbones and fine, straight nose.

Holding a bag in each hand, she entered the lobby of the building, not bothering to search for a key when she saw the doorman getting up from his seat to admit her. She flashed him a warm smile as he offered to take the bags up to her apartment on the fourteenth floor. Standing in the elevator, she wondered how much longer she would have to visit the therapist. He had said today he was pleased with her progress and hoped he could terminate treatment soon. But how soon, she wondered, was soon? Since that afternoon at the bank she had not returned to her job as manager of a small, exclusive art gallery on Madison Avenue and wondered how long her employers would allow her to be absent before seeking a replacement. She was not unduly worried, though; other galleries had sought her services, and with her fluency in Italian, French, and German she knew she would have no difficulty in finding other, suitable employment. One of the benefits of being an army brat, she mused, if a general's daughter can be called such. Wherever her father had been stationed, she had studied hard to learn the language.

On the fourteenth floor the doorman took the key and opened the apartment door. He followed Linda inside and left the bags on the couch in the living room. Linda handed him a two-dollar bill which had somehow found its way into her purse; like so many people, she detested the bills and got rid of them whichever way she could. The doorman did not object to receiving it. He touched the peak of his cap, wished her a good afternoon, and closed the apartment door quietly.

Linda shrugged herself out of the mink jacket and tossed it carelessly onto the couch. She unpacked her purchases, trying on each dress in front of the full-length mirror in the bedroom, bare feet digging luxuriously into the deep pile of the carpet. When the telephone rang, she dropped the dress she was holding and walked lithely over to the bedroom extension. She lifted the receiver and spoke into it, guessing the caller to be her father; he always rang after she had been to the therapist.

"How did it go today?" Huckleby asked.

"Better each time."

"So what did you buy yourself?"

"How do you know I bought anything?"

Huckleby chuckled richly at the question. "Because I've known you for too long."

Linda pouted at the telephone. "Are you coming over tonight for dinner?"

"Depends on what you're cooking."

"What would you like?" Linda prided herself on her cooking, as she prided herself in everything she did. She appreciated it whenever her father took an interest in food because his tastes had become simpler of late, denying her the opportunity to experiment.

"Better keep it light. It's been a rough day."

"You should let other people do the work. You're the boss."

"When I'm in a box, they can do it for me. Not before."

"Don't say things like that," Linda said sharply.

"Sorry," he apologized quickly, remembering where his daughter had been that afternoon and the reason for her visit. The last thing on her mind should be the possibility of his death as well; even mentioning it in jest could have an adverse effect. "I'll see you around six."

She blew a kiss into the phone and hung up before returning to admire herself in the bedroom mirror.

Huckleby arrived just before six, parking the Cadillac alongside the blue Mercedes. He walked briskly to the building lobby, undoing his topcoat as the doorman greeted him with a brief salute. Linda was wearing one of the new dresses when she opened the apartment door. She took her father's coat and kissed him lightly on the cheek before ushering him into the living room.

"Drink?"

"Make it a weak scotch and water." He stood in front of a Dali original which occupied the center of the room's longest wall. Linda had purchased it from the gallery, and each time Huckleby studied it, he understood it less.

Linda disappeared for a moment, then returned with a drink for her father and a martini for herself. "How's business?"

He turned away from the Dali. "Prospering, thank you."

"To the prospering business." She raised her glass in the air. "May it prosper forever and ever, amen."

Huckleby took a sip from his drink, studying his daughter over the rim of the glass, wondering how he could have fathered such a beautiful young woman. The eyes were his—Alice's had been brown, a soft, gentle color—and perhaps the erectness of her posture was also his doing, but she had inherited the coloring and complexion from her mother. He was surprised that suitors had not been knocking down the door, especially when her looks were combined with the considerable fortune attached to Howson Chemicals. Just as long as she didn't bring home some simpering liberal with no chin, a wispy adolescent beard, and a handshake like a wet fish. Anything, dear God, but that.

"Do you want to talk about Mother?" Linda asked suddenly.

"Is that what the doctor suggests?"

"It seems to be working for me." She looked at her drink thoughtfully, uncertain whether to pursue the subject. "I go over every detail of that afternoon when I'm with him. He feels that getting it out of my system as many times as possible is beneficial. How about getting it out of yours?"

"I can live with it." He looked around the room, his eyes drawn again to the Dali, the confusing jumble of lines that must mean something to someone, if only to the artist. He wondered if men visited his daughter, whether they stayed the night. Huckleby was not a prudish man. What his daughter did was her concern, and he was confident that she would always be discreet. During his entire marriage—even with the sometimes lengthy periods of enforced separation—he had remained faithful to his wife. Since her death there had been nobody else, not even an interested glance. Times change, though, and he was certain that Linda's sense of morality would be different from his own. "What did you make for dinner?"

"Simple stuff. Fish and salad. Hungry yet?"

"Soon. Let me get the drink down first. And before you make yourself too comfortable, you'd better go downstairs and move your car. One day they'll really surprise you and tow it away. Just to teach you a lesson."

41

She grinned impishly but got up and left the apartment, snatching the Mercedes's keys from the top of the telephone table.

Huckleby had eaten dinner too quickly. Turning away from Linda, he slipped a nitroglycerin tablet into his mouth, holding his breath while he waited for the constriction in his chest to pass.

"Something wrong?" Linda asked, noticing his position for the first time.

"Heartburn. It'll go away. It always does." Gradually the tightness subsided, and he grinned weakly, wiping a film of perspiration from his forehead with a pristine white handkerchief.

"Are you sure it's heartburn? Or is that your considered diagnosis and damn what the doctors say?"

"I haven't been to see any," he lied. "Anyway, it's passing now. How about another drink? Alcohol's supposed to be good for heartburn."

"Another Huckleby diagnosis and remedy all in one," Linda grumbled lightly. "You should really take better care of yourself."

While Linda prepared another drink, Huckleby turned on the television in the corner of the room and settled back to watch the news. He tuned into the middle of a report from Northern Ireland, where terrorist bombs had wrecked a public house, killing three people, injuring seven more. As Linda set down the glass, Huckleby muttered something under his breath; she asked him to repeat it.

"I said that's what we're facing here." He pointed at the television.

"Bombings by the Irish?" she asked incredulously.

"Bombings by anyone. An invasion, anything. And we're totally unprepared to counter it."

"Daddy." The single word was drawn out, almost anguished. "Please...not here, not in this apartment. Write all the letters you like to newspapers, appear at all the meetings you want, but not in my home."

Huckleby laughed and, in a rare gesture of open affection, pulled his daughter close and kissed her on the forehead.

The second drink soon went to his head, and he dozed off. When he awoke an hour later, he found Linda sitting on the couch beneath the Dali painting, watching the television. "What's on?" he asked. "More terrorism? Or a fashion show?" "Talk show." She gave him the name of the host, which meant nothing to Huckleby. He watched television so rarely—only news programs and college football games—that personalities who were household names were virtually unknown to him. Nonetheless, he shook himself fully awake and began to pay attention. The program host, a book resting on his knee, was talking to a man in his late thirties, dressed well but conservatively in a gray flannel suit. He had a ruddy, sunburned complexion, and his short light brown hair was parted high on the right side, almost at the center. What intrigued Huckleby was the man's accent, clipped, nasal. He tried to place it. From somewhere in the South? No. English? No again. Huckleby raised himself in the seat and began to concentrate.

"A lot of writers have glamorized the mercenary's life-style, Mr. Stiehl," the program host was saying. "Now you, as a former mercenary, have written a book in reply, *Killing for Cash*." He held up the book for viewers to see. On the cover, Huckleby recognized a black beret with a commando knife lying across it; above was written the title in blood red, with the name of Peter Stiehl below. "Do your own views coincide with those of popular authors?"

"I'm afraid not." Stiehl looked directly into the camera, very sure of himself as he replied. "There's a world of difference between our views." Huckleby narrowed down the accent—Australian or South African; possibly Rhodesian. "Fiction writers with no experience or inside information have romanticized the mercenary, comparing him with King Arthur and the Knights of the Round Table. Believe me, Camelot doesn't exist. There's nothing glamorous or chivalrous about being shot at, even if the money is good and tax-free. Provided you can find your employer once the fighting's over to get paid." The last remark drew a ripple of laughter from the studio audience; even Huckleby smiled.

The host waited for the noise to die down. "In *Killing for Cash,* you seem to go out of your way to show the seamy side of a mercenary's life, the inherent dangers in the profession. If it's that dangerous, that unsavory, what made you enter it in the first place?"

Again, Stiehl looked directly into the camera. "Money. Soldiering is what I do best. I held the rank of captain in the South African Army before I became a mercenary, specializing in counterinsurgency operations. Like any other skill, there is a demand for it."

"Why did you leave the South African Army?" The host knew the answer already, but he wanted to see how the audience would react.

Using a minimum of words, Stiehl narrated the search-and-destroy mission into Mozambique and his resultant forced resignation. As he listened, Huckleby began to feel a degree of sympathy toward the South African, knowing too well the sensation of being forced to quit for trying to do your best.

A shocked silence greeted Stiehl's reply, and his tanned face reddened in anger. "What would the United States do if a guerrilla band came across the border from Mexico, for example, attacked a village in Texas or California, ransacked churches, murdered the ministers, killed innocent women and children?" Stiehl snapped; this time his words were not directed at the camera—they were straight out from the stage to the studio audience. "If you remember your history, such things happened before World War One. Your government reacted by sending troops across the Mexican border, under General Pershing, to destroy Pancho Villa."

For a moment there was an embarrassed silence. Then a smattering of applause broke out, growing, sweeping over the two men on the stage. Stiehl sat back, vindicated.

"What a repulsive man," Linda said. "How can he talk of death so casually?"

Huckleby turned away from the screen and looked at his daughter. "Is he so terrible? He believes in the same things I do, the right and necessity to protect your own country. Only his country paid him off the same way the United States government paid me off. With dismissal! I'll tell you something, Linda, if I were in that television studio right now, I'd shake that man by the hand." He looked back at the television, not wanting to miss anything; when he saw a commercial for American Express, he continued talking. "I just hope those imbeciles at the White House and on Capitol Hill are watching this program. Then they'll know that it's not just Old Stoneass who believes in preventive strength."

"I suppose you'd approve of that man as your son-in-law," Linda shot back. "At least, nobody could call him a liberal."

Huckleby made no comment, turning back to the television as the commercial ended. "You mention in your book that you fought in Biafra and Angola," the host was saying, "as well as trained troops in Saudi Arabia. Have you at any time used, or would you ever consider using, your expertise to assist a communist movement?"

Stiehl shook his head. "Never. I draw a very strict line where my work is concerned. I don't believe in the communist ideology, and I would never knowingly assist it, no matter how much money was involved. Seems to me"—his face broke into a wide grin revealing perfectly white teeth—"that they're always on the opposite side anyway. I don't think they'd even want me after what we did to some Cubans in Angola."

The host quickly recognized that there was nothing to be gained with the line of questioning and changed tack. "Perhaps you've heard about the bombings in Northern Ireland tonight. Have any of the men you've worked with in your various campaigns turned to these terrorist groups or been sympathetic to them?"

Stiehl took a long time to think over the question. "In Biafra I worked with some Irish lads who had their own ideas about what to do with the British, but that's about it. I don't think any of my comrades had much sympathy for the Arabs or the other terrorist groups, though. As I said earlier, we always seemed to be fighting against the superpower that assists these people."

The host moved the conversation more directly onto the book, asking Stiehl how long he was staying in the United States before returning to his home in Port Elizabeth. Stiehl replied that he was in the country for three months to publicize the book, which was expected to reach the best-seller list. "I'm also thinking about settling down here eventually," he added. "I have a sister living in New York, and like many other South Africans, I'm worried about what's going to take place in my country over the next ten or twenty years."

Huckleby's interest in the program began to wane, and he was glad when Linda switched off the set. Checking his watch, he saw it was past nine and decided to leave. He kissed Linda goodnight and made his way down to the parking lot, started the car, and pulled onto the road. As he passed a sign for the George Washington Bridge, a sudden urge overtook him. He swung the car onto the bridge approach, paid the $1.50 toll, and headed across the Hudson into Manhattan. Doubleday on Fifth Avenue would still be open. Huckleby wanted to do what he had not done since before his wife died. He wanted to lie in bed and read before falling asleep. And he knew exactly what he wanted to read.

Killing for Cash. He chuckled happily as he thought about the title.

3

STIEHL WOKE EARLY on Saturday morning in the Mayfair House on Park Avenue and Sixty-fifth, where the publishing company kept a two-bedroom apartment suite for visiting VIPs. He had been staying there for a week while he fulfilled promotional dates. The book was already into a second printing, and the publisher's rights manager was optimistic of landing a six-figure advance for a paperback contract. Stiehl realized how fortunate he was; he had gotten around to completing the book on mercenaries when such subjects were becoming a focal point of interest. Ten years earlier it might have flopped. And in ten year's time? He refused to think about what might happen that far ahead; he lived for the present, taking each day as it came.

He showered quickly, scrubbing his scalp, feeling more alert as the steaming, tingling spray washed away the morning's sluggishness. He had gone to bed late the previous night, having dined out with a woman producer from the talk show he had appeared on a few nights earlier. She had been unable to resist the triple charismatic appeal of Stiehl as a writer, a soldier, and,

47

finally, an exceptionally personable and good-looking man. He had left her apartment just after four to take a taxi back to the Mayfair House, where he nodded easily to the doorman who let him in.

With a towel wrapped around his waist, he sat on the edge of the bed and lit a cigarette, resting it in the ashtray while he surveyed his diary. He figured he had time for a leisurely breakfast before putting in an appearance at a large bookstore on Sixth Avenue, where he was scheduled to autograph copies of *Killing for Cash*. He went to the closet and pulled out the same gray flannel suit he had worn for the television show, along with a beige cotton shirt, a faintly patterned brown tie, and heavy tan brogue shoes. As he checked his appearance in the mirror, he undid the tie and replaced it in the closet. He pulled out, instead, a plain green silk tie with a springbok emblem in the center. He decided to fly the flag; not enough people did anymore.

After eating in a nearby restaurant, he began walking purposefully toward Sixth Avenue, preferring the brisk morning air to the closeness of a cab. The bookstore was already open, and Stiehl smiled good-naturedly at those customers who recognized him from the publicity posters in the window, finding the acknowledgment pleasant. A table was set aside for him with a display unit of the book on top. He cleared a space for himself on one corner and perched there while he waited for customers to bring over their copies of the book.

"You don't look like a man who would enjoy killing," the first customer—a young woman—said as she held out her book to Stiehl.

He finished signing the page and returned the book. "I don't think you'll find that I ever claimed to enjoy killing," he said softly. "It was always a question of killing or being killed."

"What kind of soldiers were the Cubans?" a middle-aged man asked. "Were they good? Could we have taken them if we'd attacked Castro early on?"

Stiehl thought carefully about the question. He had expected some along those lines, about a soldier's capabilities, but not one where he would be required to draw a comparison between one

48

country's troops and another's. "They were out of their element in Angola," he said finally. "I wasn't. Nor were the men I fought alongside. Like Vietnam, where the majority of Americans were out of their element."

A trim young marine second lieutenant was next in line, gray eyes fixed steadfastly on Stiehl. "What was the best antipersonnel weapon you ever used, sir?"

Stiehl permitted the faintest of smiles to flicker across his face. "A bazooka," he replied simply.

"A bazooka?" The marine's eyes reflected confusion. "That's an antitank weapon, sir, not antipersonnel." Behind him, two people in the line crowded closer to listen.

"I'm referring to an incident in Biafra," Stiehl said, "where I used a bazooka as an antipersonnel weapon. It was all I had. And it was the most devastating antipersonnel weapon I've ever used."

The smile that lit the marine lieutenant's face was positively beatific. "I see what you mean, sir. Thanks for signing the book." He walked away, laughing quietly, leaving an equally amused Stiehl to face the next person.

By midday the store had sold the complete delivery of two hundred books it had ordered for the special promotion. Stiehl stayed long enough to have a cup of coffee with the manager before catching a cab to Howard Beach, near Kennedy Airport, where his sister lived. Sitting back, he estimated that if sales continued to climb, he would never have to fight for a living again. He wouldn't miss it. As he had told the first customer that morning, he had never enjoyed it. Well, perhaps he had enjoyed the fighting, the matching of wits, the plotting, but the kill had always left him cold, an impersonal action whether it was accomplished with a rifle from a safe distance or with bare hands where he could see the fear in the other man's eyes, smell it in his sweat. It was always as if someone else had stepped into his body for the final act; a chess master whose final winning move is really an anticlimax, a deed which can never match the nerve-racking battle of wits and test of skill which had preceded it.

Seconds after the taxi pulled up outside the three-bedroom house in Howard Beach, the front door opened, and a young boy ran down the path. "Uncle Peter! Uncle Peter!"

Stiehl passed some money through the taxi's open window and turned around to lift his ten-year-old nephew high into the air. "Little Peter! Little Peter!" He mimicked the boy's enthusiasm. "What have you been up to then?" He tucked the boy under his arm as if he were nothing more than a parcel and walked up to the house, where he kissed his sister, Juliet, and shook hands with her husband, Tom, who stood behind her.

"He's been nagging us nonstop all day long," Tom Brenner said. "When's Uncle Peter coming? What time? From the minute he got up this morning."

Stiehl laughed as he dropped the boy gently to the floor, holding an arm until the child gained his balance. "I would have been here sooner, but it took us this long to sell all the books."

"You sold them all? All two hundred?" Juliet Brenner asked, her thin face widening in wonder. "And you signed every single one?" Despite the fourteen years she had lived in the United States, her South African accent remained strong, as if she had made a conscious effort not to let it surrender to her husband's New York speech.

"Every one." Stiehl moved into the living room, eyes lighting up as he spotted a copy of the book on a table. He had been given ten free copies and still had nine left, not knowing people in this strange country to whom he could give them.

To his sister and brother-in-law, Stiehl was a celebrity. Even before the book had thrust him into prominence, his means of support was glamorous to them. Tom Brenner was an accountant, a man whose days were taken up with columns of figures, and Juliet's time was filled with the home and her son, who had been named after his uncle. Just as Stiehl's life seemed to be reflected in his bronzed face and healthy physique, so Tom and Juliet Brenner appeared at home in the humdrum existence of a suburban family. She was two years younger than her brother, but Juliet's face was worn, care lines creasing her forehead, thin fair hair looking straggly unless it had just been set. Her husband fitted in anywhere, early forties, chubby, double chin, and brown hair flecked liberally with gray. Only the boy seemed to have an exuberance which identified him with his uncle. His long blond hair grew to below his ears, his eyes were clear blue, and a lively inquisitiveness added strength to his skinny, immature frame.

Brenner pointed to a chair for Stiehl to use, facing him from the sofa. "Saw you on TV the other night, even let Peter stay up."

"He wouldn't have had it any other way," Juliet broke in as she was about to leave the room. "We'd have had a mutiny on our hands if we'd sent him to bed."

Stiehl reached out and pretended to clip his nephew around the ear. Peter dodged back, countering with his own open-handed punch which his uncle parried with ease. Brenner watched the interplay, jealous of the relationship which existed between uncle and nephew, yet realistic enough to know that he did not possess the undeniable flair of his brother-in-law. Although he would never admit it, he shared much of his son's hero worship for Stiehl. His brother-in-law's life-style—no matter what he claimed on television—exuded the glamor of a film set, a throwback to earlier days when as a child Brenner had gone to the theater to lose himself in some screen hero's adventures. Brenner considered himself fortunate to have a brother-in-law like Stiehl. Although he rarely saw him from one year to the next, he was content to follow Stiehl's exploits through letters. But now, with the publication of the book, perhaps Stiehl would settle down and make the United States his home. Or would the glamor disappear once this extraordinary man began to lead an ordinary life?

"What plans have you got, Peter?" Brenner wished immediately that he had phrased the question more tactfully; he did not want to appear to be prying into his brother-in-law's life. "You know, for work?"

Stiehl picked up his nephew and set him firmly on his knee, one arm held around the slim body. "I really don't know. The agent's talking a lot about movie options and all that, but I think he's doing that to keep me interested. There is a possibility of doing some technical advisory work for a film company, but that's all up in the air at the moment."

"So while you're staying in New York, where are you going to live? Your publisher's not going to keep you in luxury at the Mayfair House forever."

"I hadn't given it much thought. Life's been such that I take one day at a time, never plan too much in advance."

Juliet Brenner, returning from the kitchen with a tray of food, caught her brother's reply. "Why not stay with us? We've got the spare bedroom, and I'm sure Peter would love to have you around. If you could stand getting pestered every minute of every day."

The boy swung around on Stiehl's knee and stared intently into his uncle's eyes. "Yes! Come on, live with us! Say yes!"

"So you could show me off to all your friends? This is my uncle—he kills people for a living?"

Angelic innocence covered the boy's face. "No. I wouldn't tell them anything like that. I promise."

"Not much he wouldn't," Brenner cut in, laughing. "We'd have a never-ending stream of curious neighborhood kids, followed by their parents, upset that their precious children are being exposed to such a terrible man."

Juliet called the men when she had set the table. The boy insisted on sitting between his uncle and father, every few seconds turning in his seat to look at Stiehl. "How about it?" Brenner pressed. "Move in with us just till you get yourself straightened out."

Stiehl began to answer that he would think about it, stopping in mid-sentence as an aircraft roared overhead. "How can you stand this?" he asked. He pushed himself away from the table and walked to the window, where he stared out across Jamaica Bay. A Pan Am 747 was disappearing eastward. Clouds of black exhaust smoke marked its passage through the air.

"You get used to it," Brenner said philosophically, joining Stiehl at the window. "We're right in the flight path. The double glazing cuts down the noise a bit, but it still comes through."

After eating, Stiehl sat in the armchair, lighting a cigarette while he had coffee. He got no further than his first draw when his nephew appeared with a photograph of a machine gun, asking how it worked. "Haven't you got any homework?" Stiehl asked halfheartedly, while his sister and brother-in-law laughed. Whatever else he might have said was cut off by a whispering sound that began to penetrate the house, growing louder with each passing second until it seemed to fill the entire building. Brenner moved to the window again, beckoning for Stiehl to join him.

"That's the one I'd like to get," he said venomously, his eyes following a small shape as it soared into the sky. "Concorde. Makes the biggest racket this side of hell. We thought we'd stopped the damned thing with all the protests and demonstrations, but it didn't help. The government still gave permission for it to use New York." He turned away from the window and looked at Stiehl. "It's my dream to shoot it down one day. Me and a million other people around these parts."

Stiehl clucked his tongue disapprovingly. "That's illegal."

"Sure," Brenner conceded. "But I can still dream, can't I? How would I go about doing it? Theoretically speaking, of course."

Stiehl eyed his brother-in-law quizzically, as if seeing a side of Tom Brenner he never knew existed. "Any number of ways. Shoulder-held, heat-seeking missiles like the ones the Arabs used so successfully against Israeli Phantoms in 'seventy-three. They'd home in on the exhaust."

"I'll bear it in mind," Brenner said.

"I thought Peter's questions were the only ones I'd have to answer if I lived here."

Brenner laughed. "I'm also curious about a few things in life."

Later that night Brenner drove Stiehl back to Manhattan. He stopped outside the Mayfair House for a few moments while he pressed his brother-in-law again about moving in with the family. Stiehl could see his sister's hand in the appeal; he also envisioned a long line of single women turning up at the house if he agreed to move in. He fobbed Brenner off.

53

"She'll give me hell I didn't get you to say yes," Brenner complained as Stiehl got out of the car.

"Tell her I didn't say no either," Stiehl replied, grinning at his brother-in-law's anxiety. "It's still a maybe. Depends on too many things."

"Okay." Brenner waved a hand. "See you."

Stiehl watched the car drive through the lights on Park Avenue; then he went up to his suite on the tenth floor. As he opened the door, his foot kicked against a white envelope. He stopped and turned it over as he picked it up, seeing his name and room number. Curious, he closed the door and stood in the long hall as he tore open the envelope. The message was unsigned, only four lines asking him to be at the Windows on the World restaurant at the World Trade Center at six on Monday evening; it would be to his advantage regarding the book.

Holding the card by the edge, he tapped it thoughtfully against his hand. He wondered what it could mean. An unsigned message? A mark of rudeness on the sender's part? Or an attempt to whet his curiosity? If it were the latter, the ruse had succeeded. He was interested.

Before going to sleep, Stiehl made a note in his diary and stuck the message into his wallet. Monday was still two days away, and he had Sunday to work on first. As he had told his brother-in-law, one day at a time.

4

AN HOUR BEFORE he was due to meet his mysterious contact at Windows on the World, Stiehl stood before the mirror in his bedroom, checking his appearance closely. Underneath the left sleeve of his custom-made Harris tweed sportcoat, the fabric sagged slightly, hardly noticeable to the unsuspicious eye, yet enough to trouble Stiehl. He left the mirror and pulled an overnight bag from the closet. After opening the zipper, he withdrew a stripped-down Browning nine-millimeter automatic pistol. He assembled the weapon without even looking at it, then returned to the closet. From another bag he took a streamlined holster and the Browning's long magazine. He slipped the magazine into the butt and hefted the complete weapon in his hand to gauge the feel. Finally, he ejected the clip and sat down on the bed. Having plucked the top round from the magazine, he rolled it in the palm of his hand while he debated the wisdom of taking the gun to the restaurant. Whom was he trying to impress? Himself? Or the person who had arranged the dinner date? Did he really need to go armed on what appeared nothing more dangerous than a routine business appointment?

He looked for a long time at the round in his hand, fingering the almost invisible scratch on the bullet's steel nose. Then he pressed it back into the magazine and replaced the Browning in his overnight bag. As he waited for the elevator, he wondered why he had ever instructed his London tailor to make allowances for the holster. It was the act of a small boy intent on showing off, perhaps something his young nephew would dream up while playing with friends. Only once had Stiehl used the Browning while in civilian clothes. That was six years earlier, at a meeting in Amsterdam with a man who had offered him twenty thousand pounds for a political assassination. Stiehl had turned down the contract because assassinations were not his line of work, and at the same time he had harbored a grudging admiration for the statesman involved. The bidder had panicked, trying to cover his tracks by eliminating the South African. Stiehl had fired just one shot from the Browning before catching a plane out of Amsterdam to London, from there back to South Africa.

The doorman outside the Mayfair House flagged down a passing cab, which continued east toward the FDR Drive, heading south to the tip of Manhattan. Stiehl arrived at the World Trade Center with ten minutes to spare. He gave his name to the restaurant captain and was shown to a table for two.

"What's the name of my host?" Stiehl asked.

"I beg your pardon, sir?"

"My host. The person buying me dinner."

The captain's face remained expressionless. "He should be arriving in just a moment, sir. You were slightly early." Before Stiehl could press him further, the man excused himself.

When the waiter came, Stiehl ordered a gin and tonic. He made up his mind to give the mystery man exactly fifteen minutes. If he had not arrived by then, he would settle the tab and leave. He was already beginning to dislike the secretive arrangement, criticizing himself for having been intrigued enough to accept it.

Ten minutes passed, and Stiehl ordered himself another drink, looking out the window over the Hudson River while he waited. When he heard footsteps approaching the table, he turned around, expecting to see the waiter returning with a fresh drink. Instead, he saw a man in his late middle years, tall, erect, with short steel gray hair and piercing blue eyes.

"Mr. Stiehl?" The man extended his right hand for the South African to shake. "I'm delighted that you could accept my invitation. My name is Harlan Stone Huckleby."

Stiehl stood and shook the man's hand. The name was familiar, but he associated it with neither film nor publishing circles. It took him a few seconds to place it. "Is that with a major general prefix or just plain mister?"

"I see that I am not totally unknown to you. Good. It saves me the trouble of introducing myself further."

"We followed your case in South Africa," Stiehl said. "If it's any consolation at this late stage, I think you were in the right."

"Thank you."

"How long ago was it?"

"That I was asked to retire, to resign?" Huckleby smiled for an instant, as if enjoying some private joke. "Too long, Mr. Stiehl. We seem to share the unhappy distinction of being punished for doing what we knew was right. Only in your case, it worked out rather well."

The waiter returned with a gin and tonic, which he placed before Stiehl. Huckleby ordered a whiskey and water, which was set before him almost immediately, as if the waiter had guessed the retired general's preference.

"To an explanation," Stiehl said, raising his glass.

"All in good time, Mr. Stiehl. And I promise you the explanation will be worth waiting for." He took a slow sip from the glass before continuing. "I found your book intriguing. Especially reading it from an old soldier's viewpoint. You seem to have slipped out of some very tough situations."

"My being here, speaking to you right now, is proof of that."

Huckleby weighed the answer carefully. "Yes and no. As a

57

military man I must admit there's some question in my mind about whether you're both a competent soldier and a competent writer or whether you're just a very imaginative writer."

Stiehl stiffened, reminding Huckleby how he had reacted on the television show when the audience had shown disapproval of his attack on the guerrilla camp. "At the moment, sir, I am not interested in proving to you what I am or what I can do. I get paid to do that."

Huckleby held up his hands placatingly. "That's precisely what I intend to do, Mr. Stiehl. And to smooth your ruffled feathers, I believe every word you wrote. I have my own sources for validating the incidents you mentioned."

"What are you leading up to?"

"Before I answer that, let me ask you one question. Now that you're obviously making money as a writer, could one assume that you've retired from soldiering? Or would a challenge, a touch of excitement, and the opportunity to make a considerable sum of money make you pick up your ears and listen?"

Stiehl refrained from answering until after the waiter had taken their order; the pause gave him time to think. The meeting had nothing to do with the book. Someone was chasing him from the old life, either Huckleby directly or some organization using the retired general as its ambassador. It had learned about his background, and now it was propositioning him. But what organization was powerful enough to use a man like Harlan Stone Huckleby to make the approach?

Finished with the order, the waiter disappeared. Stiehl leaned across the table, keeping his voice low. "It depends. Excitement, yes. A little justifiable danger, perhaps. Sticking my head into a noose, most definitely no. I don't need it anymore."

"No noose. And no orders from anyone else, not even from me. You would be the top man, working out the operational plan, recruiting the specialists necessary for the job."

"What's the geographical area?" Already the conversation was following a pattern familiar to Stiehl. The gentle probe to see if he was interested, the promise that he would be in command.

58

"We can talk about the details after we've eaten," Huckleby said, leaning back as the waiter placed a dish in front of him.

Stiehl forced himself to wait, pushing his guesses to the back of his mind. He ate slowly, enjoying the meal, finishing off with coffee and a glass of port. Though the meal was excellent, he could not wait to be finished. He wanted to hear what Huckleby had to say; even to be approached by Huckleby—no matter what the assignment entailed—was a compliment. As he lit an after-dinner cigarette, he saw Huckleby stand. Stiehl followed with his eyes as the older man walked the few paces to the window, where he looked out to the Jersey shore. Five seconds passed while Huckleby contemplated the view by himself; then he turned around and beckoned for Stiehl to join him.

"Do you see that?"

Stiehl followed Huckleby's pointing finger toward the ugly lighted sprawl of Newark. "What is it?"

"Newark. Where Howson Chemicals is located. Worth about nine hundred million at today's close of market. Howson Chemicals belongs to me."

"Very nice. But I don't think you invited me up here for an education on the chemical industry. Let's get to the point. What's mine?"

Reaching into his inside pocket, Huckleby pulled out a plain white envelope, which he passed to Stiehl. The South African glanced into Huckleby's eyes before concentrating on the envelope. After tearing back the flap, he pulled out a check drawn on a Zurich bank for one million dollars made out to Peter Stiehl. His eyes narrowed when he noticed that Huckleby's signature was missing from the space above the printed name.

"This doesn't cut much ice without your autograph on the bottom."

"My signature will be there," Huckleby assured him, "once you've agreed to deliver something into my hands."

Now comes the pitch, Stiehl thought. Which country does he want knocked over? Which piddling little state in the middle of nowhere has a billion dollars' worth of natural resources that only Huckleby knows about and wants to grab for himself?

Where does he want me to arrange a coup, so he can place his own puppet in charge and milk the country dry? For some reason, Stiehl found himself feeling vaguely sorry; he had placed Huckleby higher up the ladder than that. "Okay, I'm listening. What do you want?"

"Manhattan."

"You mean where we're standing now?" Whatever he might have considered, New York's principal borough had never entered his mind. He could not keep the surprise out of his voice.

"That is exactly what I want, Mr. Stiehl. I want Manhattan. Every square inch of land, every piece of real estate bordered by the East River, the Hudson River, the Harlem River, and the Atlantic Ocean."

For Huckleby's signature on a check for one million dollars, Stiehl was prepared to listen to anything the man had to say—even to something that sounded as insane as taking over the entire borough of Manhattan. He followed the retired general out of the restaurant, down to where the Cadillac was parked. When Huckleby began heading north toward the Lincoln Tunnel, Stiehl did not even ask where they were going.

"You seem very quiet, Mr. Stiehl. Are you so frightened by the enormity of taking such an objective that you're not even curious?"

"I'm curious. Who wouldn't be? I'm just trying to figure you out for myself. When I was in the business, my usual clients were not retired American generals."

"What have you figured out so far?"

"Not too much. As I said, you're not the type of man I ever did business with. You're a solid member of the establishment, wealthy, a supporter of law and order. Reactionary. I bet you even voted for Nixon."

"I did. All three times he ran for President." Huckleby slowed down for a traffic light, then jabbed the gas pedal as it changed to green.

"Then why would you even contemplate a strike like this against your own country?"

"Because I'm a patriot. I want what's best for my country."

"Someone once pointed out that patriotism's the last refuge of a scoundrel," Stiehl reminded him.

"Don't quote platitudes at me."

Stiehl ran a hand through his hair, trying to understand what was going on. "Is Manhattan unpatriotic?" He hoped the question did not sound as idiotic to Huckleby as it did to himself.

"I'm using Manhattan because it's easy to take out," Huckleby said. "It could be anywhere in the United States. Manhattan suits my purpose because it's an island, virtually indefensible."

"And just what is your purpose?"

"To teach this country a lesson before it's too late. To show the government how susceptible the United States is to invasion by a foreign power."

Stiehl closed his eyes wearily. Maybe the newspapers hadn't been given the whole truth when Huckleby was booted out of the service, he thought; perhaps there was more to it, like insanity. "You've lost me," he admitted.

"What I'm proposing is a war game. A war game with real bullets. A real army invading Manhattan, taking it over so that the American government can see how wrong its position on national defense has been. There should be no casualties because we'll plan it carefully. But if there are, they will be totally justifiable," Huckleby said. "Especially so when you consider all the lives that will be saved once the government beefs up its defense program. And the only thing that will make it act is a sharp lesson such as this."

"And you want me to teach it that lesson, is that it?"

"Precisely. I want you to assemble a crack team of specialists—"

"There aren't that many mercenaries I'd trust," Stiehl cut in.

"I didn't mention mercenaries."

Stiehl was incredulous. "You mean regulars? That's an outright declaration of war on one country by another. You'd start World War Three."

"I didn't mention regulars either. You spoke on television the other night about some Irishmen you'd worked with in Biafra,

61

how they had their own ideas about what to do with the British."

"You're talking about terrorists, is that it?"

Huckleby nodded.

"How would you pay them? Provided, of course, that I could arrange such an army for you. A bunch of politically activated thugs to take on the might of the United States." Despite himself, Stiehl was becoming interested.

"By holding Manhattan to ransom. They can demand the biggest payoff in history. They can write their own ticket, demand whatever they're physically capable of hauling away."

"After which we'd ail be fugitives for the remainder of our lives," Stiehl said. "I don't need it, thank you very much. Just drop me off when you see a cruising cab."

"Hear me out," Huckleby said. "I'm certain that you can protect your own identity from the men you hire."

"What about you? What's to guarantee that you won't give me away?" Stiehl asked.

"I'll guarantee it. This will be the final act of my life, Mr. Stiehl. The arteries to my heart are almost gone, atherosclerosis they call it. I rely on pills to allow the passage of blood to my heart. Without them, the least exertion would kill me. I will choose my time of dying carefully enough to avoid implicating you."

"What about my fee?" Stiehl patted the envelope in his pocket. "Supposing someone puts two and two together, connects me with you that way?"

"Impossible," Huckleby asserted. "The Swiss can be relied upon to protect all confidences where money is concerned."

The Cadillac entered the Lincoln Tunnel, crawling along behind a tractor-trailer in the right-hand lane. As Stiehl leaned back against the opulent upholstery, he thought over Huckleby's words. "For one million dollars, which is about the only sane thing I can see in this whole deal, you want me to put together an army of terrorists—assuming, of course, that I can find anyone who admits to being a terrorist. Then you want me to transport them to the United States, where I will work out a plan to cut off the entire borough of Manhattan from the rest of the world and hold it long enough to get away with the biggest ransom in history. Have I got it all, or did I leave something out?"

"That's exactly it." Despite Stiehl's heavy-handed sarcasm, Huckleby was certain he had baited the hook with enough money and excitement to bring the South African out of retirement.

Stiehl laughed, a dry, echoing chuckle. "You know something? The Brits always did say the Americans had to do everything on a grand scale. They weren't kidding, were they?"

"Well?"

"I need time to think it over."

"Take all the time you need," Huckleby invited. "But you'll come in with me."

"Maybe."

After leaving the Lincoln Tunnel, the Cadillac sped north toward Fort Lee. Stiehl had still not asked Huckleby their destination. He was too busy mulling over the retired general's proposition. Recruiting an army, taking and holding a large chunk of densely populated land. Perhaps Huckleby was right, and he would join the operation. The money was an overwhelming stimulus. Besides, what excitement and challenge were there in writing anyway? Could it be done? How lucky would he be in recruiting enough men? Would they be interested? Would they be willing to sacrifice political motivation for the lure of money? Too much, to Stiehl's mind, remained uncertain.

When the Cadillac pulled into the visitors' parking lot of an apartment building, Stiehl looked up in question.

"My command post," Huckleby explained, getting out of the car.

Stiehl followed him into the building, up to an apartment on the fourteenth floor, where a blond girl opened the door. She looked with interest, then recognition at the South African.

"You're the man from the television show, the author," she said.

"Peter Stiehl." He took her hand, holding it for a moment longer than necessary as he tried to place her in Huckleby's world. He finally surmised she was his mistress. Anyone able to finance the operation discussed that evening would not quibble about the cost of this apartment, although Stiehl could not see the young woman doing Huckleby's heart condition any good.

Huckleby noticed the overlong introduction and stepped in to break it up. "Linda is my daughter," he said gruffly, drawing Stiehl away. "You'll probably get to see a lot of each other during the coming weeks, but right now we've got work to do." He led the South African over to the picture window which faced east over the Hudson River. Stiehl took in the entire panorama, the illuminated top of the Empire State Building in midtown, the sparkling twin towers of the World Trade Center, where only an hour earlier he had eaten dinner, then left to the George Washington Bridge and beyond that the affluent Bronx suburb of Riverdale.

"Nice view," Stiehl said to nobody in particular.

Linda answered him. "It's the nicest way to see New York. From a different state."

Huckleby moved in closer, and Stiehl felt he was being cut off from Linda. "Take a good look at the bridge," he told Stiehl.

Stiehl took careful note of the massive structure. The bridge was on two levels, each catering to eastbound and westbound traffic. As he watched, hundreds of vehicles scurried across, passenger cars, buses, heavy trucks going in each direction as they helped maintain the lifeline to the city. At the far end, directly over the bridge approach from the Cross Bronx Expressway, four high-rise apartment buildings rose majestically into the air, their very presence demonstrating the strength of the bridge.

"Think of a truck loaded with explosives on the lower level," Huckleby suggested. "Maybe ten tons. Even allowing the energy lost by the blast going sideways to some extent, the bridge would become inoperable. Out of action."

Stiehl's mind worked quickly. "Scratch one artery to the city. Even without detonating the truck, just by using it as a threat, you'd completely kill one entry and exit point to Manhattan. And a truck with ten tons of explosives in the Lincoln Tunnel would do the same thing for another artery. And so on and so on."

Huckleby pulled a large-scale map of Manhattan out of his jacket pocket and spread it across a table. "If we could put together a concerted, perfectly synchronized operation—in other words, a smooth military action—we could bring Manhattan to a complete halt. We could block every artery with a massive bomb and threaten to set them off if our demands were not met. We could ask for anything we wanted. No emergency operation would be capable of supplying a place with the population density of Manhattan on a day-to-day basis. They couldn't airlift, and ships would be too cumbersome. If the blockade were allowed to continue, there would be wholesale rioting in the ghetto areas, looting, burning. Manhattan would be sheer chaos. The police would be powerless to stop the rioting from spreading right down to the Battery. And if they tried to helilift in the army, we'd blow every bridge and tunnel."

"Very neat," Stiehl complimented the older man.

"Nobody will get hurt as long as they do exactly as we tell them. You see, Mr. Stiehl, it is a war game, an exercise. Our weapons will be real because they have to be. Perhaps we could bluff, use empty trucks, but I'm not willing to take that chance."

Stiehl looked down at the map again, eyes flicking over the penciled markings Huckleby had made: the George Washington Bridge, the Triborough Bridge, the Fifty-ninth Street Bridge, all the way down to the Williamsburg, Brooklyn, and Manhattan bridges, plus the smaller bridges over the Harlem River, and the Holland, Lincoln, Brooklyn-Battery, and Queens-Midtown tunnels. Never before had he realized how vulnerable Manhattan was to such an attack. Perhaps that was the reason the Indians had sold it so cheaply in the first place; they had a premonition of something like this happening. He lifted his eyes from the map and gazed out the window, imagining a truck stopping on the lower level of the George Washington Bridge, the driver locking the doors to complete an electronic booby-trap circuit before walking away and tossing the keys into the river.

"What about supplies?" he asked Huckleby.

"Being president of a major chemical company has certain advantages. I can get all the explosives we'll need, all the trucks. You just find me the right men and organize them into a first-rate strike force. Are you interested?"

"If I'm not?"

"Then we would have shared a very interesting evening, Mr. Stiehl. I have enough faith in your integrity to know that you will never repeat a single word of what has passed between us. Not even in a future book."

Stiehl pulled a pack of cigarettes from his pocket, lit one, inhaled deeply. Through the wreath of smoke which drifted upward, he looked first at Huckleby, then at Linda, taking note of the brief smile which flickered across her face.

"Well?" Huckleby's voice became impatient.

Stiehl felt inside his jacket pocket and drew out the white envelope. "Sign your piece of paper, General, and instruct your bank to open an account for me, transferring the money there. You're in command of an army again. Also, you'd better advance me some cash for immediate expenses. I need plane fares, hotel bookings, front money."

No expression crossed Huckleby's face; no handshake was forthcoming. As Stiehl had observed, he was commanding an army again; smiles and handshakes were not the order of the day. "If you wish, I'll drop you back in town. Then you can begin to make your arrangements tomorrow."

Stiehl turned to leave the apartment, waiting while Linda opened the door. As he passed the telephone, he looked down, memorizing the number.

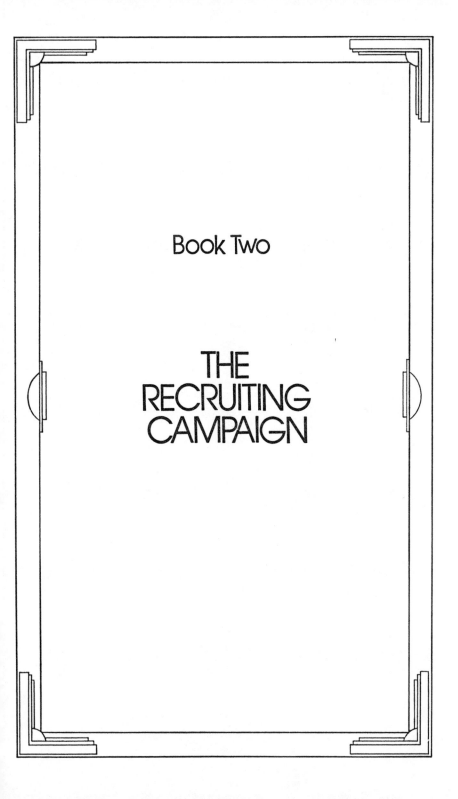

Book Two

THE RECRUITING CAMPAIGN

5

WITHIN AN HOUR of landing at Shannon Airport in the west of Ireland, Stiehl was behind the wheel of a rented Ford Cortina, heading northeast toward the six counties that constitute the British territory of Ulster. He still found his mission difficult to believe—mercenary soldier in Africa one moment, popular writer the next, and now the organizer of the biggest hijacking of all time, an operation which, in all probability, would never be surpassed outside of a state of war.

Stiehl was surprised that nobody, in an age where hijackings and extortions were commonplace, had thought of it before. Outstanding as he might have been as a military commander, Harlan Stone Huckleby did not have sole rights on the idea. But nobody had ever tried to put the theory into practice. Stiehl had to commend Huckleby on that. He even had a sneaking admiration for the man's motives, a mission that would shake up the entire United States government and force it to take a long, searching look at its military posture. Pity it hadn't taken that same long, searching look before it stuck its nose into Angola,

Stiehl thought, allowing himself a few moments for reminiscing; then I wouldn't have had to come running out as I did.

He tried to work out how long ago he had sat in the Windows on the World, waiting for his mysterious host to appear. Forty-eight hours? No more than that, certainly. The five-hour time difference was confusing his thinking. He had left Linda Huckleby's apartment in Fort Lee and stayed the night at the Mayfair House. The following morning he had made travel arrangements, then had gone to Howard Beach in the afternoon. Tom Brenner had been at work, but Juliet and little Peter had been delighted to see him with suitcases, certain that he was taking them up on the offer to move in. The delight had lasted only as long as it had taken Stiehl to tell them he was just staying overnight and would be flying to Europe the following evening from Kennedy Airport.

Now he was three thousand miles away, heading toward an undeclared war zone, preparing to leave the peace and tranquillity of the South for the nerve-racking suspense and violence of the North. Heavily armed soldiers at a British border control point checked his passport and searched the car while he stood off to the side, under the almost casual threat of a Sterling submachine gun held by a red-faced, beefy corporal. Stiehl found himself observing the search procedure from the viewpoint of an umpire, faulting the soldiers for their carelessness. If he were going to smuggle arms into Ulster, he would not put them under the back seat or in the trunk. They would be secreted in the car's double-skinned panels, hidden inside the spare tire, or wrapped in oilproof bags in the engine sump. In his eyes, the soldiers failed the test abysmally. They checked only places that were too obvious to be used by anyone but an inexperienced child. And even Ulster had not yet reached the point at which small children carried guns.

The sergeant in charge of the roadblock closed Stiehl's one suitcase, replaced it in the trunk, and slammed the lid. As the sergeant motioned for Stiehl to continue on his way, the beefy corporal lowered the Sterling for an instant, ready to raise it when the next car was stopped and the occupants were ordered out.

"You're a long way from home," the sergeant said as Stiehl began to climb into the car. "South Africa, wasn't it?"

"United States now."

"What are you doing over here?"

"I'm a writer, doing research on a projected book."

"That wasn't what it said in the passport." The sergeant gave Stiehl a slow smile. "Looked to me like you were one of us."

"Old passport. More money and less danger in writing."

The sergeant's grin remained. "Might give it a try myself sometime. But I'd sure pick a better subject than the troubles up here." He slapped the roof of the Cortina and stepped back. "Take care of yourself."

Waving in farewell, Stiehl lifted his foot off the clutch and followed the signs toward Belfast. Ten miles farther on, he pulled off the motorway into a small rest stop, where he took his suitcase out of the car into the washroom. There he closed the door of a commode, rested the case on the toilet seat, and opened it wide. He carefully deposited the neatly packed clothes in the lid. When the case was almost empty, he explored the bottom with his fingertips, seeking the spring-actuated release which had been installed. The false bottom popped back to reveal the Browning; he could not resist a satisfied smile as he remembered the British army sergeant checking the case. It would have taken a miracle, a savage turn of bad luck, for his fumbling hands to have touched off both triggers for the spring. The case had been checked by more competent searchers, United States customs officers among them, who had found nothing amiss. Stiehl had been confident that the British soldiers would fare no better.

He pulled out the automatic, arranged the holster on his shoulder, and slipped in the weapon before buttoning his jacket and putting on a light raincoat. Next, he took out a packet of powdered hair dye and rubbed it into his light brown hair, turning it darker, taking care not to smudge his forehead. Finally, he pulled a pair of tinted glasses from the case and slipped them

71

over his eyes. After repacking the case, he checked his appearance in a mirror, washed the dye off his hands, and left. The darkened hair and owlish look of the tinted horn-rimmed glasses changed his appearance dramatically, giving him a professorial air, diminishing the strength and confidence normally apparent in his face.

Back in the car, he opened his wallet and removed a transparent envelope. Inside were two gold paper initials, an inch high, stuck onto a sheet of glossy paper. He peeled off the initials and fixed them to the top of the suitcase, next to the handle. The initials read PA. He was now ready to enter Belfast.

The first thing he noticed about the city was the oppressive presence of troops; they seemed to be everywhere, rifle butts tucked into their hips, muzzles pointing into the air as they patrolled ceaselessly. Following directions in the map he had bought at Shannon Airport, he drove through the center of the city. He ignored the bombed-out, gutted buildings as he headed toward the Catholic district of Andersonstown. As he neared his destination, the soldiers appeared even more alert. Groups of two or three faced different directions as they patrolled, continually swinging around, trying to look everywhere at once. Yet the military vehicles were not so evident, as if the British did not wish to antagonize the Catholics even further with a massive show of strength and drive them even deeper into the arms of the radicals.

Stiehl found a small boardinghouse with a room-for-rent sign in its front window. A bell rang as he entered, and a woman's voice yelled, "Be with you in a minute!" Seconds later a middle-aged woman appeared from the back of the house, smiling as she saw Stiehl's suitcase.

"I'd like a room for two nights. You have a sign in the window."

"Sure. And where would you be from, Mr. . . ?"

"Adcock. Peter Adcock. I'm from Johannesburg."

"We've got a couple of rooms empty, Mr. Adcock. One in the back overlooking the yard, the other in the front."

"The front will do me fine." Picking up his luggage, he followed the woman as she began to climb the stairs. The room was furnished simply, a large bed which dominated everything, a rickety dressing table with a chair, a wardrobe, and a heavily stuffed, well-worn armchair. Stiehl hoped the bed linen would be clean.

"How much will that be?"

"Three pounds a night, in advance." The woman tried to soften the demand by adding, "That includes breakfast, of course."

Stiehl passed across two five-pound notes and proceeded to unpack while the woman went downstairs to find change. When she returned, he was in trousers and shirt, the Browning tucked away in the false bottom of the case. She gave him four pounds, waiting to see if he wanted anything else. "What brings you to Andersonstown, Mr. Adcock?"

"Business. I'm a writer for the Rand *Daily Mail*. I'm doing a series of articles on the Belfast situation."

The woman said nothing, expecting Stiehl to volunteer more.

"Could you tell me where I could find some of the more important people in the organization?" he asked. "I'll pay you for your trouble."

"I don't think I know what you're talking about. What organization?"

"The provos," Stiehl said openly. "I need to interview some of them."

"You'd be doing yourself a big favor by leaving those men well alone," the woman warned. "They're nothing but trouble. But"—she eyed the four pounds Stiehl continued to hold—"if you're set on going ahead with it, you could try a couple of the pubs. The Swan or The Carlisle." She added directions on how to reach the two public houses.

Stiehl passed across the four pounds and took hold of the woman's wrist as he fished another ten pounds out of his pocket. "There's something else you could tell me before you go," he said, recognizing the gleam of avarice that lit the woman's eyes as she saw the new prize. "I'm looking for a man. Patrick Kerrigan. Do you know him?"

At the mention of the name, the woman licked her lips nervously, debating what she wanted the most—the ten pounds in Stiehl's hand or the chance to leave the room without revealing anything about the man named Kerrigan.

"He's here someplace," Stiehl said. "I'll find him sooner or later. You may as well get the money for telling me where he is."

"What would you be wanting with the likes of him?"

"Information."

The woman reached out quickly and snatched the ten pounds from Stiehl's grasp. "You'll find him down The Carlisle most nights. Fair hair. Broken nose . . ."

"I know what he looks like. Thank you."

The woman backed out of the room, suddenly more afraid of this man in glasses than she had ever been of anyone. He had mentioned a name that was dangerous to speak out loud. Perhaps this South African was really a writer; she did not know one way or the other, but he was fooling around with his life by searching for such men.

Stiehl watched her go before closing the door. He lit a cigarette and sat down in the overstuffed armchair, sinking into its embrace, closing his eyes for a second as fatigue caught up with him. He had not slept at all on the Aer Lingus flight from Kennedy to Shannon; he had been too keyed up, working out how he could accomplish the first part of his mission, the recruiting campaign. The inflight movie had flashed past with barely a glance. Food had come and gone, plates and glasses emptied in a virtual glance. Now he was entering a game in which the odds were as heavily stacked against him as they had ever been in Africa. And the only asset he had was the name of Peter Stiehl and the reputation it carried. With a man like Patrick Kerrigan it would carry authority. Even after all these years it would demonstrate power. Kerrigan might be nothing more than a provo thug now, but he had fought in Africa, had known what the score was. And through Kerrigan, Stiehl would learn of contacts in other lands, more dedicated men who would be only too willing to act in Harlan Stone Huckleby's scheme. Stiehl needed Kerrigan. The Irishman provided the vital initial contact point; without him, Stiehl was fumbling in the dark.

Eight o'clock that evening found Stiehl in the public bar of The Carlisle Arms, a pint of warm stout in front of him, a cigarette burning in his fingers. The bar was crowded with men jostling for attention, while the women sat at tables, waiting for their boyfriends, their husbands to bring them drinks.

Stiehl took the drink to a corner of the bar where a game of darts was in progress. He had not played the game for years and was curious to see the players' skills. The two contestants took no notice of him, but the man chalking scores nodded a casual greeting.

"Want a game?"

"How much?"

"Fiver. Three-oh-one, start and finish on a double. If you don't get on the board, it's a tenner."

Five pounds a game sounded grossly exorbitant when Stiehl compared it with the beer money games he had known in the army, but the contest offered an opportunity to mix with the pub's patrons; perhaps he could pick up some useful information in the course of casual conversation.

"Chalk the next game, and you can play the winner," the man said.

Stiehl took the chalk and stood by the small blackboard, waiting for the game to begin. Three minutes passed while he chalked scores; then the game was over. He put down the chalk and accepted a proffered set of darts, standing off to one side while the winner of the previous game threw first. The man's second dart landed in the eleven outer ring for a double, and he was off. Stiehl did nothing with his first three darts and had to stand back helplessly as his opponent wiped another 127 points off his total.

"Looks like you're in trouble," one of the spectators needlessly told Stiehl. "You don't get off soon, you'll be owing Johnny Coughlin ten quid."

Stiehl shrugged his shoulders philosophically and went back for his turn. His third dart stuck lopsidedly in the double twenty, putting him on the board; it saved him the indignity of being whitewashed as the man called Johnny Couglin threw a triple twenty with his first dart and a double sixteen with his second to end the game. Stiehl handed over a five-pound note graciously.

"That's what you get for playing big time when you haven't played for years," Stiehl said, looking at his opponent properly for the first time; he saw a man in his early thirties, thick black hair and cynical blue eyes.

The winner patted Stiehl sympathetically on the shoulder. "Don't take it too hard. At least you got on the board." He passed the darts to another man and walked away from the board with Stiehl. "Noticed you when you came in. You're not from around these parts, are you?"

"Johannesburg, South Africa."

"Long way. What brings you here?"

"A man called Patrick Kerrigan."

"Who's he when he's up and about?"

"Someone I want to interview for a newspaper article," Stiehl said easily. "But that would be of no interest to you because you don't know him."

"I asked you who he was," Coughlin pointed out. "I never said I didn't know him. And who might you be?"

"Peter Adcock," Stiehl pulled out his wallet and passed across a business card he had ordered as a rush job before leaving New York.

Coughlin scrutinized the card before pocketing it. "You wouldn't be trying to pull a fast one, would you, Mr. Adcock?"

"How?"

"Like you wouldn't be working for the British, would you?"

Stiehl laughed at the suggestion. "After what the Brits are trying to do to my country? You've got to be kidding."

Before either man could say anything else, a silence descended over the pub, a momentary lapse of sound as conversation dimmed. Coughlin looked away from Stiehl, his face breaking into a happy grin. He clapped the South African on the arm. "Looks like you're in luck."

Following Coughlin's gaze, Stiehl saw a fair-haired man pushing his way toward the bar, exchanging banter with the people he passed. Kerrigan no longer had the thick mustache or the luxurious sideburns Stiehl remembered from the one time he had seen him in Biafra, but the broken nose—squashed almost flat at the bridge, then flaring out at the nostrils—was unmistakable.

"Pat!" Coughlin shouted. "Over here! Man's come all the way from Johannesburg to meet you."

Kerrigan turned as his name was called and began walking toward Coughlin, forgetting about the drink he was going to buy. "How are you, Johnny?" he asked before looking at Stiehl. "And what can I do for you?"

Coughlin answered for Stiehl. "Claims he's from some newspaper called the Round *Daily Mail* in South Africa."

"Rand *Daily Mail*," Stiehl corrected him. "I'm doing a series of articles on the Northern Ireland situation for my paper, and to get a fair assessment, I need to interview members of the Provisional IRA."

Kerrigan's eyebrows rose theatrically. "Oh, you do, do you? And what makes you think that we'd know anything about them?"

"A friend told me."

"You've got friends as well. Not here and now you haven't, boyo."

Stiehl felt himself being guided toward the street door, Kerrigan at his side, holding him by the elbow, Coughlin behind. As they reached the door and stepped out into the cool night air, Kerrigan leaned into Stiehl, his face inches from the South African's. "The Rand *Daily Mail* or whatever you say you're from is going to be minus one star reporter unless you come up with the right answers pretty bloody quick. Who's this friend of yours who gave you my name?"

"Stiehl," came the quiet, confident reply.

"Peter Stiehl?"

"Yes."

"You know him?"

"Very well. He gave me a letter of introduction to you." Stiehl handed over a long white envelope. Kerrigan snatched it away, pulled out the letter, and held it up so he could read by the light coming through the pub windows. When he was through, he passed the letter to Coughlin.

77

"Who's this Stiehl?" Coughlin asked.

"A mercenary," Kerrigan said. "And one of the best bloody soldiers who ever lived. I only saw him once, years ago, in Biafra. But all you ever heard about was this man Stiehl. The rest of the lads looked up to him like he was some kind of god." He turned back to Stiehl. "This letter asks me to give you some help. Where are you really from? What do you really want?"

"Can we talk somewhere else?" Stiehl asked pointedly. "I don't like conducting my business in the middle of the street, especially when some British patrol can stumble on us at any moment."

Kerrigan hesitated, uncertain what course to take. Coughlin watched expectantly, and Stiehl decided to push the matter. "My friend said you were a man I could rely on, someone who'd go out of his way to assist with the project I've got in mind."

"He said that about me?"

"Yes. He gave me your name because of an action you led against a Nigerian position. He said you did a thorough job, that you were a brave, resourceful man."

Kerrigan's chest seemed to expand visibly with pride. "Sweet Mary, that was a lifetime ago. Just thinking about it makes me feel kind of sentimental. Come on, we'll go to my place. The wife's over at her sister's."

With Kerrigan leading the way and Coughlin bringing up the rear, Stiehl allowed himself to be guided through the dark streets to a block of flats. After walking up three flights of stairs, Kerrigan opened a door and ushered the two men into the flat. Stiehl found himself in a small hallway with five doors leading from it. Kerrigan opened the nearest to reveal a compact living room, cheaply carpeted, a sofa and two armchairs, a small table with four chairs around it, and a black-and-white television set.

"Now what are you really here for, Mr. Adcock?" Kerrigan asked. "I assume you don't work for any newspaper."

"What about him?" Stiehl pointed to Coughlin.

"He's one of us. You chose the right person to ask questions about Pat Kerrigan."

"I made a fiver out of it," Coughlin said, grinning. "Challenged me to a game of darts."

78

"You took on the local champion, Mr. Adcock." Kerrigan laughed. "I hope it's no indication of your judgment in other matters."

Stiehl joined in the laughter, willing to let himself be the butt of amusement. But only for a moment. Suddenly he asked, "How interested would your people be in sharing one-third of a billion dollars?"

The laughter dropped from Kerrigan's face like a mask being torn away; he pursed his lips and whistled loudly. "Holy Mother of God, that's a lot of money you're talking about. What would we have to do for it? Kill every spade in South Africa and get rid of the bodies so cleverly that even the United Nations would never know it happened?"

"No. Nothing to do with Africa. But if it comes off, you'll have earned every single penny of it."

"I'm listening."

"I represent an organization in the United States that has planned an operation of immense proportions. My job is to recruit the personnel to carry out that operation."

"What's the deal?" Coughlin asked. "Immense proportions don't mean much."

"You'll find that out only if you accept. When you come to the United States, not before."

"Why us?" Kerrigan asked suspiciously.

Before Stiehl could answer, Coughlin cut in. "How come we're sharing only a third of the money? Who's getting the other two-thirds?"

"The other teams I'll be recruiting."

"Who?"

"After I leave here, I'm going to Germany. And then to the Middle East. If your people aren't interested, I'll have to share the money between the Germans and the Arabs." He saw both men pondering the point.

"How certain is the success of this operation?" Coughlin asked. "And why don't you use homegrown talent for the job? Why complicate it by importing three separate groups of soldiers?"

"It's not certain. Nothing ever is. But with the right men, it

79

should work. Recruiting such an army in the United States represents a security risk; people talk, even inadvertently. This way, by importing my army from three different areas, I'm spreading the risk, laying off my bet."

"You still haven't explained why you've come to us," Kerrigan said.

"Because I'm looking for people who are willing to risk everything to pull off this job, for the publicity they'll bring to their causes and for the arms they'll be able to buy with their share of the money."

"We don't need that kind of publicity. A lot of our support comes from the United States. How's it going to look if we take part in an operation in America, which is obviously where this thing of yours is going to take place? Let the krauts and wogs have the publicity; we'll just take the money."

"Does that mean you're interested?"

"I am. But I don't make the decisions. I'll put it to my man, arrange a meeting with him."

"When?"

Kerrigan walked to the telephone. "I can set it up now, get it over with tonight."

Stiehl nodded his approval. "You do that."

An hour later the three men left Kerrigan's flat and got into a seven-year-old Austin, which Coughlin drove. Stiehl did not even try to remember the route. There was no point; he would be returned after the meeting to where he had left his own car. He regretted momentarily having left the Browning in the suitcase, but he was certain they would not harm him. Kerrigan would back him all the way because of his alleged connection with Peter Stiehl, and no matter what shrouds of pessimism were thrown up, he could not see the provos walking away from such a magnificent payday. He found it reassuring that Kerrigan had not even shown the faintest hint of recognition; the glasses and darkened hair had thrown him completely. True, the Irishman had seen him only once in the flesh, Biafra, a million years earlier, but if he could fool him, a man who had once seen him, then strangers would be no problem.

The car stopped outside a deserted warehouse. Stiehl guessed they were within one mile of Kerrigan's home, despite the thirty minutes the journey had taken. He got out, following Kerrigan, who rapped twice on the warehouse door, then twice more after a pause of two seconds. The door swung open to reveal bare brick walls and a cracked concrete floor. Kerrigan walked inside and waited for Coughlin and Stiehl to join him. The door swung closed. Two men were standing behind it, one skinny with thick glasses and a straggly mustache, the other short and stocky, in his early forties with short red hair. Kerrigan pushed Stiehl toward the two men, but his words were directed only at the man with the red hair, as if he refused to acknowledge the other's presence.

"This is Peter Adcock from South Africa, Frank. He's come with a proposition for us."

Frank Brady studied Stiehl, letting his eyes drift over the South African. "What kind of proposition?"

"Tell him," Kerrigan prompted.

"I'd like to know who I'm talking to first," Stiehl said. "You"—he pointed at Kerrigan—"I know on a friend's recommendation. The only other thing I know about any of you is that Johnny Coughlin plays a mean game of darts."

Frank Brady's rumbling laugh filled the warehouse; he rocked on his heels, holding his sides. "Did he take you then? Johnny doesn't bother working if he can find a mug or two down at The Carlisle."

Stiehl remembered the man who had been chalking scores, all the people who had been watching the game. The chalker had recognized him as a stranger, had picked on him, asking if he wanted to play. They all must have been in on it, sharing whatever money they made from hustling strangers.

"I'm Frank Brady," the red-haired man said, "commander of the provos in this zone. The little fellow is Danny McGrath. With Johnny and Pat, we make up the tactical staff. If you've got a proposition, you're talking to the right people."

Stiehl sensed the red-haired man had an inflated ego, compensating for his lack of height. He decided to play on it, wondering how far he could go. "The right people? What do you do your

81

fighting with, darts? I need more than men who can hustle a few pounds here and there."

Brady puffed up like an angry toad. For a moment a dangerous gleam flashed across his eyes. He looked away from Stiehl and glared at Kerrigan. "Show him what we fight with! Let him see for himself!"

As Kerrigan began to move toward a pile of cartons in the corner of the warehouse, McGrath rushed forward. "Stay away from that stuff! That's not for outsiders like him to see."

"Go back to your schoolteaching," Kerrigan sneered. "This is a place for men, not boys like you."

McGrath tried to carry the argument further. Kerrigan shoved him hard in the chest, sending him stumbling into Coughlin's arms. The dart hustler held him tightly as he struggled.

"Knock it off, Danny," Brady warned. "You, too, Pat. Keep your personal feelings out of this."

Stiehl watched Kerrigan reach for the cartons and begin pulling them away from the wall, his mind registering and storing the friction between the two men. If he planned to use these men for Huckleby's operation, he needed to know everything he could about them. Brady claimed to be the leader, but could he control them?

Kerrigan finally reached the carton he wanted. He called Stiehl over. "Take a look at this. A present from a friend of ours in the Middle East. We can't seem to rely on the Americans for arms like everyone else can."

Stiehl looked over Kerrigan's shoulder. Inside the carton was a disassembled Czechoslovakian-made medium machine gun, a stand, and four cases of ammunition. He whistled, half in admiration, half in surprise. "Who loves you that much in the Middle East to send you presents like that?"

"Muammar Qaddafi," Kerrigan, replied laughing. "Loves us like his brothers, fucking filthy wog bastard. Just got this in on the last shipment, along with a load of AK-forty-sevens."

"How do you know it works?"

"We don't," Brady said from behind Stiehl. "But we plan to find out later tonight. And you'll come with us. Then, if you

82

think we can handle your job—and if we think you might have a job for us—we'll talk about terms."

"Just make damned certain where you're pointing that weapon when you start pulling the trigger," Stiehl cautioned. He had not fought his way around half the world to be gunned down by a bunch of trigger-happy Irish thugs.

Three British soldiers came out of a pub, voices loud, legs unsteady as they began to make their way back to the barracks. They knew they were taking a chance, being out late at night, but there was safety in numbers. The provos might try for one, but never for three, especially when those three were armed. Everyone knew the provos didn't like attacking anyone who could fight back.

As they stood at the bus stop, two girls in their late teens walked along the street, coats tightly buttoned. One held an unlit cigarette, fingers clasped tightly around it. They stood in line behind the soldiers, looking down the road for the bus that would not be coming for at least ten minutes.

"Got a light?" the girl with the cigarette asked.

One of the soldiers felt in his pocket and winked at his two friends as he held out a match in his cupped hands.

"Ta." The girl started to puff on the cigarette, inhaling deeply, forcing out the smoke through compressed lips.

The soldier tried to strike up a conversation. "That's what we're over here for, love. To help everyone out."

The girl with the cigarette smiled at him. "You from Liverpool?"

"Aye. You been there at all?"

"Plenty of times. My older sister lives there."

The other two soldiers moved in closer as they saw their comrade establishing a rapport with the girls. Maybe the night would not be such a bust after all, a few drinks in the pub and then the bus back to camp.

"Where are your friends from?" the second girl asked.

"He's from London. The other one's from Edinburgh," the Liverpudlian replied, pointing to each man in turn.

"I went to London once," the girl with the cigarette said. "Fantastic place."

"Bloody sight more fun than Belfast, that's for sure," the Londoner grumbled. "Nowhere to go in this bloody hole."

"That's because you don't know anyone," the girl said. "You soldiers all stick together and never get to meet the locals. There's plenty of good places to go in Belfast. We're on our way to a party right now."

"Where?" asked the Liverpudlian, his interest quickening.

The girl gave him an address. "Why don't you come with us?" she invited. "There's always too many girls at these things anyway. We were told to bring dates, but most of the fellows stay at home, playing cards, watching television."

The Liverpudlian looked at his friends; a knowing leer passed among the three soldiers. "We've got to be back by five-thirty, though."

The girl laughed, tense, brittle. "Will it take you that long to have your fun?"

The bus rumbled along, and the two girls climbed aboard; the three soldiers followed excitedly. A mile farther, they got off and walked into a side turning. The soldiers fell quiet as they realized they were going directly against specific orders given out by their company commander. Some years earlier three other soldiers had been murdered after being picked up by young girls with the promise of a party. It wouldn't happen to them, though; they were armed. Instinctively the Londoner reached down to the butt of his pistol, feeling more secure as his hand came in contact with it.

The girls went into a house, pushed open the front door, and led the way up the uncarpeted staircase. "You sure you got the right house?" the Londoner asked, becoming worried by the absence of noise. "This one looks deserted."

One of the girls turned around and put her arms around his neck, drawing closer. The soldier felt her lips press against his; her body crushed against him, stirring his feelings. "Course it's the right house," she assured him. "Can't you hear the music?"

The three soldiers listened. Sure enough, faint strains of music

84

wafted down from the top floor. They continued on their journey up the stairs and stopped outside the door from where the music was coming.

"Hold on a second," one of the girls said. "I'll just make sure it's okay to bring you in. Make sure your uniforms won't upset anyone." She winked at the soldiers. "You know what it's like; you get a few funny people who don't like the soldiers being over here." She disappeared into the room; the music increased in sound, diminishing as the door was closed. Ten seconds later she reappeared, beckoning the three soldiers and the other girl to enter.

Once inside the room, the soldiers stood like statues as they noticed the complete lack of furniture, the bare plaster walls and broken window. The only light was coming from a butane gas-powered hurricane lamp suspended from a nail in the wall. On the windowsill, a plastic transistor radio poured out pop music from Radio Luxembourg. As the first wave of surprise left them, the soldiers noticed that the girls had moved away, running across the room to join the five men there, four of them standing, the fifth lying behind a piece of machinery which looked awesomely familiar.

"Where the fucking hell did you get hold of . . . ?"

The Liverpudlian's amazed question was cut off in mid-flow as Kerrigan opened fire with the machine gun, a short, scything burst which flung the soldiers back across the room, slamming them into the wall. As they slid to the floor, blood smears left a trail of their passage.

The hammering ceased as suddenly as it had started. Kerrigan picked up the machine gun, leaving the stand and ammunition case for Coughlin. The five men and two girls hurried down the stairs to the two cars waiting outside. Within a minute they were half a mile away from the empty house, confident that the machine gun's urgent stutter had not been heard by anyone outside the building. Perhaps the following day the three soldiers would be found, or the day after that. It didn't matter; it never did. The British could not stop anything. All they could do was warn their soldiers, who would no doubt do the same thing all over again.

Despite Kerrigan's obvious hostility toward him, Danny McGrath stayed with the four other men as they entered the flat; the two girls who had been used as bait drove away. McGrath was part of the tactical staff and wanted to hear the proposition being put forward by the South African. He had as much right to be at the meeting as Kerrigan had. Kerrigan must have been in his element tonight, McGrath thought sourly, opening fire at five feet with a machine gun, just as he must have done in Biafra. But then he'd probably been shooting nothing more dangerous than women and children. Tonight was a big step up for him, killing real soldiers. And to top it all, he was acting like a bloody celebrity because this South African—who'd watched the slaughter so impassively that it made McGrath's stomach crawl—had a letter of introduction from some mercenary called Peter Stiehl who had a high respect for Kerrigan.

A schoolteacher who had been fired for bringing politics into the classroom, McGrath viewed himself as an idealist in the fight against the British, using violence only as a last resort. In his eyes, Kerrigan was nothing more than a thug, a man motivated by a bloodlust, using the excuse of sectarian divisions to kill and maim whenever the opportunity arose; he was as dangerous to the cause as he was to the British.

As soon as they had gathered in the living room, Stiehl took command of the meeting. Briefly he went over the explanation he had prepared, leaving out the name of Harlan Stone Huckleby and the reason for the operation. He told the four Irishmen it would be a strike against the United States mainland, holding an objective until negotiations had been successfully concluded for its release. He would give neither the geographical area nor the means by which it would be taken. Let them think whatever they liked, he reflected.

A short silence followed his explanation, until Brady said, "How many men do you figure you'll need?"

"From you, exactly twenty. I'll be selecting the remainder of my complement from other areas."

"Twenty's a good number," Kerrigan said, looking at Brady. "We should have no trouble in arranging that."

"There's a prerequisite," Stiehl said.

"A what?" Kerrigan asked, baffled by the word.

"Prerequisite." McGrath was unable to keep the sneer out of his voice. "It means a condition, something that must be done beforehand."

"I know what it bloody well means!" Kerrigan snapped. "I didn't hear him, that's all."

Brady swung around angrily, determined to show Stiehl who was the commander. "Shut up, the pair of you!" he hissed. Then, to Stiehl: "What's your prerequisite?"

"Nobody with a criminal record—any kind of minor offense, it doesn't matter—can even be considered for this mission. I want gray men, anonymous men. I want everyone—and that includes the four of you—to have a clean record, so there'll be no trouble obtaining visitors' visas for the United States."

Brady nodded in understanding. "We're all clear. And I'll make sure the other men I select are the same. What about you, your plans?"

"Don't worry about me. After I organize the other strike units, I'll return to the United States and map out the operation completely. When it's ready to go, I'll be in touch with you. You'll receive money for tickets and a telephone number where you can contact me once you arrive."

"When will we learn more about the job?"

"When I'm ready to tell you."

Brady stepped closer to Stiehl, looking up at the South African. "Pat Kerrigan says we can trust you because of that piece of paper you're carrying. I hope he's right, Adcock."

There was no mistaking the threat, but Stiehl chose to ignore it. "I don't think Peter Stiehl would let me down. Kerrigan's had dealings with him, and he obviously feels the same way." He walked toward the door, signifying the meeting was over.

"Good night, Mr. Brady, gentlemen. You'll be hearing from me in due course."

6

THE IRISH PART of the recruiting campaign had been easy. Once
he had located Kerrigan, Stiehl had known he would have no
trouble. The former mercenary was only too willing to help when
he had been shown the letter of introduction. And who could
resist a share in a billion-dollar payoff? Deep down, however,
Stiehl fervently wished he could have avoided being a witness to
the massacre of the three British soldiers. Killing for a reason he
could condone; senseless slaughter sickened him. He had been
forced to go along at Frank Brady's suggestion to see how efficient the provos were. It was a test for him, too, and by attending
it, he had proved himself. Above all, Stiehl wondered how the
two teenaged girls felt about their roles in the scenario, luring
the soldiers to their deaths. Not that he had much sympathy for
the soldiers; they should have had enough sense not to go roam-
ing around Belfast in the middle of the night for the promise of a
party. The sight of the Czech-made machine gun had come as a
shock, though, making him realize how much more professional-

ly armed the terrorists were becoming. He wondered how long it would be before one fanatical group came into possession of a small nuclear device. He shook his head; it did not bear thinking about.

The bus taking him from the airport at Echterdingen descended slowly into Stuttgart, and Stiehl forced his thoughts back into the present. He had called Huckleby with details of the Irish trip, notifying the general of the situation. The only drawback Stiehl could see was that Brady had been unable to supply him with any contacts in Germany, and he would be forced to start from square one. The only lead he had was a celebrated left-wing lawyer named Helmut Beider, who had defended several members of the Baader-Meinhof Gang in court, most recently on charges of robbing a bank in Stuttgart and killing two police officers during the escape. Of the four accused, two had gone to prison for life; the other two had been acquitted. If anyone knew where to reach them, Beider would. Stiehl was certain of that.

In Stuttgart, he registered in the first hotel he saw, using the name of Peter Adcock, showing the desk clerk a South African passport in that name. The Adcock passport was a belated token of gratitude from a high-ranking member of the South African government, an offering to ease the guilt brought about by Stiehl's politically advantageous dismissal from the army. Once installed in the hotel, Stiehl asked for a telephone directory in order to locate Beider. The lawyer's office was within a mile of the hotel. Stiehl set out immediately. He hailed a white Mercedes taxi and smoked during the short ride, thinking out the approach he would use.

Wearing the horn-rimmed glasses with the tinted lenses and sporting a soft tweed hat set jauntily on his head, he entered the law office. The young woman who acted as secretary-receptionist asked him his business. Stiehl produced the bogus press card from the Rand *Daily Mail*. She looked at it curiously before picking up the telephone and ringing through to the main office. Beider emerged a minute later, a man in his mid-thirties from a wealthy industrialist family who had disowned him because of his left-wing sympathies. He had long, curly black hair, dark brown eyes behind thick glasses, and a slight stoop which gave him a studious air.

"Can I be of assistance to you?" he asked in English.

"Yes, you can." Stiehl's voice was purposely abrupt, trying to intimidate the smaller man. "I'm from the Rand *Daily Mail*, South Africa. We're doing a series of articles on urban guerrilla movements. I'd like to sit down with you for a few minutes, talk about your dealings with them."

Beider glanced at his receptionist. "What appointments do I have?"

She leafed through the open diary. "Nothing till two this afternoon."

Beider nodded. "Hold any calls. Mr. Adcock, will you please come with me?"

Stiehl followed the lawyer into the office, a small room bare of all furniture except for a ponderous, old-fashioned mahogany desk, three chairs, and some steel filing cabinets. On the wall behind the desk were graduation certificates from law school and two color posters—one of Che Guevara, the other of the 1974 World Cup Champion West Germany soccer team. Stiehl found the combination incongruous: a communist revolutionary sharing wall space with eleven of the richest sporting capitalists ever assembled in front of a camera. Without being asked, he sat down, took off his hat, and lit a cigarette. There was no ashtray in the office, so he dropped the spent match onto the floor.

"What do you really want from me, Mr. Adcock?" Beider asked, settling behind the desk. The pantomime with the match had not gone unnoticed. Beider hated smoke, loathed it when people smoked in his presence, yet he felt too scared to object in this instance, as if he knew that Stiehl was aware of his fear and would capitalize on it.

"Information on the Baader-Meinhof Gang, its members."

"But not for the Rand *Daily Mail*."

"No. I want names and addresses of members who have never been connected with the organization by the authorities."

"Please continue," Beider invited the South African. "I'm listening carefully."

"I represent a political group in the United States," Stiehl said, "which is planning an operation that could net one billion dollars." He was pleased to see Beider's mouth sag by the tiniest fraction; the man could be influenced by money as well as by intimidation. Good, he knew two ways of getting through to him. "I have been appointed recruiting officer for this operation and plan to select my personnel from among the urban guerrilla groups."

"What is the operation about?"

"At the moment that remains my concern. Suffice it to say that not only will the operation net the groups a fortune, to be used however they see fit, but it will also strike a blow at the very heart of American capitalism. If you value your relationship with your friends, you'll help me and help them."

Beider pursed his lips, exhaling in a long sigh. He said nothing for fully a minute. He just sat behind the desk, staring at Stiehl.

"Well?" the South African prodded. "What about it?"

"Mr. Adcock, I am afraid you have come to the wrong man. My dealings with members of the Baader-Meinhof Gang, as they are labeled by the world's press, have always been on a strictly professional basis. Unfortunately for my reputation as a trial lawyer, the members I defended were all found guilty. Therefore, they are not available for any comment on your proposal."

Stiehl shifted in the chair, his eyes drawn to the posters on the wall. He thought he recognized one of the players on the German soccer team, a tall man with brown hair and the captain's band around his sleeve; he seemed to recall that he played for a team in New York now. "What about those defendants who were acquitted with your legal counsel?" He let his voice become harder, pushing at Beider. "The two in the Stuttgart bank raid will do to begin with."

Beider stirred uneasily at Stiehl's tone. He took a deep breath to control his fear of the man sitting opposite. "The ones who were acquitted were obviously not members of Baader-Mein-hof," was his simple reply.

"Nevertheless, I want their names and addresses."

Beider called on all his willpower to resist Stiehl. "The names you can find in a newspaper. The addresses are privileged information." He began to stand up, signifying an end to the conversation. Stiehl stood up quicker; he reached across the desk and slammed the lawyer back into the seat, towering threateningly over him. Beider closed his eyes in terror as Stiehl's powerful hands pressed down on his shoulders, forcing him even further into the chair.

"You listen to me, Beider. And listen very carefully. I'm leaving now, but I'll be back this afternoon at three o'clock. When I return, you'd better have some real answers for me. Otherwise, your illustrious clients will be looking for a new lawyer. Get it?"

Beider said nothing, only relaxing after Stiehl released his grip, picked up his hat, and turned around to leave the office. "Just remember what I said," he called over his shoulder. "By this afternoon you'd better have some names and addresses for me. Or your friends will seem like pussycats compared to what I'll drop on your head."

As the door closed behind Stiehl, Beider reached out for the telephone. His voice quaked as he asked his receptionist to find a certain number for him.

Stiehl returned to the hotel just long enough to release the false bottom of the suitcase and strap the Browning to his shoulder. Then he found a restaurant, where he ate a leisurely lunch, reading an English newspaper bought from a booth at the Stuttgart *Hauptbahnhof.* The front page was full of the murder of the three British soldiers in Belfast, with a strongly worded editorial calling for the government to pull its troops out of the North and to adopt a Shakespearean "plague o' both your houses" attitude. Stiehl agreed with the editorial. Take away the barriers, and the warring factions would probably be able to sort out their own problems; they'd be too scared to do anything else.

Remembering the route the taxi had taken from the hotel,

Stiehl set out to walk back to Beider's office, the weight of the gun reassuringly banging gently against his chest. He could imagine the telephone call Beider must have made the instant he'd left the office, the frantic summons for help to the people he claimed he did not know. There was nothing like injecting an almost lethal dose of fear into a weak man to make him act hurriedly.

He slowed his pace as he realized there was almost half an hour to go before he was due to meet again with Beider. He did not want to be early. He wanted the lawyer to have all the time he needed to make his arrangements.

A pale blue Volkswagen bus was parked outside Beider's law office. The denim-clad woman driver leaned back in the seat, arms draped indolently across the steering wheel. From time to time she would glance in the mirror attached to the passenger door, her brown eyes carefully checking the approaching pedestrians. Beider had given a comprehensive description of the South African named Adcock—tall, neatly trimmed dark brown hair parted high on the right side, almost at the center, tinted glasses, and a gray flannel suit, possibly wearing a tweed hat. She knew she would be able to pick him out easily on a sidewalk crowded with Germans.

A social science student, Magda Breitner had amassed enough hatred in her twenty-six years to last the full threescore and ten. Brought up in Nuremberg, with its heavy concentration of American military, she had learned to hate the occupiers early, gaining knowledge from her father, a former SS sergeant who had escaped detection only by the good fortune of having had his file destroyed during an Allied bombing raid. While her father had been right-wing, Magda had swung to the left, ridiculing her own family as much as she detested the Americans. So far she had participated only in mundane missions for the Baader-Meinhof Gang, acting as a messenger, envying those who had taken part in the bigger operations, the martyrs of Entebbe and Mogadishu. But her anonymity served its purpose well. She could always be relied on for the job of courier or smuggling supplies into a prison where her comrades were incarcerated. She had done well in Stuttgart when she had bribed a guard to carry in arms to the terrorists held there, allowing them martyrdom by suicide after a crack German antiterrorist unit had flown halfway around the world to end the Mogadishu affair with such precision. Now Magda waited for this South African who had threatened Beider. He had talked of an operation against the United States, the country she hated more than any other. He had talked of sums of money that were almost unbelievable. But he was also to be looked on with loathing and suspicion, the same as any of the English-speaking peoples.

Behind her, two men crouched on the empty floor of the van, peering out through the small square rear windows. Like many of the urban guerrillas, Rolf Haller came from a wealthy family, a university failure living on money from his parents in Hamburg, who owned a brewery and who believed their son was studying for his accountancy degree in Stuttgart. Instead of paying the tuition fees, the money went into the Baader-Meinhof's general purpose fund to buy weapons and explosives and to rent premises to be used as safe houses. With Haller was Horst Fischer, a teacher of English in his early thirties, a man who derived vast entertainment from teaching the language of the people he despised the most. Both men's looks reflected their backgrounds—Fischer the teacher, a thin face with lackluster brown eyes and thinning, long brown hair; Haller the brewery heir, tall and blond with clear blue eyes, an advertisement for a sports program, a man who would have looked at home on the Grand Prix circuit.

Fischer was the first to spot the man with the tinted glasses, tweed hat, and gray flannel suit. He whistled once, and Magda peered into the mirror again, watching Stiehl approach. As he came level with the rear of the van, she slid across to the passenger seat and leaned out of the window.

"Excuse me," she said in German, "can you tell me how to reach the autobahn?"

Stiehl stopped walking and looked questioningly at the girl. "Sorry," he replied in English. "I don't speak German."

Over Stiehl's shoulder, Magda saw Haller and Fischer coming around the side of the van. "In that case," she said, switching to English, "you'd better come with us. Maybe you can show us the way instead."

Stiehl felt the two men close in behind. Something hard was jabbed into the small of his back, and he allowed himself to be pushed into the Volkswagen's cargo space through the side door. There, his hands above his head, he sat back against the side of the van while Fischer patted him down, removing the Browning from its holster.

"Nice gun," the German said, hefting the automatic in his hand. "Lucky for us you didn't have the chance to use it." He operated the mechanism, chambering the top round.

"Where are you taking me?"

"For a ride," Haller replied. "To see a friend who wants to know why you go around threatening lawyers. If your answers are convincing, maybe he'll let you live. If he doesn't like them, he'll kill you."

Fischer pocketed his own weapon and sat back, facing Stiehl across the cargo space, the Browning held unwaveringly in his hand. At Haller's command, Stiehl took off his jacket and passed it over. The blond German extracted the passport and wallet and passed back the jacket. "Your name is Peter Adcock?" he asked, after pulling out the press card, an American Express card in the name of Adcock, and a forged South African driving license.

"That's what it says there," Stiehl told Haller.

Haller counted the money in the wallet before stuffing everything back and tossing it across the van to Stiehl. "Welcome to Germany, Mr. Adcock. May your stay be a pleasant one. I hope for your sake it is."

By the end of the journey, half an hour later, Stiehl's arms were aching from being held behind his neck. He lowered them gratefully as he was ordered to leave the van. While he waited for his abductors to decide on the next step, he looked around. The van had stopped in front of a tall white-painted house on a secluded street. At the junction with the main road, one hundred yards away, Stiehl could see a *Gasthaus* with cars packing its parking lot.

"Inside," Magda Breitner said, taking the Browning from Fischer.

Stiehl began to move toward the house. "Where are we?"

"Plochingen," Haller replied. "Any wiser?"

Stiehl knew where the town was, halfway between Stuttgart and Göppingen. Before flying to Germany, he had checked the area on a map, memorizing the location of towns near Stuttgart. Not that it helped him now.

"Upstairs," Magda ordered.

He obeyed. On the second-floor landing Haller went past him and knocked on the door facing the top of the stairway. A man's deep voice told them to enter.

Pushed into the room, Stiehl found himself in what was obviously intended as a bedroom, but the single bed had been moved to one side to make room for the desk which occupied the center of the carpet; a huge typewriter sat in the middle of the desk, a sheet of paper in its carriage. On the bed sat a man in his forties, dressed in crumpled corduroy trousers and a rumpled sports coat with leather elbow patches.

"This is Adcock," Magda said, shoving Stiehl in the back. Stumbling over a fold in the carpet, he pushed out against the desk to save himself from falling.

"How do you do, Mr. Adcock?" The man's English was faultless, with barely a trace of accent. "Allow me to introduce myself. Dieter Kirchmann. You have been upsetting a very valuable friend of mine, Helmut Beider. He requested that I take very special care of you."

Stiehl straightened up to face the man in the sports coat. The first thing he noticed were Kirchmann's front teeth; they seemed out of place, whiter than the rest, too large. "Who knocked your front teeth out for you, friend?"

Instinctively Kirchmann moved a hand to his mouth and fingered the two false teeth as if surprised at their presence. "A Paris gendarme's truncheon. During the riots of the sixties."

"A bit outside your territory, wasn't it?" While he had been fighting in Biafra, this man had been in France, stirring up mischief. Stiehl wondered if the gendarme had received a commendation for his work.

"We are part of an international brotherhood. Wherever we are needed, we go. One day we will even visit your country." Kirchmann dropped his hand from his mouth and smiled widely. "The French have never been the most intelligent people at instigating their own social changes. Even their revolution was a disorganized disaster."

"You didn't come out of it too well, by the looks of you."

"Far better than you are going to do. Unless you begin telling us exactly why you are here, this journey will be your last. We are not as frightened of you as Beider was."

Stiehl turned to look at the typewriter on the desk, trying to understand the words that covered the page; in German, they meant nothing to him. When he faced Kirchmann again, there was a determined set to his face that had not been there before. "Other than your name, Kirchmann, I don't know who the hell you are. And until you tell me something about yourself, I'm saying nothing more than I told Beider this morning."

"You are extremely tiresome." Kirchmann said the words softly, as if speaking to himself. "You are in no position to ask anything, only to answer." Other than giving him the name of Adcock over the telephone, with a description of the man, Beider had been useless, mumbling something incoherent about an operation that could bring in a billion dollars. Kirchmann prided himself on realism and refused to believe any operation could net that kind of money. He was uncertain what the South African wanted, but he sensed a threat. Experience had taught him there was only one certain way to deal with threats. "Mr. Adcock, I am giving you a final chance. Tell us exactly what you want; otherwise, I am going to order my people to kill you. It is as simple as that. When you stick your nose where it is not wanted, you must expect to get it chopped off."

"I'm still waiting for you to tell me what you represent," Stiehl reiterated. "I don't tell anyone my plans till I know whom I'm talking to."

Kirchmann wasted no more time. He moved his eyes to the girl and said two words. "Kill him."

Stiehl swung around and saw the Browning still pointed at him, but Magda had backed away, reaching for a telephone. When she got through, she gabbled a few quick sentences and hung up. Then she looked back at Kirchmann. "Günther's on his way right now. He'll be here in ten minutes. He can finish off the job; you know how he enjoys it."

Kirchmann seemed pleased. "Very good. Now, Mr. Adcock, you have ten minutes in which to change your mind. Because once we release you into the custody of Günther Werner, there is no such thing as an eleventh-hour reprieve."

"You're throwing away your share of a billion dollars," Stiehl said. "What are your superiors going to say when they find out about that?"

Kirchmann flushed, a deep red. "I have no superiors," he spit out, and bit his lip immediately.

"So I'm talking to the big man, the commander in chief. Think of all the trouble you could have saved yourself by telling me that in the beginning."

Stiehl felt the Browning's muzzle jabbed hard into his back. The girl's voice hissed into his ear. "You are the one who is in trouble. Not any of us."

Stiehl feinted to move. The girl stepped back immediately, holding the Browning in both hands. "Put your hands behind your neck," she ordered. "Or I will not wait till Günther gets here. I will shoot you myself."

Stiehl obeyed, clasping his fingers behind his neck. He had learned all he needed to know about the identity of the people who held him captive. Kirchmann was the leader, the decision maker, reporting to nobody. It would be Kirchmann who either approved or turned down Stiehl's proposal. He could tell the German now what he had told Brady's men, hiding the actual objective, just saying enough to interest him to the point of commitment. Or he could wait until the man called Günther Werner arrived. Stiehl decided on the latter course of action, wanting to see who else belonged to this terrorist cell.

Werner arrived five minutes later, using a key to enter the house. Heavy footsteps sounded on the staircase. The door thrust open, and Stiehl immediately recognized the kind of man who stood there—belligerent attitude, small brown eyes set closely together, broad shoulders, and a flat, almost simian face. Strong, but not too bright, Stiehl decided. Probably used as the strong-arm man, the enforcer.

Kirchmann's voice was low. "Günther, this is Mr. Peter Adcock, from South Africa. Dispose of him."

Werner stepped into the center of the room. He stared hard at Stiehl for a long moment before taking the Browning from Magda. He shoved Stiehl toward the door, followed him downstairs to the street, and held him against the Volkswagen van while he opened the driver's door. "Get in and drive where I tell you."

Stiehl hid his surprise that the man spoke English as well as any of the others. He had pegged him for an illiterate in his own language, let alone a foreign tongue. Having climbed into the driver's seat, he waited for Werner to get in.

"Go to the main road, and turn left. Keep on it till you come to a set of traffic lights." The Browning never wavered from Stiehl's side.

Putting the van into gear, Stiehl started off, trying to decide where he should take Werner out of the picture. Right now, outside the house where the others might be watching? No, he decided against it. Better let him get wherever he's planned on going, bring him back as a surprise to the others, turn the tables completely on them. Obediently he followed Werner's directions, turning left at the lights, continuing along a narrow road leading into the forest. Half a mile into the trees Werner ordered Stiehl to pull off to the side. There was a small clearing which Stiehl steered into. He turned off the engine.

"Out." The single word was accompanied by a taut wave of the Browning.

After getting out, Stiehl stood on the damp earth, hands raised automatically as the German followed him out of the driver's side. Werner was licking his lips. Stiehl guessed it was done out of anticipation, not nervousness, pleasure at what was to come. Werner was a man who enjoyed killing. Stiehl decided that he, in turn, would enjoy reversing the positions.

"You religious, Adcock?"

"If I were?"

"I'd tell you to say your prayers."

"Maybe you should start saying yours, if you can remember them," Stiehl said. He dropped his hands from above his head and began to advance slowly on Werner. Surprised at the unexpected move, the German stepped back defensively until he remembered that he held the gun. He brought it up with both hands and pointed it directly into Stiehl's face, finger tightening on the trigger, squeezing back as the slack was taken up.

Werner was still wondering why the Browning's hammer had fallen onto nothing when Stiehl knocked aside the gun and jabbed him savagely in the eyes with his index and middle fingers, blinding him. He screamed in agony and dropped the gun as he staggered back, hands clawing at his injured eyes. Stiehl was on him immediately, a shoe driven viciously into his groin, doubling him up in pain. As he toppled forward, a knee was slammed into his face. Finally, like an act of mercy, clasped hands clubbed him on the back of the neck, knocking him senseless.

Stiehl stood over the prostrate body for a minute, turning it over with his foot, waiting for signs of returning consciousness. As Werner groaned, Stiehl bent down to pick up the Browning. He ejected the top round, recognizing the slight scratch on the nose of the bullet. Pocketing it, he thought about the fortuitousness of his own private, personal fear, the horror of his one day being shot with his own gun, how it had always prompted him to leave a dummy round at the top of the magazine. It had worked this time; no doubt it would work again in the future. If he ever chose to let himself walk into a trap again, as he had done with the Germans.

Werner sat up slowly, hands to his head as he tried to focus. The first thing he recognized was Stiehl standing over him, the black hole of the Browning's muzzle reaching out to devour him.

"On your feet," Stiehl ordered. "You're driving."

Werner began to rise, gauging Stiehl's distance, his mind still numbed by the refusal of the gun to fire. Suddenly he lunged at Stiehl. The South African stepped back nimbly, feinted to counter, then slid off to one side, sticking out his foot. Werner cannoned past to fall sprawling on the ground. Stiehl raised the pistol until it was lined up on the center of the German's forehead.

"Take my word that it works now." He squeezed down on the trigger, seeing the white, naked glare of fear on Werner's face as he understood what was about to happen. At the last moment, as Stiehl's instincts told him the hammer had reached its point of return, he twitched his hand to the right. The Browning's report echoed away into the forest as the bullet smashed into the ground two inches from Werner's left ear, spraying his face with dirt. Stepping back toward the van, Stiehl allowed himself a fleeting smile. He was certain he'd have no more trouble with the big German.

Back at the house in Plochingen, he ordered Werner to unlock the front door and go upstairs. The German stood uncertainly on the landing. Prompted by the Browning, he opened the bedroom door.

"What happened to you?" Kirchmann gasped in surprise as he saw Werner's bruised face, blood trickling from his nose, his lips split.

"I happened to him," Stiehl said, stepping into the room behind Werner, understanding the gist of Kirchmann's question. "You're playing with the professionals now, not the amateur dramatics you normally indulge in. You shouldn't send a bullyboy out to do a man's job."

Kirchmann assumed a blank expression at Stiehl's unexpected reappearance. "We did not really expect you to return, Mr. Adcock."

"I didn't expect it to be otherwise." Stiehl shifted his gaze from Kirchmann to take in Magda Breitner, Haller, and Fischer. Aside from Kirchmann, the others were too stupefied by his

101

return from the grave to move or speak. "I assume you're the leader of this group, Kirchmann, so what I have to say is for your ears only."

Kirchmann appeared not to have heard the remark. He was looking from Stiehl to Werner, his head shaking in unbridled admiration. "I have never known Günther to fail us before, Mr. Adcock. Especially when he holds the gun. How did you accomplish it?"

Werner answered for Stiehl, trying to excuse himself in Kirchmann's eyes. "He tricked me, tricked us all. The top round in the magazine was a dummy. The same thing would have happened to any of us who tried to use that gun."

"Oh?" Kirchmann seemed impressed by the simple ruse. "And you accuse us of amateur dramatics, Mr. Adcock. It would appear that you have a genuine flair for them yourself. But"—he spread his hands in a gesture of finality—"you have proved your point most admirably. Let us talk."

"To you alone."

"Of course." Kirchmann clapped his hands, waving the other members of the group toward the door. The last one out, Werner, gave Stiehl the benefit of a long, malicious stare; there was no mistaking the threat contained in the small eyes.

"Günther doesn't like you, Mr. Adcock."

"I don't give a damn what he likes or dislikes."

"Foolish. A very foolish attitude. He is a mean person, strong as well. He—how would you say it?—likes his work, derives a certain satisfaction from making people suffer. Be sure that you do not give him the chance for revenge."

"I'll bear it in mind." Stiehl holstered the Browning, feeling no need for it alone in the room with Kirchmann. Beider tipped you off, just as I wanted him to. I assume you're all members of Baader-Meinhof."

"For want of a better title, yes," Kirchmann conceded. "In our own eyes, we are the instruments for change, concerned people trying to establish a more just social system."

"Yes, yes, yes, spare me the propaganda speech." Stiehl waved aside the explanation of Kirchmann's political ideals.

102

"But you wouldn't be opposed to a small venture where the payoff could be in the region—"

"Of one billion dollars." Kirchmann finished the sentence for Stiehl. "You mentioned that figure before. Whom do you represent? What do you want us to do?"

"Whom I represent is my business. Your only concern is getting your part of the job done and earning your share."

"I am listening." Kirchmann leaned back on the bed, his head against the wall, legs drawn up, knees tucked underneath his chin.

Stiehl kept his voice low, confident the other group members would be listening outside the door. "I need your help in completing a mission in the United States. It'll have the biggest payoff in history. Interested?"

Kirchmann's eyes blazed with a fanatical enthusiasm usually reserved only for a political action; there was no need for a reply.

7

"ADCOCK, I do not trust you."

Outside the small apartment where Stiehl sat, the temperature was in the high nineties; the noon sun blazed down on the almost deserted streets, turning them into dry, baking caldrons of heat. Moslem gunmen, toting Russian-made AK-47 assault rifles, patrolled ceaselessly, ready to repel any incursions the Christian militiamen might attempt. In the distance could be heard the occasional rattle of small-arms fire, punctuated by the heavier, more threatening echo of artillery. Stiehl guessed the artillery belonged to the Syrian forces which had moved into Lebanon, ostensibly to keep the warring factions apart, but now taking sides with their Moslem brothers.

He turned from the window, eyes accustoming themselves to the darkness of the room as he faced the man sitting opposite. By the door stood another man, dressed in combat fatigues and a kaffiyah which covered half his face; his hand never strayed from the Makarov pistol in his belt.

"Give me the chance to earn your trust, Doctor," Stiehl offered. "That is all I ask."

The man weighed Stiehl's words carefully. As head of the Marxist-oriented Popular Front for the Liberation of Palestine, Dr. George Habash would like nothing better than to participate in a strike against the United States, the guardian of the hated Zionists. But he remembered his history too well, especially the sage advice about Greeks bearing gifts. This man Adcock, who had come to him with a proposition for striking against America, was a South African. Next to the United States, South Africa was Israel's staunchest supporter. What reason would a South African have for making an offer such as this? "How would you prove your good intentions?" Habash asked. "Have you any suggestions?"

Stiehl took a long time thinking out his answer, not wanting to show that he had worked out everything in advance. From the moment Dieter Kirchmann had given him Habash's name and details of how to contact the Arab leader, Stiehl had known this would be the toughest part of the recruitment campaign. But Huckleby wanted terrorists for his operation—that's what he was paying for—and by God, Stiehl would deliver him an army of terrorists. "I'll do a job for you. A mission in Israel. I'll have no trouble getting into the country. Tell me what you want done."

Habash beckoned to the guard standing by the door. The man came forward and bent while Habash whispered a rapid torrent of Arabic into his ear. The man replied, then stepped back to resume his post by the door.

"We have a man in Tel Aviv," Habash said. "You will contact him. If you perform the task he sets you to our satisfaction, we will talk again. If you do not, you will never leave Israel." He stood up, and the guard opened the door. "Good day, Adcock."

Stiehl flew from Beirut to Cyprus, where he waited four hours for the flight to Ben-Gurion Airport. This time he used his own passport, hiding the one in the name of Adcock in the secret compartment of his suitcase. A taxi took him to the small restaurant the name of which Habash had given him. He entered, sat down, and ordered coffee. Before it came, the restaurant owner joined him.

"*Salaam.*"

"Do I know you?" Stiehl used the four words he had agreed upon as a sign of recognition.

The restaurant owner came back immediately. "No. But you will." He stood up and walked through the restaurant. Stiehl followed, forgetting about the coffee. The man led the way upstairs to a small, dingy apartment and bolted the door after Stiehl had entered.

"There is a bus," he said, "which runs from Tel Aviv to Jerusalem. Sometimes it is filled with many tourists. The doctor says you will prove yourself by destroying this bus."

"How?"

"Come. I show you." The man led the way farther into the apartment. In the single bedroom he pushed aside a worn chest of drawers and pried up the floorboards below. Stiehl leaned over to watch the man uncover a metal box. Inside were two kilos of plastic explosive and detonators. "I will make this for you. You will leave it on the bus."

"When?"

"I will have it ready by tomorrow morning. You will board the bus for the run to Jerusalem. When it stops at Petah Tikvah, just outside Tel Aviv, you will get off."

"And leave the package?"

"Yes. But a warning. You will be watched the entire time by one of my men. Should you do anything other than what I have told you, you will be killed immediately."

"And afterward?"

"You will report back here to me. If I am pleased by your work, I will send the appropriate message to Dr. Habash." He replaced the floorboards and pushed back the piece of furniture. Stiehl made no attempt to help him.

From the apartment Stiehl returned to the center of town. In

Dizengoff Square he melted quickly into the thronging mass of people, confident of losing any tail the restaurant owner might have put on him. He found a telephone booth and asked the operator for a government number. She put him through.

"Eli?"

"Yes. Who is this?" the man asked in Hebrew.

"Speak English," Stiehl said. "I was never good at ancient languages."

There was a pause, then: "Peter?"

"Yes."

"I'll be damned!" There was no way Eli Romberg of the Mossad—the Israeli intelligence agency—could mask his surprise or pleasure at the unexpected call. "Where are you, you villain?"

"In Tel Aviv."

"On business?"

"In a way." Before Romberg could ask more, Stiehl continued. "Remember when you let us down in Angola?"

A long silence came from the other end of the line before Romberg spoke again, apologetically. "I'm sorry about that, Peter. We could not help ourselves. The Americans . . ."

"I know. But I need a favor now. A big one. I figure you owe me that much."

"Can I ask why you need this big favor?"

"No. But I'll make a trade. In return for your help, I'll give you a name and an address in Tel Aviv that your people would like to know all about."

"What are you up to, Peter?"

"One day I'll tell you, but not right now. Will you help?"

Romberg let out an exaggerated sigh. "Tell me what you want, and I'll give you at least a thousand official reasons why I can't help you."

"But you will."

"Yes, Peter. I will."

Stiehl returned to the Arab restaurant at ten the following morning. His contact was waiting for him.

107

"The bus leaves in forty-five minutes. When you get off at Petah Tikvah, leave this under the seat." He handed Stiehl a plastic briefcase. "It is all set."

Stiehl took the case gingerly, wondering whether to look inside to make certain it was safe to carry. "What if the bus doesn't leave on time?" He had visions of himself being blown to pieces before the bus even left Tel Aviv; this was his first trip to Israel in almost six years, but he clearly remembered that bus timetables meant very little.

"Then leave it in a store, a marketplace, or somewhere, and walk away."

"What about your man?"

"He will be there. Make no mistakes."

"I won't," Stiehl said softly. "I don't make mistakes."

The bus left on time, and Stiehl sat back, the briefcase tucked between his feet. He hoped the Arab knew what he was doing and the damned thing would not go off before Petah Tikvah. As the bus chugged through the Tel Aviv suburbs, he made a mental list of the expenses he would charge Huckleby over and above the agreed one million dollars. The most hazardous duty he'd ever pulled came nowhere near sitting with a live bomb between his feet, which even a jolt might set off. He looked around the bus, trying to spot his tail, but there were too many people of mixed nationalities to pick out a single Arab. The Americans he could recognize easily enough. Their loud clothes betrayed them if their voices did not. He picked up a few English accents; even one South African, a young girl with long blond hair who reminded him of Linda Huckleby. He would have to look her up when he returned to the States. That is, if he ever got back, he thought, as he looked at the briefcase between his feet.

At the outskirts of Tel Aviv the bus stopped, and three men boarded. Two were soldiers carrying Uzi submachine guns; the other was a middle-aged man in gray trousers and a white, open-necked shirt. The two soldiers sat down behind Stiehl, while the civilian chose a position across the aisle.

A mile farther, as open country began to take over from buildings, the driver pulled the bus off the road and switched off the engine. Several passengers began talking excitedly in half a dozen different languages, each trying to be heard over the other. Stiehl sat waiting, almost laughing out loud at the scene. Even when he was in Israel during the Six-Day War as an official observer for the South African Army, the Israeli soldiers had acted like this. He was dumbfounded how the entire defense force managed to operate with so many different languages spoken. That was when he had first met the man sitting across the aisle from him. Eli Romberg had been an intelligence officer then, before he resigned to take up an appointment with the Mossad. When Stiehl glanced across the aisle to see what Romberg was doing, the Israeli winked.

From the front of the bus came the driver's voice, yelling in Hebrew above the general commotion. "We can go no farther for a while. The engine is overheating, and I must let it get cold before I can check the coolant level." He repeated the words in English, surprising Stiehl with a strong American accent. "You may just as well leave the bus and walk around till I find what the trouble is. You will be more comfortable outside because the air-conditioning unit will not work with the engine not running."

Passengers began to rise, grumbling to each other about the bus line's inefficiency. Stiehl also stood, leaving the plastic briefcase on the floor, and moved into line behind Romberg. The two soldiers were the last to leave. One knelt down by the seat Stiehl had been using and taped a small square object to the case. He hurried off the bus and joined the others, pushing them back.

Thirty seconds later, when the fuse on the demolition charge ran out, a double explosion ripped through the bus, the lesser blast of the charge, followed by the thunderous detonation of the plastic. Everything within a ten-foot radius of Stiehl's seat was destroyed beyond recognition. The bus rocked on its axles, a mortally wounded giant breathing its last, before settling back on an even keel. Windows blew out as people screamed and dived for safety. There were no casualties.

"Nobody move!" came the shouted order from Romberg.

Stiehl froze, looking at Romberg, mentally complimenting him on the smoothness of the operation. The Israeli intelligence officer had been given little time to plan, but Stiehl doubted if the job could have been done more efficiently with a year's preparation.

"*Ata! Atzur!*" one of the soldiers yelled as a swarthy youth edged away from the group of stunned passengers. "You! Halt!"

The other soldier took up the cry. "*Atzur! Acheret nerei!* Halt or I shoot!"

The youth spun around, hand flashing toward his waistband. Out came a small-caliber pistol. Before he even had the time to raise it, one of the soldiers dropped to his knee, sighted quickly along the barrel of the Uzi, and squeezed the trigger. The burst of six bullets slammed the youth squarely in the center of the chest, a tight shot group that could have been covered by a fist. His mouth gaped open, blood frothing from his lips as the bullets punched him back. The pistol flew up into the air and landed at the feet of one of the passengers. Romberg stepped forward quickly to pick it up before going over to the body of the youth. Stiehl joined him.

"Very slick."

Romberg seemed not to hear. He was staring at the pistol, breaking it open, dropping out the ammunition. "Look at this, will you, Peter? He'd have blown off his hand if he'd pulled the trigger." He showed Stiehl the amount of play in the weapon. "This thing must have been used as a hammer."

Stiehl looked down at the dead youth; he could have been no older than seventeen. "You did him a favor. Who wants to walk around without a hand?"

Romberg looked curiously at the South African. "Do not mock death, my friend. Not even when it comes to visit an enemy. You, more than anyone, should know that." He threw the pistol to one of the soldiers, then turned to face the passengers.

"On behalf of the Israeli government, I apologize for what has happened today. Believe me, none of you was ever in the slightest danger; we had the situation monitored very carefully from the outset. Another bus will be along shortly to take you the remainder of the way to Jerusalem." He turned to Stiehl. "Now we had better get you to Petah Tikvah so you can take the bus back to Tel Aviv."

"The news story will come out all right?"

"Trust me. You'll give me that name in Tel Aviv?"

"When he's done one more thing for me."

An army jeep drew up. Romberg and Stiehl got in, leaving the two soldiers to supervise the passengers waiting for the replacement bus. "You're not going to tell me what this is all about, are you?" the Israeli asked resignedly.

"Not yet," Stiehl said with a smile. "But one day I'll let you in on all the secrecy."

"Sure," Romberg said disgruntledly. "And one day our farmers will produce a pig with cloven hooves that chews the cud so I can eat bacon without offending God." He signaled for the driver to move off.

Stiehl returned to the Arab restaurant early that evening. The story of more than a dozen people dying in an explosion aboard a bus leaving Petah Tikvah covered the front pages of newspapers. Inside the restaurant the patrons were listening to the news on an Arab radio station, gathered from details supplied by the Israeli official information service. From Lebanon, Dr. George Habash had claimed responsibility for the Popular Front for the Liberation of Palestine.

"You did well." The restaurant owner congratulated Stiehl.

"Your young friend did not. He was found with a pistol at Petah Tikvah. Instead of surrendering, he tried to shoot it out with an Israeli Army patrol. He was killed instantly."

"So I heard. But a dozen of them for one Arab is a good exchange. They will be gone long before us at such a rate. Do you go back to Beirut now?"

"To see the doctor."

"He will be pleased to welcome you. This action has shown that you are one of us. You are to be trusted."

"Thank you. When will you send the message?"

"It is sent already. As soon as news came through on the radio of the explosion."

"Good." Stiehl shook hands with the man and went outside. He stood on the narrow sidewalk for thirty seconds; then a Mercedes sedan drove up, followed by two army trucks. Troops raced

111

into the restaurant. A minute later they brought out everyone who had been inside. Stiehl pointed out the restaurant owner.

"He gave me the bomb," he told Romberg. "Just do me one favor."

"Another one?" Romberg asked.

"All right. Another one. Hold him incommunicado for at least six months."

Romberg grinned at the request. "He'll be lucky if he ever gets to stand trial. But do *me* a favor—don't spread that around. We don't want the United Nations more upset with us than they are already." He shook hands with Stiehl and got back into the Mercedes.

As the restaurant owner had promised, Habash welcomed Stiehl with open arms on his return to Beirut. The atmosphere of hostility which had cloaked the first meeting between the two men had disappeared. Habash insisted on taking the South African around the Moslem-held section of Beirut, showing him the fortifications and arms captured from the Christians. Stiehl tried to remember all he could, so he would be able to pass the information on to Romberg and from there to the Christians.

"Tell me your requirements again, Adcock," Habash requested as they ate in the apartment, waited on by one of the guards.

"Twenty men. Good men. All able to speak English. All with clean records so they will be able to obtain visitors' visas to the United States."

"Visas are no problem," Habash cut in. "I can get any amount of Libyan diplomatic passports."

"Even better. Of those twenty men, three must be trained pilots, able to fly a large jetliner out of New York for the escape."

Habash listened thoughtfully. "I know of three such men. They are Syrians who are now fighting alongside us. They are in the camps, instructing our antiaircraft teams to repel the Israeli terror bombers that kill our women and children. No, I do not think my complement of men will be difficult to arrange. We have many people wishing to carry the fight to the enemy. Perhaps the hardest part will be deciding how to choose only twenty men from among so many thousands. And"—he made a gesture with his hands—"a share in one billion dollars will buy much equipment. Even our friends in Russia are not unhappy about being paid in American dollars."

"I'll leave you then," Stiehl said. "Until you hear from me, you will do nothing."

"Other than selecting the men, absolutely nothing. It has been a pleasure meeting you, Adcock. Perhaps not for the Israelis, but certainly for me."

Stiehl could not resist a smile. He just hoped that Habash did not know why he was smiling.

8

THREE HOURS remained before Harlan Stone Huckleby was due to pick up Stiehl from the TWA terminal at Kennedy Airport. Stiehl had called thirty minutes before boarding the flight, waking Huckleby before dawn to give him the news that the recruiting campaign had gone successfully; the first step in the operation had been completed. That was one headache out of the way as far as Huckleby was concerned, something he could never have accomplished without Stiehl's assistance. Now came the part that he alone could do; even Stiehl, with his multifarious contacts, would be unable to pull this off as well as he could.

Huckleby surveyed the pile of papers on his desk at Howson Chemicals a final time before filing them away in a drawer. There were written orders from himself, and confirmations from his warehouse manager, that 150 tons of explosive had been shipped from Howson Chemicals' manufacturing plant and stored in the company's Newark and Long Island City warehouses, allegedly a canceled order awaiting a new buyer. Beneath the notations on the explosives was a short memorandum

114

from the company's transport manager that fifteen trucks, each with a ten-ton load capacity, had been specially leased in addition to the company's normal fleet and painted steel gray instead of Howson Chemicals' traditional red and blue. Huckleby knew the trucks would be traced back to his company and to him as president, as would the sudden increase in the storage of explosives without a corresponding buyer's order. He did not care. What was the point of teaching the United States the most important lesson it would ever learn if nobody knew who the teacher was? And Stiehl? He could look after himself; he was being paid enough to take his chances with the rest of them, even if he was having no part in the actual operation. Huckleby was certain that after the mission was over, the South African would simply disappear, taking his money with him. He would never be connected by police with the theft of Manhattan. The man covered his tracks too well.

The TWA flight touched down two minutes behind schedule, just as Huckleby was steering the Cadillac into an empty space in the Terminal Four parking lot. He got out and began walking hurriedly toward the terminal when he felt the familiar tightening in his chest. He took a nitroglycerin pill to ease the pressure and slowed down. By the time he arrived inside the terminal the constriction had ceased.

Stiehl came through customs twenty minutes later, his single piece of luggage swinging from his hand. Having strolled past Huckleby with no sign of recognition, he waited on the sidewalk for the older man to catch up. As they walked toward the car, Huckleby asked about the trip.

"Sixty men are waiting on my word. What's happening here?"

"My side of it's all in order. I've requisitioned—sorry—put in purchase orders for the explosives. Everything should be in storage by now. My transportation manager's lined up the extra trucks. We can start working on the next phase of the operation now."

They reached the Cadillac and got in. Huckleby drove the short distance from the airport to the home of Stiehl's sister in

115

Howard Beach. He slowed down to let off his passenger. Stiehl told him to keep driving; he did not want Juliet to see him in Huckleby's company. When this was all over, he wanted nobody ever to remember seeing him with Huckleby.

"Drop me at a real estate office," Stiehl said. "I have to see about a command post for myself."

Huckleby nodded, understanding, pulling up at the first real estate office he saw. Stiehl got out of the car, fumbled in his jacket pocket, and slipped something over his eyes. When he turned around, the tinted glasses had changed his face completely. He finished off the impromptu disguise by fishing a crumpled hat out of his case and jamming it over his head. Huckleby swore he could have passed him on the street without recognizing him.

Inside the real estate office, Stiehl watched the Cadillac drive away before turning to the girl sitting at the closest desk. "I'm looking for a furnished apartment," he said, the South African completely gone, replaced with a clipped English tone. "I want something for three months while I'm working over here. My name's Adcock." He passed across a business card. "London correspondent for the Rand *Daily Mail,* on temporary assignment in New York while our regular man's on leave."

"I'll see what I can find for you, Mr. Adcock." She leafed through a catalog, lifting it up when she reached the desired page. "There's the top half of a two-family house. Five hundred dollars a month."

"Could I see it, please?"

She led Stiehl out to the back, where an old Mustang convertible was parked. He got in, pulling up his jacket collar as the wind whistled in through tears in the soft roof. They completed the journey in less than ten minutes. Stiehl guessed the house to be no more than two miles from his sister's home. He followed the girl up an external flight of stairs to the apartment, waiting while she found the right key on the bunch she had taken from the office.

A quick survey of the apartment was all Stiehl needed to say he would take it. The furniture was cheap, but he had no plans for staying any great length of time. As the girl tried to show

116

him the kitchen, he broke into her sales pitch and asked to see the master bedroom. She looked at him crossly, then led the way through the apartment.

"In there," she said curtly, not bothering to accompany him.

Stiehl pushed open the door with his elbow and walked inside. He headed straight to the window, making certain he touched nothing with his hands. The window offered a splendid view of Jamaica Bay, the water only three hundred yards distant, with no tall buildings to block his view. As he turned away, he caught a glimpse of a British Airways jumbo roaring low overhead on its final descent to Kennedy Airport.

"I'll take it," he said, rejoining the girl in the hallway.

"Two months' rent in advance, please. First and last. As a security."

Stiehl pulled out a fat roll of hundred-dollar bills from his trouser pocket, the remnants of Huckleby's expense fund. He peeled off ten and passed them to the girl, who stuffed them into her purse immediately, as if scared the new tenant might change his mind.

"I'll give you a receipt when we return to the office, Mr. Adcock."

"Thank you. Do I get to meet my landlord?"

She shook her head. "They're a very elderly couple who spend most of the year down in Florida; they have a condominium there. We look after everything for them."

Back at the real estate office, Stiehl took the receipt from the girl, asking her to send his copy of the lease to the apartment. He then caught a taxi to Kennedy Airport, where he used a washroom's privacy to remove the glasses and tweed hat, hiding them in his suitcase. As Peter Stiehl again, he caught another taxi to his sister's home. She was delighted when he told her he would be moving in.

Linda Huckleby was barely awake when the telephone rang at seven-thirty the following morning. She pushed her eyes open with her hands, trying to focus on the room, then on the white Princess telephone occupying the bedside table. Who could be calling at this hour? Her father? But why, for God's sake, so early?

"Daddy?"

"Try again, sweetheart. Right sex, wrong relationship."

To Linda, still half asleep, the voice sounded like Humphrey Bogart's, but nobody she knew did the impersonation that well—especially at seven-thirty in the morning. "Who is this, please?"

"The man from south of Kilimanjaro."

Weariness vanished, and pleasure took its place as she recognized the South African accent Stiehl had slipped back into. "Don't they sleep where you come from?"

"Hell, no. How do you think we get these great complexions? We just stay up and drink all night long."

Linda shook her head in disbelief at the call. She had given up on ever seeing Stiehl again after that first lightning visit to the apartment. She had sensed an interest on his part, but it had come to nothing. Even when she had asked her father what had happened, he had shrugged his shoulders and said that Stiehl had his own business to attend to.

"I think you owe me an apology, Mr. Stiehl." She made it sound very formal.

"Oh? For what?"

"For taking so damned long to call."

"How come you're so certain I was going to call?"

"Why else did you look so carefully at my telephone number when you left here that night?"

"I've been out of the country," he said, amazed that she had noticed what he considered a surreptitious action. "That's why I called so early. I'm still on European time."

"Promoting your book?"

"No. Working."

"Killing? For cash or otherwise?"

Something bothered him about the tone of her questions. He was uncertain whether she was teasing or putting him down. "Does killing have some kind of fascination for you?"

"Good heavens, no! But it does seem to be what you do best. Or is it something to do with my father?"

118

Stiehl did not answer immediately. "I called you to find out what you're doing today," he said at last. "Not to get the third degree of my life."

"In about half an hour I'll get up. Then I'll shower and have breakfast. After that, I may go shopping."

Stiehl began to feel on firmer ground. "How could a girl as lovely as you improve herself with something out of a shop?"

"Just watch me." She laughed. "Or have you got a better idea?"

"Meet me for lunch in the city."

"Where?"

"Make it the library on Fifth and Forty-second. Southwest corner at twelve-thirty."

"What better place to meet a writer?" She laughed again, and Stiehl began to feel easier. "See you then."

From a shop doorway Stiehl watched Linda approach their meeting place. A brisk wind whipped her flaxen hair around her shoulders, sweeping it across her face, making her brush it back every few seconds. He stood admiring her for almost a minute, the way she dressed, how she complimented her figure and coloring with the tan suede jacket and chocolate slacks which flared out over sensible but expensive shoes. Over her shoulder was a capacious soft leather purse from Italy.

"Waiting long?" he asked, walking up behind her.

She turned to face him, her blue eyes sparkling. "Almost a minute. Another five seconds, and I'd have stood you up."

He took her hand and kissed her on the cheek, smelling the light fragrance of the perfume she'd dabbed on her neck. "I think you would have given me at least ten seconds."

"You're very confident. But then I suppose a man who has commanded armies like my father must be confident."

He held her arm as they began to cross the road. "Never an army. Nothing quite so grand. Tell me something, Linda. Have you got something against soldiers?"

She seemed to soften, as if a defensive wall had disappeared and she were willing to let Stiehl see a little deeper into her.

"Not really. It's just that I've been surrounded by military uniforms for most of my life. Even though my father's been retired for more than ten years, he still acts like he's in uniform."

"Let's postpone any deep discussion till after lunch," Stiehl said, wanting to nip this particular conversation in the bud. "I was never one for talking on an empty stomach."

"I'm not really hungry anyway," Linda said. "I had a late breakfast." Without waiting for Stiehl's reply, she waved down a cab and directed the driver to the Guggenheim Museum. "I'm going to give you an afternoon of New York culture," she said as they settled in the cab. "Relax and enjoy."

They walked around the museum for the better part of two hours. Stiehl felt like a dog on a leash, following Linda wherever she went, stopping wherever she stopped, listening attentively to whatever she had to say about each exhibit. Somehow he found himself enjoying the experience, even to the point of forgetting he had missed lunch. Some galleries followed, then at Linda's suggestion, they had dinner at the Four Seasons, where, for the first time since meeting the girl at the library, Stiehl had time to collect his thoughts.

"I never killed anyone for the sheer hell of it," he said suddenly.

The unexpected comment took Linda by surprise. A few seconds passed before she could relate it to the telephone conversation of the morning. "Why did you kill?"

"To achieve an objective. Or to protect myself and my men. Which amounts to the same thing."

"Explain." She leaned back as the waiter began serving. "Why are soldiers necessary? I don't recall my father ever explaining it very satisfactorily."

Stiehl thought the question over. "Any country which values its freedom needs an adequate defense force. Otherwise, it's in danger of being invaded. The poorest, most undeveloped country in the world has something another country wants . . . even if it's only fleas."

"That doesn't explain where the mercenary comes in."

"We're utilized by small countries which cannot afford their own standing armies. We fight on contract."

"Do you like the life, the fighting?"

Stiehl replied with a question with his own. "Does the CPA who lives in Connecticut enjoy commuting every day to his office in New York? It's the same thing, part and parcel of his job."

"Would you ever consider fighting again?" An inner force which Linda could not understand prompted the questions, as though it were determined to learn all it could about the South African.

"Who knows? If I make a fortune writing, of course not. If I were short of money, I'd have to work again—just like that CPA in Connecticut."

She toyed with the spoon, looking at her reflection in the bowl, upside down on the concave side, enlarged to grotesque proportions in the other. "I've seen you twice in my whole life, Peter; three times if we count the television show. Before, it wouldn't have mattered to me in the least to read that some mercenary soldier called Peter Stiehl had been killed in some unimportant, unpronounceable corner of the world, fighting for some cause that had no meaning. Now I think it would."

Stiehl began to feel vaguely uncomfortable; someone was getting closer to him than he liked. "I'm not sure I follow you."

Linda looked up from the spoon, staring wide-eyed across the table. For all her apparent sophistication, she suddenly looked very vulnerable to Stiehl. "Knowing you, if only for a few hours, would somehow make it seem more personal if you were killed. Maybe it's just a selfish reason for hoping you don't go back to your old business."

"Would it ease your mind if I made a solemn promise never to return to it?"

"Would you?"

"Of course not." He grinned broadly and was relieved when Linda responded. "Come on, let's finish up and get out of here before you have me in tears about the rotten life I've led."

From the restaurant they caught a cab to where Linda had

121

left her Mercedes. As she slid into the driver's seat, Stiehl hesitated, wondering if he was presuming too much by taking the passenger seat.

"What are you waiting for?" she called, opening the other door. Stiehl got in and made himself comfortable. "Are you still going ahead with that plan for Daddy?" She had seen her father sign the check.

"Has he said I am?"

"He's avoided talking about you."

"Then what do you think?"

"I think you are."

"Why?"

"Because he's started talking about the operation a lot since he brought you up to the apartment. How he's going to show his old pals in Washington that he's right and they're all wrong. Old Stoneass coming to the rescue again."

"Pardon?"

"Old Stoneass . . . my father's army nickname."

"Oh, I see." Stiehl sank back into the seat, trying to register exactly what Linda had said. He was irritated with Huckleby for his lack of discretion, no matter how much he trusted his daughter. "What do you think about it?"

"It's insane, frankly. The whole idea. But he's my father, so who am I to argue?" She concentrated on driving for a moment, then added, "For one thing, Daddy's not the criminal type."

"I've noticed," Stiehl said dryly.

"And what he's proposing is a crime, right?"

"I think the majority of legal experts would term it as such." Stiehl couldn't help the smile that spread across his face at her naïve question.

"Do mercenaries normally include the crime of the century in their portfolios?"

"No."

"You don't need the money he's giving you."

"Not at the moment I don't," Stiehl acknowledged. "But who's to know what's lurking around the next corner? An extra million stashed away never goes to waste."

"So it comes down to why," Linda pressed. "Why are you letting yourself get all mixed up in this?"

Watching the road, Stiehl tried to think of a reasonable answer he could give Linda. And himself. Why? It always came down to that single word in the end. So why this time? No moralistic reasons. No threat. No passionate involvement. "The challenge," he said finally. "It's something that's never been done before, and I think I can put together the operation to do it."

"Thanks for not trying to fob me off with a load of bullshit," Linda said. "But damn it! This isn't some godforsaken piece of jungle that nobody cares about it. This is Manhattan, a city in its own right with a population of millions. I know Daddy says nobody will get hurt if the city does as he demands, but something can go wrong. You know that. I'm not so concerned about the city, but I don't want anything to happen to Daddy," she finished lamely. "Or you."

"Do you love your father?"

"I don't have to love him. I don't have to love you either. But I know both of you."

Stiehl wondered how much Linda knew about her father's heart disease and whether she understood the significance of the illness when Huckleby had made his plans. "Caesar crossed the Rubicon," he said softly. "He couldn't go back. Neither can we."

An air of resignation tinged her voice when she next spoke. "I didn't really think I'd succeed in putting you off, but can you blame me for trying?"

"You're not thinking of doing anything stupid, are you?"

"The police?"

"As good an example of stupidity as any."

"No." Her voice was firm in its denial. "Major General Harlan Stone Huckleby, United States Army, retired, is still my father and commands my full loyalty. There's no way I could point a finger at him. I owe him too much. As I said before, I don't want to see anyone get hurt. I know what being hurt is all about."

"In what way?"

She began to tell Stiehl about that afternoon outside the bank, the numbing terror and the burning tragedy all rolled into one. She was surprised at how calm her voice sounded as she related the details. Stiehl listened intently until she finished.

"Is that the reason why your father chose Manhattan for his little exhibition?" he asked. "He wants a two-edged sword. A lesson to his old pals in Washington and a crushing blow against New York because he figures your mother died through police inefficiency."

"Yes."

"He neglected to tell me that bit."

"Does it make any real difference?"

"Not really. Even without his motive, Manhattan's probably the most dramatic place to prove his theory of military weakness."

Long shadows fell across the Mercedes, and Stiehl was surprised to find they were crossing the George Washington Bridge into New Jersey. Through the span, he could see the lights of Linda's building. When they arrived, Linda left the car in the guest parking space and went upstairs, where she made a gin and tonic for Stiehl and a martini for herself. Holding the drink, Stiehl stared out at the illuminated span of the bridge from the picture window. Pinpoints of light moving across gave the position of traffic.

"Seeing it happen already?" Linda asked.

"Trying to figure out where the snags could arise is more like it," Stiehl admitted. "Your father's imagination and my planning might not have foreseen every contingency."

The taunting, teasing quality which she had used on the telephone that morning returned to her voice. "You're making it sound as if even the great Peter Stiehl could be guilty of misjudging something."

Stiehl put down the drink, turned around, and cupped her face in his hands, staring into her eyes. "I hope I'm not. I hope to God I'm not."

She stood on tiptoe as he lowered his face to hers. Their lips

124

brushed, drew apart, then came together a second time. Her arms snaked around him, feeling the strength in his body; she clasped her fingers tightly together to lock him to her. Stiehl was mesmerized by Linda's eyes. They were the most unusual shade of violet he'd ever seen, a hypnotist's weapons if she so chose. He felt her fingers tugging at his shirt, the delicious sensation of her nails running across his bare back, his own throbbing anticipation that he could not ignore. Her lovely eyes closed in bliss as he picked her up and carried her toward the bedroom.

The dream woke him again. It never really changed. The same scenes had replayed in his mind during the many months since the dream had started to torture his sleeping hours. Funny, Linda was still asleep. It must have been his own voice that awakened him, screaming that he should save himself. It was always the same. Trapped, cut off in a hostile country, hundreds of miles from safety. He was not even certain there was a haven in his dream. Everyone was filled with some kind of insanity, and Stiehl reckoned the dream was his share.

The nightmare was filled with burning buildings, people dead and dying, a population of hundreds of nameless, faceless people all bent on destruction. They were after him, and this time there was nobody he could turn to, no ally, no hope of salvation.

He had dreamed the scene infrequently at first, but recently it had invaded his sleep more often. And it never ended; he never found the sanctuary he sought, nor did his pursuers catch up with him.

He got out of bed and stood naked on the carpet. Then he began to pull on his pants. If they ever caught up with him, he wanted to have his pants on. Naked bodies in bed were fine, but they looked bloody stupid doing other things.

His actions woke Linda. She sat up in bed, surveying him with the same detachment she had shown when inspecting the Guggenheim treasures. "Leaving?" she asked. "I thought the military had very strict penalties for deserters."

He sat on the edge of the bed, his back to her. "No, I'm not going anywhere. Just the adrenaline beginning to flow, I guess. Talking about the operation with you, watching out the window before. Preaction nerves. Happens to even the most experienced soldier. Ask your father about it."

"Come back to bed," she whispered, putting her hands on his shoulders, massaging him gently. "I know a wonderful remedy for making nerves go away."

"What would your father say if he could hear you?" He turned around to see her reaction.

Her eyes narrowed for an instant, eyebrows contracting. "I'm a very grown-up person, and what I do is no concern of my father."

"When you're with other men, maybe," Stiehl said, driven on by some indefinable force to learn more about the man who was employing him. "But what would he say if he knew I was up here with you?"

"Peter, he probably does." Linda began to laugh, falling back onto the pillow. "Do you really believe he hasn't got the slightest idea? Why do you think he tried to separate us the first time you came up here? He could see a mutual attraction; he just didn't want anything to come between you and the work he's hired you to do."

"If he knew, he wouldn't mind?"

"He wouldn't fire you," Linda said pointedly. "Take my word for it, he wouldn't mind. If he's really concerned about his daughter, what could be more reassuring than to know she's being looked after by a best-selling soldier? Even if he is a mercenary?"

The final remnants of the nightmare vanished as Stiehl recognized the comedy of Linda's answer. He collapsed alongside her on the bed, torn by helpless laughter.

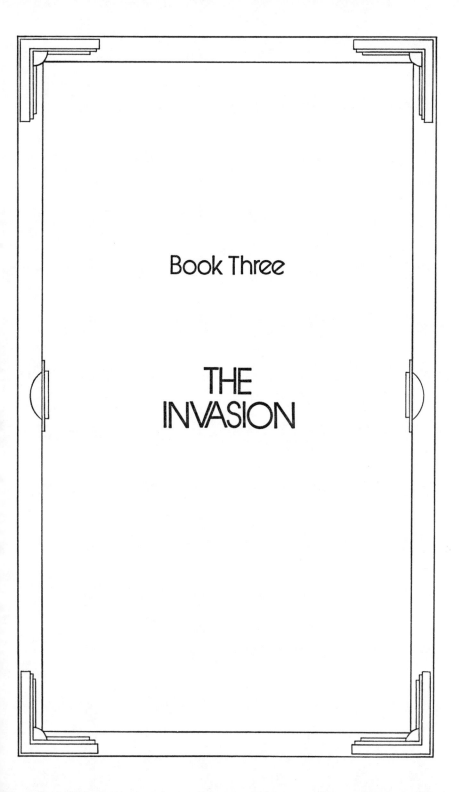

Book Three

THE
INVASION

9

TOWARD THE END of May Peter Stiehl's handpicked assault force began to embark upon the most audacious hijacking of all time. Working closely to Stiehl's timetable, with tickets bought from funds he had provided, the sixty soldiers entered the United States in small, unsuspicious-looking groups at different ports over a three-day period.

At New York City . . .

At Washington . . .

At Buffalo . . .

And at Boston, a particularly fitting point of entry for the Irish contingent commanded by Frank Brady. Brady had visited Boston before and had some distant cousin living there, but looking up relatives was the farthest thing from his mind. The flight across the Atlantic had passed without incident; now he wanted to get his party of four—himself, Johnny Coughlin, Patrick Kerrigan, and Danny McGrath—to the meeting point in New York without incident.

Brady knew all about the animosity that existed between Kerrigan and McGrath, but he'd included both men because of their different specialties. Kerrigan was a fighter, a man who'd punch his way through any obstacles to reach his objective. McGrath's analytical mind made him a perfect planner. Together they complemented each other, Brady thought; if only they could get on together.

While waiting in the terminal for the New York bus to depart, Kerrigan began to romanticize about the impending operation. He compared it with the action he had known in Africa. Coughlin and Brady took little notice of him, used to his nonstop chatter, but McGrath became irritated.

"What was in that Nigerian camp you took out?" he snapped at Kerrigan. "Women? Or just children? You must have reveled in it, shooting at helpless kids who couldn't fight back."

Kerrigan refused to let McGrath's antagonism dampen his own high spirits. This operation for which the South African Adcock had recruited them would separate the men from the boys. He knew Brady respected McGrath, but that did not matter to Kerrigan. He wanted the operation to show McGrath up for the weed he was and let it demonstrate that Kerrigan was still the soldier he knew himself to be.

He stopped talking and began to whistle instead, a sad, lilting song of the Republic. The whistling served only to make McGrath more edgy. "Why don't you shut up, for Christ's sake!"

Kerrigan swung around on the seat. "If you're so jumpy now, what are you going to do when the shooting starts? Wet your pants and start crying for mummy?"

"I can take care of myself," McGrath replied churlishly, not knowing why he was bothering to answer. "Don't worry about me."

"Oh, but I do," Kerrigan said, wanting to see how far he could push McGrath. "Especially if you're standing behind me, then I'm bloody worried."

Brady, who had been watching two policemen question a long-haired youth with a rucksack, spun around. "Knock it off, the

130

pair of you!" he hissed. "You're like a bloody bad husband-and-wife act, nagging and arguing with each other the whole time."

"Tell that to the hero." McGrath sulked. "Thinks I'd put a bullet in his back if I got the chance."

"Me?" Kerrigan laughed, determined to have the final say. "I don't let things like that worry me. Danny would be too scared to pull the trigger even if I was carrying a white stick."

Coughlin, who had also been watching the police officers at the far side of the terminal, joined in the conversation. "Danny's all right, Pat. He's just a bit too intellectual for you to understand."

"That's what the school board must have thought when they chucked him out of his teaching job," Kerrigan said. "That he was too intellectual for anyone to understand." He rolled on the seat with laughter, happy when Brady and Coughlin joined in, even happier when McGrath turned away, his face reddening.

While Kerrigan, Brady, Coughlin, and McGrath traveled down from Boston on the bus, Hashim Nissouri, Gamal Aktouri, and Ahmed Nassim rode up from Washington, D.C., on the Metroliner, their Libyan diplomatic passports duly stamped. The three men had been obvious choices for Habash in Beirut to contact; their stock in the PFLP had been high ever since they had murdered an Egyptian diplomat who was one of the prime movers for peace with Israel.

Like Brady's Irish, the Palestinian faction was traveling in separate groups. Paralleling the three men on the Metroliner from Washington to New York were three Syrians, sitting on a Trailways bus, their thoughts not so much on the coming operation but on the aircraft they would be required to pilot. Mahmoud Assar, Hassan Basri, and Abdul Wasim had been commercial airline pilots before the Yom Kippur War had given them the opportunity to fly Mig 21 fighters, although the Syrian Air Force had never been committed in the battle. Disenchanted with their country's unwillingness to continue the fight once the United Nations had stepped in, they had left Syria for Lebanon

131

to offer what assistance they could to the Palestinians. When the Syrians had invaded Lebanon during the Moslem-Christian civil war, the three men had believed their country was finally going to declare itself on the side of the Palestinians, and they would be able to train with more than just words and underpowered weapons. Their disappointment had been shattering when they recognized that Syria was interested only in annexing part of Lebanon and would pay no more than lip service to the Palestinian cause. Habash's approach with a mission to fly a passenger airliner out of New York's Kennedy Airport had come like a sunbeam on a dull day, a lifesaving opportunity to be clutched with both hands. They had never flown the DC-10s or 747s they would find in the United States, but Habash had supplied them with flight manuals he had received from Stiehl. They all were confident that when the time came, they would not be found wanting.

Dieter Kirchmann's group, including Rolf Haller, Magda Breitner, and Günther Werner, was the last of the German squads to arrive. Having flown from Frankfurt to Toronto, they bused down overnight across the American border at Buffalo. A stickler for precision, Kirchmann had spent the whole of the previous day at Frankfurt Airport, seeing off the other units, ensuring they caught their flights, stressing that they call the number he had given them the moment they arrived in New York. If anything went wrong with the coordination of the mission, Kirchmann's group would not be responsible.

On the long overnight trip down the New York Thruway, Kirchmann stayed awake, using the time to go over his selection of personnel. Had he done right by including Günther Werner? True, the man had no criminal record and had obtained a visitor's visa easily, but he had been humiliated by Adcock. Kirchmann had known Werner for long enough to realize that the hulking strong-arm man did not forget or forgive willingly. He had warned Werner that he would tolerate no disobedience, but somehow he foresaw trouble and wished he could have chosen

132

another man instead. But who else was there? He had stripped his personnel roster bare to come up with twenty members who had no police record. Thanks to the German authorities' effective crackdown, Werner had been forced upon him. Kirchmann hoped that the South African would understand.

Kirchmann turned in the seat to look at Werner, breathing heavily as he slept. Across the aisle, Haller and Magda Breitner also slept, their reading lights turned out. Only Kirchmann's light was on, throwing a single circle of brightness across him, the sole illumination in the entire bus apart from the driver's instruments. Wearily he reached up and flicked off the switch, plunging the bus into darkness. If only Ulrike or Gudrun were with us, he thought. But they both were dead. And Gabrielle was in prison. Maybe we'll all end up that way, dead or in prison. But not this time, not before we pull this one off.

Günther Werner awoke just after seven-thirty in the morning as the Greyhound bus passed through the toll gates at the end of the Thruway. He stretched noisily in the seat, shouldering Kirchmann roughly, waking him.

"Where are we?" Kirchmann asked.

Werner shrugged his broad shoulders. "How should I know? Wherever it is, I just wish to hell we were there already." He stood up and walked to the rear of the bus, shoving aside a man's legs, glaring down at him as he woke with a start, daring him to complain. In the washroom he relieved himself, passed wind noisily, and left without washing his hands. Two girls who occupied the rear seat by the washroom stared at him as he came out; he just grinned. When he returned to his seat near the front of the bus, Magda and Haller were also awake, leaning across the aisle, talking in muted tones to Kirchmann. Haller looked as fresh as if he had slept in a proper bed and taken a shower; the blond hair was neatly combed, and the blue eyes were alive and sparkling with the excitement of what was to come. And Magda—to Werner she always looked good. The long brown hair softly falling over her forehead made her look like a schoolgirl, innocent, the perfect camouflage. Werner had tried several times without success to get her into bed. He figured she was a lesbian; any woman who did not want to go to bed with him had to be.

"Do you all have the number to call?" Kirchmann asked as Werner sat down. "In case we become separated."

The other three nodded. Haller and Magda had memorized it. Werner had written it on a cigarette pack.

"According to the bus schedule, we are due into New York around nine o'clock, so we should be picked up by ten. By Adcock or whoever he sends over to pick us up." As he mentioned the South African, he looked at Werner for a reaction. No expression gave away Werner's thoughts.

"Then what happens?" Haller asked. "After we are picked up?"

"Only our Mr. Adcock knows," Kirchmann said. "But no doubt we'll find out."

Werner lost interest in the conversation and slouched down in the seat. Ignoring the sign that said smoking was allowed only in the rear three rows, he pulled the pack of cigarettes from his pocket and lit one. A man occupying the seat in front turned to glare angrily, but the brooding face which stared back cut short his protest. The bus driver, glancing in the rearview mirror as he smelled tobacco, was not so easily swerved from his duty.

"You wanna put that out, mac?" he called over his shoulder. "Can't you read?"

Werner lifted his eyes in surprise, catching those of the driver in the mirror. He said nothing, leaving the cigarette in his mouth.

The bus driver tried again, his voice waking any passengers who still slept, alerting them to the tiny drama that was taking place.

Still, Werner did nothing, puffing away as if he had not heard. The driver shook his head, pulled the bus off the road onto the soft shoulder, and turned off the engine. The passengers' eyes followed him as he left his seat and stood over Werner.

"You wanna put it out? Or you wanna walk the rest of the way?"

Werner made no move to comply, challenging the man with his eyes. Kirchmann, Magda, and Haller stirred uneasily. Suddenly Kirchmann reached out and grabbed the cigarette, pulling it from Werner's mouth; he slid open the window and dropped the cigarette into the road. "You will have to forgive him," he said to the driver in English as Werner erupted into a torrent of German abuse. "He does not understand English, only German."

"Yeah, well, maybe he'd better start learning some," the driver said, relieved that the situation had been handled for him. He turned away and went back to his seat, started the engine, and pulled onto the road to continue the journey. Werner swung around, face red, eyes blazing.

"Who the hell do you think you are?" he snarled at Kirchmann.

"I am in charge, that's who I am. You will do as I damned well say. Remember what I told you before we left. You are to obey every order given to you. There will be no trouble. We are involved in something too big to have it fouled up by your stupidity. Am I understood?"

Werner looked left to where Haller and Magda sat, as if seeking support from them. He found none. Their eyes accused him. He began to smile as if accepting their criticism, closed his eyes, and went back to sleep. When he awoke, it was just after nine, and the bus was pulling into the Port Authority building in midtown Manhattan.

"Get up," Kirchmann said. "We've arrived."

Werner looked around at the people standing in the aisle, waiting to disembark; others were reaching up into the overhead racks for small cases.

"Stay together," Kirchmann cautioned. "If we do become separated, you each have the number to telephone Adcock and arrange for transportation."

Outside the bus, they collected their suitcases and went into the terminal, standing aside as the last of the rush-hour crowds pushed past. Werner moved his small suitcase from one hand to the other as he followed his comrades from the bottom level of the terminal, past the armed forces police desk to the main floor. There Kirchmann located a bank of telephones, put down his case, felt in his pockets for change, and dialed the memorized number. As Kirchmann waited for the call to be answered, Werner began to edge away. He lost himself quickly in the swirling mass of people that filled the terminal, letting himself be swept toward the exit on Eighth Avenue. He did not need Kirchmann or the others. He had the telephone number. For the first time in his life he was in New York. Why let the opportunity go to waste? He was damned certain that after the South African's plan went through—whatever the hell it was—none of them would ever set foot in New York again.

By the time Kirchmann put down the telephone, having spoken to Stiehl at the Howson Chemicals head office in Newark, Werner was at the junction of Eighth Avenue and Forty-second Street, his eager eyes taking in the movie marquees, the burlesque shows, the offers of cheap sex.

When Stiehl arrived in Huckleby's Cadillac to pick up the Germans at the Ninth Avenue exit of the bus terminal Kirchmann's rage at Werner's disappearance had reached a crescendo. He had remained at the exit with the baggage while Haller and Magda scoured the terminal to look for the missing member of their squad. They had reported back at ten-minute intervals, always with the same news—there was no sign of Werner; he had totally disappeared.

"Can you wait a few minutes?" Kirchmann asked anxiously as Stiehl rolled down the car window. "One of my people is missing."

"Who?" Stiehl adjusted the dark glasses. He had taken to wearing them permanently, just as he had dyed his hair darker with a strong tint.

"Günther Werner. You remember him, of course?"

Stiehl remembered clearly the way he had taken out the big man. "I know who you mean," he said wearily. His voice reflected the fatigue he was beginning to feel, the constant running back and forth from New Jersey to pick up each new squad as it

136

arrived, driving them back to the specially cordoned-off warehouse at Howson Chemicals which had been fitted out like an army barracks. So far everything had gone off without a hitch. Each unit had followed instructions to the letter. Now Werner had screwed it up. "Did you have to bring him with you? Was there nobody else?"

"Nobody," Kirchmann admitted. "We stripped our organizational structure clean for this operation. You asked for a lot."

"Has he got the telephone number?"

"Yes. I made certain that each member of my squad had the number. In case something like this happened."

"Get in then. You and the others. When Werner finally surfaces, he can call up."

"And if he does not surface?" Kirchmann left the question hanging in the air.

"Then we start out a man down. Get in."

Kirchmann took the bags from Magda and Haller, threw them into the trunk, slid into the back seat, and closed the door. Seconds later they were bouncing along Ninth Avenue toward the Lincoln Tunnel.

First he had to get rid of the suitcase. Werner looked around the unfamiliar area of Forty-second Street, wondering where he could leave it. Dare he take a chance and return to the bus terminal, use one of the lockers there? Or would Kirchmann and the others be looking for him still? Would they leave for Newark without him if their transportation arrived while he was still missing? He walked into a stand-up snack bar and ordered a cup of coffee and a frankfurter, trying to waste thirty minutes, by which time he felt it would be safe to return to the terminal. Of course, Kirchmann and the others would go on. They knew Werner had the telephone number written down on a cigarette pack; they would expect him to follow through as best he could.

He ordered a second cup of coffee and took his time drinking it. After he finished, he retraced his steps to the bus terminal. Continually keeping alert in case he should spot Kirchmann or one of the others, he left his case in a locker. There was no sign of them, and he began to feel more confident. What would he say when he met with them again? That he had got separated, swept away by the bustling crowds which thronged the terminal? They would have to believe him; they could not do otherwise. Unburdened of the suitcase, he returned to Eighth Avenue, looking wondrously at the advertisements for sexual gratification. He had money in his pockets, an advance of two hundred dollars given to each of the German squad by Kirchmann as an emergency fund. Well, what he felt now was an emergency. How could a man go into battle without first having had a woman to soften the privations which must surely come?

Werner crossed over Forty-second Street and continued north on Eighth Avenue before stopping outside a burlesque house which advertised sadomasochistic fare. Studying the illustrations on the marquee made him lick his lips in anticipation. Even this early in the morning the theater was open, but he moved on. He knew exactly what he wanted, what he could never get in Stuttgart, or in all Germany for that matter. He had read stories of New York, young girls who were still children being led into prostitution by their pimps. Such practice would never be allowed to flourish in Germany, nor would he ever find a young black girl in his own country. Kirchmann and Adcock could wait.

Something plucked at his arm. He turned around to see a Puerto Rican youth brandishing a piece of colored paper. "Check it out," the youth said. "Best show in town." Werner took the flyer and scanned it. A half-naked girl beckoned to him from a crudely executed line drawing. He was about to screw up the piece of paper and throw it onto the sidewalk when he changed his mind. He had to start somewhere; it might as well be here.

"You won't regret it," the youth called after him. "Time of your life. Guaranteed."

Inside the theater foyer, Werner found himself facing a cash desk. "Ten dollars," a woman told him. "That's all you have to pay for a date with one of our girls."

He passed across a ten-dollar bill. "What do I get?"

"Friendship," the woman answered with a smile.

His eyes adjusted to the darkness as he walked inside. A hostess, a young white girl in a kimono, came to meet him, the practiced smile pasted on her face. "Anything special?" she asked.

Werner felt the crotch of his pants begin to tighten. "Young." The word seemed to stick in his throat. He had never been anywhere like this before; even The House of Three Colors in Stuttgart was a kindergarten compared with what he sensed was happening here.

"Everyone's young here."

"Black."

"Try booth number five."

He walked past the hostess and entered the booth, closing the door behind him. The only piece of furniture was a couch; soft music was piped in through two overhead speakers. On the couch was a young black girl, hair frizzed up, dressed only in a bra and panties. Werner guessed she was no more than fifteen.

"Come in and sit down, honey. Make yourself comfortable."

He slumped down on the couch next to her, his hand immediately thrusting its way between her thighs. She recoiled from his touch and held up her own hand.

"Hey, don't you go getting no ideas."

"I paid my money," he protested.

She laughed at his words. "What you paid was an entrance fee, that's all. Entitles you to a little company, a little conversation, maybe a kiss or two. Nothing more. Where you from anyway?"

"Germany."

She laid a hand on his thigh, moving it gently, massaging him, heightening his anticipation even more. Her palm was hot, sticky with sweat; he could feel it penetrating the fabric of his trousers. "Can show you a real good time if you like, honey. Much better than down here."

"Where?"

139

She rolled her eyes expressively. "Upstairs. Got a private little room with a big soft bed."

"How much?"

"Twenty-five." She saw him begin to hesitate and added quickly, "It's worth every cent. Half and half."

"What?"

"Half and half," she repeated. "Half suck, half fuck." Her hand moved to his stomach, pressing, rubbing, tantalizing his senses. His muscles tensed automatically. "Give you something real special to remember New York by."

"Come on." He stood up, waiting while she slipped into a kimono. Taking his hand, she led him from the booth to a staircase. The room on the second floor had an old-fashioned brass bedstead with a stained mattress. The absence of sheets did not worry Werner. He began to undress immediately, throwing his jacket onto the bare wooden floor, stepping out of his trousers, kicking them aside. He grabbed hold of the girl and threw her down onto the bed, forcing her legs apart.

"Hey! Take it easy!" she cried out. "You don't want to blow your twenty-five in one go." She sounded frightened, scared by Werner's force. He enjoyed that. "Don't you wanna get sucked off first?"

For answer, Werner drove into her, a thrill of pleasure as he heard her gasp in pain. He took his weight on his elbows, looking down into the girl's dark, scared eyes. "You ever had it like this before? A man so strong?"

She played up to him, deciding it was the safest thing to do. "Honey, you're the strongest. You're a real big man." Christ, if he carried on like this, she'd need stitches by the time he finished.

He began to move, slowly at first, then with an ever-increasing rhythm, thrusting deeply inside her, shaking the brass frame of the bed with his exertions, hearing her cries as a stimulant. As he began to climax, he noticed that the girl was no longer crying; her attention was on something else in the room, eyes turned away from him. Despite his preoccupation, he turned his head,

140

shocked into disbelief by what he saw. Another black girl, dressed in jeans and a dark sweater, was creeping out from underneath the bed, reaching for his jacket. Even as he watched, she picked up the piece of clothing, ran toward the door, threw it open, and raced outside.

Werner's roar of rage echoed through the room. He pulled himself out of the girl on the bed, spilling sperm over the mattress as he struggled to his feet. Without sparing the girl a second glance, he threw on his trousers and pounded barefoot into the hall, down the stairs, out the back door into an alleyway.

"Come back here, you bitch!" he bellowed in German; his passport and money were in the jacket.

The girl glanced back to see how far behind he was. The action cost her the lead as she tripped over an uneven piece of concrete, arms flailing for balance, the jacket spinning from her grasp. Werner was on her in four strides, discomfort from the concrete on his bare feet forgotten as he lifted her up and smashed a huge fist into her face. Behind him a man yelled, and Werner turned around to see people erupting from the club's back door. He picked up the girl as if she weighed no more than a piece of paper and flung her bodily at the advancing crowd before stooping to scoop up his jacket and running toward the end of the alleyway. He had no idea where it led, driven only by the knowledge that he must escape. Ahead, a tall figure in a dark blue uniform loomed closer, shouted commands to stop. Werner paid no heed, driving on toward the patrolman, who had been alerted by the girl's screams. He brushed aside the uniformed figure and broke for the street he could see ahead. Another shout ordered him to halt. He stepped in some broken glass and yelled in pain as it cut deeply into his foot, but never did he slow his pace. Another figure appeared ahead of him, blocking out the view of the street that meant freedom to Werner. The patrolman's partner was bent low, squatting, hands held out in front, something dark and shiny in them. Werner barely had time to recognize the revolver before it bucked in the policeman's hands. He staggered as the bullet smashed high into his

141

bare left shoulder, regained his balance, and dived at the patrolman. The gun bucked again, and Werner crashed into a pile of garbage cans, sending them flying, spilling their contents as his own brains were spilling from his shattered head, where the second thirty-eight bullet had found its mark.

10

TWENTY MINUTES AFTER the shooting death of Günther Werner by one of two patrolmen answering a call to a disturbance, word of the incident reached the offices of MetroCity Television on Broadway and Forty-ninth Street. After twenty-three years in the communications field, station owner Charles Kohn thought he had seen everything, heard everything. But the odd circumstances surrounding Werner's death—running barefoot and bare-chested through the streets at ten in the morning—intrigued even the overweight, balding Kohn. He removed his gold-rimmed glasses, wiped them carefully with a Kleenex tissue, and put them back on. Rereading the news flash, he wondered what kind of depravity had led the dead man to risk running barefoot through the broken glass and debris which littered the area. He also wondered why it had taken two police officers to subdue him; not only to subdue him but to shoot him twice, killing him. Never a dull moment, Kohn thought, pressing down the intercom switch.

"Yes, Mr. Kohn," the secretary answered.

143

"Babs O'Neill in yet?"

"Just arrived."

"Tell her I want to see her." He flicked the switch into the off position, perusing the news flash yet again, making himself fully aware of the facts.

The door to his office opened a minute later. At thirty-five, Babs O'Neill was the station's foremost news personality, a tall, slim woman with blond hair and an engaging manner which had rocketed her to the top of the station's popularity poll. What did not show through was her toughness, a quality which had enabled her to fight her way up in her chosen profession with all the tenacity of a hungry wolverine. After only two years with the station, she had been given her own evening news show, winning the slot against stiff competition from older, more experienced reporters.

"Still working on that Times Square piece?" Kohn asked. He never bothered asking Babs how she was feeling or even offering her a token "good morning." They both were professionals. First and foremost came the station, and neither wasted time with the fripperies of courtesy.

"Yes." She sat down without being asked, the only member of the MetroCity staff ever to make herself comfortable in Kohn's office without an invitation. Her relationship with Kohn was unique among station personnel. She could take whatever liberties she liked as long as the end product stayed high in the news ratings. Only once had she ever let him down, when she had blown up a story about a pad operating among the city's sanitation workers, trash collectors who were refusing to remove garbage from industrial areas unless they were paid off by the companies concerned. The embarrassment at being found out an exaggerator at best—a liar at worst—had lasted only as long as it had taken Babs to bring in a fresh, true story. After a month even the sanitation workers had ceased picketing outside the studio, finding better causes.

"How far are you into that piece?" Kohn asked. "Almost ready to run?"

"Another couple of weeks, I guess," she replied. "I've made

the rounds of the sex-for-sale shops, the massage parlors, the theaters. What I want to do now is a good piece on the specialty shops, where you can buy whatever kinky equipment you want for your own particular perversion."

"Don't look at me when you say that," Kohn said defensively. "I'm strictly a straight from squaresville."

She laughed lightly at his protest. "Everyone knows about you, Charlie. The closest you ever get to an orgasm is when the ratings come out and good old MetroCity's right up there at the top of list."

Kohn made no attempt to deny the accusation. Since the breakup of his marriage ten years earlier, his sex life had been nonexistent. He spent too much time and energy running the television station, trying to make a small independent compete successfully with the major networks. He did not have the money the networks had, but he managed well. It always helped when your main evening news show was one of the best, centering on the local issues to make New Yorkers tune in. Not that Babs, of all people, should be reminding him of his sex life. After six years of marriage Babs's husband had decided he could no longer stand to share her with the rest of the city and had called it quits.

"Take a look at this," Kohn said, passing across the news flash. "Maybe this guy was involved in something to do with that porn piece you're working on."

She reached across the desk and removed the slip of paper from Kohn's hand. "What else would he have been doing?" she asked. "Nobody runs around that neighborhood without a shirt or shoes unless he's up to something. He was lucky he had time to pull up his pants." She sat still for a moment, pondering the incident, deciding how best to tackle it. "I'll run it as a straight piece in tonight's news. Whatever else we learn, we can include in the porn feature."

Kohn nodded in agreement. "Whatever you think best, but you'd better get onto this one quick. Go out there, see what you can find. Grab ahold of Jerry and take him with you."

"He's outside now, having coffee," Babs said, referring to Jer-

145

ry Rosen, the station's top cameraman. Rosen had won awards for his work and was as well known in his own field as Babs was in hers.

"Tell him he hasn't got time for coffee. Otherwise, drink it in the car."

Babs gave Kohn her most endearing smile. "Jerry's been out all night on that fire over in Brooklyn and you won't even give him time for a cup of coffee to wake himself up. Do you know why we all love you and work so hard for you, Charlie? Because you're so fucking considerate, that's why."

Kohn managed to suppress the rare smile he could feel coming. "He's got five minutes to finish it," he said gruffly.

The two patrolmen who had participated in the shooting stood off to one side of the squad room, watching disinterestedly as the girl who had been beaten up by Werner was questioned. A bandage covered her smashed nose, and sutures had been inserted into her lips, making speech difficult. On a bench in the corner of the room sat the frizzy-haired girl who had led Werner up to the room. She was dressed now, bent forward as she choked back tears, waiting for her turn to be interviewed.

"Let's try it all again, honey," a plainclothes officer said to the beaten girl. He was a man in his early fifties, haggard-looking with doleful brown eyes that were tired of seeing all that passed before them; thinning gray hair was combed straight back, and his shirt collar and tie were undone. "You're saying this guy took off after you for no reason at all. Just beat up on you because the mood took him."

The girl nodded, the faintest of movements.

"Then why the goddamned hell wasn't he wearing any shoes? And where was his shirt? Why was he carrying his jacket?"

The girl said nothing. She touched her injured nose gently, wondering what had hurt more—the beating itself or the medical attention she had received before the interrogation started.

"He was in bed with your friend over there, right?" the man asked, leaning closer to the girl. "You were hiding somewhere in the room, and you made off with his jacket. Only he spotted you doing it." Still the girl volunteered no information, and the haggard-looking man kept talking. "He caught up with you and beat the shit out of you, which you damned well deserved. How am I doing so far?" He leaned back in the chair, not really expecting an answer, just knowing through gut feeling that his deductions were correct. Christ, it happened all the time, but what a break for the poor German slob. Visits New York and gets ripped off by a couple of teenaged hookers. Then he gets his head blown off because he panics after beating up one of the girls. Fun City, what a joke.

His thoughts were interrupted by the arrival of a young detective. "We've traced that telephone number on the cigarette pack, Inspector Denton. It's a chemical company over in Newark."

Inspector Eric Denton looked up at the man, taking a piece of paper from him. "Thanks. I'll give them a call later on, try to find out something about this"—he peered down at the official form on his desk—"Günther Werner character. In the meantime, get ahold of the Immigration and Naturalization Service. Find out anything you can about this guy. See if there's a name we can contact, someone over here Werner was going to see."

"Okay, Inspector. I'll see to it."

Denton went back to the girl, his earlier aggressive attitude deserting him. "Where you from, kid?"

"Milwaukee,"

"How old are you?"

The answer came out in a whisper. "Seventeen."

"Try again."

"Sixt . . . " She faltered and began crying. "Fourteen."

"Ran away from home and caught the bus to New York, huh?" Denton said as if talking to himself. "Some fellow was nice to you at the bus station when you first got in, that how it happened?"

There was no need for the girl to nod. Denton knew the answer already. He must have run into hundreds of them since taking charge of a vice unit to crack down on teenage prostitution. And each one made him sicker than the last. He swung around in the chair, spotted a policewoman, and called her over. "Get these

147

two kids over to juvenile. See about getting them back to where they belong, whether their families want them back or not. And see if you can get them to tell you anything about the scum that got them into this racket. Maybe we'll get lucky and nail a few of the bastards."

He got up from the chair, went into his own small office long enough to pick up his jacket, and started to leave. When he was almost out of the squad room, he remembered the piece of paper the detective had given him. He stopped by a telephone and dialed the number, wondering why a German tourist should have the telephone number of Howson Chemicals scribbled on a cigarette pack.

The warehouse at Howson Chemicals' Newark base resembled a barracks from the inside. Collapsible cots lined the walls, lockers beside them. A field kitchen took up most of the center space, its fumes ducted through a specially cut vent in the roof. Stiehl had seen to it that enough provisions had been brought into the warehouse to last his army for a month, stored in chest freezers until used. The strike units were doing their own cooking, eating off paper plates, using plastic cutlery, which could be thrown away without arousing suspicion. Other than Stiehl, the only person connected with Howson Chemicals who knew about the visitors was Huckleby himself. They had chosen a warehouse well away from the center of business activity, one which had been empty for almost a year. Nobody had seen the different units arriving from New York. Nobody would see them leave. As far as the company's employees were concerned, the warehouse was still empty.

Tucked away in a corner was a small glass-enclosed office, furnished with a desk and chair, filing cabinet, and telephone. It was there that Stiehl now sat, checking his roster to make certain all the personnel were present in the warehouse. They had been forbidden to leave, but he was taking no chances. Since Kirchmann's news earlier that morning about Werner's separation from his unit, Stiehl was doubly on the alert for something to go wrong. Silently he cursed the big German, wishing he had not jerked his hand aside when he fired the Browning in the forest that day. He could have done himself a big favor by shooting Werner there and then.

The telephone's insistent ring intruded into his recriminations. Werner, he thought as he reached out to lift the receiver. Must have decided it's time to check in, join the others. Nobody else had the number except Huckleby. The telephone had been specially installed; it was listed as a Howson Chemicals line, but the only people using it would be those connected with the operation ringing through to announce their arrival and to request transportation from New York.

"Adcock here." He was curious to know what excuse Werner would have for splitting up from the group. Stiehl felt the need to make an example of the man, put everyone else straight before there was any more disobedience. As he spoke, he shifted the tinted glasses, wondering if they were responsible for the headache he was getting.

"I'm sorry," a voice said. "I didn't catch the name."

An alarm triggered instantly in Stiehl's mind. His headache was forgotten, as was the example he intended to make of Werner. This wasn't a German accent; this was American. Was it a misrouted call, or had something gone terribly wrong? "Adcock."

"Of Howson Chemicals?"

"Yes. Who is this?"

"It's the police, Mr. Adcock. Inspector Denton, New York."

"Oh?" What the hell were the police doing, calling this number? And why the New York police? Newark was not in their area of jurisdiction.

"We're wondering if you can help us, Mr. Adcock. Would the name Günther Werner mean anything to you?"

"Werder?" Stiehl mispronounced it purposely.

"Werner," Denton repeated. "Günther Werner. A West German national."

"No. Doesn't mean a thing to me. What does he have to do with us?" Stiehl's heart was racing. Obviously Werner had got himself into some kind of trouble, but what? Stiehl did not know

149

whether it would affect the operation, and he could not ask this police inspector for details of Werner's predicament without appearing too inquisitive.

"We found your telephone number on a cigarette pack he was carrying," Denton explained. "Guess you should know what the fuss is all about. This man Werner was shot to death about an hour or so ago by a police officer while attempting to escape after beating up a hooker. Other than his passport and some money, plus German documents, the only thing we could follow up was your telephone number."

"Germany, huh?" Stiehl tried to think of a way he could make Denton believe he was helping. "I can't say definitely he had nothing to do with us. Some of our best scientists are German, what with Germany being a world leader in chemical products. Listen, what did you say this man's name was again?"

Denton repeated it for the second time.

"Tell you what," Stiehl offered. "Leave it with me, and I'll ask around our German employees. Maybe he was a relative of someone over here and was coming to see them."

"How long do you reckon this will take?"

"Hard to say. We're a pretty large company. But I'll get it done as soon as possible."

"Thanks, Mr. Adcock. Call me if you get something. I'd appreciate it." He gave Stiehl the number.

"Okay, Inspector. Rest assured that you'll have our fullest cooperation." Stiehl hung up, hoping his apparent sincerity would throw the police off the trail. He knew he would have to get back to Denton eventually, but he would be able to satisfy the police inspector by saying he had turned up no connection at all. Anyway, there was no connection between Werner and anyone at Howson Chemicals, and Denton would have to work damned hard if he wanted to find one.

Stiehl looked around the warehouse for Kirchmann and spotted him on the bunk below Magda Breitner. The German leader appeared to be sleeping. Tough. As far as Stiehl was concerned, now was as good a time as any to tell him not to put a candle in

150

the window for his comrade. At least, he wouldn't have to worry about Werner's creating any more problems.

Denton was still curious about the scribbled telephone number on the cigarette packet. So this man Adcock claimed to know nothing about Günther Werner. Why should he know anything? Adcock was obviously one of the lower cogs, and Denton had learned long ago that the only way to accomplish anything was by going directly to the top; you never bothered with the peons. He picked up the telephone again, asking for information. The operator gave him a different listing for Howson Chemicals. When Denton asked about the number he had called earlier, he was told it was a new listing, no more than four weeks old.

A woman's voice answered when he dialed the number given by information. "Howson Chemicals. Can I help you?"

"What's your president's name? This is Inspector Denton of the New York Police Department."

"Harlan Stone Huckleby, sir. Do you wish to speak with him?"

Denton was familiar with the name, remembered it from the many news stories. "Please. And do you have an Adcock—" The question was cut off in midstream as the switchboard operator transferred the call.

"Mr. Huckleby's office."

Denton identified himself again. "Is Mr. Huckleby there, please?"

"Just a moment, Inspector. I'll check." A pause; then the girl came back on the line. "Putting you through."

"This is Huckleby. How can I help you, Inspector?"

"We're looking into a police shooting on this side of the Hudson, sir. Man who was killed carried a West German passport in the name of Günther Werner. Does the name mean anything to you?"

"Nothing at all," was Huckleby's immediate reply. "Is there any reason why it should?"

"I was just wondering, that's all. You see, he had one of your

151

company telephone numbers scribbled on a cigarette pack. What about the name Adcock? Does that ring a bell?"

"It should," Huckleby replied, wondering just what the hell was going on. "Adcock's my South African manager. Working over here right now. I'll put you through if you like. Is he in any kind of trouble?"

"No, nothing like that. But the number on the cigarette pack was Adcock's direct line. I spoke to him a few minutes ago."

"Then why did you call me?"

"Because I was curious why Werner would have Adcock's direct line number, especially when that number has only recently been activated. If he were going to call someone at Howson Chemicals, surely he would have gone through the main switchboard."

"I'm sorry, Inspector Denton, but I can't help you there."

Denton hung up again, no nearer to solving the riddle of the telephone number than he had been the first time. Over the Hudson River, in Newark, Huckleby was agitatedly picking up the telephone, calling through to Stiehl in the converted warehouse, demanding to know what had gone wrong.

Jerry Rosen lugged the heavy camera up the steps to the police station. The ever-present Pall Mall drooped from the corner of his mouth as he followed Babs into the musty atmosphere of the station; behind him tagged the sound man.

Babs went straight to the desk sergeant, waiting for Rosen to catch up with her before she spoke. Babs knew the value of the camera, how it mellowed people's attitudes if they thought there was the slightest possibility of their being on television that night. Automatically Rosen began to focus, zooming in on the desk sergeant's face as he waited for Babs to turn on her charm.

"I understand this is where they took the girls involved in the Günther Werner shooting," she began.

"Upstairs." The sergeant directed his reply at the camera Rosen was holding, unaware that it was not exposing film. Nor was the sound equipment working.

"Thanks." Babs turned around and marched steadfastly toward the stairway leading to the squad room, disregarding the shout from the desk sergeant that she was not allowed up. Halfway up the narrow stairs, she met Inspector Denton coming down. One of them had to give way. In a tribute of chivalry, Denton turned around to go back the way he had come, leading Babs and Rosen into his office.

"You hear bad news pretty quickly," he greeted her.

"I'm paid to," she said. She sensed Rosen and the sound man moving in behind her, filming as she spoke, taking down the words and actions. Denton held up a hand to ward off the camera's lens, but Rosen took no notice, moving around to the other side of the small room to catch Babs and Denton in profile.

"What happened this morning, Eric?" she asked; she had established a first-name basis with Denton years earlier when they had first met.

"What did you hear?" He sat back in the chair, hands clasped across his stomach. With Babs, it was like being at the dentist: It paid to sit back and get it over with.

"I heard there was a shooting by one of your cops. An unarmed man was killed."

"A man was killed resisting arrest," Denton corrected her. "After he had already severely beaten one girl and assaulted a police officer."

"Okay. So what was it all about?"

"Hooker pulls a john into bed. While they're screwing, another girl takes off with the john's jacket. Contains his passport, money, the works."

"Passport?" Babs queried.

"Passport. Federal Republic of Germany. Must have just got into town. We're checking him out with the INS right now."

"So why the shooting?"

"As soon as this girl snatches his jacket, the guy jumps off the hooker he's screwing and takes off after her. Just throws on his pants, no shoes or shirt. Was beating the crap out of her when two patrolmen answered a disturbance call. He took care of one

153

of them. Would have taken out the other one as well if the cop hadn't blown him away first. Big strong guy. Let you see him down the morgue if you like."

"Thanks, Eric, but no thanks." She ran Denton's words through her mind. "Could you run all that by me one more time? It's not going to look very good for your image if all that language about hookers and screwing comes out on prime time television, what with impressionable kids watching as well."

Denton laughed loudly. "Wouldn't do you much good with the FCC, either, when license renewal time rolls around again." He repeated the details for Babs, selecting his words more carefully.

"Nothing else?" she asked when he was finished.

"Only a telephone number. Scrawled on a pack of cigarettes. Two-oh-one prefix and a number. Belongs to Howson Chemicals over in Newark, the chemical corporation run by General Harlan Stone Huckleby. I spoke to him awhile back, but nobody over there seems to have the faintest idea who this guy Werner is."

"What kind of cigarettes?"

Denton opened a desk drawer and withdrew an orange pack. "Ernte Thirty-two. All the writing's in German, so I guess that's where they're made."

"Maybe it's a German telephone number," Babs suggested. "Has nothing whatsoever to do with Howson Chemicals."

Denton looked thoughtfully at the scrawled numbers on the face of the pack. "I never even thought of that. You're probably right. Who knows? Maybe it's not even a telephone number. Could be anything, I guess. Bank account number, insurance number, anything."

Babs decided it was time to leave. "Just make sure you watch yourself on MetroCity tonight," she told Denton.

"Wouldn't miss it for anything in the world," he promised. "Now I've got to get on with some work. If I hear of anything, you'll be the first to know. Even before the chief."

"Thanks." She turned to Rosen, who was removing the camera from his shoulder. "Let's go, Jerry."

"Right with you."

154

The MetroCity crew trooped out of Denton's office. As the door swung to, the inspector smiled. Like hell she'd be the first to know.

The information he'd been expecting from the Immigration and Naturalization Service reached Denton early that evening. Günther Werner had entered the United States the previous day at Buffalo, New York—which Denton already knew from the I-94 form stapled into the dead man's passport. His destination had been listed as New York City. Further checking revealed that Werner had flown in from Frankfurt to Toronto earlier the same day, accompanied by three other German nationals, who had crossed the border with him in a Greyhound bus. All four Germans—three men and a woman—had listed the same New York City hotel as their address, The Gallic Arms, a small establishment on West Twenty-ninth Street, near Fifth Avenue, which catered to budget-minded tourists. A quick telephone call by Denton ascertained that neither Rolf Haller, Dieter Kirchmann, nor Magda Breitner had taken up his or her reservation. They had simply disappeared.

A multitude of nagging thoughts erupted in Denton's mind. If they were coming to New York, why had they flown to Toronto first, then suffered the discomfort of a cramped twelve-hour bus ride? Why hadn't they flown direct? It didn't make sense.

He tried again. Four German nationals had entered the United States through a devious travel route and then vanished into thin air. All except one of them, of course, who was lying in the morgue, his head split in half, courtesy of the NYPD. Denton liked it even less. He had been in the department too long to let an oddity like this slip by. He wanted an answer, even if it meant telexing Interpol and the German authorities.

155

11

BY THE FOLLOWING MORNING, Stiehl had thrust his fury at Werner's disobedience to the back of his mind. He saw no point in dwelling on it; the man was dead, and the chapter closed. It was unfortunate that the idiot had scribbled the telephone number on a cigarette pack, not memorizing it as others had done, so that it could be ferreted out by an alert detective. But Stiehl could see no way of Denton's connecting the operation he was planning with Werner's death. Both he and Huckleby had denied knowledge of Werner, although Huckleby had been justifiably worried about the call from Denton. Stiehl had calmed him down, thankful that the retired general had remembered his cover of Adcock, the company's South African manager, in Newark to work on new products being introduced.

Stiehl entered the converted warehouse at nine o'clock, as most of its inhabitants were finishing breakfast; he wondered who had done the cooking, not that he really cared. His own breakfast had been prepared by Linda Huckleby, at whose Fort Lee apartment he had spent the night. The dream had woken him again at four in the morning, the same never-ending sequence of burning buildings, screaming crowds intent on his blood, the chase through unfamiliar terrain with no sanctuary. He wondered if there was any significance, whether the dream portended some future disaster. Best not to think about such things; that was how you began to make mistakes.

He stood watching the squads for a moment; then he clapped his hands loudly, bringing everyone to attention. "Good morning. You have five minutes to finish off whatever you're doing; then I want you sitting on the closest bunks." He watched as the activity increased before walking into the glass-enclosed office. When he emerged, he was carrying a wide rolled-up piece of paper, which he tacked to the warehouse wall, leaving a blank sheet of paper across it.

Five minutes later the breakfast articles had disappeared. The three squads crowded around Stiehl, some sitting on the edges of bunks, others squatting cross-legged on the floor. Cigarette smoke filled the air.

"No doubt you've all heard by now what happened to one of our number yesterday morning." Some of the men nodded their heads. "His name was Günther Werner, from Dieter Kirchmann's group. Werner believed he knew best and could disobey my instructions. If he had not been killed by the police, I would have executed him myself when he arrived here. The man endangered our entire operation by his thoughtlessness. He went outside my instructions, an act which I will not tolerate. If this mission is to succeed, I must have complete authority, unanswering obedience to any command I give. Is that understood?"

A muted assent greeted the question. Stiehl looked around the gathered faces, seeking out Kerrigan, who he believed represented his strongest support in the camp. The broken-nosed Irishman nodded solemnly. Stiehl moved his gaze to take in Danny McGrath, wearing jeans and a blue cotton shirt, the heavy glasses pushed high on the bridge of his nose.

"And you?" Stiehl asked. He knew why Brady had included the former schoolteacher, for his planning capabilities, but he still did not trust him completely; he viewed him as an intellectual idealist, a combination which had never appealed to Stiehl's better judgment.

"I'm all for you," McGrath acknowledged. "You're in charge."

"Very good." He turned back to the wall and removed the sheet of white paper to expose a large-scale map of Manhattan, including the borders of Queens, Brooklyn, the Bronx, and New Jersey. "That is your target, the objective of this mission. The entire borough of Manhattan."

A whistle of admiration erupted from Kerrigan's lips, cut short the instant it had started. Stiehl waited a few seconds until he had complete silence. "I trust that whistle does not mean you think this operation is impossible, Kerrigan."

"No, sir!" Kerrigan stood up. "But when someone offers you the crown jewels on a solid gold platter, only a corpse would show no emotion."

Stiehl smiled at the response. "This is Manhattan, the principal borough of the city of New York, and the main nerve center of the United States' financial institutions. Not only is the taking of Manhattan a plausible operation, but the odds will be heavily weighted in our favor. With the exception of a scattered handful of attacks by Puerto Rican extremists, New York City has never been the target for any kind of operation. We will have surprise as our ally, and we will be using the most audacious plan ever devised to steal, if you will, the entire island. There is no reason in the world why it cannot succeed."

"How much money will be involved?" The question came from Dieter Kirchmann. "You originally mentioned one billion dollars. Have you revised that figure at all?"

"No. I mentioned the sum of one billion dollars as a rough estimate. You must realize that when you cut off the entire borough of Manhattan from the rest of the world, you can demand whatever you like for its release. It could be considerably more than one billion dollars. I know for a fact that there are forty billion dollars in cash and negotiable securities in the vault of the First National Bank of Manhattan alone. What we take depends on what we are physically able to haul away."

158

"How do you propose to take over Manhattan?" Brady asked. He felt he had to promote himself more. The South African seemed to have developed a rapport with Kerrigan because of their mutual acquaintance, and Brady sensed that he could lose control of the Irish squad.

"I'll explain that when I'm ready."

McGrath raised a hand in the air, wavering, uncertain whether to ask his question. Stiehl noticed and pointed to him quickly. "Yes. What is it?"

"Manhattan seems like a huge objective. Why not just seize something like the Statue of Liberty? The Americans value that highly; they'd pay to get it back."

"A number of reasons. First, the Statue of Liberty is located on a small island, which we would have to defend. We could probably take it over during the day and have hostages, but we'd still need to get off the island. If we did not get what we wanted and blew it up to show we meant business, we would have nothing left to bargain with. And it could always be rebuilt."

Brady stuck his hand up in the air for another question. "If we're splitting whatever money we get as ransom among the three groups represented here, who's paying you and your principals?"

It was the wrong question. "That is my concern," Stiehl replied coldly. "My principals have their own motives for financing this operation. Those reasons are not open for discussion." He looked around briefly to see if there were any more questions; there were none. "What I have to say next I want you all to listen to very carefully. If anyone wishes to back out now, before I go over the operational plan in detail, he may. He will be given a ticket back to his point of origin, and nothing will be said about it. Once I explain the operation, there will be no backing out."

There was no mistaking the threat contained in the final sentence. The squads sat quietly, mulling over the proposition, each individual looking around to see who would take Stiehl up on the avenue of escape. Stiehl waited for fully two minutes, his eyes roving across his audience, certain that there would be no withdrawals. To pull out now would be to lose face, and he was sure

159

that none of the groups would want to be seen as weak by the others. Satisfied, he continued speaking. "As you will see from this map, Manhattan is an island, joined to the boroughs of Queens, the Bronx, and Brooklyn, and the state of New Jersey, by a series of rail and road bridges and tunnels. The ferry system to Staten Island does not concern us, nor do the heliports as they would prove impractical for use in lifting a blockade. We are going to cut Manhattan off from its surroundings by a combination of blowing up, blocking, and taking hostage its bridges and tunnels. Once we have accomplished that, we will be able to demand whatever we want as a condition for lifting the blockade."

"How do you take a bridge hostage?" Kerrigan asked. "We haven't got the manpower to withstand any kind of concerted assault from an army unit."

"Let me finish," Stiehl said. He produced a pointer and laid the tip on the map. "North of the Triborough Bridge, which connects the Bronx, Queens, and Manhattan, we will set charges to blow all road and rail bridges spanning the Harlem River up to where it runs into the Hudson River. Simultaneously selected teams will carry explosives onto all subway and main-line trains running in and out of Manhattan, from New Jersey, Queens, Brooklyn, and the Bronx. At a predetermined distance inside the tunnel from the last Manhattan station, you will stop the train by pulling the emergency brake handle and announce there is a bomb on board. The bombs will be timed to detonate together. They will, of course, be booby-trapped as a defense against attempts to defuse them. The explosions will be powerful enough to wreck the coaches, jamming them across the tracks."

"What about the men who place the bombs?" asked one of the Arabs.

"They will surrender themselves to transit police once the trains are cleared of passengers."

"How do they get away then?"

"They will be rescued, as you will see from the next step of the operation." Stiehl returned to the map and moved the pointer to the George Washington Bridge. "Once the bridges north of the

Triborough have been made inoperable, and the rail system blocked, we will move onto the major bridges and tunnels." He moved the pointer as he spoke, holding it against each location for as long as it took him to identify it.

"That leaves us with the George Washington Bridge between Washington Heights in Manhattan and Fort Lee, New Jersey. The Lincoln Tunnel between midtown Manhattan and Weehawken, New Jersey. The Holland Tunnel between lower Manhattan and Jersey City, New Jersey. The Brooklyn-Battery Tunnel between Brooklyn and South Ferry at the southernmost tip of Manhattan. The Brooklyn, Manhattan, and Williamsburg bridges connecting Brooklyn to Manhattan, the Queens-Midtown Tunnel and the Queensboro Bridge between Queens and Manhattan. And, of course, the Triborough Bridge. These we will take hostage." He paused to draw breath, scanning his audience, seeing that he had each member in his grasp.

"After the train system has been brought to a complete halt and the Harlem River bridges blown up, trucks will take up positions on the remaining bridges and tunnels. They will each be loaded with approximately ten tons of high explosive, radio-controlled from a command post which I, alone, will know about. The drivers will leave the trucks, locking them to complete an electrical circuit which will detonate the loads if anyone tries to tamper with them. With one flick of a switch, we will then be able to sever all these massive links between Manhattan and the rest of the world. Manhattan produces nothing, so all food has to be shipped in. If Manhattan's lifelines, and Manhattan itself, are put out of action, the banks—the nerve centers of the Western financial world—will cease to function. Furthermore, unless the blockade is lifted quickly, Manhattan will become a scene of rioting because we will make certain much of the police force is deployed elsewhere."

"What about the drivers of the trucks?" someone called out. Stiehl looked up crossly, trying to spot who had interrupted him; he could not.

"After locking their vehicles and throwing away the keys, the truck drivers will assemble at the Wall Street Heliport, Pier Six on the East River. They will find their own way and wait there for transportation to Kennedy Airport. I believe the city of New York will be only too willing to provide that transportation to ensure the survival of its major lifelines. Just as it will provide our one billion dollars and the release of the men held in the subway bomb incidents."

A stunned silence greeted the simple audacity of the plan. Then Kerrigan stood up and clapped his hands loudly. "Mr. Adcock, you can count me in all the way. I'm proud to be a part of it."

Stiehl smiled. He had been right all along about Kerrigan's support. True, the Irishman was not the leader of his group, but Stiehl was certain his enthusiasm could sway his comrades. "Thank you. And I'm equally pleased to have you with me. Perhaps you all would like to talk it over among yourselves or get some rest. You'll be going into action during the next few days, touring New York as it's never been toured before. By the time we have finished preparing you'll all know more about the city than any cabdriver."

Leaving the map on the wall, he returned the pointer to his office, locked the door, and left the converted warehouse.

As soon as Stiehl left, the terrorists gathered in their respective groups, discussing the enormity of the plan. Kerrigan, as he had displayed when Stiehl was present, backed it all the way, describing it in the same sentence as brilliant, magnificently conceived, and absolutely foolproof. McGrath jeered, calling him a fool blinded by dreams of his own glory. Only Brady's intervention, diving in between the two men, stopped the situation from developing into a fight.

The Germans, too, were impressed. Kirchmann had been fearful that Werner's disobedience would incriminate his entire squad, but Stiehl had made no sweeping indictment. He had been content to let Werner's death serve as a warning to the others and then forget about the entire incident.

Only among the Arabs was there trepidation, a worry brought about by the immensity of the operation. They could understand hijacking a single aircraft or staging a nighttime foray into Israel. Cutting off an entire borough of millions of people and holding it indefinitely against the world's mightiest power for the largest ransom in history were beyond their scope, like crossing the desert barefoot with no water. They argued quietly among themselves, discussing the possibilities. One man alone seemed truly pessimistic: Omar Baroudi, a Palestinian dentist turned freedom fighter. Baroudi had lived in the United States five years earlier, when he studied at Fairleigh Dickinson University in New Jersey. He knew more about the Americans than did his colleagues. They might be swung easily into backing this madcap scheme, sacrificing themselves for someone else's glory, but doubts assailed him. He drew Hashim Nissouri, the Arab group leader, off to one side, out of earshot of the others.

"This man Adcock is mad," he said simply.

"We can do it." Nissouri replied. "Do you see the other groups, the Irish, the Germans? They are confident. Dr. Habash chose us because we are men. Do not let us down."

"You forget that I have lived here," Baroudi stressed. "I know the Americans better than any of you. If I had known what this operation entailed, I would never have consented to be a part of it. I would have continued my fight from the camps in Lebanon, where I belong."

"You cannot back out now. We will not let you. You will disgrace all of us."

"It cannot be done," Baroudi repeated. "That is what I am trying to tell you."

"We will ask the others," Nissouri decided. "See what they have to say." He drew Baroudi back to the group of Arabs. Gamal Aktouri and Ahmed Nassim looked up questioningly as Baroudi and Nissouri approached. The other sixteen men, including the three Syrian pilots, were absorbed in their own conversations.

"Omar is having second thoughts," Nissouri said. "He says because he has lived here, he knows more than any of us. The Americans will never let us get away with such a mission."

Neither Aktouri nor Nassim said anything, but they moved in

closer, threatening. Baroudi held up his hands in a gesture of surrender. "I was only trying to help," he said softly. "If the rest of you are for this scheme, I am for you."

A smile touched Nissouri's lips. He was unable to conceal his pleasure at seeing the Arab group whole again; now nothing could stop them from going down in Palestinian legend as heroes.

As darkness fell, Stiehl walked past the warehouse, checking that the blackout curtains were in place. No chinks of light shone through from the inside. His orders on total security were being obeyed. Even the faintest glimmer of light would reveal that the warehouse was in use.

A hundred yards distant from the warehouse was a small wooden shack, once used as a dispatch office, now taken over by Stiehl for his personal use. He knocked twice on the door and walked inside, adjusting his eyes to the dim redness of the night-light. Two men were seated at a table, playing cards, squinting in the semidarkness; a third man stood by the window, infrared glasses held to his eyes as he kept the warehouse under constant surveillance. In one corner, three M-16 rifles were stacked army-style.

"Everything okay?" Stiehl asked, helping himself to coffee from the percolator on the floor.

One of the cardplayers tossed in his hand and stood up. "Nothing doing anywhere, Colonel." He addressed Stiehl by the rank he had held in Angola when he had led the three men out of Cuban-controlled territory back to the safety of the border.

Stiehl nodded, satisfied. Funny how a professional relationship came in useful again, he thought, looking from one man to the other. He remembered telling them to keep in touch when they had parted company. Who would have thought they would be working for him again, especially on a project like this? The three Americans had no idea what the project was, and for twenty-five thousand dollars each, they were not particularly interested. All they had to do was keep the warehouse under guard, make certain that nobody tried to leave.

"I'll be sacked out in the main office," Stiehl said, turning toward the door. "You've got the number. Any problems, get straight through to me."

"Will do, Colonel." The cardplayer waved cheerfully and picked up his hand again, going back to the game as if the interruption had never occurred. It pleased Stiehl that the man with the infrared glasses had never acknowledged his presence in the shack; his attention had remained on the warehouse the entire time.

Omar Baroudi lay awake, listening to the rhythmic snoring of the man in the upper bunk, watching the mattress sag each time the sleeper moved. He had to get out of here. Nissouri and the others were as insane as the South African. They had no chance of getting away with an operation like this. It was a fool's dream, nothing more, and he wanted no part of it.

He rose quietly, slipped into his clothes, made certain he had his passport, and padded stealthily across the warehouse floor to one of the toilets. Nobody stirred. Standing by the toilet door, he listened carefully to be certain he had disturbed nobody. Then, with an excruciating slowness, he tiptoed across the floor, lifted the latch, and slipped out into the cool night air. He stood by the door for a minute, looking around the empty loading yard, seeing lights in the distance from the main business area and, beyond that, the lights of Newark. He had no idea where to go. He did not have the money for airfare back to his own country. Perhaps he could go to the Libyan United Nations delegation and ask for money back to Lebanon. Or would they turn him over to his own people as a traitor? Baroudi harbored no doubts that the Libyan government had been informed about an impending operation in the United States; otherwise, why would it have issued the diplomatic passports? Perhaps he could buy their favor by telling the Libyans exactly what was planned.

Satisfied that he was alone in the yard, he began to gain confidence. He walked briskly, soft-soled shoes making no sound on the asphalt. He would go into Newark. Maybe he would find money there, a robbery, anything to give him the airfare he needed. Praise be to Allah that he had seen this thing for the

165

madness it was. Let the others have their throats slit like so many sheep at the slaughter if that was what they wanted; he would rather die on his own terms.

Something hard pressed into his back. A hand stronger than a vise clamped over his mouth, cutting off the scream of panic which would have woken the people sleeping in the warehouse. As Baroudi tried to understand what could have happened, a bomb exploded inside his head, driving consciousness away.

Baroudi came around ten minutes later, emerging from the blackness into a hell filled with dim red light, which eddied and swayed like a foundering boat in front of his eyes. He tried to move, to steady himself against the waves of pain that battered the inside of his skull, but could not. His hands were pinioned tightly behind his back, held there by the same iron grip that had cut off his scream of panic. Voices swept over him, questions which were fired in English.

"Where were you going? Why did you leave the building?"

He screwed his eyes tightly shut, then opened them slowly. Stiehl's face came into gradual focus, a blur at first, features defining themselves as he became accustomed to the red light of the dispatch hut. On either side Baroudi felt the presence of other men; a third, behind him, held his arms in an unrelenting grip.

"I am asking for the last time," Stiehl said. "Where were you planning to go?"

"Home!" Baroudi burst out. "I was going home! You are mad! Your plan is mad!" There was something different about the South African. It took Baroudi a few seconds to realize he was not wearing the tinted glasses.

Stiehl appeared satisfied with the answer. He turned away from the Palestinian and walked toward the window to stare out into the blackness of the night. "Were you by yourself?" he asked eventually. "Or were others involved?"

"Nobody else." Baroudi licked thick lips, the tip of his tongue coming into contact with the long hairs of his mustache. "I am the only one with enough courage to leave. The others are like

sheep. They will follow you anywhere, even to their deaths."
Stiehl turned back to the Palestinian. "Courage is a blessing,"
he said; the smile which appeared on his face made Baroudi
flinch. "Provided you are wise enough to know when to use it."
He opened a cupboard in the corner, rummaged around for a
moment, finally producing a length of thin, strong twine. While
one of the guards held Baroudi over the table, Stiehl roped his
wrists, cut the twine, then tied his ankles together, leaving just
enough slack for the man to take short walking steps. Finally, he
looped a length of twine over Baroudi's head. Tossing the left-
over twine into the table, he opened the door of the hut and
pushed Baroudi ahead of him with the muzzle of the Browning.
By the time he closed the door two guards had gone back to
playing gin rummy; the third had resumed his position by the
window with the night glasses.

The warehouse was in pitch-blackness when Stiehl opened the
door. He slipped the dark glasses over his eyes and stood still,
holding the twine around Baroudi's neck, listening to the sounds
of an army sleeping. From one corner came snoring; from somewhere else came the rustle of a mattress, the squeaking of
springs as a man moved. Stiehl reached out and turned on the
lights, banging on the wall with the butt of the Browning.

Frank Brady was the first to wake, sitting up in his bunk, eyes
wide open, instantly alert. He looked first at Stiehl, then with
undisguised amazement at the bound figure of Baroudi. Leaning
over, he prodded Kerrigan, who was sleeping in the lower
bunk.

Stiehl watched the warehouse come to life and acknowledged
the puzzled stares. Behind the tinted glasses, his eyes flicked
over faces, noticing how the Irish, Germans, and Arabs had all
made their own ghettos, separating each group from the other.
He held Hashim Nissouri's gaze for a long moment, inviting a
question from the Arab leader.

"Why is Omar Baroudi tied up?" Nissouri asked. He left his
bunk and walked barefoot across the floor, dressed only in a pair
of baggy underpants.

"Get your people together," Stiehl said. "Then I'll tell you."

He waited another half minute before moving into the center of the floor. "This man"—he jerked the twine around Baroudi's neck like a dog on the leash—"has betrayed us. He was caught attempting to desert."

Kerrigan was the first to react, as Stiehl had guessed he would be. "Kill the bastard," the Irishman growled. He looked around his own group, locking eyes with Danny McGrath, wondering if the four-eyed dummy would dispute even this with him. McGrath slowly nodded his head in agreement.

"And you?" Stiehl looked at Kirchmann. "How do you think we should deal with deserters?"

The German stuck out the thumb of his right hand and turned it down, an emperor pronouncing the sentence of death on a fallen gladiator.

"Nissouri? He's your man. You brought him with you. You heard the warning I gave before revealing the operational plans. What do you want me to do with him?"

Nissouri appeared uncomfortable at the prospect of deciding Baroudi's fate. He had sympathy for the man because he was a Palestinian like him. But if he showed softness, he would be damned in the eyes of the other groups. "He is no longer one of us. Kill him."

Stiehl jerked the twine savagely. Baroudi crumpled to the ground, landing on his knees, unable to stop his face from hitting the concrete. The shout of pain turned into a hysterical scream of fear as he felt the muzzle of the Browning jammed hard behind his right ear. Stiehl looked up for a brief moment at the ring of faces surrounding him; then he squeezed the trigger.

"Your men can clean up the mess," he told Nissouri, not looking down at the body on the floor or at what was left of Baroudi's head after the Browning's nine-millimeter slug had done its work. "We'll arrange to dispose of the body tomorrow. Good night."

He walked away quickly and closed the door, hungrily breathing in the cool air as he sought to wash away the taste of bile in his mouth. Like so many necessary throughout his life, the cold-blooded execution had been distasteful, but job enjoyment was not one of the requirements for the operation in which he was involved. A nerve of steel was, determination was, even if it meant callously killing a man who had enough brains to be afraid, so that he might teach an indelible lesson to other possible deserters.

By the time he reached the dispatch hut he was feeling better. The shot had not been heard outside the warehouse, but the three guards had guessed what had happened. None of them made any comment as Stiehl stood watching the card game for fifteen minutes, smoking two cigarettes before deciding to return to bed. When he left, the man at the window turned to his colleagues at the table.

"Hasn't changed one little bit, has he?" His voice contained a touch of the Midwest. "Just glad he's on our side."

"You can say that again," one of the cardplayers muttered. "If he was any different, we'd all be pushing up Angolan daisies right now."

The lookout laughed and went back to sweeping the night with his glasses.

12

A HIGH WALL faced Inspector Eric Denton, as smooth as glass and seemingly insurmountable. In the four days which had passed since the death of Günther Werner, he had made no headway into his investigation of the three missing Germans. Queries telexed to both German police and Interpol had produced no information. Denton doubted that either of the law enforcement agencies would be able to supply any news to help him.

Item, he scribbled down on a yellow pad lying on his desk: "A German tourist gets killed by a cop after beating up a hooker who was trying to rip him off." "So what else is new?" he added in parentheses, before scratching it out. Item: "The three German tourists the dead man crossed the U.S. border with—Dieter Kirchmann, Rolf Haller, and Magda Breitner—never checked in at their intended destination, and they've all disappeared from the face of the earth." Item: "The police inspector heading this self-appointed investigation into their disappearance when he's

170

got a million other things to do wishes someone would tell him what the hell's going on."

Disgusted, he threw the pencil onto the desk and opened the office door. Outside, two detectives were questioning an elderly woman who had been mugged. Another detective was sitting back in his chair, feet propped up on the desk while he listened to a telephoned complaint. When he saw Denton looking his way, he rolled his eyes, clapped a hand over the mouthpiece, and shouted across the squad room, "Got some nutty broad here who's just seen Martin Bormann and Josef Mengele disguised as countermen in the Forty-seventh Street Deli."

Denton grinned, forgetting all about his own problems for a moment. Reports of Nazi war criminals he knew how to handle. A bunch of missing Germans in the city presented a different, more sinister puzzle.

Leaving the building, he headed for the restaurant on the corner of the block. He got no farther than twenty yards to his anticipated lunch of pastrami on rye when a woman's voice made him halt. "Eric! Inspector Denton! Can you give us a minute?"

Heart sinking, he turned slowly toward the road, recognizing the white Ford station wagon with the red MetroCity sign emblazoned on the side. He wished she'd quit calling him by his first name; if anyone on the department heard her, he'd think he was her pet cop.

The passenger door of the Ford opened, and Babs O'Neill sprang out. "Yeah, I know," Denton said wearily. "You were just passing by and thought you'd look me up, right?"

"Of course," she answered brightly. "We're doing some research for a Times Square porno series."

"So where do I fit into it? And get that goddamned thing out of my face!" He raised his voice as Rosen got out of the Ford, aiming the camera at him.

Babs delayed her answer long enough to look at the crowd of people which had begun to form. The power of the camera, she thought; it never fails. "What about that murder on Eighth Avenue the other morning?" she asked, speaking loudly so the onlookers could hear, playing to her unexpected audience.

"Which murder? What morning? We get a lot of murders. Or don't you ever watch the news?" He began to move away, embarrassed by the public interview.

"Werner," Babs prompted, keeping in step as Denton walked toward the restaurant. "Günther Werner, the German tourist who beat up the hooker who was ripping him off."

"Werner was not murdered," Denton pointed out. "He was shot by a police officer in self-defense, as the investigating board will undoubtedly prove." He continued walking, turning away from Babs. When he entered the restaurant, he took his regular seat at the end of the counter, close to the kitchen. He was not unduly surprised when Babs took the seat next to him, with Rosen still in tow.

"Will you tell me what's happening on that case?" she asked.

"Buy me lunch, and I will. You must have an expense account that allows you to take starving cops to lunch now and again."

"I do. What do you want?" She pulled out a twenty-dollar bill from her purse.

"Pastrami on rye. And coffee." He looked along the counter to where Rosen sat; the sound man had stayed in the car. "You buying your partner lunch as well? Or does he have to pay his own way?"

Babs gave vent to an exasperated sign. "I'll buy everyone in the city a goddamned lunch if you only tell me what's going on in that case."

"Let me eat first," Denton said. "Then I'll tell you. It's been a rough morning."

The orders came, and Babs picked up the check, asking for a receipt. Limiting herself to cream cheese on whole wheat and a black coffee, she finished first and waited impatiently for Denton. "Well?" she asked, when the inspector had swallowed the last bite. "What about it?"

Denton wiped his mouth with the paper napkin. "Thanks for lunch. Now you're entitled to know everything I do about the Günther Werner case."

"Which is?"

"Which is"—he paused for effect, enjoying the suspense he

172

was building up—"absolutely nothing. No leads have turned up, except for the fact that three German nationals Werner traveled with from Frankfurt to Toronto before taking a Greyhound down to New York have all disappeared."

"How do you mean disappeared?" The initial burst of anger at Denton's negative answer had gone, replaced by a growing interest.

"Coming over the border from Canada, they had to fill out I-ninety-four forms for the INS. That's the white form with personal background and destination that gets stapled into the passports of people visiting the United States. There are two copies, one of which the INS keeps for its—"

"Yes, yes, yes," Babs said irritatedly. "I know all about I-ninety-four forms."

"Werner came into this country with three other people, two men and a woman. Rolf Haller, Dieter Kirchmann, and Magda Breitner. All of them, Werner included, listed The Gallic Arms on West Twenty-ninth Street as their address while in the United States. None of them ever checked in. The reason for Werner's failing to take up his reservation is pretty obvious. What happened to the three other Germans is a mystery."

Babs filed the names away in her memory. "What's happening about it now?"

"What's all this got to do with a porno story on Times Square?" Denton asked suspiciously.

"Nothing. I'm curious, that's all. And I did buy you lunch."

Denton looked past her to Rosen, who was checking his camera. "Immigration's looking into it. I've also telexed the German police and Interpol to see if there's anything known on the three missing characters. I always get a bit nervous about krauts who disappear, especially when they're on my beat."

"Can't say I blame you," Babs said, standing up. "Not after what happened at Entebbe and Mogadishu. Let me know if you find out anything."

Denton crossed himself earnestly. "Like always, you'll be the first to know, Babs. Cross my heart."

"Before the chief?"

He smiled at her. "Before the chief."

"You're such a liar," Babs whispered. "Even for a cop, you're such a fucking liar." She returned his smile nevertheless.

Having removed the glasses, Stiehl passed a handkerchief over the dark lenses, wiping away the greasy smears caused by perspiration. He would be glad when the operation was over, when he would be able to discard the simple disguise he had adopted and wash the color rinse out of his hair. Not that he really needed it, he mused; the only involved person who had seen him in the flesh was Kerrigan, and then only for a minute a lifetime earlier, when he had been wearing a forage hat and fatigues. Of course, the glasses and hair coloring were necessary for his other dealings— the apartment in Howard Beach for which he had registered in the name of Peter Adcock, British correspondent for the Rand *Daily Mail.* Far safer to carry the game all the way than to risk being caught out when it came time to change from Stiehl to Adcock.

He replaced the glasses, assuming the actions of a man who really needs them, blinking rapidly as he tried to readjust his focus. He leaned against the rail of the Circle Line boat as it sailed slowly past upper Manhattan and looked south at the George Washington Bridge, half lost in the haze which drifted across New York. Next to him stood Frank Brady, Johnny Coughlin, Kerrigan, and McGrath and four other members of the Irish squad, all appearing totally relaxed, acting like other tourists on a cruise around Manhattan. Never a lover of water, Stiehl was grateful that this would be the last time he would shepherd his charges on the Circle Line tour, pointing out the various bridges, explaining which spans would be destroyed and which ones would be taken hostage. He was beginning to feel like a tour guide, especially when he considered the many different nationalities of his army.

As the boat neared the George Washington Bridge, Stiehl looked past it to the luxury high-rise apartment buildings overlooking the Hudson from Fort Lee. He tried to estimate which windows belonged to Linda Huckleby's apartment and whether she was looking out. Probably in the city shopping, he thought

174

wryly, remembering her extensive wardrobe. He'd like to see more of her, but the intensity of the preparations for her father's operation precluded his visits. He wondered how Linda felt about the mission and what would happen to her when it was all over. Did she know what her father planned as the finale? Was she far enough over her mother's violent death to be able to cope with it? Stiehl knew he had to be around when it was over, to help her through. Without him to lean on, she would be lost. For some reason he found the idea appealing.

He felt someone nudge his arm and tore his eyes away from Linda's building, pushing the girl from his mind. McGrath was looking at him, a question forming on his lips. "What are those buildings over there?" The Irishman pointed to four high-rise blocks which stretched up from the New York side of the George Washington Bridge. "Apartments?"

Stiehl scoured his memory for information. He had read up extensively on the history of each bridge involved in the operation and remembered something about the buildings. "They're apartments. Built on the bridge approach from Route Ninety-five, the Cross Bronx Expressway." He paused, looking carefully at McGrath. "Are you thinking what I'm thinking?"

McGrath nodded. The others gathered around, as if alerted by telepathy. "Our plans call for the use of one truck loaded with explosives on the George Washington Bridge, right?"

"Carry on," Stiehl invited.

"Supposing we use two? Put the second truck directly under those apartment buildings? If threatening to blow the bridges and tunnels causes enough panic to make the city pay up, think what threatening to bring down those buildings will do, with people inside."

"That should present an added incentive to our demands," Stiehl agreed. McGrath had come through, the planner among the Irish. He wondered what effect the former schoolteacher's ingenuity would have on his feud with Kerrigan. "We'll incorporate it into our operational plan."

Smiling broadly, McGrath turned back to his comrades, accepting their congratulations. Only Kerrigan refused to join in, annoyed at himself for not being the one to think of such a simple ploy. Stiehl decided to keep a more watchful eye on the two men; then he permitted his attention to wander back to Linda's apartment, again thinking of the girl, wondering what she was doing. Was she thinking of him as he was thinking of her?

Wearing jeans and a windbreaker, Rolf Haller boarded the middle car of the uptown E train at Lexington Avenue. As the train rattled out of the station, he pressed down the button of a stopwatch, looking through the window as the train gathered speed and passed into the tunnel. After twenty seconds in the tunnel, he pressed the stopwatch again and read its face. He noted in a small diary that thirty-two seconds had elapsed.

Driving a Chevrolet Nova rented in the name of Howson Chemicals, Hashim Nissouri, Ahmed Nassim, and Gamal Aktouri rode along the center lane of the Grand Central Parkway through Queens toward Manhattan. Traffic thickened as they approached the Triborough Bridge, cars joining the stream from the Brooklyn-Queens Expressway.

"Over there," Nissouri said, pointing left toward Long Island City. "That is where you will start from, the secondary staging point."

The other two men grunted acknowledgment as they glanced at the sprawling area of decaying houses and factories. Aktouri had enough to do controlling the car in the middle of all this traffic without looking where Nissouri was pointing; he had never believed there was this much traffic, this many cars and trucks in the entire world, let alone on one street. On the approach to the bridge, he disregarded the solid white line and pulled over to the right lane, cutting off a tractor-trailer which had joined the traffic flow from Hoyt Avenue; the rig's driver gave the Nova a long, derisive blast of the horn.

"Careful," Nissouri whispered agitatedly. "No accidents. No police."

"You worry about your own business!" Aktouri shot back. "I will worry about the driving."

Nissouri sat back, absently watching the cars which swept by them. His thoughts were on Omar Baroudi, how the fool had caused his fellow Arabs to lose face in front of the Germans and the Irish. "If only we could have caught him before Adcock did," he muttered. Neither of the other two men in the car paid any attention to him. "We would have made him pay, dishonoring his comrades, his family, the whole Arab cause." He grimaced as he thought about the dead Palestinian. Now both the Germans and the Arabs were a man short, two men down in all. Nissouri wondered if Adcock had taken into consideration the possible premature loss of men, or would he be forced to compromise his plan or find replacements elsewhere?

He felt the Nova slow down as Aktouri came off the bridge, following the signs to Manhattan. A long sweeping curve to the toll booths lay ahead. Nissouri tapped Aktouri on the arm. "This is where you leave the truck, so that it threatens the connection to Manhattan. Right in the middle here. Lock it up, and walk away."

All three men glanced at the dashboard clock. Two minutes had elapsed since they had passed the point where the explosive-laden truck would be positioned at its takeoff point. The truck would not be as fast or as agile as the Nova, but on the other hand, it would not have to fight against such a heavy flow of traffic. Two minutes it would be. Nissouri marked down the time as Aktouri tossed three quarters into the basket of the exact change lane. The light turned green, the bar flicked up, and they were through.

At midnight the fifty-eight remaining members of the assault force sat listening to Stiehl in the converted warehouse. He kept it short, knowing they were tired after spending three days traveling around the city, driving, using the subways, the Conrail and PATH trains to New Jersey, the Long Island Rail Road, checking on times, identifying locations, making themselves totally familiar with the lifelines to the borough that would become their prize.

"You've all done very well," he commended them. "Especially

177

since we're under the added strain of being two men short. If we had to go right now, I'm certain that none of you would fail. But there is one more crucial factor. The weather. It is imperative that we have hot weather. So I apologize now, in advance, for having to force you to wait longer than necessary. We cannot move without hot weather. Until I have a long-range forecast that guarantees me exactly what I'm looking for, you're all going to have to sit around and wait. I'll try to make the waiting as easy as possible. Film shows will be provided, so will books, playing cards, chess sets, et cetera. Any questions?"

Abdul Wasim, one of the three Syrian pilots, thrust a hand into the air. "Mr. Adcock. Is any information yet available on the type of aircraft we will be flying?"

Stiehl smiled at the question, seeing a way he could deflate any tension that might be creeping in. "I'm afraid not. It's not as though we could order a plane beforehand without tipping off the authorities." He was pleased to hear the wave of laughter which swept over his audience at the answer; it proved that the tension had not yet set in, that creeping, nagging, destroying force that disrupts even the best-laid plans, turns one man against another for no apparent reason, splits an army right down the middle. "When the time comes, we'll need a wide-bodied aircraft, DC-ten or Seven-forty-seven. I don't think we can afford to be too fussy about what we get."

He looked away from Wasim, noticing Kerrigan sitting cross-legged on the floor, next to Danny McGrath, whispering to him; the loathing on Kerrigan's face was unmistakable even from where Stiehl was standing.

"Kerrigan!" he called sharply. "Is it something you'd like to share with the rest of us?"

Taken by surprise, Kerrigan looked up. "No," he protested. "I was just complimenting Danny here for his idea about the second truck, telling him what a bright boy he was."

"Do it on your own time," Stiehl said, disbelieving every word. "Not when I'm speaking." He turned away and walked into his office.

Kerrigan moved closer to McGrath. "Bet you think you're hot

stuff, don't you? 'Our plans call for the use of one truck loaded with explosives on the George Washington Bridge,'" he mimicked. "'Supposing we use two?' Bet you think you're real smart now."

McGrath stared at him. "Stay away from me, Kerrigan. I'm warning you for the last time."

"You warn me?" Kerrigan laughed. "You're shitting in your pants at the thought of this job, aren't you? Why don't you try to run away, get back home to Belfast?" He had pleasurable visions of McGrath receiving the same summary justice meted out to Baroudi. "Go on, take off. I swear on my mother's grave that I'll wait five minutes before yelling copper."

McGrath's expression was one of pure venom.

13

STIEHL HAD BREAKFAST Saturday morning at his sister's home in Howard Beach. Although he had taken up her offer to move in with the family, since the arrival of his assault force he had been absent most of the time. He told Brenner and Juliet that he was traveling on business, working with the technical staff of a film company which had bought the option for a war story; the excuse seemed to satisfy them. After breakfast he caught a taxi to the Pan Am terminal at Kennedy. He disappeared into the building's cavernous bowels and emerged five minutes later, wearing the tinted glasses and tweed hat, to take a different taxi to the furnished apartment in Howard Beach which he had rented in the name of Peter Adcock. His sister had remarked once about the darker color of his hair; he had feigned embarrassment, claiming that he was being paid back for conceit. In trying to cover up some gray hairs which had crept in, he had overdone the treatment, darkening his hair too much. She had not asked him again.

Before entering the furnished apartment, he pulled on a pair of white, tight-fitting gloves, the type worn by film editors. He traced a pattern with the tip of his index finger in the dusty apartment as he walked into the master bedroom overlooking Jamaica Bay. Pulling up a chair to the window, he sat down, lit a cigarette, and gazed serenely out over the water. Every few minutes an aircraft would roar overhead, shaking the house, appearing seconds later in the viewfinder frame of the window. Stiehl could understand how the neighborhood's residents felt, how their animosity toward the airlines had grown with the increase in power and noise, until the Concorde had finally descended on them like some earth-shattering bird of prey.

At precisely ten-fifteen, the newly installed telphone rang. Stiehl reached over and lifted the receiver.

"Adcock."

"This is Huckleby. What's the situation?"

"My men are ready, sir. I trust that your equipment is the same."

"Everything is prepared," Huckleby replied. "In both Newark and Long Island City. The new trucks are loaded with a ten-ton capacity and have been driven to their staging points. Spares are split between both points. The wiring will be installed by your specialists when we're ready to roll."

"Good. Where will you be staying once it begins?"

"Fort Lee. The apartment."

"What about Linda?"

"She'll stay in a hotel. After we've finished, I don't think that apartment will be lived in for a long, long time. They'll make a museum out of it," Huckleby said. "Her story is that we had a fight and I threw her out."

Stiehl gripped the receiver tighter as it threatened to slip out of the cloth glove. "What about my weather report? Have you got it yet?"

"Yes."

"Then bring it over here. We'll go for a ride and discuss the remainder of our work." He hung up and returned to aircraft watching.

Huckleby arrived just over an hour later, announcing his pres-

181

ence with a short double blast of the Cadillac's horn. Stiehl locked the apartment door, peeled off the gloves, took the outside stairs two at a time, and walked toward the car. He slid into the front passenger seat, and Huckleby drove off.

"Where is it?"

"Glove compartment." Huckleby took his right hand off the wheel long enough to point at the compartment. "In a brown envelope."

Stiehl extracted the National Weather Service report and began to read. An exceptionally hot spell, lasting three to four days, was due to start Monday, with temperatures in the high eighties, low nineties, and accompanying high humidity; there was also a possibility of scattered electrical storms. Stiehl memorized the details, replaced the envelope, and slammed the glove compartment door. "We go on Tuesday night," he said. "That gives me time to make certain the whole team's combat-ready."

"You don't want any longer?" Huckleby asked in surprise. "Is three days long enough?"

"Probably more than enough. I've already executed one man for desertion and lost another because he disobeyed instructions. I don't want to take a chance on anyone else dropping out on me because of nerves. They've been cooped up all week in that warehouse, only coming out to travel around New York like a bunch of goggle-eyed tourists. I want the operation over and done with. As soon as possible."

"ASAP," Huckleby said. He guided the car onto the Belt Parkway, heading toward Brooklyn, paying little attention to where he was going. "What will you be doing after Tuesday night or Wednesday morning?" he asked Stiehl.

Was the old general getting maudlin? Stiehl wondered. "Planning on spending my money. All one million dollars of it. And you?"

"Who knows?" Huckleby gave out a dark, humorless chuckle. "Maybe getting ready to make my peace with my maker, trying to get Him to understand why all this had to be done."

"Do you think He will?"

"If He'd been through what I've been through, He would."

"What about Linda? When it's all over."

"I was hoping that might become your concern," Huckleby said.

"You'd better explain that." Stiehl remembered his own thoughts about the girl, how he had reconciled himself to being around when she would need someone. He still wanted to hear it from Huckleby's mouth. "I didn't take your daughter as part of the deal, along with the million dollars."

"She thinks a lot of you," Huckleby explained. "Linda's a bright girl. Sophisticated. Cultured. Yet everyone has a basic animal instinct, a primeval drive, if you like. You satisfy all facets of her personality, all her needs, her desires. Your writing has been published, one book only, admittedly, but it shows you must have some literary skill. So that puts you okay with Linda's cultural side. And you're a killer. That appeals to her animalistic side."

Stiehl breathed out heavily. "I had this all out with her once before."

"When you went to the Guggenheim?"

Stiehl made no attempt to hide his surprise. Obviously Huckleby knew everything about his daughter's relationship. Stiehl wondered if the girl had even told her father how many times they had made love that first night. "When we went to the Guggenheim, that's right. I stressed then that I've never killed anyone for the sheer hell of it. Whatever I've done was always for a reason—my life or theirs. Never for kicks."

"That makes your appeal even greater," Huckleby said. "You're tough enough to hold your emotions in check. You've got the power, but you use it wisely. Whichever way Linda looks at you, you can't go wrong."

"Is your daughter the reason for this drive?"

"One of them. She's all I have left, and I want to make certain someone will keep an eye on her."

Stiehl said nothing during the remainder of the drive, running Huckleby's words over in his mind. It was almost like a bribe: Look after the girl—she's in love with you anyway—and the million dollars he was being paid for the job would seem like peanuts with the fortune Linda would inherit from Howson Chemicals, not to mention the considerable sum of money Huckleby had already transferred to her. Nice to know that the old boy wasn't above a bit of bribery and corruption and didn't limit his talents to hijacking major cities.

When they returned to Howard Beach, Stiehl put on the white gloves and unlocked the Cadillac's trunk. Inside were two wooden crates, occupying all the space. Huckleby waited while Stiehl took one up to the apartment, then returned for the other.

"Until that time," Huckleby said, holding out his hand. "Thank you for helping make this possible."

Stiehl took Huckleby's hand and held it for an instant longer than he intended to. He suddenly felt close to the older man, as if seeing for the first time the anguish he had been through. "Good luck, General." Without another word, he picked up the remaining crate and went up to the apartment, not looking back as the Cadillac drove away.

Inspector Eric Denton surveyed the telex sheet in his hands with a combination of glum disbelief and numb horror. The German police had replied—though God alone knew what had taken them so long—and the initial worries Denton had harbored about the disappearing Germans were beginning to take on a far more sinister shape. He read the words again, willing them to change, knowing they would not. "Reference your inquiry on Dieter Kirchmann, Günther Werner, Rolf Haller, Magda Breitner. All at one time or another have been under observation as suspected Baader-Meinhof sympathizers."

The name at the bottom of the sheet meant nothing to Denton. All he could think of was three possible German terrorists loose in New York City.

He crumpled the piece of paper and flung it viciously at the wall, wondering what he should do first, which panic button he should push, where could he pass the buck most efficiently. The chief? FBI? After a second, he decided to push it straight upstairs. As his hand hovered over the telephone it rang.

"Yeah, Denton!"

184

"Inspector Denton? Babs O'Neill."

He swore under his breath. Did this goddamned broad have a nose for trouble? Could she sense it? She and that goddamned cameraman Rosen, just what he needed right now. "What do you want?"

She ignored his gruff tone. If Denton had his own problems, that was his lookout. "Anything new on the Günther Werner case?"

"Not a damned thing! Now don't bother me about it anymore!" He cut her off, then picked up the receiver immediately. While he waited to be put through to the chief's office, he tried to think of the most tactful way of telling the old man that a bunch of bomb-toting, gun-waving kraut terrorists was running amok in New York City.

In her office at MetroCity, Babs O'Neill sat studying the telephone thoughtfully, teeth biting on her lower lip as she concentrated. Denton might have avoided her in the past, even poked occasional fun at her, conning her into paying for lunch as he had done at the restaurant, but never had he been downright rude. What had made this usually patient man fly off the handle? A row with his wife? Male menopause? He was just about the right age. Or had she mentioned something that had acted as a trigger to his rage. Günther Werner; could there be something? A new piece in the jigsaw puzzle which gave it a completely different complexion? Denton had admitted over lunch that he'd telexed Interpol and the German police. Had he received a reply?

Without telling anyone where she was going, she left the studio and caught a taxi to the police station. Denton was out when she arrived; she had missed him by five minutes.

"Left here in a hell of a rush," a sergeant explained, flattered at being sought out by the television personality. "Looked like he had the devil himself on his heels."

"Do you know where he went?"

"Can't say I do. Brass doesn't confide in us lowlifes. Why don't you try asking Lieutenant Jones over there?" He pointed to a tall black plainclothes officer who was coming down the stairs from the squad room. "He might know."

She turned and walked quickly to the black police officer. "Hi, I'm Babs O'Neill from MetroCity."

"I know, ma'am. How can I help you?"

"I'm looking for Inspector Denton. It's very important." She breathed in deeply, steeling herself for the lie, hoping she was professional enough to carry it off. "I might have a lead on one of his cases, that Günther Werner, where the other three Germans have gone. I heard something that might be useful to him."

The black police officer smiled broadly. "Reckon he could do with all the help he can get on that one." Babs's heart jumped at the words. "He's downtown, FBI headquarters, getting their help in finding those krauts before they start pulling any of their terrorist tricks over here."

"Terrorists?"

"That's what the message from Germany said," Jones replied. "Say . . ." He hesitated as the first suspicions filtered through his mind. "I thought you said you knew where they were, what this was all about. What the hell do you know, lady?"

Babs spun around and raced out of the building before Jones could make any move to stop her. She flagged down a passing cab and sat excitedly in the back as she began to plan the exposé she would deliver on television. They'd make a special spot for her. Bump off one of the sitcom reruns to make space, maybe even cut into the baseball game scheduled for that evening.

Blond hair arranged in a contrived casualness, the blue costume without a scrap of lint to mar its finish, Babs sat in front of the camera, watching the news show director count off the seconds. He swung down his arm in a final gesture, and Babs launched into the opening, over which she had labored.

"Within the past hour this television station has learned that there are three German terrorists—members of the Baader-Meinhof Gang—loose in New York City."

She waited long enough for her initial words to sink into the television audience, letting them absorb the significance.

186

"The names of the three terrorists being sought by police are Dieter Kirchmann, Rolf Haller, and Magda Breitner. A fourth member of the group, Günther Werner, was killed by police." She went on to give details of the shooting, picking up the pace of the report as she neared the part about Denton.

"In charge of the investigation into the disappearance of the three Baader-Meinhof Gang members is Inspector Eric Denton, who at this moment is liaising with agents of the Federal Bureau of Investigation and with officials of the Immigration and Naturalization Service to establish their whereabouts and apprehend them.

"Although the three missing Germans listed The Gallic Arms on West Twenty-ninth Street as their destination in the United States, the reservations have not been taken up. They have simply disappeared, absorbed into the huge mass of people who make up this city." She looked past the camera for an instant and saw the producer holding up his thumb and forefinger in a circle. Next to him stood Charles Kohn, the station manager; he was grinning.

"Denton was alerted earlier this evening by German police about the link between the Baader-Meinhof Gang and the four German nationals—Werner, the man who was killed, Kirchmann, Haller and Magda Breitner." In a moment of charity, she decided to lighten up on Denton, going outside her prepared script. "This information from Germany was in reply to a query Inspector Denton made following the shooting death of Werner. When checking how Werner had entered the country, Denton learned that he had been accompanied by three other German nationals on an aircraft from Frankfurt to Toronto and then on the bus down to New York. Certainly Inspector Denton's outstanding work on this case has to be commended fully. But unfortunately for all of us who live and work in this city, Denton's intuition and perseverance are not enough. Three terrorists are somewhere among us, and the police do not even have a photograph to circulate yet.

"We will keep you informed if there are any further developments in this case." She straightened the papers in front of her

187

as the red light disappeared from the camera. Kohn came rushing forward, lifted her out of the chair, and kissed her on the cheek.

"You were wonderful! Fantastic! Any second now our switchboard will be lighting up like a Christmas tree. You've just started the biggest panic since Orson Welles did his number with *War of the Worlds*."

"I hope so, Charlie," Babs said, suddenly feeling very tired. "I sure as hell hope so. I just pray we're not barking up the wrong tree."

Jerry Rosen came over as she walked off the stage. "Great story. How did you dig up that stuff on Denton?"

She appreciated his praise. "Persistence, Jerry. Sheer old-fashioned persistence. Plus dumb luck and an angry cop." She took a cup of coffee someone held out to her, then turned to Rosen. "You ready to go out?"

"Where?"

"Mayor's office. I think we'll be getting a string of denials out of there soon. Might as well get ready for it."

Percy Scrivens had been mayor of New York City for six months, during which time he had endured a garbage strike, a teachers' strike despite the Taylor Law, a February filled with a record-breaking fifty-one inches of snow in two separate blizzards, and now a city-wide panic because of three possible German terrorists.

During the garbage strike he had joked on television that the unions were testing the resolve of the city's first black mayor. The teachers' strike had given him the opportunity to lose friends among the school administration by saying that perhaps the kids would learn more out of school than they ever would in it. The blizzards, he told New Yorkers, had been sent by God. When he received news of the three missing terrorists, he said nothing at first, unable to think of anything other than God's being a southern bigot who really had it in for him.

A Democrat in the tradition of New York mayors, Scrivens had sought election on a platform of conservatism, shedding the liberalism which had all too often been the undoing of his predecessors. Tall and slightly chubby with a clipped mustache and short hair that was turning gray at the sides, Scrivens had seen too often how a liberal attitude exacerbated city problems instead of solving them. He had promised reform of the city's cumbersome welfare system, a scything cut in unnecessary services, a raising of the examination standards for city jobs. Nobody would be able to claim that the forty-four-year-old native of the Bronx was favoring his fellow blacks; he made certain of that. The electorate had loved him—especially the blue-collar workers—shunning the pleas of his enemies in the Democratic Party who referred to Scrivens behind his back as the black Republican. Now, after six months of torture, having given up his partnership in an East Side law firm, he had been unable to put one of his campaign promises into action. The string of emergencies, culminating in the present panic, had taken up all his time.

Scrivens knew he was walking a tightrope when he ran for public office. Just as John F. Kennedy had done during his short tenure in the White House as the country's first Catholic President, Scrivens knew he would be judged on his ethnic background, his blackness. If things went wrong while he was in office—and God, how much worse could they possibly get?—they would go wrong because the city had a black mayor. If they went right, even to the point where he was reelected in three and a half years, they would go right because he had enough brains to surround himself with people who knew what they were doing. His color would never be a political issue if everything worked well, only if things continued to go wrong.

The telephone began ringing within thirty seconds of Babs O'Neill's going off the air. Alone in the living room of the cooperative apartment he preferred to use on East Sixty-fifth Street, instead of moving into what he considered the wasteful splendor of Gracie Mansion, Scrivens gazed gloomily at the instrument. Which newspaper? he wondered. Or which TV station? Doesn't the mayor get any rest?

He picked up the receiver, heard the caller identify himself as

189

being from The New York *Times,* and went into the reply he would give everyone until he had fully assessed the situation. "As far as I know, it is a totally uncorroborated story put out by MetroCity. When I have further information, I will hold a press conference. Thank you for calling." He replaced the receiver, then changed his mind and left it off the hook, covering it with a pillow from the couch. Maybe he should have moved into Gracie Mansion and let his staff handle incoming calls. He walked to the red unlisted telephone. When he got through to the police commissioner, the official was as baffled as Scrivens.

"What about this cop Denton?" Scrivens asked.

Police Commissioner Alan May, one of Scrivens's first appointments, took a long time answering. He was as surprised by the news as Scrivens and was still trying to adjust himself to it. "One of my top men. I'd vouch for him any day. All I know about him and these three missing krauts is what I just heard on the news. I've got men out now, checking with the FBI, trying to find Denton. Maybe he's learned something that'll put us all in the picture a bit more."

"Do your inspectors normally go off grandstanding like this?" Scrivens asked sharply.

"He's not grandstanding!" May shot back, always anxious to defend his department. "He was following a normal investigation procedure. He was checking into the disappearance of three visitors from Germany, using foreign law enforcement agencies to assist him. Now it turns up that these three—Breitner, Haller, and Kirchmann—may have affiliations with the Baader-Meinhof Gang, so Denton's doing what he should be doing. He's taking the investigation further. I'd say he's done some damned good work, used his initiative. That woman's news story hasn't helped us at all. I'd just like to know where she picked it up."

"So what do we do?" Scrivens was conscious of how many news media people must be trying to get through to him. Pretty soon they'd be hammering on the door if the security guard in the building's lobby let them through.

"Deny it," May said with growing conviction. "Say that O'Neill woman's full of shit. You can be damned sure she's started a panic, so it's up to us to calm it before it gets out of hand. It'll give my people a better chance to clear things up as well. Call her a liar, and remind people about that sanitation pad story she once ran, how there was no truth in that."

"Okay, I'll do it that way. But when you're getting on with your work, just remember that I run this city. I appointed you, and I want to be kept informed the moment anything breaks."

"I'll do that, Mr. Mayor."

Scrivens pressed down the receiver rest, released it, and dialed his aide. In a situation like this, the mayor could not be elusive. He had to be in the forefront, giving direction. The only way he could do that was with a press conference, where he would do his damnedest to stain that O'Neill bitch as a sensation-creating liar and bury her and her goddamned station.

When Police Commissioner May reached his office at eight-thirty Saturday evening, the jacket of his brown suit was undone, a button was missing from the middle of his white shirt, allowing his stomach to poke shyly through, his trousers were badly pressed, and his black shoes were scuffed. Appearance, as always, was the last thing on his mind. "No commissioner ever ran an efficient department by parading around like a tailor's dummy," he was fond of saying. He ran the department by working sixteen hours a day, seven days a week, and cleaning his shoes when he could find the time to stop at a corner shoeshine stand for two precious minutes.

Denton was waiting for him, having been called back from the FBI's New York office to explain his actions. He did this quickly, merely duplicating what Babs O'Neill had said on her news show.

"How the goddamned hell did that woman find out all this?" the commissioner demanded. "The mayor's calling a press conference right this minute to deny every single word she said."

"Christ knows where she got it from," Denton said wearily. "She called me up earlier to ask if there was anything new on the Werner shooting; she was trying to tie it in with some series on the porno industry her station's planning. And she wanted to know what had happened to the three krauts Werner had arrived with; she knew that much. She got through to me as I was reading the telex from the German police. I was short with her—who wouldn't be under those circumstances? Maybe she smelled a rat and dug further."

"From one of your men?"

"I don't know. Something could have slipped. She's clever enough to trip someone up."

"So what's the FBI doing?" May asked sarcastically. "Looking smart and well dressed as usual?"

"Checking. Cross-checking. Which is all they can do at the moment. They're pulling immigration lists of all foreign nationals who entered the country when those Germans did, the day itself, two days back, and two days after. They're bracketing the time to see if anyone else doesn't fit."

"Oh, great!" May exploded. "That should take them the next five years."

"Only in the East," Denton said. "If there is anything going down, it'll be in this area. Otherwise, why would those krauts have registered an address here?"

"If they were planning something here, why did they go to the trouble of busing down from Toronto, not land at Kennedy like any normal traveler would do?" May asked in return.

"Maybe they did."

"Huh?"

"Maybe they did," Denton repeated. "Maybe those four weren't alone. That's why the Feds are checking lists now. Maybe there were more of them, so they split up in case a big load would look suspicious." Denton had arrived at that conclusion on the way over to FBI offices. He wondered how long it would take Babs O'Neill to draw the same conclusion. "I gave the Feds your number; they'll be calling me here if anything turns up."

May was uncertain whether he wanted anything to turn up or not.

Mayor Scrivens faced the barrage of arc lights in his City

Hall office with composure and confidence. He even managed to joke with the reporters who crowded around him, microphones thrust in his face, television cameras zooming in, camera strobes popping off into his eyes.

"I have been in touch with Police Commissioner May," he told the assembled newspeople, "and he has assured me that there is absolutely no truth in the story put out by MetroCity Television a short while ago." He waited while the reporters turned to look at Babs O'Neill, who stood in their midst. Her face turned red, not from embarrassment at being called a liar, but from fury.

"I don't make up my stories, Mr. Mayor! I don't have to lie! I'm not running for political office!" she shouted, the words seeming twice as loud in the sudden hush which followed them. "I received my information on those three missing Germans from a very reliable source."

"The same source who gave you your lead on the sanitation payoff racket?" Scrivens taunted her. "Very reliable." He was gratified to hear the ripple of laughter which swept through the other reporters. Dog eat dog; he liked that. Wound the bitch by reminding her of a mistake, and let the rest of the pack devour her; keep them all out of his hair.

"How about a cop?" Babs shot back. "Is that reliable enough? Or are your cops liars?"

"The one you spoke to obviously was. Or maybe he was seeing how gullible you really are." He turned his attention to the other reporters. "Now, let's get away from sensation and back to simple facts. You're all here because you want to know what's going on, and your readers and viewers also want to know what's happening. First, let me assure you there is no need for panic. True, a German national was killed the other morning. You all know about that; it's old news, the Günther Werner shooting. And he was on vacation with three German friends."

"What about their disappearance?" one man called out. "Is that for real?"

"That is true," Scrivens conceded, feeling himself in complete control of the situation now. He'd dumped that O'Neill bitch on her fanny; now the others were eating out of his hand. "They were booked into a hotel, The Gallic Arms, on West Twenty-ninth Street, and never showed up. But let me ask you a question. Supposing you were in a foreign country with a friend, and that friend got killed by a cop because he was breaking the law in a particularly vicious way. What would your reaction be? Would you show yourself and admit to being a friend of such a person? Take a chance on getting involved? Or would you run and hide because you were either too embarrassed to come forward or too scared of what might happen to you because of your association with the dead man?"

A thoughtful silence greeted Scrivens's question. The mayor knew he was on the way to calming public fear. He just hoped to God that Police Commissioner May or the FBI came up with something pretty damned quick.

While newspapers and other stations reported Scrivens's words faithfully, Babs O'Neill turned to the attack. She knew the audience was hers, waiting for her next words no matter what Scrivens maintained. She blasted him for clamping down on the news, trying—with the help of a suspiciously silent police department and Federal Bureau of Investigation—to make out that nothing was wrong. She had managed to start a panic, and she was not going to let up. Even if her credibility and job were on the line.

"There are times," she concluded, eyes fixed on the camera, "when it is right and proper for an elected official to keep certain information under a cloak of confidentiality, to keep quiet in the public interest. If Mayor Scrivens believes this to be one of those times, he is sorely mistaken. We, the people of New York City, have the right to know what is happening in our midst. And if Mayor Scrivens continues to deny us that right, the citizens of New York will see to it that his tenure at City Hall will never be forgotten. Or repeated."

She paused for breath, pondering the final words she had written in without Kohn's knowledge, wondering if she should go through with them and really put the fear of God into everyone watching the show. What the hell, what could she possibly lose? Scrivens had done her a favor by bringing up the old sanitation payoff ghost in trying to brand her a liar; the worst that could happen if she went ahead was to be branded a liar again. She'd survive.

"That is, those citizens who escape from the holocaust threatening us. They will never forget Mayor Percy Scrivens. From MetroCity, this is Babs O'Neill saying good night."

In the living room of his sister's home in Howard Beach, Stiehl watched the MetroCity news report with growing apprehension. God damn that Werner! Again he cursed himself for not finishing the man when he had the chance. None of this would have happened if he had not pulled aside the Browning at the last instant.

"Sounds grim," Tom Brenner said, slumped in an easy chair, eyes glued to the screen. "Nowhere's safe from these lunatics anymore."

"It's the press," Stiehl said. "This woman has obviously got hold of some snippet of information, wrong to begin with, and now she's trying to save face by building on it." He thought ahead to Tuesday night, only seventy-two hours in the future, when the operation was scheduled to begin. Should he bring it forward by twenty-four hours? Start on Monday night instead? He would still have the hot weather on his side if the forecast were correct.

"Could they do any damage, just the three of them?" Brenner asked his brother-in-law.

"One man can do a hell of lot of damage if he's determined enough and doesn't give a damn about his own skin. But I think we're all theorizing too much. Your mayor has denied the story, and everyone—except for that O'Neill woman—apparently believes him. "Maybe"—he grinned widely—"they'll do you and your neighbors a favor and blow up the Concorde for you."

Brenner's face relaxed into a smile. "Then I'm all for them."

Denton sat in the commissioner's office, staring at May

195

slouched behind his desk. Every few seconds the inspector's eyes would flicker to the telephone, willing it to ring, wanting it to be the FBI with information on the missing Germans. Then he could go home and forget about this damned thing. Jesus, what a way to spend a Saturday night!

When it did finally ring, just after ten, Denton snatched at the receiver, pulling it away from May's chubby hand. "Commissioner's office!" he barked. "Denton speaking."

It was the FBI, but the news they had for Denton was unwelcome. His face turned ashen as he listened, grunting monosyllabically every so often. When the one-sided conversation was over, he looked across at May.

"Sitting comfortably, sir?"

"As comfortably as I'll ever be. What's so bad that you ask that?"

"The Feds have done their homework. Hundreds of their guys are on this case, plus a whole bunch of inspectors from the INS. To begin with, on the day before Werner got wiped out, on Sunday, a group of twenty Arabs entered the country at Washington, in four separate flights, all carrying Libyan diplomatic passports. Not that the passports mean anything, but the Feds have checked with the Libyans, and they're refusing to give any information on the men."

"What were the names of the men?"

"There's a messenger on the way round here right now with a list," Denton answered quickly, eager to get on with the details of the conversation. "The Feds have done a lot of checking on other I-ninety-four information, and they've come up with plenty of discrepancies, with entry points covering New York, Buffalo, Washington, and Boston."

"Go on, man," May urged. "Go on."

"Other than the three krauts we already know are missing, plus Werner, would you believe that another sixteen Germans did not take up their hotel reservations in New York?"

"Sixteen more?"

Denton nodded. "And how's about this for the capper? Twenty sons of Erin did the same damned thing."

"Jesus, the Feds must have bust a gut on this one," May interrupted.

"I'm not worried about the FBI's efficiency ratings," Denton said. "All I'm thinking right now is that sixty people—Irish, Arabs, and Germans—have disappeared, all probably in this city. Scratch Werner because he's in the morgue, so we'd better make that fifty-nine. There could be even more to come or some we've missed. But what bothers the hell out of me is that Ireland, the Middle East, and Germany are hotbeds for some of the more lunatic terror gangs."

"You think we're in trouble?" May had no idea how stupid the question sounded.

"Trouble?" Denton laughed hoarsely. "Don't make jokes about it, sir. We've got a fucking war on our hands."

Midnight was the time watchman Harry Briggs liked best. He could wander down to the edge of the Hudson and listen to the waves lapping against the dock, his mind taking him back sixty years to when he had been a child, bathing in the very same river. Of course, you couldn't do it now, he reasoned sadly. Pollution would kill you stone dead inside a minute. Kids of today didn't know what they were missing, a swimming pool a mile wide stretching down from West Point to the Atlantic.

He walked closer to the water, shining his flashlight to help him pick his way among the washed-up debris, the soles of his gumboots sinking into the soft mud. Then he froze. The flashlight's beam picked out the bedraggled figure of a man, skin bloated by immersion in water, eyes closed, hair sticking to his forehead, mustache drooping. Briggs knelt to get a better look. Two feet away he recoiled in horror. Drowned men he'd seen before, plenty of them. This one was different. Half the head was missing, hacked off or blown away.

The watchman began to walk backward, almost tripping over garbage, unable to tear his eyes away from the corpse. Finally, with a tremendous effort of will, he turned around and started running for his hut and the telephone it contained, his speed belying his seventy-two years.

* * *

Police Commissioner May slumbered fitfully on an army bunk set up in the corner of his office, while Denton remained in the chair, eyes closed, feet up on a table. Denton knew he should be home in bed, getting some rest in preparation for the work that would certainly follow if his hunch was correct—that New York was about to become the target for a concerted terrorist blitz— but he refused to leave the office in case the Feds came up with anything else to make his nightmare a little blacker.

He must have fallen asleep. When he next looked at the clock on the wall opposite May's desk, the hands showed ten after five on Sunday morning. A shadow loomed over him. Denton thought it was May until he saw the commissioner still stretched out on the bunk.

"Inspector Denton?" the smartly dressed young man asked.

"That's me, son," Denton said, shaking himself awake. He stood up, yawned and stretched. God, his mouth felt like dried leather; he tried to look away from the young man as he spoke, knowing his breath must smell as bad as it tasted.

"We thought you should be made aware of this." The FBI agent thrust a sheet of typed paper into Denton's hands.

Denton began to read, uncomprehending at first, wondering why the Feds wanted him to have information on some floater's being fished out of the New York side of the Hudson. Until he came to the name. "Baroudi? Wasn't that one of the guys who came in with the Libyan mob at Washington? Where's that list your people sent over?" He saw it lying on top of the desk, picked it up, and scanned the names.

"That's right," the agent answered. "Baroudi was one of them. Omar Baroudi. He hadn't been in the water that long, only a few days. Water didn't have a chance to destroy his prints, so we ran them. Not that we tied him into this other thing. NYPD lifted the prints as a matter of course, then checked our files because they had no make on the guy."

"How come you had him?"

"We didn't. Immigration did. Studied dentistry here a few

198

years ago. Went to Fairleigh Dickinson University in New Jersey."

Still clutching the message, Denton walked across the office and shook the commissioner awake. "Guess what the mailman brought? You can scratch another of the visitors. This one turned up floating in the Hudson. Drifted onto shore a short while back." Denton turned back to the federal agent. "What are your men doing about it now?"

"Checking again with the Libyans. Baroudi was entered into the country on one of their diplomatic passports."

"Fat lot of good that'll do you."

"We tend to think the same, sir. But we try." The agent forced a tired smile onto his face as he left the office.

"We've been invaded," Denton said to May. "A foreign force is in our midst, and we don't know who they are or where to find them. The only photographs we'll be able to get will be from our consulates where the visas were issued or from passport offices in Britain and Germany, which will probably be next to useless."

"So what do we do?" May asked helplessly.

"Sit tight and keep extra alert. Hope that when they do strike, they pick something we're capable of defending. And pray they recognize the Geneva Conventions covering warfare."

Police headquarters released news of the appearance of the drowned man in a carefully worded statement which omitted any reference to his being associated with an intensive federal search. He was described as a member of the Libyan United Nations staff. The report concluded with the statement that police were continuing their investigation and were hopeful of a speedy solution.

Most of the people who heard the early-morning news on Sunday took little notice of the item. Except for Stiehl, who was playing with his nephew while his sister and brother-in-law slept late.

"I have to go out, Peter," Stiehl said suddenly. "Urgent business that I should have attended to yesterday."

199

Disappointment was etched on the boy's face. "But, Uncle Peter . . ."

"Another time. I'll make it up to you, I promise." He went up to his own room, quickly packed a small case, made certain he had the glasses, and left the house. Twenty-five minutes later, as Peter Adcock, he was in the furnished apartment, white gloves covering his hands as he telephoned Huckleby.

"Have you heard the news?"

"What news?"

"The employee I terminated has been found and identified. I am beginning the operation tomorrow night, advancing it by twenty-four hours."

"Are your men ready?"

"As soon as I contact the squad leaders. Are you ready?"

"Yes."

"Then good luck." He cut Huckleby off, then telephoned his sister's house, telling her he had been called away on business and would be out of town for the next two or three days.

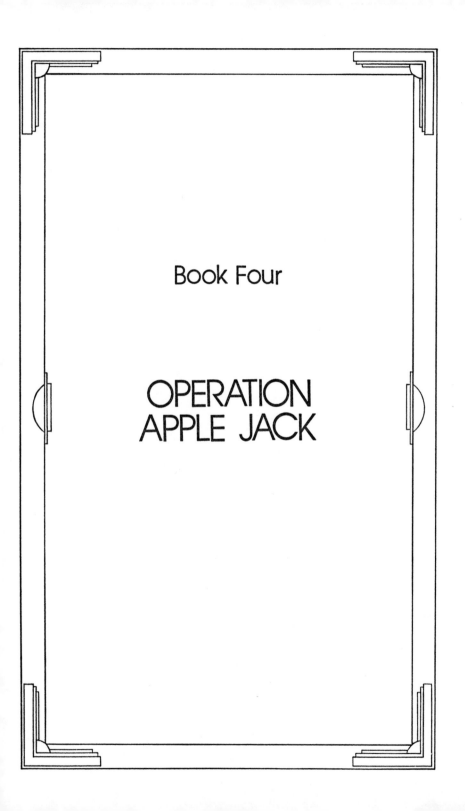

Book Four

OPERATION
APPLE JACK

14

THE HAZE which New York woke up to on Monday remained above the city the entire day, trapping the air underneath, making it almost unbreathable for the millions of people who lived and worked below. The high pollution count combined badly with the ninety-degree maximum temperature reached at two-forty-three in the afternoon, without even the slightest breath of wind to disturb the seething oven. By six in the evening eleven heat-related homicides had been recorded on police blotters. Disputes reached a flashpoint in the sweaty caldron of the city: an argument about pushing in the subway; a difference of opinion in a bar over the Yankees and the Red Sox; a cut-up driver on the FDR Drive who would normally shake his head in despair at another driver's stupidity. A gun or a knife had appeared, the act over in a millionth of a second, irreversible, another statistic to be blamed on the heat by a defense lawyer pleading his client's case in court.

Inspector Eric Denton's shirt was soaked through with sweat, light patches across the chest and back, deeper, heavy areas underneath his arms. The air-conditioning unit in the squad room had broken down shortly after midday—the third time in two weeks—and the assortment of hastily purchased fans did little to relieve the humidity. Some detectives had taken off in air-conditioned private cars, cruising around the neighborhood; others were slouching in the air-conditioned movie houses along Forty-second Street to cool off. Denton had stayed behind, collating information received from British, German, and Israeli security agencies on the three groups of terrorists suspected to be in the city. Working with federal agents, Denton and his men sorted through the sparse collection of photographs wired from around the world—all admitted by their sources to be at least three years old—plus photographs from the consulates where the non-immigrant visas had been issued. No other records were available. Stiehl's insistence that no person with a criminal record was to be included had paid off handsomely. Denton was stuck. He had names taken from the I–94 forms, visitors who had not checked into their stated destinations and were untraceable, and some outdated pictures. Other than that, nothing. Even the usually efficient Mossad could offer little. The Arabs Denton asked about were not on Mossad files. The Germans could supply only the possibility that some members of Kirchmann's group had Baader-Meinhof affiliations. And the British had nothing on Frank Brady's men.

In desperation, Denton looked at the two federal agents in his office, their faces, like his own, glistening with sweat. "Anyone fancy a cold beer?" he asked.

Neither man needed a second invitation. Denton picked up his lightweight jacket and led the way to the nearest bar. Whether he was on duty or not, he wanted something cold inside him before he had to confront Police Commissioner May with the news that the department had absolutely nothing to go on.

For Babs O'Neill, the story on the missing Germans was running dry. She had exhausted all possibilities in the two days since Mayor Scrivens's press conference and knew that her audience would be lost irretrievably if she kept on the same track without offering any new developments. Together with Jerry Rosen, she stood in Charlie Kohn's office, debating the next step of their campaign.

"Denton's the guy closest to the action," she said. "He's our only chance."

"So stick with him." Kohn was beginning to debate the wisdom of continuing on a collision course with the major networks, which had relegated the story to the bottom of the pile. He wondered whether MetroCity should follow suit. "The pair of you, stick to Denton like leeches. Follow him home, everything. Do you know where he lives?"

"Bayside."

"When he goes to Bayside, follow him there. Camp outside his house. Maybe he'll be so sick of the sight of you, he'll tell you something just to get you off his back."

"Are we allowed to sleep?" Rosen asked sarcastically. "Or are you going to shoot us full of pep pills?" The question drew an approving glance from Babs.

"You can sleep," Kohn said. "Just do it standing up outside Denton's house, with a camera in your hands at all times." He stopped talking suddenly, swinging around to face the bank of three color television sets which flanked one side of his office. From left to right, they showed the CBS, ABC, and NBC evening news shows. Kohn turned down the volume on ABC and NBC, up on the CBS Channel 2 program as the newscaster announced that police were still seeking the three missing Germans.

"Right at the end," Kohn breathed. "Like a postscript." He turned back to look at Babs, flicking off the volume. "Are you sure that's where your story doesn't belong?" It was the first time he had openly questioned her handling of the story. "Should we swallow our pride, Babs? Relegate it?"

"No way." The firmness of her rejection prevented any argument on Kohn's part. "We're going to stay with Denton, not let him out of our sight. That son of a bitch knows a damned sight more than he's willing to tell us. We'll get him, though."

Kohn remained anxious. He had to answer to his shareholders, and right now it looked as though O'Neill were running the station, not he. He was beginning to question his decision to let her have so much of the bit. She was running away so quickly that he found it impossible to keep her in check. "Just make sure you do," he murmured, closing the meeting.

Dusk was falling as two motor launches slipped away from the docks on the New Jersey side of the Hudson River. They headed upstream to pass underneath the George Washington Bridge, then turned east toward the Spuyten Duyvil rail bridge that spanned the entrance to the Harlem River where it meets the Hudson. The lead boat pulled over to the stone pier which supported the bridge in midriver. While Johnny Coughlin held onto the pier to keep the boat from drifting away, Frank Brady scrambled up onto the stonework. The two men in the second boat watched for an instant; then the engine note rose as it headed on toward the next span, the Henry Hudson Bridge, joining Manhattan to the Bronx. The two Irishmen in the second launch were certain Brady and Coughlin were all right.

Working quickly, Brady placed four thirty-pound rolls of plastic explosive along the base of one of bridge's main struts, where it was anchored to the stone pier. When detonated, the explosive would kick the strut out from the pier, collapsing at least the middle part of the span. Next, he took four detonators, wound guncotton around each one to ensure a double kicker, and pressed them into the plastic. Setting aside the loose wires, he turned to the timer, taping it to one of the girders, setting the device, hooking up the battery. Lastly, he connected the detonator wires to the battery and timer. Knowing the condition of most of the city's bridges, Brady was certain that even a hand grenade blast would probably make the span unsafe, but one hundred and twenty pounds of high explosive would do a far more efficient job.

He scampered back to the waiting boat and fell onto the floor as Coughlin gunned the engine. They passed the second launch at the Henry Hudson Bridge, where one man was setting charges in the supports while the other remained in the boat. Brady waved as the engine's thrust carried them past, on to the next bridge.

Standing at the living-room window of his daughter's apartment in Fort Lee, Harlan Stone Huckleby lowered the binoculars as the two boats passed underneath the George Washington Bridge on the first leg of their journey. The operation was under way. All thanks to a South African named Peter Stiehl, a man he had seen on television, discussing a new book of all things! He laughed silently at the memory, finding it ludicrous that the world's greatest city would soon be brought to its knees by a man who had beaten his gun into a typewriter, only to resurrect it at the sound of one million dollars. He wondered what Stiehl would do with the money. Flee the country? Not that there seemed to be much point. The police would be looking high and low for an Englishman working on temporary assignment for the Rand *Daily Mail*. Only two people knew the real identity of Adcock. He and Linda. Linda would never turn him in, that was for certain. How do you rat on the guy you've fallen in love with? Huckleby asked himself. He recalled the night when he had first seen Stiehl on the television show, how he had hoped someone at the White House was watching, and how Linda had mocked him, saying he would probably approve of someone like the South African as a son-in-law. He smiled at the memory. Yes, he might just approve of him.

Reluctantly Huckleby pushed such thoughts from his mind. He looked down at the gray steel panel of lights and switches that stood in front of the window. There were eleven switches in all, each pushed into the off position, each with its own red light. When all the lights came on, it would signify that contacts had been made in each of the eleven explosive-filled trucks. Then he would be able to control the destiny of the bridges and tunnels that were Manhattan's lifelines. A simple flick of a switch, and a bridge would blast apart at a crucial point, a tunnel would be ripped open letting in the East or Hudson River, or the apartment buildings on top of the George Washington Bridge approach would come tumbling down like a pack of cards, their foundations wrecked by the earthquake explosion from beneath. But that was not the idea. It would suffice to show the government that it could be done, that the country's defenses were so weak that a group of quasi-military thugs could walk in and take over the nation's largest city with impunity.

He picked up the telephone and dialed the number of the furnished apartment in Howard Beach. It was answered before the first ring was complete.

"Adcock."

"Huckleby here. I have just seen the launches going north."

"They're on time. Let's hope everything else goes just as smoothly," Stiehl said before hanging up.

A sound behind Huckleby made him turn. Standing in the center of the living room was Linda, a leather suitcase on the floor beside her.

"Are you going?" he asked.

"Yes." There was a trace of strain in her voice. "Where's Peter?"

"Where he's supposed to be. Out of harm's way."

"You can still call this whole thing off," Linda said. "You've proved to yourself that it can be done, that you were right. Isn't that enough?"

"I always knew I was right. It's my old friends who need the lesson," Huckleby replied. "They have to know it can be done. Then they might pick themselves up and do something about it before some country invades us for real. Don't worry," he added, "nobody will be hurt. Zero casualties." He fiddled with one of the switches, caressing the top, dreaming of how easy it would be to flick it downward once the corresponding red light was glowing. "Go on, go to your hotel and get out of this." He hoped she would not embarrass him with a display of tears; let her at least have inherited enough of his backbone to avoid a messy farewell.

Linda did not disappoint him. After kissing him lightly on the cheek, she tilted the leather suitcase back on its wheels and began to walk toward the door. He wondered how she would fare with the police when this was all over. Her alibi would be strong, and the only person who could revoke it—himself—would not be around. How would she feel when she learned how ill he had been, how it had been the little white pills that had kept him alive for this one last military operation? Would Stiehl tell her? Perhaps during a moment of intimacy, when secrets were liable to be let out? Would she be proud of the way he had kept his illness a private affair, refusing to burden others with it?

By the door Linda stopped and turned around, looking back into the apartment, gazing at her father. He turned away and stared out of the window, fervently wishing she would just leave, not draw it out like this. He was sending her away, wanting her to go; these were moments he needed for himself.

He heard the door close but did not look around. Instead, he picked up the binoculars again and swept the river, focusing finally on the massive steel structure linking Fort Lee with Washington Heights, panning to the high-rise apartment buildings on the bridge approach from the Manhattan side, watching them loom up in the gathering dusk. Lights were twinkling in the apartment windows as day faded. Huckleby wondered if the occupants had any idea of the part they would soon play in a colossal drama.

A cloud of diesel exhaust fumes belched out into the evening air as the first truck left the Newark site of Howson Chemicals. Behind the wheel was Gerd Havlicek, one of Kirchmann's men from Munich. Twenty-eight years old, Havlicek was a printer by trade, a man whose grudge against management and the giant corporations which ruled his life had led him into Kirchmann's circle. On the surface, Havlicek had been a model employee of the massive printing firm, never missing a day, never participating in union negotiations to squeeze more money from the firm. Underneath, he had festered. He sabotaged the company's computer-controlled presses three times. A dropped screw here, a quick piece of work with pliers there, all seeming accidents which could have been caused by carelessness on someone's part, costing the company time and money.

Havlicek had met Kirchmann a year earlier through a friend, a girl who had suggested he could make his disenchantment with the system into a far sharper weapon. Since the meeting the acts of sabotage had stopped as Havlicek waited for the moment he would be called upon to act in a more concerted strike. Never in his wildest fantasies did he believe that one moment would occur in the United States.

The headlights of other trucks from the Howson Chemicals plant disappeared in his rearview mirror as he increased speed, heading for the New Jersey Turnpike and from there to the George Washington Bridge. He pulled off at a rest stop as instructed and sat in the cab, quietly smoking. Every so often he would look at the luminous hands of his watch, willing them to move faster, to reach that time when he would set off for the final part of his journey.

On eastbound Route 80, another of the specially leased ten-ton trucks pulled into a rest stop, and Wolfgang Herzlein turned off the engine. Herzlein had hated the Americans for as long as he could remember, having grown up in Heilbronn, with its enormous military base in the middle of town. The GIs and their fat wives, hair in curlers, had rushed around the town as if they owned it. Herzlein's father had worked at the post commissary until he had been fired for buying a jar of Maxwell House instant coffee from an American sergeant who had been making money in black-market dealings; the sergeant had gone unpunished.

When race problems had ripped the Heilbronn base apart in the late sixties, Herzlein had joined those Germans who egged on the white soldiers. They had succeeded to the point where the body of a black corporal from a Seventh Army artillery unit had been found beneath a pile of tarpaulins. The army had then stepped in, restricting all personnel to the base and rooting out the troublemakers. The German civilians who had added fuel to the fires slipped away unnoticed, retiring to hate the Americans from a distance. Herzlein's work had not gone totally unnoticed in other quarters. Kirchmann's group had contacted him for news of further developments that might make good propaganda. For ten years he had done nothing but report on the American presence, waiting for the opportunity to act. Now, at a rest stop on eastbound Route 80, in New Jersey, his opportunity had come.

Leaving the Howson Chemicals New York City warehouse in Long Island City, Gamal Aktouri pulled the ten-ton truck to a stop on Hoyt Avenue, close to the Triborough Bridge. As he sat waiting for the hours to pass, almost unaware of Ahmed Nassim sitting beside him, Aktouri's mind wandered to the men in the other trucks, the Arabs, the Germans, the Irish. Where were they now? In position? Or had something gone wrong with one of the units? What about the subway bombers and the men in the launches who would paralyze the northern bridges? He had no way of knowing how the parallel operations were progressing, no contact with either the command post or the other units. All he could do was wait until one-thirty in the morning, the time when Manhattan would writhe in terror.

Tonight was a night America would never forget, a night the entire world would never forget. Pearl Harbor would pale into virtual insignificance beside it. And he, Gamal Aktouri, from the refugee camps in Lebanon, would play a part in it. He would return to his people as a hero, ready to lead his own army into Israel when the Palestinians went home.

Two men were also in the ten-ton truck heading for the inbound tube of the Lincoln Tunnel, Danny McGrath and Patrick Kerrigan. All the other trucks had backup drivers, except for the two going to the George Washington Bridge, but why, wondered Kerrigan, did he have to get stuck with this slimy four-eyed bastard? He knew the answer. Stiehl had drawn him off to one side as the truck assignments had been made. Despite McGrath's contribution to the operation through his idea about the apartment buildings over the George Washington Bridge, the South African did not trust him completely; he wanted Kerrigan to keep an eye on him.

Kerrigan pulled the truck off the road into a prearranged rest stop, turned off the engine, and began humming to himself.

Knowing McGrath did not smoke, Kerrigan lit a foul-smelling cigar, which he puffed heavily. The confined space of the cab soon filled with thick gray smoke.

"Do you have to smoke that bloody thing?" McGrath choked.

"Sure, and why not? Condemned men always get a last smoke," Kerrigan mumbled, the cigar jumping up and down in his mouth, its end glowing bright as he puffed. "Haven't you heard of that tradition?"

"We're not condemned men."

Kerrigan grinned wolfishly in the darkness. You would be if I had my bloody way, he thought. You sure as hell would be, Danny Boy.

The motor launch containing Brady and Coughlin reached a pier near the heliport a minute before the second boat. The boats' cargoes had already been discharged at the bridges above the Triborough. There was nothing left to do now except wait.

Rolf Haller set down the two heavy suitcases as he fumbled with a token at the turnstile of the Lexington Avenue stop for the E and F trains. After dropping the token into the slot, he slid the cases underneath, pushed his way through, picked up his baggage, and descended the escalator to the station's only platform. A glance at his watch told him that another ten minutes remained before he was due to act out his part of the operation. He sat down on the sturdier of the two cases, hoping that no passing transit patrolman paid too much interest to him.

While Haller waited, Horst Fischer was drinking a cup of coffee at one of the many fast food stands which dotted Grand Central Station. Having finished the coffee, he dropped the plastic cup into a trash can, picked up his two cases, and began following the blue arrows to the IRT subway. He went down two flights of stairs before he reached the Flushing-bound platform. He brought a paper and sat down to scan the pages, wondering if there would be any news of German football. A keen fan, he had even followed the team to Argentina for the World Cup. He had

212

liked Argentina; many people spoke German, and he had felt at home. Perhaps he would even go back there to live when this was all over. After all, many other Germans had made the trip to escape pursuit from the law.

In other trucks, in other stations, Stiehl's attack units waited patiently. Truck engines were turned off, drivers and co-drivers hearing their own heartbeats over the noise of passing traffic. Tension increased as the minutes ticked away.

In stations, each soldier had two suitcases, their targets the subway and main railroad tunnels which channeled trains in and out of Manhattan. Some, like Magda Breitner—whose target was the tunnel between Manhattan's First Avenue and Bedford Avenue in Brooklyn—waited with sneers on their faces as they watched transit police officers pass by without the slightest suspicion. Others, like Kirchmann, waiting at Penn Station for the Newark train, kept their minds completely blank, trying to relax before battle commenced.

15

Since Harry DeLeon could speak Spanish fluently, the New York Police Department had assigned him and other Spanish-speaking officers to North Manhattan six years earlier in an attempt to create a better relationship between police and the people of Spanish Harlem. Maybe the department was pleased with its strategy, but DeLeon was not. He would have been far happier ending his career in Brooklyn Heights, near where he lived with his wife and children. But like it or not, he had worked the desk in North Manhattan efficiently, his mind shielded from the violent crime which swamped the area by the vision of the small home he had bought outside Fort Lauderdale for his retirement six months hence. If he had managed to take nineteen and a half years, he could take another six months. Especially so when he knew that he had been putting in as much overtime as possible during the past six months to qualify for a higher pension. Florida would do a lot to compensate for the scars inflicted by the job.

214

A half-empty can of warm Coke sat on the desk in front of DeLeon, his third of the hour as he tried to fight off the cloying heat, which had not eased with the coming of nightfall. He wished the criminals would observe the heat as well, take a vacation till it was all over and more comfortable for the police to catch and book them. But DeLeon had been in the business too long; he knew it did not work out like that. The hotter it got, the worse tempers became. Until they exploded into senseless violence, knifings, beatings, shootings, with the culprits usually as pitiable as the victims. Then DeLeon's Spanish would be tested, explaining rights to those suspects who did not speak English sufficiently well, translating detectives' questions, trying to make it easier for everyone concerned; when he heard the stories, he wondered why more murders weren't committed.

DeLeon looked up from the Coke as a patrolman came through the station door, holding a middle-aged Puerto Rican by the elbow, guiding him toward the desk.

"Wino, Sarge. Blind drunk and pissing against the side of a car."

Nodding, DeLeon wondered where the man had managed to get enough money to make himself that drunk. Living on welfare probably, but always enough in his pocket for a bottle of cheap wine or a number in the blind hope of pulling off the big one. "Take him through. Make sure he doesn't puke on anyone." He watched the man stagger along in the patrolman's steady grip before turning back to the door as another officer entered. This one had a handcuffed youth, pushing him roughly into the station house.

"What did he do?" DeLeon asked. "Knife his mother for a quarter?"

The youth understood, spit at DeLeon, but missed, striking the desk. The patrolman shoved him viciously in the back. He fell to the floor, hands behind him, unable to stop his face from striking the wooden planks. When he looked up at DeLeon, his nose and mouth were bleeding, and hate blazed from his dark eyes; it made DeLeon feel sick.

215

"Relieved an eighty-year-old woman of her purse," the patrolman said, kicking the youth in the ribs. "Using this in case she put up a fight." He held up a shining switchblade.

"Get it over with," DeLeon said. "And make sure nobody sees you kicking him. They might not be as understanding as I am."

"Sure." The patrolman reached down and dragged the youth to his feet. "C'mon, turkey. Let's see what we can break for you."

DeLeon looked at the Coke again, asking himself why it took ten years for six months to pass.

In the distant sky, a flash of light exploded infrequently. The thunderstorms, for now, were far away. If New York was lucky, the storms would miss the city altogether. Up at Indian Point, two of the nuclear reactors were down. One was in the process of having its core refueled, its used radioactive rods replaced with fresh ones. The other reactor was down because a slight crack had been discovered in the building housing the reactor, and a complete structural examination had been ordered.

The hot night was putting a strain on all of the utility's generating capacity, but so far there had been no problems. Surplus power was coming in from upstate New York, across the river from New Jersey, and from New England. The men in the Manhattan energy control center had no reason for concern; everything was functioning just as it had been engineered to.

There had still be no indication of any problem when three men broke into the center. With stocking masks pulled over their faces, they looked as if they had missed the bank or the jewelry store they should have been in and had stumbled into the energy control center by mistake. There was no mistake, though, in the way they swiftly bound and gagged the utility men. Then everyone waited. Up in Westchester County, three electrical transmission lines came tumbling down, prompted by timed explosive charges. The crumpled towers collapsed, cutting the cables bringing power into the city from upstate and New England. On the meters, the technicians and the gunmen watched the loss of available power to the city. Within seconds a blast severed the

Hudson-Farragut transmission line coming into the city from New Jersey. Again, the results showed up on the control center meters.

Now, without outside power sources, with Indian Point only able to offer one-third of its normal supply, with hundreds of thousands of energy-consuming air conditioners sucking up power to cool a hot, sticky night, something had to give or the whole city would be blacked out. One of the gunmen made the charitable action, saving the city by sacrificing one of the boroughs. The Bronx. While he threw the switch to shed load to that borough, he also broke it, making certain that nobody would be able to restore power to the Bronx for quite a while.

Peter Stiehl's three Angola veterans left the building without having uttered a word, got into a panel truck which they had parked several blocks away, and sped to the Bronx to complete their mission.

In upper Manhattan, Sergeant Harry DeLeon looked up in question as the lights flickered for an instant before returning to full power. Another blackout? Just what was needed in the middle of a heat wave. He dropped his gaze to the patrolman standing in front of his desk, holding two teenaged suspects in the rape and robbery of a sixty-year-old woman.

"Must be the boys upstairs sticking a suspect's finger in the light socket again," DeLeon said, keeping the grin off his face as he watched the two youths flinch. "Wish to hell they'd stop doing that, keeps dimming the damned lights. Go on, take them up." As the patrolman led them away, DeLeon turned around and laughed.

Rolf Haller checked his watch as the uptown E train thundered into the Lexington Avenue Station. One minute to eleven. He got up off the suitcase, picked up both of them, and waited at the center of the narrow platform for the train to stop. Inside the car he sat down, keeping the two suitcases in front of him. As the doors slid closed and the train began to roll toward its next stop—Twenty-third and Ely in Queens—he pressed the button of the stopwatch and peered down at its face as the seconds ticked away. When thirty-two seconds had elapsed, he stood up and pulled the emergency brake handle.

The E train screamed in protest, cars rattling as the emergency brake was applied. Passengers were flung out of their seats, sent scrambling onto the floor, parcels and packages flying in all directions. Haller watched it all with a smile on his face, held secure by his grip on the steel stanchion. As the train stopped with one final jarring grind, the passengers began to rise, glaring angrily at the man who had pulled the handle.

A door at the end of the car opened, and the conductor came out, cap missing, a mixture of puzzlement and fury on his face. "Who pulled that handle?" he demanded.

Before anybody could point the accusing finger at him, Haller confessed. "I did."

"Why?"

"Because there is a bomb on this train. No"—he looked down at the suitcases—"two bombs. Each of these cases contains twenty-five pounds of high explosive. If you do not do exactly as I tell you, I will detonate them now, and we all will die. If you obey my instructions, nobody will be hurt."

The conductor licked his lips nervously, unable to decide whether Haller was bluffing or not. "What do you want?"

"I want you to abandon this train. Everybody. Do not make any attempt to move it farther along the line. Just empty it here, and lead the passengers back to Lexington Avenue. You have five seconds to comply." He noticed some of the passengers begin to slide away nervously. "Well?"

"We'll get off," the conductor said. He returned to his cab and called through to the motorman, telling him what Haller had said. Thirty seconds later, the motorman appeared, confronting the German.

"What the hell is going on here?"

"Exactly what I told your colleague. These two cases are filled with explosives. They are also booby-trapped in case somebody should try to disarm them. I want this train cleared and everybody taken back to the last station. There I will surrender myself to the police."

"You're damned right you will," the motorman said. "I've already called my control."

"That was very wise of you." Haller complimented the man. "Now please see that my orders are carried out."

The motorman took a final look at the suitcases on the floor in front of Haller. He nodded once and went back through the train, telling passengers that the train had broken down and they would be led back to Lexington Avenue. The conductor went to the rear car, opened the sliding door, and helped the passengers down onto the railbed. As they passed Haller, standing with the suitcases, they avoided looking at him, as if the motorman had told them what was happening. The motorman was the last to return, and Haller held out a hand to stop him.

"I surrender myself to you," he said. "The driver of a train is like the captain of a ship, no?"

"Have you really got explosives in there?"

"I can show you now if you really wish to find out," Haller offered.

"Don't bother." He took hold of Haller's arm and led him through the remaining cars, treating him gently as if the German could detonate the bombs from a distance. The conductor on the track helped Haller down; then the whole line began walking back up the tunnel toward the lights of the Lexington Avenue Station.

Five transit police officers—four men and a sergeant—were waiting on the platform when the line of evacuated passengers arrived. They bent down, helping people up onto the platform, seeking out Haller as the motorman delivered him.

"Okay, what's all this crap about bombs on the train?"

"Exactly what you heard from your driver. There are fifty pounds of high explosives on the train, timed to go off later tonight. Nothing you do will stop it. If any attempt is made to tamper with the bombs, they will detonate automatically."

"And what do you want to stop them from detonating?"

219

"I want nothing," Haller replied calmly. "There is nothing you can give me."

The sergeant turned away, trying to think. Why the hell did this have to happen when he was on duty? He did not know what to do other than turn the man over to higher authorities, let them sort it out. And in the meantime, the uptown track for both the E and F trains was blocked by a train with a bomb on board.

The headlights of the panel truck picked up fleeting shadows as Stiehl's three mercenaries drove eastward along the blacked-out 138th Street in the South Bronx. Since traffic lights were not working, the truck paused as it reached each intersection and passed across as quickly as possible. This was no area for three whites to walk through during the brightest hours of daylight, let alone get involved in a traffic accident during a blackout.

"Anything yet?" one of the men asked.

"Not yet," the driver replied. "Reckon they're waiting to see if it's a real blackout or just a temporary power failure. Should we give them a lead?"

The man who had asked the question laughed. "These dudes don't need a lead when it comes to looting. Look what they did in 'seventy-seven."

"Maybe they don't believe it could happen again so quick." The driver slowed down while the man in the farthest seat rolled down his window. A group of young blacks followed the pickup with their eyes as it passed, their faces almost invisible in the darkness, only their clothes giving away their position. The man bent down to pick up something from the floor of the truck, a round object, made of metal, with a curved handle coming down from the top.

"Ready when you are."

The driver brought the truck to an almost total stop. The man in the right seat pulled the pin on the phosphorus grenade and lobbed it with an underhand motion at the glass window of a clothing store. It hit the glass, shattering it, and rolled inside the display, where it exploded in a flare of white fire, setting the shop alight. Within seconds, bands of black youths converged on the scene, some just watching, other braving the roaring flames to steal what clothing was undamaged. Along the street, other groups of youths, taking the grenade explosion as a signal, broke into stores, smashing windows, tearing off doors, confident that with the blackout the burglar alarm systems would never ring through to the police stations.

"Time to go home," the driver said, gunning the engine. He blasted the horn as three youths ran across the street in front of the truck, two of them carrying stereo equipment, the third a color television set.

When Haller arrived handcuffed to the sergeant at transit police headquarters, the place was in pandemonium. Telephones were ringing; personnel were running this way and that as if a major panic had broken out.

"What's happening?" the sergeant asked a lieutenant, catching him by the arm as he scurried past.

"Everything. The whole goddamned world's gone bananas. First we got a blackout in the South Bronx, so we've got nothing moving up there. On top of that, we've got a bunch of nuts who've stopped trains under the water with bombs on board. Subways and main-line railroads."

"What!" the sergeant yelled, almost unable to believe what he had heard. "That's why I'm bringing in this guy. He pulled the brake on the uptown E between Lex and Twenty-third and Ely. Said the two suitcases with him were full of explosives and wanted the train cleared."

The lieutenant stepped back to take a good look at Haller. "Better get him upstairs with the rest. They've already brought in two others, a man and a woman. And from reports, there's a whole bunch more on the way. Where are you from?" he added to Haller.

"Germany."

"That's what the hell I figured."

"What do you mean by that?" the sergeant asked the lieutenant, perplexed. "How the fuck did you figure that?"

"The two upstairs are from Germany. Plus we've got some

Arabs and Irishmen coming in to join them. I'll be up in a minute. Then we'll try to get to the bottom of this mess."

The sergeant turned around and stared after the disappearing figure of the lieutenant, trying to understand everything that had been said to him.

"May we go now, please?" Haller asked impatiently, tugging at the handcuffs which held him to the sergeant. "I would like to see my friends."

"Your friends?"

Haller nodded. "That is correct. My friends."

By eleven-fifteen on Monday night Mayor Percy Scrivens was adamantly certain that God was a bigoted southern bastard who really had it in for New York City's first black mayor and was determined to nail him to the first convenient burning cross. Having left his East Side apartment the moment he heard about the blackout in the Bronx, he arrived at City Hall only to learn that a greater emergency had the city in its grip. The looting which would undoubtedly run across the entire Bronx paled into insignificance beside the news Police Commissioner Alan May relayed to him at City Hall. Some organization had cut all rail links between Manhattan and its neighbors, forcing trains to be abandoned with bombs on board. If nothing were done, the bombs would blast the cars apart, blocking the tracks for God only knew how many days.

"And they all surrendered?" Scrivens asked May incredulously when the police commissioner had finished bringing him up to date.

"Every single one of them. Without a fight," May replied. "They were as cooperative as hell. We've got them at headquarters now. But you'd better hear this. They're all Germans, Arabs, and Irish."

"Denton!" Scrivens gasped.

"You'd better believe it, Denton. That's what he's been going on about all this past week, checking with the German, British, and Israeli authorities. He suspected something all along, and he was damned well right about it."

222

"So what do we do now?" Scrivens's question reflected the absolute futility he felt.

"First things first," May advised. "This blackout might be nothing to do with the trains. It could be a coincidence, happening just like last time because the system was overloaded. We won't know what caused it till Con Edison gets back to us. But you've got to do something about the looting up there."

"What?"

"I suggest we take some extra units out of upper Manhattan and send them into the Bronx. The Bronx divisions can't cope with what's happening up there by themselves. They need help."

"So do it," Scrivens said.

"What are you going to do?" May asked.

"I'm going to police headquarters where you've got those train people. I want to see what's going on for myself."

May shook his head. "Good luck."

The telephone call from Charles Kohn startled Babs, who was on the verge of sleep in her Greenwich Village apartment. She sat up in bed, shaking her head to dispel the drowsiness before reaching out for the bedside extension.

"O'Neill."

"Babs, it's Charlie. You been listening to the radio or television?"

"Are you kidding? It's almost midnight, and I'm exhausted from running around after Eric Denton." Automatically her hand stretched out and turned on the clock radio by the telephone; music greeted her ears, and she fumbled with the channel selector till she found WINS. "What's it all about, Charlie?"

"They've got a blackout all over the Bronx. South Bronx is going crazy right now, looting, firing buildings, the lot. Looks like it could spread."

"Blackout? Looting?" Sleep vanished. Something began to come through on the radio and she turned up the volume, listening to Kohn and the newscaster simultaneously.

"There's everything happening up there, Babs," Kohn said, raising his voice to compete with the radio. "You've got to go. I

223

want live coverage. A remote color studio and crew are already on the way. A car should be picking you up in about ten minutes."

"What about Jerry?" She did not know why she asked about him. Maybe it was habit; when a big job was going down, she had to have the best.

"I'm just going to call him. You can pick him up on the way uptown."

Another voice came onto the radio. Babs held the telephone receiver away for a moment, listening to the new flash which had broken into reports on the blackout. "Charlie," she said breathlessly, bringing the mouthpiece back to her lips, "what about the trains?"

"What trains!" Kohn almost screamed. "I told you, the driver's coming for you."

"Something just came up on the news about all the trains with bombs on board stuck in the tunnels. All rail links are blocked, in and out of Manhattan."

"I don't know anything about that," Kohn said. "Just get ready to go up to the Bronx. We'll keep that under control. We'll keep you in touch with what's happening on the trains. Get yourself dressed. The guy should be with you in any minute."

She hung up and began to dress hurriedly, jeans, blouse, and a cotton jacket. While she moved around the apartment, she kept the volume of the radio turned up, trying to learn more about the trains. No new information was forthcoming while she remained in the apartment. When she heard the radio car driver honking loudly from below, she left the apartment in such a hurry that she forgot to turn off the clock radio. Another news flash, less than a minute later, echoed around the empty apartment that police had released information about the bombers being German, Irish, and Arab.

Two police officers, a lieutenant and a sergeant, entered the stranded E train from the rear and walked swiftly through the empty cars until they reached Haller's suitcases.

224

"What do you reckon?" the lieutenant asked, taking off his cap and jacket, kneeling down to inspect the locks.

"The guy said they were fixed," the sergeant reminded his superior. "Could be the locks. Then we'd have to cut through the side to insert a scope."

The lieutenant cracked his knuckles, the sound loud in the silence of the empty train. "We'd better make up our minds damned soon. Otherwise, they'll go off by themselves." He opened the small case he had brought with and took out a sharp, heavy-bladed knife. He pressed the point gently against the side of one case.

"You going to use a shield?" the sergeant asked, indicating the two clear, strengthened plastic shields they had brought with them.

The lieutenant laughed humorlessly. "What's the point? One of these babies goes up, a sheet of four-inch cement wouldn't help." He put away the knife and took out a set of feeler gauges, used by mechanics to adjust spark plug and distributor contact point gaps. Gingerly he inserted a sixteenth-of-an-inch feeler under the lid of one case, moving it along, feeling for any possible wire which could activate the booby trap. There was nothing he could feel. He repeated the process on the second case; again nothing.

"Got to be the locks," he said, putting away the feeler gauge, wiping sweat off his forehead. God, it was hot down here, over a hundred if it was fifty. "I'm cutting away the side of this case. Okay with you?"

"Sure," the sergeant said. "Go ahead."

The lieutenant picked up the knife and pressed the point into the imitation leather of the case, slitting the material neatly. As the entire side came loose, he picked it up to inspect the contents of the case. Both he and the sergeant saw the packed plastic before they caught a glimpse of the wires attached to the side of the case, triggers for the booby trap. The case blew apart in their faces, setting off its companion, wrecking the subway car, derailing other cars, and buckling the rails.

When the dust and debris settled, the uptown E train was jammed securely across the track.

Denton arrived at Police Plaza after being awakened at his Bayside home by a uniformed patrolman with a car waiting outside. Even before he was informed about the train bombs and the terrorists who had surrendered themselves, Denton was certain it had something to do with the Irish, Arab, and German visitors who had disappeared after entering the country. An operation of this magnitude could not be anything else; it would be too much of a coincidence for a large group of potential terrorists to be in the New York area and for the train bombs to have been placed by a different group.

Federal agents were also present when Denton arrived. Together they inspected the terrorists, standing in a long line, hands manacled, chained to each other, gazing back openly at Denton's surveillance. Satisfied, Denton walked away from the line and joined Commissioner May.

"See that one, third from the end?" he whispered to May. "That's Rolf Haller, one of the Germans who entered the country with Werner."

"Recognize any of the others from the photographs we got?"

"Maybe. That must be Magda Breitner next to him; she was the only woman in the group."

"But we've got only thirty-one people here," May said, running his eyes over the line, counting. "Your investigation revealed sixty possible terrorists."

"Scratch Werner and the Arab Baroudi."

"Okay, so fifty-eight," May conceded. "That still leaves us with twenty-seven missing. Where are they? What are they up to?"

Denton shrugged his shoulders. "I haven't got a clue. But you can be damned certain they're up to some shit connected with this."

A uniformed sergeant interrupted them. He was holding a piece of paper in his hand, which he passed to May. The police commissioner read it twice, his face turning white before he passed the note to Denton. "Our friends in the line weren't joking about booby traps being on those train bombs."

Denton read the message about the sergeant and lieutenant's being blown up aboard the E train as they tried to disarm Haller's bombs. He passed the sheet of paper back to May and stormed across the room. Grabbing Haller by the front of his shirt, Denton lifted him clean off the floor. Magda Breitner, chained next to him, stumbled as she was jerked around by the sudden maneuver.

"You hear what you've done, you kraut son of a bitch!" Denton screamed, saliva flying from his mouth into Haller's face. "Two men have died trying to disarm those bombs you left." He threw Haller back against the wall; three people on either side of the blond German fell over as Haller's body weight dragged them back.

"You were warned not to try and disarm those bombs," a voice said from the other end of the line. Denton swung around to find himself looking at a pasty-faced man with long brown hair and two obviously false front teeth.

"You'd be Kirchmann, wouldn't you?" Denton said, suddenly associating the man with his visa photograph.

Kirchmann was surprised by the unexpected identification. "Yes, I am. How do you know?"

"Because we've got every police force in the free world helping us to catch you scum, that's how the hell I know. And we're going to nail the other twenty-seven of you before you do any more damage."

Kirchmann smiled graciously as if receiving a compliment. "I would be interested to know how you arrive at the conclusion that there are only twenty-seven more of us, Mr. . . ?"

"Denton. Inspector Eric Denton of the New York Police Department. Sixty of you came into this country. Thirty-one of you are standing here right now. Two of your number are where they belong. Dead. According to my subtraction, that leaves twenty-seven."

"Very good, Inspector. But useless information. You will catch none of them before they have completed their assign-

227

ments. You did not catch any of us. Everyone here delivered himself into your custody. As for Werner and Baroudi, they were expendable."

"I don't give a shit whether we caught you or whether you turned yourselves in. You're still in custody."

Kirchmann smiled again. "For how long, Inspector Denton? For how long?"

Denton understood Kirchmann's question only too well. Desperately he tried to think what the remaining members of the group could hold as a hostage in exchange for their captured comrades. What else where they planning? Surely the blocking of all rail links was not the objective of their whole crazy scheme. Christ, he'd give up his pension if only he knew what was going down.

After being confined to desk duty, Sergeant Harry DeLeon looked on his trip over the Willis Avenue Bridge into the South Bronx as a welcome relief. He was becoming a police officer again, a riot gun clutched in his hands, the thirty-eight weighing comfortably on his hip as if it belonged there.

He was struck immediately by the darkness of the entire area as the car came off the bridge and swung onto the Deegan as far as 138th Street, the worst area of looting. Although the street-lights were out, DeLeon could see the fire tenders trying to quench the increasing advance of flames from burning stores. Police cars were abandoned in the middle of the street as officers took cover inside doorways, dodging bricks tossed down at them from the roofs of buildings. As DeLeon got out of the car, something smashed into the fender. He bent down to examine the dent left by a brick. Only it was not a dent. It was a small, perfectly formed round hole. From a bullet.

Someone, a police officer, screamed at him to hurry, to run for cover, to throw himself flat beside the car. DeLeon did none of these things. Instead, he looked up, just in time to see a flash of gunfire from a sixth-floor window as someone fired out into the night, the mass of police cars and uniforms providing an irresistible target. The next instant a sledgehammer smashed into DeLeon's chest. As he fell back to the ground, choking out his life's blood, the three police officers who had been with him in the car opened up with riot guns at the window from where the single shot had come. High above the night's chaotic noise, a scream tailed off. A rifle clattered to the ground. The body of a fifteen-year-old boy plummeted to the sidewalk.

"Let's get the hell out of here!" one of the officers yelled.

"What about Harry?"

"Leave him there. We can pick him up later on."

"Poor fuck. Was gonna retire in six months." The police officers sprinted for the cover of doorways, ready to shoot at anything not wearing a uniform.

At fifteen minutes before midnight the MetroCity station wagon crossed the Willis Avenue Bridge from Manhattan into the darkness of the Bronx, pulling off the Deegan at 138th Street. The driver halted beside the studio's remote unit, which was parked about one hundred yards short of the cluster of police cars and fire engines. Babs and Rosen continued on foot, working as they walked, Babs talking into the microphone she held, Rosen filming. The sound man tagged behind.

Babs tried to say something to the two men, but the words were lost in the crackle of flames, the shouts of police and fire officers, the occasional rattle of gunfire. She raised her voice and pointed.

"Over there, Jerry!"

Four police officers were crouched in a doorway, riot guns and rifles raised as they tried to protect a fire crew from snipers. Babs ran on ahead and ducked into the doorway to ask the four men about the situation. Rosen moved in right behind her, getting everything down on film. When Babs turned around from the police officers, she caught Rosen in an eye-to-eye confrontation. "How about we move to the fire trucks, Jerry? Ready to risk it?"

"What are we waiting for?" He nodded for the sound man to

follow. They began to run across the street and stopped as they came to the figure of Sergeant Harry DeLeon stretched out in death. Rosen started to focus in on the body.

"What happened to him?" Babs asked.

"Shot through the chest."

She shuddered. "This is turning into something wild, like Detroit in 'sixty-seven. All we need now is the National Guard."

It was Rosen's turn to shudder. "We've got enough corpses already." He straightened up, finished with DeLeon. "We don't need any more."

As they neared the fire captain, Babs turned around once more. "Reckon we can win an award with this story, Jerry?"

"Why not? Something good always comes to a lucky few from disasters. Might as well be us."

16

AT ONE MINUTE before midnight the two suitcases left aboard the abandoned Flushing-bound IRT Number 7 by Horst Fischer exploded, wrecking the center car and derailing cars on either side, strewing debris across the tracks. It would take at least two days for the wreckage to be cleared, the track repaired, and the line reopened. Within the next five minutes the other train bombs exploded, cutting subway and rail links into Manhattan.

Mayor Scrivens received the news from the subway control center at Grand Central Terminal without any show of emotion. He felt totally drained, all nervous energy sapped from his body by the catastrophic series of events which were being unleashed with such devastation against the city. He had no doubt that Denton had been right in his fear of terrorist activity against the city, but where would it end? The blackout must have been their work, along with the train bombs, designed to create confusion among the police. What, he asked himself exhaustedly, came next?

Heavy footsteps made him turn to see Police Commissioner May. The official's fat face was grim, lips stretched into a thin, straight line as he approached the mayor.

"What now?" Scrivens asked.

"Just got word in from Con Ed," May replied. "They found their employees trussed up like a bunch of turkeys in the energy control center."

"Anyone hurt?"

"Not a scratch. Just their dignity bruised. Three armed men broke in and gagged them. Then they shut off the Bronx."

"How long till the damage is repaired?"

"Hard to say, but a day at least. The South Bronx is going to have to do without power for a while. They've got an army of technicians working on the damage, but whoever blew those transmission lines did a damned professional job. There's a lot of splicing to do."

"Transmission lines?" Scrivens felt as if he were losing contact with the rest of the world. "Blew them?"

"Yeah. When the three gunmen were sitting in the control center, the lines came down. Someone had rigged explosive charges on them. According to Con Ed, we'd have lost the city if the load hadn't been shed almost immediately. One of the raiders shed the load for us, to the Bronx, then destroyed the switch so it couldn't be put back on."

Scrivens tried to understand the reason for the action, but it was beyond him; he had other things to worry about. "What about the looting and rioting?"

"One police officer dead, guy named DeLeon. Four firemen injured. Four looters and two snipers dead."

"Are the reinforcements from upper Manhattan helping?"

"A bit. We've cleared the whole area, sent them all into the Bronx. I'm praying"—May closed his eyes for a moment—"that nothing happens in Manhattan right now. Because that's about all we're left to work with. Nothing."

"None of the suspects said anything yet?"

May shook his head. "They're acting like a bunch of dummies, standing in a long line with their mouths buttoned shut. Denton's managed to identify a lot of them with the information and photos we got from abroad."

"What happens next?"

"I wish I knew. Denton wants to cut loose on them with a rubber hose, beat it out of them. But we can't let him do that," May added sarcastically. "We're a civilized country, remember?"

"Too damned civilized," Scrivens said, turning away from the police commissioner as the telephone rang. It was for May. A second police officer had been shot to death.

In Howard Beach, Stiehl lay comfortably on the bed, a small portable color television set on the dressing table tuned into MetroCity. Scenes of the looting and rioting in the South Bronx flashed across the screen, shadowy figures of police running along a street, seeking the shelter of parked cars as they tried to spot sniper positions, returning fire with a ten-to-one ratio. The picture faded; then Babs O'Neill's face came into focus, talking breathlessly as she tried to explain the latest developments. The snipers were being ferreted out, and police had orders to shoot looters on sight, she said. Gradually the worst areas were being cleared, although reports coming in from other precincts showed that the looting was spreading, although less viciously than on 138th Street. A brief but heavy thunderstorm had blown into the area, helping control the fires and dampening the spirits of the looters.

The picture cut suddenly, replaced by the grim face of Mayor Scrivens, caught unaware, looking sideways, talking to someone at police headquarters before he realized he was on the air.

"We have been invaded," he said simply, "by an international army of terrorists."

Stiehl wondered how painful it was for the black mayor to admit he had been wrong on the very television station he had earlier accused of lying about the terrorists.

"I have been in touch with Albany," Scrivens continued. "The governor has promised to send in State Police and National Guard units to assist our own police department. At the present time the worst rioting and looting have been stopped, but it is spreading to other parts of the blacked-out Bronx. The subway service to Manhattan has been cut off, and we will not know the full extent of the damage until crews have managed to clear the blocked tunnels. But I hand out this warning to any man or woman watching who might be connected with what is happening. You will be found. You will be punished severely. More than thirty of your comrades have already been captured and will face trial and lengthy prison sentences for their part in tonight's infamy." Scrivens worried for a moment that he sounded too much like Roosevelt after Pearl Harbor.

"We may be on our knees at the moment, but we are far from finished. Like the phoenix from the ashes, we will be resurrected to smash you no matter where you try to hide."

The picture disappeared, replaced by another shot of the South Bronx. A police officer was throwing up his riot gun to blast away at some unseen target.

Stiehl lay back on the bed and gazed serenely at the ceiling. Good luck, Mr. Mayor, he thought. You haven't captured anyone yet, nor will you. If you think what's happening now is bad news, stick around for a while, wait for the knockout punch. Boy, had those three guys ever done a job up in the Bronx, starting a riot all on their own. Despite his admiration for the way the three men had handled their assignments, Stiehl was disturbed by the injuries to the police and fire personnel. He had considered the possibility, had tried to justify it to himself as an acceptable risk. Now he found himself thinking about the police officer who had been killed, DeLeon. Young guy, old guy? Was he a family man? Kids? The short newscast from Babs O'Neill had said that he was only six months away from retirement.

Shaking off the momentary depression, Stiehl picked up the telephone receiver in a white-gloved hand and dialed the number of the apartment in Fort Lee. Huckleby answered.

"It's all going according to plan," Stiehl said.

"So I hear from the television. I can see the glow from here,"

234

Huckleby replied as he looked through the picture window across the Hudson to the South Bronx. "Your men did well."

"Cops are getting killed. I didn't want that to happen."

"Justifiable casualties," Huckleby said philosophically. "We have no control over life or death once the battle starts. You should know that."

Stiehl sensed a difference in Huckleby's voice, an animation, an excitement which he had never noticed before, as if the man were warming to the havoc he was creating, enjoying it.

"I'll get back to you when the next move happens," Stiehl said, hanging up before Huckleby could reply. As he lay back on the bed again, his thoughts turned to the retired general. He had doubted his sanity once before, when Huckleby had made the initial proposal; he had wondered then if there had been more than was in the newspapers about Huckleby's retirement from the army. Stay calm, he prayed. Remember, this is a lesson, not Armageddon.

The thought of the high-rise apartment buildings on the approach to the George Washington Bridge—filled with vibrant, living people—made Stiehl's blood run cold.

In her room at a midtown Manhattan hotel, Linda Huckleby was also thinking about her father. Zero casualties, he had told her as they parted. Had he really meant it? Or had he known innocent people would be killed?

What of Peter Stiehl? What was he doing even now? Was he thinking of people like the police officer DeLeon? Or was he concentrating solely on his mission, blanking everything else from his mind, ignoring the suffering that was taking place all around him?

She looked at the telephone, a simple connection that could take her to either her father or Stiehl. She could call her father and beg him to call it off before it went even further, plead with him as she had never pleaded with anyone. Would he listen? If she called Stiehl, would that help? Stiehl could not reach her father. Twenty miles separated them, and it was her father who controlled everyone's fate from the apartment in Fort Lee.

Picking up the receiver, she tried to think what she could say to her father. As the switchboard operator answered, Linda hung up. It was pointless. Any calls to Fort Lee would be traceable, implicating her in this madness. That had been the idea behind her staying in a Manhattan hotel while the operation took place. What better alibi could she have? If she had known anything about her father's plan, would she willingly have stayed in the center of the maelstrom?

She turned back to the television again to watch her father's dream unfold. Like the rest of the city, there was nothing she could do but sit and wait.

Far away from her Greenwich Village apartment, entrenched in the ravaged South Bronx, Babs O'Neill felt more at home than she had in years. The action was all around her, news being made, and she was a part of it.

"How about a couple of shop owners?" she asked Rosen. "Most of these places are mom-and-pop shops, with no insurance. Good human-interest angle to see how they're reacting."

Rosen looked along the street, catching a glimpse of a group of people standing in front of a broken shopwindow. As he began to close in, he recognized two of the police officers Babs had interviewed earlier. With them was an elderly black couple; the man was looking dumbfounded into the plundered appliance shop while the woman was crying.

"Over there!" Rosen called to Babs, who was looking elsewhere. "There's your story." He broke into a jogging run, the heavy camera beating a familiar tattoo against his shoulder.

Babs's voice was laced with sympathy as she confronted the elderly couple. "Was this your store?"

The man nodded. "Small electrical appliances, secondhand stuff, repairs. Look"—he pointed into the smoldering carnage, steam rising from the floor where firemen had hosed—"there's nothing left. What they didn't steal, they burned."

"Were you insured?" Babs knew the answer before she even asked the question; she wanted her viewers to hear, to wring an extra tear from them.

"Who would insure us?" the woman asked tearfully. "No insurance companies come 'round here no more. They're in business to make money, not lose it."

"How long have you been here?" Babs asked. She felt Rosen move in closer, zooming in on the woman's tearstained face.

"Ten years," the man replied. "Neighborhood was all right then. Not like now."

"You getting all this, Jerry?" Babs whispered.

"Every tear." He swung the camera away from the woman, back into the smoking shop, then out again, to the man, his lined face looking in stupefied amazement at what had been his livelihood.

"What will you do now?" Babs asked.

The man grimaced, signifying that he did not really care if the building fell down on top of him; nothing worse could happen than had taken place already. "What can we do? All our money was in the shop. Maybe we'll get a government loan like last time and work to pay it back. Maybe we'll just move away from here."

Somewhere in the distance a single rifle shot barked out, answered immediately by the combined roar of half a dozen riot guns. One of the police officers with the elderly black couple looked nervously over his shoulder, realizing how exposed the small group was. "Better move it on out of here," he said gently to the black couple. "We can come back later on."

"Tough," Rosen said as they walked away from the destroyed shop.

"You bet," Babs agreed. "And all we're doing is making headlines out of their grief."

Rosen looked at her strangely. "You going soft on me?"

She stopped to wipe something from the corner of her eye. Then she smiled at him, an expression that seemed strangely out of place on 138th Street that night. "No. Just a little older and a little wiser. Guess it happens to everyone."

Rosen chuckled. "Don't let Charlie Kohn hear you say that. He'll start looking for someone else to fill your spot."

"Fuck Charlie Kohn. He knows what he can go and do." She

237

laughed and went looking for other victims of the night to interview.

Stiehl watched Babs O'Neill's latest report from the stricken South Bronx with only one eye, finding little of interest in the stories of police gallantry. He was trying to divorce himself completely from what was happening in the Bronx, as if he wished he had nothing to do with the casualties there. They were not acceptable to him. They were not just statistics. They were innocent people getting hurt through no fault of their own, a situation he desperately wished he could have avoided.

He walked across the bedroom to the two wooden crates he had taken from the trunk of Huckleby's car when they had last met. After opening them, he removed the contents and began to assemble them. The he turned out all the lights and opened the window overlooking Jamaica Bay. He gazed out into the night, hearing the roar of an aircraft passing overhead, seeing its navigation lights wink on and off.

At one-fifteen on Tuesday morning a haggard Mayor Percy Scrivens held his next press conference at police headquarters. Standing in front of the manacled terrorists—whom the newsmen insisted on using as a backdrop for the conference—Scrivens straightened his back and looked into the probing eyes of the assembled television cameras.

"I have been in touch again with the governor," he began, "and I am happy to report that I've assured him our own police department is bringing the situation in the Bronx under control. There will be no need for either State Police or National Guard units to be sent into the city. Right now Con Edison crews are working to restore power and service, and we should be back to normal in that respect by some time this afternoon." He coughed into his hand as the heat of the television lights made his throat go dry.

"Regarding the subway and railroad tunnels in and out of Manhattan, I'm afraid the news is not so good. Work on clearing the tracks and removing the wrecked trains cannot begin yet.

Until a lengthy inspection has been made to ensure it is safe to work down there, the Transit Authority cannot allow the clearing to begin. Please, I urge all commuters, unless you have urgent life-or-death business in the city today, stay at home. Only buses will be running. Everything else will be out of action. Do not attempt to bring your cars into the city as police barricades will be operating on all bridges from six in the morning. You will only be turned back and cause greater confusion. Stay home with your families until we can get the mass transit system back to normal."

Denton stood off to one side, watching the mayor, his mind only fractionally on the speech. He was feeling like the manager of a baseball team in the field, trying to stop a runner scoring from third when there was only one out. What was the opposing manager planning to bring the runner home? A squeeze play? A sacrifice bunt? Should he bring in his own third baseman for the bunt and try to mow down the runner at home plate? Or was the batter going to hit away, try to bring the runner home with a deep fly ball to the outfield?

What had happened so far that night was a concerted action. A blackout causing looting and rioting in the South Bronx, one of the city's worst areas, followed by the decimation of the entire rail system into Manhattan. What came next? Where were the other men whose names the INS investigation had turned up? What were they planning? What could it be that would tie in with the two operations already carried out? Something was missing. Somewhere there was a link between the things that had happened. But damn it; he couldn't see any connection at all.

He began paying attention to the press conference again as Scrivens wound up his prepared speech and began to answer questions from the reporters.

"The men standing behind you all surrendered, Mr. Mayor. Doesn't that strike you as odd that they should give themselves up?" an NBC reporter asked. "It's as if they were expecting to be rescued or exchanged for something."

Scrivens looked uncomfortable at the question, one that he

had hoped would not come. "I assume you mean that their colleagues"—he used the word distastefully—"are planning to take over something in this city and use it for a ransom demand. The thought has crossed our minds as well, rest assured about that. Our police department has mounted extra guard on all accessible political and financial institutions. Any further attempts to wreak havoc on this city will go unrewarded."

"What about the police units which have been shifted out of upper Manhattan to the South Bronx?" asked a bespectacled woman from the *Daily News*. "To me, that seems as if whoever is planning these strikes wants the police out of Manhattan. Could they deliberately have started the trouble in the Bronx for the express purpose of drawing police strength out of Manhattan? Can the remaining police units cope with any emergencies which might now arise in Manhattan?"

Scrivens was gaping stupidly before the woman had the opportunity to finish the question. So was Police Commissioner May. And Denton. Of course! Why the hell hadn't they thought of that? A decoy. The whole mess up in the Bronx, the attack on Con Ed, the blackout and resultant riots were a decoy, designed to draw police away from the next area the terrorists would hit, the borough of Manhattan, probably the main objective of their attack.

Before either Scrivens, May, or Denton could speak, a clipped, carefully enunciated voice broke into the silence which had descended over the large room.

"Would the ladies and gentlemen of the American press care to hear what will happen next?"

All eyes swung to Dieter Kirchmann. He stood silently for a moment, basking in center stage, an actor acknowledging the effect he has made with a superbly timed entrance. He looked at the clock on the opposite wall, following the red second hand as it reached the twelve; the minute hand clicked sharply onto one-twenty-two.

"At precisely one-thirty, in eight minutes' time, explosives will destroy all the bridges over the Harlem River. I am offering you

240

this warning because we do not wish to see any American civilians needlessly killed. Our enemies are not the people of the United States or of New York. They are our brothers, our sisters, trodden underfoot by the capitalists and imperialists who rule this country. We wish the American people no harm, no harm at all," he added, seeing the cameras and microphones swing toward him.

Denton was the first to see the significance of what was happening. Quickly he pulled the police commissioner and mayor aside, away from the mass of newspeople crowding around Kirchmann.

"Manhattan's being systematically cut off."

Scrivens regarded him blankly, his mind still reeling from the revelation of the bombs on the northern bridges. "What do you mean?" May asked.

"We've lost our underground rail links. Half the police are up in the South Bronx, and now those bridges are going to blow. They'll never get back."

"Of course they will," May broke in sharply. "We haven't got the time to find those bombs on the bridges and defuse them, but we've still got the other road bridges and tunnels. They can come back over the Triborough ramp."

"Sure," Denton said sarcastically. "You think whoever planned this little caper didn't take that into consideration? How long do you think we'll have those other bridges and tunnels?"

Scrivens broke away from the small group, but May pulled him back roughly. "Where are you going?"

"The governor. Those state troopers and Guard units I told him we didn't need. We want them now."

May released his grip. Scrivens scurried across to a telephone, picked up the receiver, and began talking agitatedly, brushing away newspeople who gathered around him once Kirchmann stopped talking.

"What about those bombs?" Denton asked.

"Forget it," May replied. "We'd never find them in time. I'll order units to keep those bridges closed in case anyone gets blown up with them. We've just got to protect the bridges and tunnels we've got left."

"From what?" Denton asked. "We still don't know what we're fighting against."

"Miss O'Neill! Miss O'Neill!"

The station wagon driver's strident voice cut across the noise on 138th Street, stopping Babs and Rosen in their track. They turned around to see the man racing toward them, shirt open, chest heaving with exertion.

"What is it?" Babs snapped.

"Mr. Kohn. He's just been on the line. All the Harlem River bridges are being blown up in five minutes. We've got to get back to Manhattan before we're cut off."

Neither Babs nor Rosen needed further urging. Fifteen seconds later they were back in the station wagon, the driver gunning the engine as the vehicle roared toward the Deegan Expressway, followed by the big remote unit. They cut off at the Willis Avenue Bridge, skidding right at the inoperable traffic lights at the bottom, the driver holding down the horn, flashing his bright beams on and off to clear a path through sparse traffic that was braving the blackout. In the mirror, he saw the remote unit following suit. The station wagon jumped into the air as it accelerated toward the ramp leading to the bridge, closing the gap to the police line barricade that had been set across the approach. Two patrolmen waved flashlights at the oncoming vehicles.

"They're blocking the ramp!" the station wagon driver yelled.

"Go through it!" Rosen screamed back. "Ram it!"

"Hold tight," the driver warned. He pressed down harder on the gas pedal, gave three warning blasts on the horn, and smashed through the flimsy wooden barricade. The occupants of the station wagon caught the briefest glimpse of two startled faces as pieces of the gray-painted barricade flew into the air. The next moment the station wagon was on the metal roadbed of the bridge, veering across the four empty lanes to the off ramp leading down to the FDR Drive, the remote unit close behind.

242

"Stop the car, and aim your main beams at the bridge," Rosen ordered. The station wagon braked to a sharp halt as it reached the FDR, and Rosen held out a hand to stop Babs from flying forward. He jumped out of the car, camera on his shoulder, focusing back on the bridge.

"Where would it be?" Babs asked breathlessly.

"The bomb?"

She nodded.

"Probably somewhere in the supports coming out of the concrete bed in the river. Must have used a boat to get it there. Or maybe it's on one of the struts coming into the shore," he explained, pointing the camera down to the water. "That's if there's a bomb there to begin with, not just a scare."

"What do you think's going on, Jerry?"

"I'd say your story was right all along. You had a scoop, and nobody would give you credit for it. Not even Kohn."

"Dear Charlie," she murmured in a disparaging tone. "Too scared about our credibility if the story turned out to be a bust."

Rosen began thinking about their one and only unfounded story when a loud crack sounded from the direction of the bridge. "Oh, oh, there it goes! Look out!"

An orange flash was followed by a loud roar, changing to a series of earsplitting cracks as the bridgework shuddered under the strain of the explosion. Rosen reached out with one hand and pushed Babs to the ground as a blast of hot air attacked them. Something heavy swung through the air and landed with a crash on the pavement six feet from where he was standing. He took no notice of it. Standing upright, he filmed steadily as the metal framework of the bridge began to break up, struts dropping off into the seething river below, sending up fountains of spray.

The bridge made a final almighty effort to shrug off the damage done to its supports by the bomb. With a wheezing, dying groan, a large section of span dropped away and crashed in a solid lump into the water with a roar of thunder that blotted out all else. Water sprayed over Rosen; a sheet thrown into the air smashed into him with the force of a tidal wave. He staggered back, almost fell, and grappled with the camera to prevent its sliding from his grasp. Two hands reached out to support him. He looked down and saw Babs on her knees, holding his legs to stop him from falling.

"Big bang," he said, regaining his balance. "Wonder what they used, an atom bomb?"

"Hardly." Babs stood up and steadied herself. "Come on, we'd better get back to the studio before Charlie puts out an APB on us. Provided there are any police left in Manhattan to carry it out."

Stiehl turned away from the window and looked back into the bedroom, his eyes caught by movement on the television screen. He wondered what news coverage was being given on other channels and turned the selector to a major network. The scene was identical to the one he had just left. He switched a second time; again the picture was the same. It took him a moment to realize that MetroCity's coverage was being patched onto the major networks because it was so good. He found the realization vaguely amusing. Out of wars and similar disasters came fame and awards for newspeople. These two—O'Neill and Rosen— looked as if they were well on the way to one right now, with their coverage of the Bronx looting, the destruction of the Willis Avenue Bridge, not to mention their having the story before anyone else did, only to be branded as liars by the mayor. Stiehl wondered if they had any compassion for the people they were filming, those who had been the worst affected by the night's events. Or were they too interested in making a comfortable niche for themselves in the annals of news reporting?

He turned down the volume and sat on the bed, wishing the whole operation were over. Just another twelve hours, and he could throw away the tinted glasses and white cotton gloves forever, wash the dye out of his hair, throw away the false passport, the business cards from the Rand *Daily Mail,* and the other forged documents. He could deposit them all on the trash heap of memories along with the name of Peter Adcock.

244

17

THE DESTRUCTION of the bridges over the Harlem River was the signal for Stiehl's drivers in the specially leased ten-ton trucks. At different points outside Manhattan—in New Jersey, in Queens, in Brooklyn—diesel engines growled into life, sending clouds of black exhaust smoke into the air as the trucks closed in on the stricken borough for the final assault.

Traffic was light as Gerd Havlicek left the New Jersey Turnpike. Humming to himself, he continued north toward the George Washington Bridge at a steady fifty miles an hour. It took him a few seconds to identify the melody on which he was concentrating—"Lili Marlene"—and he wondered what had made him select that particular tune. War. What he was doing reminded him of a war movie. And why not? He was going to war.

He glanced down at the empty seat beside him, at the large white placard with the heavy black printing that read: "Caution. This truck is loaded with ten tons of high explosive. Any attempt to interfere with this vehicle will cause it to explode." Havlicek chuckled loudly, banging a fist on the steering wheel as he imagined the havoc the sign would cause.

And the even greater havoc if someone chose to ignore it.

Patrick Kerrigan eased the heavy truck down the sharp bend leading to the Lincoln Tunnel, one eye on the road, the other on the brightly lit skyline of midtown Manhattan across the Hudson River. Almost there, he thought. Just another few minutes, and I can dump this thing and walk out of the tunnel into Manhattan. He looked sideways at McGrath, perched on the edge of the seat, nervous, the tension and excitement of the moment showing behind his thick glasses. You, too, Kerrigan thought. Going to dump you as well, boyo. Get you out of my hair once and for bloody always.

"Got any money?" he asked McGrath.

"What for?"

"For the toll, you stupid git. We need money to get into the tunnel."

Grudgingly McGrath felt in his jacket pocket, pulled out his wallet, and handed Kerrigan a five-dollar bill. "That enough?"

"I don't know. It's a dollar fifty for a car. Don't know what it'll be for us." He took his right hand off the wheel, reached out, and snatched the wallet from McGrath's grasp. "I'll take what I need."

"Hey! There's more than two hundred dollars in there."

"Don't worry. You'll get it back." Kerrigan slowed the truck to a gradual halt by the toll booth, where he passed across a twenty-dollar bill and waited for change and the receipt the attendant insisted on giving. As the truck began to move toward the mouth of the tunnel, he stuffed the wallet into his own pocket. Where McGrath was going that night, he would not be needing money.

Wolfgang Herzlein waited behind the short line of cars at the toll booth of the George Washington Bridge, eager for his turn to come. His target was the four high-rise apartment buildings on

246

the far side of the bridge, over the Cross Bronx Expressway approach.

"Where you heading tonight?" the toll booth clerk asked.

"Why?" The question caught Herzlein off guard.

"All the bridges to the Bronx are out, blown up by some nuts."

"Long Island City," Herzlein lied. "Delivery of plastic resin. I'll be using the Triborough."

The clerk handed Herzlein a receipt. "Take care. God only knows what's going on over there, but from radio reports it sounds like World War Three's broken out."

"Thanks for the warning." Herzlein stepped on the accelerator, and the truck roared away. As the lanes from the toll booths converged onto the bridge, he looked left and saw a truck similar to his own. Havlicek, he guessed, ready to leave his gift to the city of New York. He honked and saw the other truck's lights flash in response.

In the other truck, Havlicek grinned in the darkness as he recognized Herzlein. They had the bridge sewn up. He hoped that Herzlein would wait for him underneath the apartments so they could walk together into Manhattan, two triumphant soldiers.

On Hoyt Avenue, near the Queens side of the Triborough Bridge, Gamal Aktouri turned the ignition key of his truck for the fifth time, his foot pressed down on the pedal. Beside him, Ahmed Nassim tensed with the stirring of excitement; they were on their way.

The starter motor whirred, but the engine refused to catch. Aktouri's anxiety increased. What was wrong? Why didn't the damned thing start? Was it flooded? In desperation, he floored the pedal and held it down as he turned the key again, trying to clear the fuel line. He tried the key one more time. Still no response was forthcoming.

"Damn you!" he cursed loudly. "Damn you a million times! Why don't you start?"

* * *

In Fort Lee, Huckleby stood by the living-room picture window with his binoculars focused on the illuminated span of the George Washington Bridge. He could make out a large vehicle entering the toll booths, but at that distance he could not be certain it was one of his own.

In front of him, all but four of the red lights on the control panel were glowing. All had flashed on within the past minute. Every truck but the two for the George Washington Bridge, the Lincoln Tunnel, and the Triborough Bridge was in position, their booby-trap mechanisms, activated. If he flicked one of the switches now, ten tons of high explosive would rip apart a bridge or a tunnel. His fingers drifted down to the last light to come on, that of the Queens-Midtown Tunnel. He had wanted to send two trucks to each tunnel, one for the inbound tube, one for the outbound. Stiehl had overruled him, quoting the overkill theory. One truck full of explosives would be enough to put all tubes of a tunnel out of commission. Besides, there were not enough men now to crew the eleven trucks they were using; two trucks had had to go with only one driver.

As Huckleby stood there, another light flickered on, glowing red in the darkness. Kerrigan and McGrath were in position. The Lincoln Tunnel was also his.

Kerrigan turned off the engine, leaving the truck stopped diagonally across the inbound tube's two lanes. Behind, he could hear the angry blasts from drivers who had been following the truck, but he paid no attention. Before he locked the doors and completed the circuit, he had one more chore to attend to.

"Danny, here's your wallet back."

McGrath turned in the passenger seat, hand outstretched. Kerrigan's fist caught him flush on the point of the jaw, knocking him across the cab. His head struck the door pillar, and consciousness departed in a kaleidoscope of flashing light.

"Be seeing you, Danny Boy." Kerrigan chuckled as he stepped down from the cab and locked the door. "But not, I hope, for a bloody long time."

"Get that fucking truck out of here!" an indignant voice yelled as Kerrigan reached the pavement. "You can't leave it there!"

He turned around and saw a gray-haired elderly man storming around the side of the truck. "Can you read as well as you can shout?" Kerrigan asked.

"What?"

"Read what's written in the window." Kerrigan began to walk down the tunnel, glancing back over his shoulder as the driver read the warning notice in the truck's windshield. He laughed uproariously as the man backed away hurriedly from the truck and ran back to his car, shouting at the other stalled drivers.

Doesn't take much to start a panic, Kerrigan mused. Just ten measly tons of dynamite. Ten minutes later, as he neared the Manhattan end of the tunnel, he dropped the truck keys down a drain and waited for the police to arrest him. He did not spare a moment's remorse for Danny McGrath.

Gerd Havlicek drove the ten-ton truck slowly along the lower level of the George Washington Bridge, his eyes peering into the semidarkness where Herzlein's taillights had disappeared. As he approached the twin support towers on the New York side of the bridge, he slowed down. If the truck exploded here, the blast would put gaping holes in both levels of the bridge and damage the support towers. If the bridge itself did not come down, it would be unusable till the towers were repaired, and that could take up to a year. He turned off the engine and checked he had left nothing behind. As he placed the placard in the windshield, he spotted on the periphery of his vision blazing headlights coming toward him, swerving left and right as the driver tried to keep the car in the center lane. Havlicek jumped out of the cab, locked the door to activate the electronic circuit, and threw himself to the ground. A blue 1972 Buick LeSabre roared past, three people inside, the driver obviously drunk. Havlicek got to his feet in time to see the sedan go completely out of control, swerve to the right, crash into a guardrail, and rebound upside down into the path of another car. There was a grinding scream of metal as three more cars plowed into the accident, but Havlicek was no longer looking. He was running, past the accident, anxious to get to the end of the bridge, where Herzlein would be waiting. The multiple accident had nothing to do with him. The police could sort it out when they arrived, if they dared to come on the bridge when there were two heavy trucks full of explosive waiting for them.

As he passed close to the guardrail, he flicked the truck keys into the water, losing sight of them immediately.

One red light still had not jumped into life on Huckleby's control panel. Either something had gone wrong with the Triborough Bridge truck, or else there was a malfunction in the circuit and the red light would never come on. Huckleby did not have the time to wait and find out. According to the schedule he had worked out with Stiehl, all the trucks should have been in position. The time had come to make the first phone call. He picked up the receiver and dialed police headquarters in Manhattan.

"Mayor Scrivens." Thanks to the massive television coverage being given to the night's events, Huckleby had not been forced to waste time by calling Scrivens first at City Hall; he knew exactly where to find him.

"Who wants him? He's very busy at the moment, accepting only priority calls."

I'll bet he's very busy, Huckleby thought savagely. "This is a priority call. Top priority if you value the safety of Manhattan."

Scrivens came on the line seconds later, puzzled by the call. "This is the mayor. To whom am I talking?"

"Names are unnecessary," Huckleby countered. "Leave it to suffice that I am the man responsible for the series of misfortunes plaguing your city tonight."

"Look, mister," Scrivens growled, "you've picked a poor time for practical jokes. Call me back some other time, and we can both have a good laugh."

"Mr. Mayor, let me assure you that I am the man responsible. I am holding Manhattan's fate in the palm of my hand. Manhattan has been attacked and conquered. Right now I have placed

250

trucks containing ten tons of high explosive on all remaining road bridges and tunnels into Manhattan. Except for the George Washington Bridge, where I have two trucks, one of which is directly beneath the high-rise apartment buildings on the approach to the bridge from the Cross Bronx Expressway. Now do you believe me, Mr. Mayor?"

"You're mad!" Scrivens screamed.

"Not as mad as you will be if you do not listen to my demands and obey them."

Scrivens became quiet. "What do you want?" he asked softly.

Huckleby thought he heard a click on the line, another party listening in, police trying to trace the call. He had to be quick. "The trucks can be detonated by radio control from my command post. They are also booby-trapped in case your men try to interfere with them. Notices are posted on each truck to that effect."

"You haven't told me what you want yet." Scrivens's tone was normal, as if he were being coached by someone to keep Huckleby talking for as long as possible.

"We want the vault of the First National Bank of Manhattan Building opened. We expect anywhere in the region of one billion dollars—no securities, please—to be delivered to a fully fueled seven-forty-seven at Kennedy Airport by noon. If this is not done, you will be asking Washington for federal aid to replace your bridges and tunnels."

"That's it?"

"We want the release of all the personnel you now hold for the subway bombings, plus the release of the men who are now surrendering to police from the bomb trucks. They are to be taken to the Wall Street Heliport and held there until they are joined by the four men who fixed the bombs to the Harlem River bridges and a further three men, who will pilot the aircraft at JFK. When all are present—fifty-seven men and one woman—they will be helilifted to the waiting seven-forty-seven and put aboard with the money. If this is not done, we will blow the bridges and tunnels."

251

"Anything else?" Scrivens asked, trying to keep Huckleby on the line.

"The aircraft will be given clearance to take off from Kennedy at midday. Any interference with it, while on the ground or in the air, and we will blow the bridges and tunnels.

"Finally"—Huckleby began to speed up his words, anxious to terminate the conversation—"I want television coverage of what is taking place. So I will be able to see that my orders are being carried out. I want"—he looked across the room to the color television, which was tuned into MetroCity—"the crew working for MetroCity to do all the coverage, from the arrival of my people at the Wall Street Heliport, their transportation with the money to Kennedy Airport, and the takeoff."

Scrivens sensed the call was about to end and tried desperately to continue it. "I don't know if I can help you there. That decision is up to MetroCity—" The phone clicked in his ear, and he knew that the caller had gone. He looked across to Police Commissioner May, who shook his head in silent answer to the unspoken question.

"Couldn't trace him. The phone trap's out; otherwise, we'd have nailed him in seconds. We've got to do it the old-fashioned way now. Just our luck, the computer breaks down tonight of all nights. All we know is we're dealing with a nut."

"Some nut." The bitter words came from Denton, who had been listening on another extension. "He's nuts enough to have worked out all this and got it rolling."

Another telephone rang. Denton picked it up and spoke briefly before breaking the connection. "Police just picked up two krauts who left a ten-ton truck loaded with explosives in the middle of the Queens-Midtown Tunnel. They turned themselves in. Tunnel's being cleared, blocked off."

May dug a finger into his already loosened tie knot, dragging it down even farther. "Better get some men over to those apartments on the George Washington Bridge. Evacuate them before we have an even bigger disaster on our hands."

Still another telephone rang. May waited until Denton had

finished the short conversation. "Which tunnel this time?" the police commissioner asked wearily.

"A bridge. A ten-ton truck parked on the Queensborough Bridge's lower level."

"More Germans?"

"No. Irishmen this time."

May began whistling to himself, lips pursed tightly together, breath escaping between the slight opening in the center. Like Gerd Havlicek, who had hummed a melody on the way to the George Washington Bridge, it took May a few seconds to realize what he was whistling. When he did, he blushed, then grinned in embarrassment.

"Hardly the opportune time to pick a tune like that," Scrivens said, recognizing the old nursery rhyme.

"Guess it isn't at that," May acknowledged. Nevertheless, he continued whistling "London Bridge Is Falling Down."

Gamal Aktouri closed the engine compartment cover of the ten-ton truck and climbed back into the cab. Neither he nor Nassim had been able to see much and doubted if their amateurish fiddling with the accelerator linkage had done any good. Even in the daylight they could have accomplished little. Neither knew much about engines, especially the huge power plants the Americans loved to put into their vehicles.

Closing his eyes and offering up a silent prayer, Aktouri turned the ignition key again and listened tensely to the starter motor crank over the engine. To his surprise, it caught once, died away, then caught again, snarling into life, making the whole truck vibrate. They had fixed it! The realization took a few seconds to register on them, baffled by the surprise that the linkage had been stuck and their probing had freed it. A good omen, Aktouri decided; men who knew little about machinery fumbling in the darkness and solving the problem. Next to him, Nassim yelled in triumph.

Happier in his own mind, Aktouri pointed the heavy truck toward the bridge and pressed down hard on the pedal. They were starting out five minutes late and had to make up whatever time they could. Ahead of him was the ramp onto the bridge, used by trucks as they came off Hoyt Avenue after being rerouted around Grand Central Parkway, where commercial vehicles were prohibited. He shifted up, pressing again on the accelerator, the shame of being late dulled by the exultation of finally reaching his objective.

The remaining police divisions in Manhattan—those which had not been stranded in the Bronx when the bridges blew—acted with commendable alacrity on Police Commissioner May's order to block all bridges and tunnels and allow nothing but emergency traffic to enter. On the other side, police in Queens and Brooklyn and Port Authority police from New Jersey set up barriers to warn motorists off. Only on the George Washington Bridge was there activity as police cars and ambulances sped along the lower level to the scene of the multiple accident. Slowing when they neared Havlicek's truck, they glanced nervously at it as urgent messages came over the airwaves about the booby-trapped vehicles left on the bridges and in the tunnels. Two ambulances and three Port Authority police cars arrived almost simultaneously at the accident scene. Men jumped out of the official vehicles and began opening the doors of smashed cars, helping out drivers and passengers, placing them into ambulances, which then sped westward to the Jersey end of the bridge. It took three minutes to clear all but one of the cars, the 1972 Buick LeSabre which had caused the pileup. Both sides of the car were smashed in, and the roof was crushed almost flat, making it impossible to free the unconscious occupants without heavier equipment. Shining in flashlights, the police could see all three occupants were bleeding profusely, the driver from a gash above his eyes; the two passengers, a boy and a girl, were lying across the back seat like broken dolls, eyes gazing blankly at the shattered roof.

"Reckon they're alive?" a police officer asked.

"Just about." The reply came from a black paramedic who

had seen worse cases in Vietnam, but not much worse. "If you look close, you can see their chests rising and falling. It's a near thing right now. Let's try to force those doors. Otherwise, we'll have corpses on our hands."

"What about that?" The policeman jerked a thumb in the direction of Havlicek's truck.

"Fuck it. We've got something else to worry about right now." The paramedic attacked the passenger door with a crowbar, trying to force it off its hinges, arms bulging, eyes popping from their sockets with the exertion. "Come on, man!" he snapped at the police officer, who was still staring in terror at the truck. "Don't stand there gaping! Lend some muscle!"

The policeman tore his eyes away from the truck and joined in the struggle against the door, trying to push his fear of being blown into the Hudson River to the back of his mind.

On the New York side of the George Washington Bridge, fifty police officers and firemen raced through the four high-rise apartment buildings, trying to evacuate them before it was too late. Many of the tenants were up, glued to their television sets as the drama of the night continued to unfold, not comprehending that their homes were a part of it. When police or firemen hammered on the doors to tell them about the truck below, the exodus was swift. Others, who were sleeping, took longer to warn, each minute becoming more precious as time passed.

In one apartment lay tragedy. Three men sat around a table, small polythene bags between them as they carefully doctored pure heroin with milk sugar for retail sale on the streets of the city. As the door threatened to break under a furious hammering from outside, one of the men reached down for the shotgun on the floor beside his chair.

"Who's there?" he yelled as his two colleagues scooped the heroin off the table and into a bag.

"Police officers. We're evacuating the building."

The words died as a shotgun blast ripped through the flimsy wood of the door, killing the officer who had knocked, wounding

255

two more standing beside him. The next instant a fusillade of bullets smashed into the apartment as four more police officers returned the fire before carrying on to the next apartment.

They would worry about filling out shooting reports later. If, indeed, there was a later.

Aktouri had the truck up to forty-five miles an hour when he spotted the hastily erected police barricades across the Queens entrance to the bridge. Ahead were two patrolmen, waving at him to stop. Pressing down harder on the pedal, he swerved the wheel at the last moment to catch one of the policemen with the fender, sending him spinning away into the darkness. Through the barricade, he hammered across the bridge, staying right for the lane which led down to Manhattan, getting ready to slow down as he approached the long curve where he would leave the truck.

Sergeant Calvin Coolidge Campbell had been with the NYPD for eleven years. Supervising the barricade on the ramp from the FDR Drive up to the bridge, he heard the truck coming from behind and turned around to look. So far the Triborough had been the only bridge to escape the terrorists' attention; he knew the truck he heard meant only one thing. He left the barricade and began to run toward the truck. Gasping for breath, he raced up the ramp in time to see both doors open and two men jump out. The driver turned around to lock his door. Then both men came loping down the ramp toward Campbell.

"Hey, you!" Campbell yelled. "You can't leave that truck there. Drive it off the bridge."

Neither Aktouri nor Nassim said anything. They slowed their pace and waited for Campbell to reach them, their arms raised, preparing to surrender.

"Did you hear what I said, motherfucker?" Campbell screamed. "Get that truck out of here!" He grabbed Aktouri by the shoulders, shaking him like a dog.

"Move it yourself," Aktouri said. "If you can."

"Give me the keys!"

Aktouri reached into his pocket and held the keys invitingly under Campbell's nose. As the police sergeant moved to grab them, Aktouri swung around and tossed the keys away into the night. They arced over the parapet of the ramp into the blackness below. "Now move it," he sneered.

Campbell pulled out his service revolver and clubbed Aktouri across the side of the head. Then he yanked Nassim's arms behind his back and marched the Palestinian toward the truck. "I'll show you what I'm going to do, you fucking little creep. I'm going to open that truck door, and you're going to drive it away." Campbell had started engines without keys before; this one would be no different.

"You cannot." Panic appeared in Nassim's voice. "The truck is wired to explode if you interfere with it." Nassim was terrified. He was facing the unexpected and did not know how to react. All he was supposed to do was surrender himself with Aktouri, like the others. This lunatic police officer was not supposed to be here, acting like this.

"We'll see what I can and can't do." Campbell could hear, coming up behind him, the running footsteps of the police officers who had been manning the barricade with him. He threw Nassim against the truck and then lined up his revolver on the door lock.

"No!" Nassim screamed, envisioning the fiery martyrdom which beckoned him. "For the love of Allah, no!"

The first shot slammed into Nassim's right shoulder as he threw himself in front of the door. Spinning around, he tried to keep his balance by clinging to the mirror on the door. He was only vaguely conscious of the second shot as it whistled inches from his head to shatter the door lock.

The force of the explosion was felt five miles away. Buildings shook and windows shattered as far downtown as Fifty-seventh Street. The entire Manhattan ramp of the Triborough Bridge disappeared, the area around the truck atomized, sections farther away ripped apart into huge chunks of steel and concrete, which bombarded the immediate vicinity like a heavy artillery salvo. When the dust cleared, the Triborough Bridge was an amputee, its main span leading from Queens still standing proudly across the East River, the Bronx ramps damaged, the Manhattan ramp totally obliterated.

In Fort Lee, Huckleby heard the blast clearly. He checked his control panel and saw that the final light which had flickered on moments earlier had gone out again. Mentally he struck the Triborough Bridge from his list of hostages. He picked up the telephone and called New York police headquarters again.

"One of your men has obviously not heeded instructions," he told Scrivens. "You can see for yourself what has happened. The Triborough Bridge has been destroyed."

Scrivens said nothing, and Huckleby guessed correctly that the mayor was too shocked to react.

"Remember that I control the destiny of the other bridges and the tunnels, Mr. Mayor. I have the only set of duplicate keys which will open the truck doors and deactivate the circuits. You will receive them only when I am satisfied that all my conditions have been met."

"Do you realize what you've done?" Scrivens finally managed to speak, amazed that he could keep his voice so level.

"Not me," Huckleby corrected him. "Someone else. By disobeying my explicit instructions. All blame for this rests on your head as the mayor of New York City. Whatever happens tonight is your fault. They will blame you and your administration if I choose right now to destroy the Lincoln Tunnel and bring millions of tons of water crashing through it. Think about that, Mr. Mayor. The choice is yours."

Scrivens began to lose control again. "We're doing all you asked," he blurted out. "Everything. Your men from the trucks are being taken to the Wall Street Heliport. So are the men and the girl we're holding for the subway bombings. We're doing it all."

"What about the television crew?"

"For Christ's sake, I'm only human! Give me a break!"

Scrivens clamped a hand over the mouthpiece as Denton passed him a piece of paper. On it were scribbled the financial costs of the bridges and tunnels when they were built. The mayor felt his stomach begin to rebel as he read. Triborough Bridge, completed in 1936 at a cost of more than $63 million, including land; Brooklyn Bridge, opened in 1883 at a cost of $25 million; Queensboro Bridge, finished in 1909, more than $20 million; $200 million spent on the George Washington Bridge. The figures made him shudder. Each bridge would cost at least ten times its original price to rebuild now, and the tunnels would be even more. He looked back at Denton, who was mouthing something at him.

"Keep him talking," Denton whispered.

"We're doing everything we can for you," Scrivens pleaded. "You have to be patient."

Huckleby was about to hang up when he noticed flickering red and white emergency lights on the lower level of the George Washington Bridge. He picked up the binoculars with one hand and scanned the span, trying to identify the vehicles. Were they trying to deactivate the trucks? Had the police realized something that neither he nor Stiehl had foreseen?

"What are those police cars doing on the George Washington Bridge?" he snapped at Scrivens. "Quick, answer me before I flick a switch."

"What police cars?" Scrivens turned to Denton. "What the hell's he talking about?"

"There's been a big accident there. Three kids are still trapped inside a wrecked car."

"Great." Scrivens relayed the information to Huckleby, not knowing whether to believe it himself.

"Get your vehicles off the bridge," Huckleby warned. "Otherwise, you will lose Manhattan. If you wish to speak to me anymore, do it on television." Hanging up quickly, he realized almost too late that he had been on the telephone far too long. At police headquarters Scrivens put down the receiver and looked hopefully at Denton.

"Too quick," the police inspector said. "They were getting close when he cut off."

"Any idea of the general area?"

"No. Another ten seconds, and they reckon they'd have had the exchange."

"But we know he's calling from some place where he can see what's happening on the George Washington Bridge," Scrivens said. "Surely we can pin something down on that."

"I'll get onto it," Denton volunteered. "In the meantime, we'd better get those guys off the bridge before that nut blows up the damned thing." As he picked up the telephone, someone passed him a message about the shootings in the high-rise apartments over the Cross Bronx Expressway. He looked at the note irritatedly before crumpling it into a ball and throwing it at a trash can; he needed a drug-related shooting right now as much as he needed a hole in the head.

Five minutes later Mayor Percy Scrivens appeared on television. His face was gray without the benefit of cosmetic application, and his eyes were begging from the screen.

"Whoever you are," he began, voice quaking, "I beg of you to let those ambulances and police cars finish their work on the George Washington Bridge. There has been a serious accident there. Three young people, all critically injured, are still trapped inside a car. If they are not rescued immediately, they will almost certainly die. Please telephone me and say it's all right for the paramedics to continue working."

Huckleby stormed across the Fort Lee apartment and turned down the volume of the television, furious that his orders to clear the bridge were being questioned. He dialed through to police headquarters and asked for Scrivens again, rage rising in his voice as he screamed at the mayor.

"I don't care about any goddamned accident! Just get those cops and vehicles off the bridge!" He slammed down the phone, hands shaking while he tried to remember where his pills were. Taking one, he waited for it to take effect, to ease the pressure in his chest. Five minutes passed before he could pick up the binoculars and focus on the bridge again.

* * *

Linda had seen enough. She turned off the television, left the room, and caught the elevator to the hotel lobby. At the desk she asked the receptionist for five dollars' worth of quarters. Then she walked into the street, looking for a phone booth.

How many people had died in the Triborough Bridge blast? she asked herself. The men driving the truck, probably, although that mattered little to her. Had there been more police casualties in the blast? What of people living nearby? How many more had died?

She found a phone booth and dialed the Fort Lee number. The operator cut in, telling her to deposit twenty-five cents for the first three minutes. Linda hoped three minutes would be enough; she did not want the operator coming back on the line while the conversation was in progress.

"Hello?" Her father's voice was breathless. The excitement of his dream coming true, she guessed.

"Daddy? It's Linda."

"Linda?" His voice was incredulous. "Why are you calling?"

"To ask you stop this madness."

"I can't stop it!" he yelled. "It's too late. Get off the phone. They'll trace the call from the hotel."

"I'm not at the hotel."

"Then go back there." Huckleby dragged the receiver over to the window, trying to see what was happening on the bridge.

"You said nobody would get hurt," Linda said. "People are being killed everywhere."

Huckleby ignored his daughter's voice as he stared down at the bridge through his binoculars.

"What about the Triborough Bridge? And those injured kids on the George Washington Bridge?"

"What injured kids? What are you talking about?"

"Those kids the mayor just spoke about on television."

"I'm looking at the bridge right now," Huckleby rasped. "It's empty except for my trucks. The mayor's lying. There's been no accident. He's trying to make me look like a bastard!"

"Why would he lie like that?" Linda asked.

"How should I know? Maybe he thinks I'll soften if there are some injured kids on the bridge. But I know better than the mayor. I can see what's going on, and there are no injured kids. Believe me, Linda, there's nothing there."

She gulped, unwilling to disbelieve her father. Was he really looking at the bridge? Could he really see nothing? "What about the cops who were killed?" she asked. "The two in the train that blew up, the ones up in the Bronx?"

"Do you believe that as well? It's propaganda, Linda. All of it."

"The Triborough Bridge is also propaganda?"

"They set it off on purpose. That's what I would have done. The mayor's in a war, and when you're in a war, you try to make the other guy look bad. Believe me, I know." There was a break in the conversation while Huckleby scanned the bridge again, waiting to see the ambulances and police cars begin to move. "Linda, you're not thinking of doing anything, are you? You'll hurt yourself and Stiehl if you do. You can't hurt me, and you can't stop me. Nobody can."

An interrupted buzzing sounded in Linda's ear. The three minutes were up. She looked at the remaining quarters in her hand, trying to decide if she should continue the call. What was the point? Her father hadn't listened to a damned word she'd said. She hung up and began to walk back to the hotel, distraught for failing and realistic enough to know that she could never have succeeded.

Had her father been telling the truth about the George Washington Bridge, that there were no injured kids there? She didn't know what to believe anymore.

With the assistance of a Port Authority police officer, the black paramedic had the driver's door of the Buick halfway off its hinges. He could reach in and offer comforting words to the three youngsters trapped inside, but it would take at least another ten minutes to rip the door clean off and remove the injured occupants.

"Hey, you guys!" a voice called from behind.

The paramedic and the police officer turned around, forgetting about the Buick for a moment. They saw a police sergeant standing by a car, radio mike in his hand.

"What is it?" the paramedic yelled back.

"We've got to pull out. All of us."

"What! Are you crazy, man? Move out when we've almost got them out of the car?"

"Mayor's orders."

"He's the mayor of New York!" screamed the medic. "I work out of New Jersey. Screw him." He turned back to the door to lean on the crowbar again, hearing metal rend.

"Those two trucks are gonna blow up right now if we don't hightail it out of here!" the sergeant yelled. "You wanna get killed as well? You wanna be a fucking hero, you go right ahead and be one, but we're pulling out."

The medic eased his pressure on the bar, wiping a white sleeve across his sweaty face. He'd been a hero once, in Vietnam, a Silver Star for crawling into the middle of a vicious firefight to assist two wounded soldiers, and two bullets in his side to prove it. Did he need to be a hero again?

Wearily he thrust the crowbar into the tear he had made in the side of the car, pushed one more time, and stood up. He walked back toward the police sergeant, quickening his pace as the police car started up and swung around. Poor bastards, he thought bitterly, looking back at the mangled Buick, then at the truck. Poor bastards. What a night of all nights to pick for a smash up.

Scrivens breathed an audible sigh of relief when he received information that the police cars and ambulances were being removed from the lower level of the George Washington Bridge. That was one battle over in his fight to save the city. Now he had to come up with a billion dollars in a hurry; otherwise, that lunatic would start flicking his switches.

"We've managed to locate Mr. Stonechap," Police Commis-

263

sioner May said to Scrivens as he came off the phone after hearing from the Port Authority police at the New Jersey end of the bridge.

"Who?"

"Stonechap," May repeated. "David Stonechap. President of the First National Bank of Manhattan."

"How did he sound?"

"Not too thrilled. Bank presidents don't like being called up in the middle of the night to be asked for the keys to the vault."

"I'll speak to him in a minute," Scrivens said. He turned to Denton. "What about those three kids trapped in the car on the bridge? Any identification on them yet?"

Denton held up a piece of paper. "I've got it here. Car's registered to a Joe Troiano, out in Astoria. His son's driving, a kid named Tony. Went over to Jersey with a couple of friends. Boy named Al Crochetti from Elmhurst and a girl from Astoria called Anita Carli." Denton lit a cigarette, begged minutes earlier from a patrolman. He thought he'd kicked the habit two years earlier, but tonight's tensions were excuse enough for anything. He drew deeply before continuing to speak; the action made him look ten years older, and Scrivens realized how the anxiety of the night was getting to all of them.

"I've got the girl's mother coming over here now. In a police car," Denton explained as he saw the query on Scrivens's face. "The barricade on the Queens-Midtown Tunnel will be lifted to let them through. She's going to make an appeal over television for those three kids."

"Just as long as that nut can't see what's happening over in Queens as well."

"My bet is he's located around Washington Heights, Riverdale, maybe even in Jersey at some place like Edgewater, Cliffside Park, or Fort Lee," Denton said. "Probably in a high rise where he can look out over the bridge and off to the side a bit, so he can see what's happening on the lower level. Even if we found the place—and that would be like looking for a needle in a haystack—there's nothing we could do. Before we got in there and took him out, he'd flick his switches and destroy everything."

"What's happening then?" The question came from May.

"Police units are collecting in the high-rise areas, wherever the tenants have got a good view of the bridge. They're not doing anything more than that at the moment. They dare not."

"Damned right," Scrivens said. He looked up as a police officer waved at him from a desk, holding a telephone receiver in the air. "What is it?"

"Mr. Stonechap's still holding, sir."

"Thanks." Scrivens took the telephone. "Mr. Stonechap, this is Mayor Percy Scrivens of New York City. We've got a problem here, and we need your help." He was spared the trouble of explaining all that had happened when the bank president assured him that he had been following the drama on television. "We need to remove a billion dollars from your bank, sir. In cash, by midday."

David Stonechap had heard a lot of requests in his business career, but this one, he had to admit, surpassed all the others. His bank had propped up Arab oil-producing countries in the days before they had started to siphon off enough of their own money; it had headed up multibank loans to Japanese and German businesses. Two of Stonechap's brothers had been governors of states, and his younger brother, Franklin, was now Secretary of State.

Stonechap was used to handling power, to being among those who handled it, squeezing and being squeezed in return. Solid, unflappable, somehow so involved in the larger issues of the world that the mundane events of life seemed to pass him by, Stonechap was at first tempted to turn down the request from Scrivens, dismiss the whole thing from his mind, and return to watching it from a safe distance. Nobody had ever asked him to open the vaults down at corporate headquarters. While an individual branch might be robbed now and then, nobody had ever taken money out of the main offices without the correct procedure.

"Mr. Mayor, as much as I appreciate your terrible dilemma, you have to realize that a request of the type you have made is not something we normally encounter in the banking community. I am responsible to my board of directors, my shareholders. It would be difficult, if not impossible, for me to authorize the removal of such an enormous sum without prior consultation."

"Listen, Mr. Stonechap. I'm not asking you to give us this money. It's a loan. We'll pay it back."

"Oh? I didn't realize that New York City had a Triple A rating these days as far as arranging loans was concerned," Stonechap observed acidly. "May I ask what the other banks have said to your request?"

"There are no other banks. They're not involved." Scrivens swung his gaze around the room; everyone seemed to be watching him, as if the fate of the entire borough of Manhattan rested firmly on his ability to make this call successful. "The terrorists want it all from your bank. It's simply a matter of convenience. Somehow they know you have at least forty billion dollars in cash and securities downtown, and it's close to the heliport."

Stonechap paused to think, wishing he had been on summer vacation when the call came through, in the South of France, where he would not have been bothered with this. "If First National came to the aid of the city, as I said, I would have to speak to a few members of my board. More important, I think what you are asking will require a federal guarantee of indemnity. In addition, I will have to consult with the various insurance companies, as well as the security company which installed the vaults and other equipment.

"And there is a final point." Scrivens groaned as he listened. "The legal liability the bank faces. And which I will face personally as a result of aiding these terrorists."

"What do you mean?" Scrivens asked. Christ, by the time this guy got through talking it would be midday, and they would be no closer to getting anything done.

"I mean the Treaty of Belgrade," Stonechap said coldly. "Surely you've heard of that."

"Yes," Scrivens muttered.

"I am sure you're aware that the United States signed that treaty, which specifically spells out that no nation which is a party to the treaty will do anything to assist international terrorists. I don't know how the State Department is going to react, or the rest of the world for that matter. And"—Stonechap enunciated carefully—"we are an international bank."

"Are you trying to tell me that you won't cooperate?" Scrivens asked incredulously.

"No, I am not. Given the correct circumstances, I believe we can approach this predicament positively. It will take several phone calls and a bit of time. Since time is one of the more crucial factors, I will say good night to you, Mr. Mayor, unless you have something to add. I'll get back to you as soon as I can inform you of the arrangements I have made. Is that all right with you?"

"Yes, yes, quite all right," Scrivens answered. There was little more he could say. What he could think was a different matter. As far as he was concerned, Stonechap was a first-rate son of a bitch. But then all bankers probably were. At least this time Scrivens had to deal with only one.

"Now what?" Denton asked when Scrivens had related the conversation with David Stonechap.

"From a bank president to a national President." Scrivens ordered one of the police officers to get through to the White House. "Looks as if our southern Baptist friend is going to get one last chance to make good his promise about never letting New York go under."

Denton grinned sourly. "I don't think his comments were made with this kind of situation in mind."

"We'll see," Scrivens said. "We'll see."

In a hastily convened meeting of the National Security Council, the President of the United States briefed members on the latest developments from New York. A fervently religious lawyer from North Carolina who had passed through the Tarheel State governorship on his climb to the White House, the President knew how vital it was to his reelection hopes that he be seen doing all he could to help the country's principal city; the principal city when it came to getting a Democrat into the White House. He had been elected only by the grace of New York's

Democratic bloc, edging his way in the final lap past the Republican incumbent, who had seemed set on repeating his tenure as President. Now the city would be watching carefully, seeing how the President lived up to his election promises of not casting New York City off like some tired old piece of clothing.

"Well, gentlemen, I do believe we have a difficult nut to crack." The chief executive played deliberately upon his strong southern accent, broadening it instead of trying to tone it down.

"I do appreciate your all getting here as fast as you could, and I do apologize for any inconvenience I may have caused." The last words were directed at Secretary of State Franklin Stonechap, brother of the president of the First National Bank of Manhattan. "When we signed at Belgrade, I don't believe any one of us ever thought that such a massive and dangerous situation as the one now developing in New York would ever occur. Assuming we are obligated to observe the treaty, then I would say we are going to have to refuse to do anything to help the city. That would be construed as giving in to the terrorists' demands. Can anyone at State give us some guidance on that part of the question?"

Franklin Stonechap had rushed to the meeting in an old pair of jeans and a sweat shirt, leaving his yacht, which was moored at Annapolis. He had developed a fairly good relationship with the President, despite the hard campaign they had waged against each other for the Democratic Party presidential nomination.

"I hate to be caught with my pants down—or my jeans in this case—but I'm afraid my people are still working on it." Franklin Stonechap tried to sound relaxed, feeling that was the best position to adopt in the face of crisis. "We haven't had much time on this one, as you can imagine. We are opening communication with the major signatories to alert them of the situation. Personally I think that given the information we're getting out of New York—taking it to be accurate—we have no option but to step in and help the city meet the terrorists' demands. There isn't much choice. Financially"—he tried not to sound as if he had the slightest intention of injecting humor into the discussion—"it's a bargain. I know I'd hate to have to pay for rebuilding all those bridges and tunnels. Neither the state nor the city could afford to foot the bill, so that means the money would have to come from Washington. I think you'd have a fight on your hands in Congress about getting any aid through, Mr. President. As far as what giving in would mean internationally . . ."

"Yes," the President prompted. "What would it mean?"

"I think our friends would stand by us. And our, well, let's say the countries which are not so friendly to us, they wouldn't support us no matter what we did."

"I say we call their bluff!" The Chairman of the Joint Chiefs of Staff had listened to the diplomats for too long. "Let them blow the bridges and tunnels. The Corps of Engineers can put up pontoon bridges across the Harlem, Hudson, and East rivers to take care of the most urgent needs while the bridges and tunnels are repaired. We can supply the city with a Red Ball Express type of operation. We have to honor that Belgrade Treaty, or we make a mockery of it, and nobody else will ever feel obliged to honor it."

Thick fair hair tumbled onto the President's forehead as he shook his head vehemently. "It would be cheaper for us to lend the city the money than have to repair all those bridges and tunnels, in addition to all the problems that would occur with those structures out."

"Whole bridges would not be destroyed," the Chairman of the Joint Chiefs argued. "Just where those trucks are. A lot of the blast's energy would be lost. And those apartment blocks on the George Washington, have they been cleared?

"Yes. But there would still be casualties. The buildings would come tumbling down like packs of cards. The cost would be in the tens of billions to repair everything. Franklin's right; at a billion dollars it's a bargain. We must help the city out, lend it the money, back up the First National Bank of Manhattan."

"And the terrorists' deadline is midday, right?" the Chairman asked, looking at his watch; it showed two-twenty. "We have another nine hours and forty minutes. Can everything be arranged by then?"

"Yes," Franklin Stonechap answered.

"And we're just going to let those thieving bastards get away with it, is that the idea? Americans are lying dead, and we are going to give these murderers money and a plane to leave in?"

"We're letting them get away with it," the President agreed, "for as long as it takes to find out where they have landed. Then we'll attempt to extradite them. Of course, we may run into a problem there since we can be pretty damned sure they won't go to a country which has signed the Belgrade Treaty."

The Chairman of the Joint Chiefs snorted derisively. "So you can kiss them and the money good-bye."

"I'm willing to take a chance on that," the President said. He had made up his mind. The federal government would guarantee the loan made to the city by the First National Bank of Manhattan. It was the only way he could see himself out of the predicament. And it was the only way he could see of assuring himself of the New York vote when the next election came rolling around. Domestic politics took precedence over foreign treaties.

At the Wall Street Heliport the scene was one of jubilation. Although still manacled and chained to one another, the subway bombers were not letting their restricted circumstances detract from their moment of triumph. They chatted excitedly in German, English, and Arabic, discussing how they had performed their individual tasks. When Frank Brady, Johnny Coughlin, and the two other Irishmen who had set the charges on the Harlem River bridges were brought up to join the captured terrorists, a great roar of welcome greeted them.

Standing among a group of heavily armed police officers, Babs O'Neill knew that she had reached the pinnacle of her career. Whatever happened after tonight would be only an anticlimax. Never again would she be in on the ground floor of such earth-shattering events, predicting them in the face of ridicule, covering them as they came true. Babs could sense the animosity of the police officers and wondered how much more pressure would be needed for them to start using brute force to intimidate the prisoners. She admired the police for their discipline and decided to include a piece about it when the drama was over and the terrorists were safely aloft in their commandeered aircraft. She would praise the New York Police Department as it had never been praised before. And Inspector Eric Denton, wherever he was now, would be the man she lauded most.

Rosen pushed his way through the group of police officers and stood next to Babs. "Scrivens has just gone off the air," he whispered. "Kohn wants another report from us."

She picked up the thread of the story immediately, knowing that MetroCity was the only network covering the events. She had been as surprised as she had been pleased when the mystery man controlling the operation had selected her to provide sole coverage of the transfer to Kennedy Airport. MetroCity and New York were no longer her only stage. Now the whole country, the entire world were watching her. She walked quickly to the mark Rosen had made for her, raised the microphone to her mouth, and began speaking.

"The number of surrendered terrorists here at the Wall Street Heliport in lower Manhattan has grown to thirty-five with the arrival of the four men responsible for placing the charges to destroy the Harlem River bridges," she began. In front of her, Rosen panned the camera from one end of the line to the other, catching clenched fists raised in gestures of triumph, chains and manacles notwithstanding.

"According to the orders of the man masterminding this operation, twenty-three more men are still to arrive, bringing the total to fifty-eight, although there is some doubt about the fate of the men on the Triborough Bridge. Tonight New York was truly invaded, and we are powerless to do anything about it other than pay up and watch these terrorists fly away in triumph from Kennedy Airport at midday. I have just heard from the mayor's office that the President of the United States has agreed to guarantee whatever amount of money is carried away today. The money will undoubtedly be arriving here as soon as arrangements have been made for its transfer." She wished there had

271

been more time to prepare the story, polish it up, make it more professional. But did it really matter? Hers was the only game in town.

"Meanwhile, overseas reaction up till now has been mixed. The Soviet Union, we understand, has called the decision to give in to the terrorists a serious violation of the Belgrade Treaty and has questioned the current administration's resolve to keep its word on other important issues. At the same time there has been no condemnation of the terrorist act itself.

"In London the British government has labeled the crisis a grave dilemma for the United States which apparently cannot be solved without injury no matter what choice is made. Consequently the British government is refusing further comment on American actions but officially condemns the actions of these international brigands." Babs paused for as long as it took to draw breath, then carried right on.

"The French, reportedly, have made no comment yet. But we are told that the West German government is meeting in an emergency session to determine what assistance, if any, can be offered at this stage."

Three more men appeared, shepherded by police officers, to join the line of terrorists. Taking the microphone with her, Babs intercepted the party. "Can I have your names and what part you're playing in this drama?"

The three men looked at each other, grinning. "I am Mahmoud Assar," one replied, "the captain of the aircraft that will fly us out of here. This is my first officer, Hassan Basri, and my second officer, Abdul Wasim"

Rosen caught the small group in his viewfinder, holding the picture until Babs had finished. "That just leaves us with the truck drivers," she continued. "Then we will have the whole army up here." She stopped as another ragged cheer split the air. Patrick Kerrigan appeared, his face splitting into a wide smile at the reception. He walked toward Brady and Coughlin, pulling two patrolmen with him. Babs moved in closer with the microphone, looking for color, a conversation in English between

272

the terrorists; behind, she could sense Rosen closing in with the camera.

"Where's Danny?" Brady asked. Kerrigan's smile became even broader. "Sleeping like a little baby, he was, when I left him."

"Where?"

"In the Lincoln Tunnel. Locked in the truck."

"You killed him?"

"No. He'll do that favor for himself if he tries to get out. He had it coming, Frank. If anyone ever had it coming, it was that little bastard."

"Christ!" Brady protested. "The police will get him when this is all over. They'll crucify him."

"Good. It couldn't happen to a nicer bloke." Kerrigan lifted his hands so that one of the police officers could join him to the main chain.

Babs turned away, facing Rosen again. "As you may have heard from that conversation, some dissension has apparently broken out within the terrorist ranks. One man has been locked in the cab of the truck in the Lincoln Tunnel. If he tries to escape, he will break the electrical circuit and set off the explosives, killing himself and wrecking the tunnel. It appears that some of the planning which has gone into this incredible operation might be coming undone because of the one great unpredictable factor. Human nature. This is Babs O'Neill at the Wall Street Heliport in lower Manhattan switching you back to our main studio for other developments."

Huckleby listened to the report from the heliport dispassionately. So another man was down, a victim of a vendetta apparently, locked in the Lincoln Tunnel truck, unable to get out and join the others because he knew he would set off the booby-trap mechanism. Left there for the police and the city to take revenge on when everything was over.

The picture faded from the screen while a disembodied voice announced a return to police headquarters, where another development was taking place. Interested, Huckleby turned from the picture window to concentrate on the television. When the picture formed again, he was looking at a middle-aged woman, her face awash with tears as she beseeched the camera.

"Please, I, Lucia Carli, beg of you, whoever you are, to let my daughter, Anita, be rescued before she dies. She is my only child, all I have in this world since my husband died. Are you that heartless that you would let an innocent child die? Please, on my knees I am begging you. Let my daughter be rescued."

Huckleby's mind went totally blank for an instant. Then a terrible rage began to consume him, a blinding white fire that the mayor should try to soften his stance with a picture of this pathetic woman, crying on television, pleading about her child. The girl was a casualty. All battles had casualties. Huckleby was prepared to take them; that's what had made him such an effective commander. Why should he give a damn about the girl anyway? Nobody had cared about his wife when the police had opened fire on the bank robbers; they'd just blazed away, and to hell with anyone standing in the line of fire. He picked up the phone and dialed through to police headquarters once more, his eyes never leaving the crying woman.

"Scrivens! Get that woman off the screen this minute, or I'll flick every switch right now. Do you hear me?" He saw the woman's face disappear as the camera at police headquarters swung around until it found and focused upon Scrivens, standing by a desk, phone in hand.

"I don't give a damn about that girl!" Huckleby screamed, his voice booming back at him from the television set as the call was relayed live. "Why should I care? Your city killed my wife. Now your city can let this girl die as well. You're to blame, Scrivens! Do you understand me? You're to blame for everything that happens tonight! Not me, Scrivens. You!"

18

IN THE FURNISHED apartment in Howard Beach, Peter Stiehl sat bolt upright in his chair by the open window as Huckleby's voice echoed from the television set. He was unable to believe what he had heard, as if he had dreamed it. But he was not dreaming now, and Harlan Stone Huckleby was not the dream he normally had; that was burning buildings, people running, chasing, not a madman on television. He got up and telephoned the apartment in Fort Lee, steeling himself for a confrontation with the man whose fingers were on the switches.

"Huckleby! Have you gone bloody crazy?"

The hysteria which the retired general had displayed during the televised conversation with the mayor was still evident in his voice. "I'm not the crazy one!" he shouted back at Stiehl. "They are! Scrivens! All of them! Crazy to think I'd care about some injured kid!"

Stiehl took a deep breath. Of all the crises he had ever faced, this was the toughest. "You listen to me," he said slowly, spacing out each word, hoping Huckleby would be calmed by his voice.

"And you listen damned good. Otherwise, I'll blow your cover right now."

"What do you mean?" Huckleby's words were quieter. Stiehl was having the effect he wanted.

"Just listen, and don't interrupt. I came into this thing for two reasons. One, for the money. Two, there would be no indiscriminate killing. That's the way it's going to remain. Nobody from the city was to be killed intentionally or left to die intentionally. What happened at the Triborough Bridge was an accident. Something went wrong somewhere, though God knows what. The same as those people hurt in the Bronx rioting and the two cops from the bomb squad who tried to defuse that bomb on the train. But I will not allow you to leave those kids on the bridge to die. If I don't hear on television within the next five minutes that you've called Scrivens back and allowed him to send out the ambulances again, I'll blow the whistle on you. Do you understand that?"

"How do you know it's not a plot to defuse those bombs? They tried it with the train. Maybe they want to try it here."

"Nobody in his right mind would risk tampering with the trucks," Stiehl answered. "Not after what happened at the Triborough Bridge."

Huckleby began to scream again, and Stiehl feared he had lost him. "You're not here! How do you know what the hell they're planning to do on that bridge? I can see what's going on. I know they're up to something."

"Huckleby." Stiehl's voice became ominously quiet. "You've made two mistakes already tonight. The first was telling Scrivens that you could see what was happening on the bridge because you pinpointed your approximate position for him. Your second mistake was coming out with that shit about the city killing your wife."

"What do you know about my wife?" Huckleby cut in, his voice going quieter. "Who told you anything about my wife?"

"Linda told me. That was why you picked New York to give this demonstration to the government. I don't give a damn about that. All I'm concerned with is that you've given the man clues to work on. Don't make a third mistake. If I don't hear on television that those ambulances are back in position on the George Washington Bridge, rescuing those kids, I'm cutting out of here. Your name and location will go straight to the police, and"—here comes the crunch, thought Stiehl; this will either settle him or blow what sanity he's got left right through the top of his skull—"Linda will be implicated in it right up to her lovely neck."

Huckleby faltered. Nobody had ever spoken to him like this before either during his military career or as president of Howson Chemicals. Stiehl's tone shocked Huckleby enough to think carefully about what the South African had said. Linda; he couldn't let her get mixed up in this. It had always been the plan to keep her out of it. Would Stiehl drag her into it even if it meant implicating himself? How far was the South African prepared to go? "All right," Huckleby said at last. He had to agree. He still needed the South African, just as he had needed him all along. "I'll call Scrivens and tell him he can send the ambulances back. But ambulances only. No police cars."

"That's fine by me. Just make sure you do it. I'll be watching carefully."

Huckleby waited a minute, trying to clear his head. The conversation with Stiehl, violent one moment, calm the next, had started the pain again. He could not remember where he had put the pills. He tried to control his breathing, waiting while the tightness subsided. Then he dialed through to police headquarters. "Scrivens? I've changed my mind. You can send the ambulances back onto the bridge. But ambulances only, nothing else."

"Sure," Scrivens said. More than ever he was convinced he was dealing with a madman, a totally irrational human being who had somehow got his head together for as long as it took to conceive the hijack plan and put it into operation. "Ambulances only."

The picture of Scrivens disappeared from the screen. In its place was the tear-streaked face of the woman Huckleby had

277

seen before. He moved uncomfortably as her liquid brown eyes sought him out.

"Thank you, mister. A mother thanks you for your mercy."

"Here we go again," the black paramedic sang out as the ambulance swung onto the bridge. "Hope that crazy son of a bitch hasn't got itchy fingers, wherever the hell he is."

The lead ambulance roared past Havlicek's truck with barely a second glance from the medics occupying it and screeched to a halt by the mangled LeSabre. The black paramedic picked up the crowbar he had dropped when the evacuation of the bridge was ordered and began tearing away at the Buick's door again, widening the hole he had made, working with a frenetic fever. With a final, almighty thrust, he ripped off the last hinge. The door dropped onto the roadway, a torn edge of metal catching him across the shin. He took no notice of the blood which stained his white trousers or of the six-inch gash from which it had sprung. He gritted his teeth to blot out the pain and carried on with his work. He could get a tetanus shot and stitches later. Right now he had to get the occupants of the car to safety. He leaned in and gently pulled at the driver, working with another medic to put him on a stretcher. Then the boy in the back seat, finally the girl, crooning to her as he set her down on another stretcher.

"Gonna be all right, baby. Everything's gonna be all right." He wheeled the stretcher back to the waiting ambulance, lifted it in, and jumped into the back, slamming the doors.

"Let's get the hell out of this place!" he shouted at the driver, clapping his hands loudly.

"Look at your bloody leg!" one of the medics screamed as the ambulance began to move toward the New Jersey shore, siren and lights working unnecessarily to clear the already empty bridge.

The black paramedic glanced down and felt his stomach contract as he surveyed the damage to his shin. Then he got hold of himself, remembering Vietnam. "I've seen plenty worse. Now give that kid some oxygen. I can get fixed up later on."

278

For the fifth time in as many minutes Inspector Denton played back the recording of Huckleby's conversation with Mayor Scrivens when the evacuation of vehicles from the bridge had been ordered, following the mother's televised appeal. The words "your city killed my wife" intrigued Denton. He was certain that a clue to the mystery man's identity was contained in them. And a clue to the man's motive for this tremendous strike against the city. Revenge. Simple revenge. But for what? Because the city had killed his wife? Had the woman been killed by a cop? Run over by a bus? Had she been a crook killed in the progress of a crime? Denton played the tape one more time, then called Police Commissioner May over to listen.

"What do you make of it?" Denton asked.

"Vengeance, pure and simple. For something that happened here or something this guy thinks happened."

"Sounds pretty real to me," Denton commented. "We somehow killed his wife. I figure it's a cop who shot and killed someone."

"Could be," May agreed halfheartedly. "At least, we've got a name for him now."

"Oh, how come?" Denton sounded surprised.

"Not his real name. Just a working title. The Avenger."

"Great, just great." Denton chuckled, surprised that he could find anything to laugh about under the circumstances. "I'll just go check if he's listed in the Yellow Pages."

"No. Not the Yellow Pages," May said. "Why don't you try getting together a search team and going through files? Any case where a married woman was killed. Pull the files, and see what we come up with."

Denton grimaced at the mountain of work involved. "By the time we do that our Avenger might have identified himself for us."

"And then again, he might not. Get some men onto it right away. Cops, clerks, anyone. Tell them what to look for."

"Okay," Denton said. "Maybe we'll get lucky." He did not really think so, not when the idea came from a civilian appointee who was trying to do detective work. Nevertheless, he got onto the telephone and put the search into operation.

Illuminating the beautifully manicured lawn of David Stonechap's home in Franklin Lakes, New Jersey, the police helicopter's searchlight picked out the lone figure waiting there. As the chopper touched down, Stonechap sprinted forward, head bowed against the miniature cyclone blown up by the whirling blades. Seconds later, with Stonechap occupying the copilot's seat, the craft soared skyward, heading east toward New York.

"You realize there's nothing I can do until the time locks open," Stonechap told Scrivens when he arrived at police headquarters. There was a way around the locks, but Stonechap was not prepared to call in the security agency just yet.

"What time will that be?"

"Eight-thirty. Another four hours from now."

"Let's see what the lunatic says to that." He took the television microphone, waiting patiently for his cue as he faced the camera. "I have with me Mr. David Stonechap, president of the First National Bank of Manhattan. Mr. Stonechap has assured me that the bank's main vault will be opened, but it will be impossible until the time locks open at eight-thirty." He hoped the man was listening, was receptive, and would not fly into a rage, as he had done when the trapped girl's mother had appeared.

"In any event," the mayor continued, "it will take at least till then to organize everything. Mr. Stonechap has questioned your schedule, by the way. Even if the money starts to move at eight-thirty, he is certain it will be impossible to transfer such a large sum in such a short time. It may take longer. But we are carrying out your demands as quickly as possible."

That last statement isn't strictly true, Scrivens thought. Stonechap had said it would take less than an hour to get things organized, but just to make any delays creditable, he should state publicly that there was a time-lock delay. Staff would enter the vault as soon as they had set up a system to move the money smoothly. At least they had a head start on the work, Stonechap had explained. More than $150 million in old bills with serial numbers already recorded had been stored in the bank, awaiting transfer to Washington for burning. Additionally, there was $200 million in freshly printed bills in the vault awaiting distribution to banks in New York and New England.

"There's another point in our favor," Stonechap had told Scrivens. "Very few people have ever seen one billion dollars in one place. I am certain these people you're dealing with are not among the select few. Nor are they likely to stop and count. So while we deliver as much as time allows, I don't think it will be nearly one billion dollars. I wouldn't worry, though. They'll be happy enough to see all those bags that we use for just a quarter of a billion or so."

Scrivens pondered all these points as he stood in front of the camera, wondering what to say next. Off to one side, and out of sight of the camera's eye, Denton whispered, "Get his approval of the loading schedule."

Scrivens nodded. To viewers it looked as if the mayor's nerves were playing up, the tension of the endless night finally getting the better of him. "I understand you are wary of telephoning me at police headquarters," he began, "because of the possibility that we will trace your call and identify your location. We will not do this because we believe you when you say you can set off all the bombs on the bridges and in the tunnels before we could stop you." Anything to keep this madman calm. "Let's play it this way. If you agree to Mr. Stonechap's proposal about the money, that it cannot be collected until after the time locks have sprung open, make your agreement known by not telephoning. Telephone only if you disagree. Then we will try to work out a new solution. If I do not"—he wiped a hand across his brow, sweaty from the heat of the television lighting—"hear from you within five minutes, I will assume that you agree to the proposal." The red light on the camera faded, and Scrivens turned away. On a television set in the corner of the room, he could see that MetroCity had switched back to Babs O'Neill at the Wall Street Heliport. She was talking to one of the Germans, a young woman, asking her what they hoped to achieve with all the money. Scrivens wondered which way MetroCity would swing during the next mayoral election, especially after the way he had claimed its top newsperson was a liar. It was too far away, he decided. He shouldn't start worrying about his reelection prospects for at least another couple of years.

Her father had lied. Linda was certain of it. Lied about everything, the injured kids on the George Washington Bridge, the deaths and devastation everywhere. But far worse than the lies—and unforgivable in Linda's eyes—had been her father's screaming rejection of the crying mother's plea for mercy. He had changed his mind moments later, but Linda was certain that Stiehl was behind the about-face; a telephoned threat, enough to make Huckleby do what the South African wanted.

Linda began to seriously wonder if her father would keep his word to the mayor to turn himself in with the duplicate truck keys once his army had escaped. Or would he decide to go out in one momentous finale, blowing up every truck and severing all of Manhattan's umbilical cords, destroying more lives, making his revenge on the city more important in his own eyes than the lesson he was giving the government? She knew he was a dying man anyway and had resigned herself to the fact. Not that Huckleby had ever told her anything. His physician had shared the confidence with her mother, feeling she had the right to know. Both Linda and her mother had never let Huckleby know that they were aware of his condition. They had let him continue to feel he was keeping the trouble to himself, playing up to his ego.

Now it was different. His heart condition meant everything. Living on borrowed time, a physician's expertise, and his own company's pharmaceutical knowledge—what could he lose if he decided to go out in a fiery hell of his own making?

19

BY NINE in the morning the lead vehicles carrying ransom money from the First National Bank of Manhattan arrived at the heliport. Heading the convoy was a police truck with four heavily armed officers riding guard, flanked by two police cars. Another truck, flanked by motorcycle cops, brought up the rear. The lead vehicle came to a halt and was surrounded immediately by more police officers. They were taking no chances in case of a robbery attempt. A money shipment of this size publicized on television and radio when half the force was stuck in the South Bronx was an inviting situation.

Denton and May were waiting under a gray sky that was daubed here and there with solemn black clouds; the humidity was already reaching levels of discomfort. Canvas satchels and paper carrier bags full of money moved past the two men into the belly of a helicopter. They watched in numbed fascination as the seemingly never-ending human chain of blue uniforms passed the money, a swift reciprocating action like the engine of a car, connecting rods and pistons, gears, and shafts, all marrying together to form one slick mobile unit.

"How much do you reckon we've got so far?" Denton asked.

"God only knows," May was honest enough to answer. "But it's a damned sight more than you or I are going to pick up when we retire. If," he added meaningfully, "we ever live to retire."

Denton's eyes went dreamy for a moment. May was uncertain whether the police inspector was thinking or just plain tired. "There's just one thing I want to do before I call it quits," Denton said. "Get the bastard who organized last night's little caper, pin him to a cross, and bend the nails over."

May chuckled humorlessly, his stomach bobbing up and down inside his shirt. "You, me, and twenty million others. But I don't think our Avenger is going to be quite so accommodating."

Another vehicle began to unload its cargo. Denton and May stopped talking as they watched the new procession take shape. Bags of money were passed into the open side of the helicopter until it could take no more. The door sighed closed. Amid a cheer from the gathered terrorists, the helicopter lifted up, heading for Kennedy Airport.

On the ground, Frank Brady darted forward to inspect one of the satchels, to find out if the money inside was genuine. The chain through his manacled arms pulled him back sharply. He glared angrily at the closest police officer, who pretended not to notice.

A clattering overhead relieved the attention on the constantly growing pile of money. All eyes lifted as a second helicopter hovered steadily at one hundred feet above the landing zone. As it began to descend, another triumphant cheer poured from the throats of the manacled terrorists.

Babs O'Neill was talking into a microphone, describing each new event as it happened without really knowing what she was saying. She was too caught up in the drama that was unfolding in front of her eyes; her professionalism had been swept away by the excited pounding in her stomach. She was no longer a journalist. She was a part of what was happening, a character on history's stage. So, too, was Rosen. Plugged into the MetroCity communications network and being patched across the country, if not the world, his movements were automatic, the lens of the camera following the descriptions given by Babs. Occasionally he would take his concentration off a subject—the gleam of triumph in a terrorist's eyes, or the sweat on a police officer's face as he struggled with the cases full of money—and glance at Babs. There was a serenity about her, Rosen decided, as if she had found a kind of peace. Or was it the indisputable knowledge that this day comprised the peak of her career, of both their careers? And everything from here on in would be only an anticlimax?

Huckleby lowered the field glasses from the George Washington Bridge the moment he recognized Mayor Scrivens's voice coming from the television set. He turned around to watch the black mayor's face fill the screen. Scrivens needed a shave; his shirt collar was undone and grimy, and the tie knot was dragged halfway down his chest.

"Whoever you are, wherever you are, your aircraft is ready." The words were spoken softly, without emotion, a sign of defeat, ultimate shame at giving in to the last of the ransom demands. "As you specified, it is a wide-bodied plane, a Boeing seven-forty-seven, fully fueled, and waiting for you at Kennedy Airport. Kennedy and LaGuardia airports have both been closed to all traffic to allow your men free access to the sky. There will be no interference with the passage of your men to the airport or to the aircraft itself once it is airborne."

Huckleby listened approvingly, moving back to the picture window and sweeping the Hudson with the field glasses. He could see Havlicek's truck at the far end of the lower span, next to the support towers. Herzlein's ten-tonner, underneath the bridge apartments, was out of sight.

Again the mayor's voice penetrated the room, gripping Huckleby's attention. "As we do not have a name for you, not yet anyway, we have given you one of our own. You are listed in police and federal files as the Avenger since you obviously think you are avenging yourself on New York City for some imagined wrong. I tell you this now, and listen carefully. No matter where you disappear to after this is all over, no matter what hole you crawl into, we will hunt you down. Your file will remain open under the name of the Avenger for as long as it takes to bring you to justice. For murder. For extortion. For as many counts as possible after this night's infamy."

Standing by the picture window, Huckleby shook his head angrily. He was not an avenger; why couldn't they see that? He was a teacher, giving the United States a lesson before it was too late. The damage to property, the deaths didn't mean a damned thing—they all were justifiable. If Scrivens couldn't see it, posterity would. When the Soviets tried to invade and were repelled by superior American forces, the country would thank Huckleby for what he had done. Americans would be grateful to him for showing them the way.

God damn that Scrivens! "I am not the Avenger!" Huckleby screamed at the television, tears springing to his eyes.

"I am a patriot!"

News of the aircraft's readiness was reason for another sustained bout of cheering at the Wall Street Heliport. Excitedly Brady turned to Coughlin and Kerrigan, the manacles and chains which joined them totally meaningless. Even the predicament McGrath found himself in, alone in the Lincoln Tunnel, unable to escape, meant nothing. Maybe Kerrigan had even been right. There had been nothing but bad blood between the two men. If he had to choose, Brady would opt for Kerrigan any time, for his fighting spirit, for his guts. McGrath was a thinker—you could find them anywhere. A man of action like Kerrigan was rarer.

"Got your bathing suit?" Brady asked Coughlin. "We'll be needing them soon. And suntan lotion where we're going."

Coughlin laughed loudly, his merriment a mirror of what was taking place around him. "Think we'll go down well in Saudi Arabia or one of these other wog countries? Might even go into the oil business ourselves, open up a few wells."

286

"Your ones would gush Guinness," Kerrigan gibed.

"Could always go to work with our Palestinian friends over there," Brady observed, nodding his head in the direction of Hashim Nissouri, who was talking earnestly with the three Syrian pilots.

"Fuck that for a laugh," Kerrigan said. "I'd just as soon those wog bastards never got on the plane. Same goes for the krauts. We're the only ones here with any class; the rest are a bunch of scum."

Amid the scenes of jubilation, not one of them gave a single thought to the man with the tinted glasses whom they knew as Peter Adcock or to the organization he purported to represent, the organization which had made the entire operation possible.

Mayor Percy Scrivens pulled a white handkerchief out of his pocket and mopped his sweaty forehead as he read the latest police report. The riot situation in the South Bronx had been brought completely under control; other small pockets of rioting and looting had also been suppressed. Additionally, Con Edison technicians had worked like Trojans to repair the damage caused by Stiehl's mercenaries, restoring partial power to the borough. All that was left to do now was pick up the pieces and try to apportion blame. Perhaps on the people who had rioted or on the system which had taught them how to riot. Right now Scrivens did not give a damn where the blame belonged. The headache in the Bronx was over, and it did not matter whether it had been a genuine migraine or just a hangover; he had found a cure for it. Now he could concentrate more fully on the main event, the transportation of the money and terrorists to Kennedy Airport and the release of Manhattan from its ring of terror.

He indulged in a moment of self-pity as he reviewed the situation. He knew exactly where the blame for the whole mess would fall. Where it could only fall—right onto his own shoulders. Because he was black. The bigots would have a field day. Just as they would if he were Puerto Rican, Catholic, or Jewish. He looked around the room at police headquarters, where until recently the captured terrorists had been held. Denton and Police Commissioner May were at the heliport. There was a dearth of familiar faces. As his gaze settled for an instant on the television screen, where Jerry Rosen's camerawork put four Germans on view, a police lieutenant approached.

"Just got this in, Mr. Mayor." He handed Scrivens a sheet of yellow lined paper. Scrivens read it quickly. The hastily assembled search team had come up with eleven immediate possibilities for the Avenger's identity. All were men whose wives had been killed either as a direct result of police activity or through police mishandling of a situation. They ranged from a cabdriver to a bar owner, from a chemicals company president to an unemployed longshoreman. Scrivens shook his head sadly. Some of the men had cause to hate the city, there was no doubt about that, but where could any of them have come up with an army like the one which had invaded Manhattan?

"Get ahold of Police Commissioner May for me," he told the lieutenant. "Or Inspector Denton. Either one. They're at the Wall Street Heliport."

"Right away, sir." The lieutenant walked to the nearest telephone. As soon as he had made the connection, he waved to Scrivens.

"The commissioner?"

"No, sir. It's Inspector Denton."

Scrivens took the phone. "Denton? It's Mayor Scrivens. How much money has been flown out so far?"

"About seventy-five million, they tell me." Denton's voice sounded a million miles away to Scrivens, as if the police officer were holding the mouthpiece away from his lips.

"Have you seen the list of suspects your search team turned up?"

"Yes." Denton's voice became clearer. "They just radioed the names over here."

"Anyone there who strikes you as being a quick pickoff?"

"No," Denton answered. "All we can do is check if each person on the list is at home. There's nobody at work today; they can't get into the city. Except for those who don't have their place of business in Manhattan."

"Are you coming back here at all?" Scrivens asked.

` "What do you want me to do?" Denton suddenly felt sorry for Scrivens and guessed correctly what was going through the mayor's mind. City's first black mayor, and he gets hit with a pile of shit like this. Poor bastard's probably going out of his mind looking for friends.

"Where will you work best from?" Scrivens asked. "Over at the heliport or back here at Police Plaza?"

Denton laughed dryly. "Where would I work best from? With this little lot, I'd say from a missile launcher somewhere in the middle of the Atlantic Ocean, just waiting for these sons of bitches to pass overhead. Tell you what, I'll just check that all the suspects' homes are being hit; then I'll be on over. The commissioner's staying here. I'll pick up everything at headquarters."

Denton explained to May that he was returning to Police Plaza. As the car taking him from the heliport moved off, more trucks passed, loaded with money from the First National Bank of Manhattan. Looking at the convoy, Denton wondered where the terrorists were going to spend their money. And what they were going to spend it on.

After regaining consciousness in the cab of the truck in the Lincoln Tunnel, McGrath had sat perfectly still for hours, scared that even the slightest movement would set off the massive bomb. There was no radio inside the cab; he had no idea what was happening. Only that nobody had been down the tunnel since he had recovered from Kerrigan's blow.

The tunnel was as he had always imagined the grave to be—quiet, eerie, the ghosts of traffic which had swished through over the years coming back to haunt him.

He had toyed with the idea of opening a window and escaping that way. He knew it was useless. Adcock, the man they were working for, had seen to that. To ensure that police would be unable to smash their way into the vehicles, he had installed unbreakable plastic windows and linked their mechanism into the booby-trap circuit. Once the doors had been locked, the windows could not be opened without triggering a detonation.

The police would eventually come for him. They would have the duplicate keys once the others had flown away with the money. They would take him out. Charge him with everything, make him the scapegoat for the entire operation. He'd be a martyr when he didn't want to be one. And that pig Kerrigan would be laughing himself sick.

Would the police kill him out of hand? Or would they save him for a show trial, trying to use him to go after the others? Maybe he'd give them information on Kerrigan, where he could be found if he ever went back to Belfast, all his haunts. But nothing else. He'd tell them nothing about the others, Brady, Coughlin, and the rest. Why not? he thought suddenly. None of them probably gives a damn about me. They'll accept whatever lies that oaf Kerrigan tells them and let it go at that. McGrath's hands clenched into rigid fists as he thought about Kerrigan. The bastard, the bloodthirsty gorilla. He should never have got into the truck with him; he should have anticipated something like this happening.

He closed his eyes behind his glasses and tried to think. He'd never been inside any kind of jail, not even a stinking British prison. But he had heard the stories. Tales of the treatment handed out by British guards to Irish patriots. Would the American jails be any different? They might even hand him over to the British! No, he calmed himself, of course, they wouldn't. His crime had been committed in the United States, in New York. They'd make him serve his time there. Or maybe New York would reinstate the death penalty for this. The possibilities conjured up by that thought made him shudder uncontrollably. Not swinging on the end of a rope, but convulsing like an epileptic in the electric chair, muscles taut as voltage flowed through him. That's what they did in the United States. That and the gas chamber. Which would it be?

* * *

290

Denton had forgotten all about the two years he had not smoked. He lit another cigarette and flicked the spent match through the open window of the police car taking him back to Police Plaza. He was thinking hard, not wasting the short journey in idleness. Did any of the names his search team had found stand out? Had he reason to suspect that one of the eleven people pinpointed in the list was the mastermind behind the operation, the Avenger, as he had become in Denton's mind? Even a plain, old-fashioned gut reaction would have been welcome, something which selected one of the group as a prime suspect. Or threw them all out as improbables.

He cast his mind back to the beginning of the operation. The riot in the South Bronx, following the blackout. No, that wasn't it. Farther back than that. To Baroudi's body being washed up? No again. Babs O'Neill's revelation about the possibility of a combined terrorist attack against the city, a piece of sheer sensationalism which had come alarmingly true? Nothing there. Farther still, to where it had all started. To death of a man named Günther Werner in strange circumstances, running half-naked through the Times Square area early in the morning, only hours after arriving in the country. There was something about Werner's death that nagged at Denton. But for the life of him, he could not persuade it to surface in his confused mind.

One telephone among many rang at police headquarters. A police sergeant took the call and passed it immediately to Mayor Scrivens.

"What is happening with the money?" a voice demanded. Scrivens recognized the Avenger. "How much has been delivered so far?"

"You're watching television, same as everybody else," Scrivens retorted, wanting to keep the man on the line in the hope the telephone people would eventually be able to trace the call.

"Don't get smart with me!" the voice screamed. "I can blow you up. I can destroy you in seconds. How much has been delivered?"

Scrivens fixed his eyes to the television set. He saw Babs

O'Neill's face, followed an instant later by a shot of bags being loaded onto a Sikorsky Skycrane. "About a hundred million's been delivered so far. One load's already gone to Kennedy to be transferred to your aircraft."

"I want some of my men to go with the next load," Huckleby said. "To guard the money."

"They'll go in chains with a police escort," Scrivens replied.

"No tricks."

"No tricks," Scrivens promised.

"Send that camera crew as well. The one covering it for MetroCity."

"Maybe they'd like a break," Scrivens said; he knew he would. "They've put in a long shift." He caught the eye of a detective talking into another phone, trying to get the call traced; the man shook his head.

"I've also put in a long shift." Huckleby's voice began to rise again. "They can work just as well as I can. I want to see what is happening out at Kennedy. I want to see that you're not trying to trick me. You know what would happen if you tried to trick me, don't you?"

"Yes," Scrivens said, his voice sagging with fatigue. "I know what would happen. You'd blow up all the bridges and tunnels and leave us stranded." He looked at the detective on the other line again and caught the faintest glimmer of hope in the man's eyes. "What happens after the seven-forty-seven takes off with the money and your men? What do we do then?"

"One man," Huckleby said slowly, "will stay behind from a position of surveillance. He will have the control panel which activates the bombs in the trucks. Only when he is certain that the aircraft has reached its destination will he arrange for you to receive the duplicate keys for each truck, so that you may deactivate the circuits and disarm the bombs."

"Where is this destination?" Scrivens asked. He saw the detective give him a thumbs-up signal and knew he had to draw the conversation out a little further. The Avenger was getting careless, staying on the line this long. Maybe he was also tired, his

292

guard dropping. "That could be sometime tomorrow when they get there."

"Only I know the destination," Huckleby replied. "Not even the captain of the aircraft has been told. He has sealed instructions which he will open only when the aircraft has taken off. Then you will also know."

"Why all the secrecy now?" Scrivens yelled into the mouthpiece as he realized Huckleby was about to hang up. The question fell on a dead phone. Disgusted, he turned around to see the detective busily scribbling something on a pad in front of him.

"Well?" Scrivens felt it was a useless query; he was certain that the elusive caller had escaped detection again.

"Jersey," the detective said excitedly. "Somewhere in the Cliffside region. Fort Lee, Edgewater, somewhere around there."

"Nothing more?" The area figured, Scrivens thought. Denton had guessed the calls were being made from that region; you could see the whole George Washington Bridge from there.

"No, but you can bet it's a high rise," the detective answered, echoing Scrivens's thoughts. "There aren't too many of them." He ripped the sheet from the pad. "I'll get onto the commissioner. He can contact the Jersey authorities to close in on all likely buildings."

What good will that do? Scrivens wanted to ask, but he did not have the heart to destroy the detective's optimism. Even if they located the Avenger, they'd never be able to take him out before he pulled every switch on his goddamned control panel. We're still stuck until he decides he's played with us long enough.

Each minute that dragged past was pure torture for Linda Huckleby. Each minute brought with it the possibility of another death, the culmination of another lie her father had told her. He was mad. He had to be mad to have dreamed up this wild, dangerous scheme in the first place. And in his madness, he had not known truth from fiction when he had told her about it or when he had enlisted Stiehl's assistance.

293

But she could stop it. She could stop it all. Other than Stiehl, only she knew from where the operation was being masterminded. Could she remain anonymous through it all? Walk away with a clean slate? That had been the plan. Certainly the police would trace her because Huckleby was controlling the city from her apartment. But she would say she had argued with her father and had left the apartment since she did not want to live in a home he had bought for her. She had no idea that he planned to use the apartment for his command post. The police would be able to do nothing to her. They would have no evidence linking her to the scheme.

Her eyes strayed to the telephone in the room. She willed herself to walk the four paces required to reach it, pick up the receiver, and ask the switchboard operator to put her through to police headquarters. Somehow her feet stayed fixed to the floor, unwilling to obey the simple command put out by her brain, unable to betray her father.

The driver of the police car looked nervously to his right. He saw Denton sitting rigidly in the seat, ashes from the cigarette in his mouth spilling over his trousers.

"You all right, sir?" Christ help us, the driver thought, the son of a bitch has had a heart attack in the middle of it all.

Denton seemed not to hear the question, nor did he notice the ashes on his legs. Staring through the windshield of the car as it barreled along the empty street, his eyes were wide open, focused on some distant spot.

"Pull in," he ordered the driver as he took the cigarette from his mouth and tossed it through the window.

"What's the matter?"

"Just pull in, damn it!" Denton waited for the car to come to a complete halt before he unlatched the radio mike. "Get me the commissioner. Quick!" He fidgeted while the call was made, cursing himself for not having spotted the connection earlier. That telephone number Günther Werner had scribbled on the pack of German cigarettes: the New Jersey number of Howson

Chemicals. Of course, it hadn't tied in at the time, but it sure as hell did now. Otherwise, why was Harlan Stone Huckleby's name on the list of possible suspects with a revenge motive against the city? His wife had been killed because a police unit had tried to play hero. That was why Werner had the number in his possession when he arrived in New York. So he could report in. One of an army of international terrorists arriving in New York and reporting to his commander. Huckleby was behind the whole damned thing. That would account for the hundreds of tons of high explosive now sitting at critical points around the city, the massive transportation plan required. Huckleby would have the whole damned thing at his fingertips, working through his corporation's normal channels.

"The commissioner's on the line, sir." The driver's voice shocked Denton back into reality.

"This is Denton. Call off all the search squads except for Harlan Stone Huckleby in Upper Montclair. He's our man. Tell Jersey to hit the place right now, but I bet he's not home."

"General Huckleby?" May sounded incredulous. "The president of Howson Chemicals?"

"Yes, General Huckleby. Remember Günther Werner, the kraut who got killed by the cops at the start of this whole business? He had a telephone number for Howson Chemicals scrawled on a pack of cigarettes." Denton racked his brains, trying to place circumstances, names, times. "I tried the number and got some guy called Adcock. Then I called Huckleby himself. He denied all knowledge of anyone called Werner and said that the guy I first spoke to, this Adcock, was the company's South African man or something, over here to hone up on new products. That's when I forgot about the whole thing, thinking the number was a German exchange, since it was written on a pack of German cigarettes."

"I'll see to it," May promised. "By the way, the telephone company's got a partial trace on the last call, somewhere in the Fort Lee, Cliffside Park area of Jersey. Right by the bridge."

"What do you know?" Denton said, half in wonder, half in

annoyance that it had taken so long to get a trace. Damned marvelous that the phone trap would be out when they needed it most. "I'm on my way into Police Plaza right now. I want to be there the next time that nut calls up to speak to Scrivens. Maybe our knowing who he is will tip him over the edge, make him give it all up before those bastards get off the ground at Kennedy."

"And maybe it'll make him throw a few switches just to keep his hand in," May warned. "Be careful, we're dealing with a madman."

"No shit." Denton replaced the mike and ordered the driver to carry on. He sat back and willed himself to be patient, just long enough to wait for the next call to come in. Then they would see how tough the Avenger's nerve was when he realized his identity was no longer a secret.

The heavy drapes were closed tightly, leaving the master bedroom of the Howard Beach apartment in virtual darkness. The only light came from the television, reflecting a rainbow of colors onto the opposite wall, where Peter Stiehl sat, a cigarette held loosely between the index and middle fingers of his right hand, his eyes taking in the events on the screen. The morning had been unnaturally quiet, no sounds of aircraft taking off from Kennedy, nothing except the chorus of birds making the most of the unexpected opportunity of having the sky to themselves.

Stiehl stood up to stretch himself, first his arms above his head, then his back, finally his legs, relieving the cramp caused by prolonged inactivity. Soon he would be out of here, finished forever with Peter Adcock of the Rand *Daily Mail*. Again he would be himself, Peter Stiehl, soldier of fortune and best-selling author. Maybe his next book would be about the long night just finished. A title came to mind almost immediately: *The Night They Stole Manhattan*. Repeating it a few times, he decided he liked the sound of it. The book might even be another best seller, but it would also put him behind bars for the rest of his life. Perhaps it would be best if he never attempted to write another book. Just leave it at the one; he certainly would never need money again after tonight.

He turned his attention again to the television set. Money was being loaded onto the skycrane, with members of his group following it triumphantly. Stiehl looked down at his watch, pleased that everything was still going according to schedule. They would be taking off at midday. He spared a moment to think about McGrath, trapped in the Lincoln Tunnel. He knew the feud between McGrath and Kerrigan had been bitter, but he had never expected Kerrigan to leave McGrath trapped in the truck. Not that it mattered. McGrath would spend the remainder of his life in jail, unless he tried to escape from the truck, and Stiehl did not think he had the courage for such a drastic step. The Irishman could not put the finger on him. All he could do was point to a man named Adcock. And the police, unless they were incredibly inept, would already be looking for a man named Adcock. No, McGrath would be no problem.

Stiehl wondered about Huckleby as well. He was still uncertain whether the man would give himself up to the police with the truck keys as he had promised to. Stiehl had misjudged him badly. The man had hidden his craziness well when they were together, using patriotism as his reason for the strike against Manhattan. Even when Stiehl had learned from Linda her father's reason for selecting New York, he had not been unduly concerned; he'd even found something to admire in the retired general's taking the opportunity to add a little personal revenge to the scheme. But when those kids had been trapped in the wreck on the George Washington Bridge, Stiehl had realized how mad Huckleby was. Now there was no way of knowing which way he would turn, what he would do.

All Stiehl could do was pray, and he had given up that habit so long ago he could not even remember how to begin.

New Jersey State Police and FBI units raided Huckleby's house in Upper Montclair and the Newark headquarters of Howson Chemicals simultaneously, while a team from New York hit the Long Island City warehouses. Of Huckleby, there was no sign. His housekeeper in Upper Montclair had not seen him for two days. The staff at the head office and at Long Island

City were of no greater help. Police specialists tore all three premises apart. They knew what they were looking for: any scrap of information that would definitely tie in Harlan Stone Huckleby with the attack on Manhattan or give the location of where he was overseeing the operation.

One unit found the order forms for the excess explosives in Huckleby's desk, stapled to the leasing forms for the trucks. While they were searching for more information, two FBI agents broke into the apparently abandoned warehouse, finding the bunks, the field kitchen, and other debris from the terrorists' stay; the map of Manhattan was still on the warehouse wall. Another agent entered the locked dispatcher's hut, where he discovered three M-16 rifles and a pair of infrared night glasses, all meticulously wiped clean of fingerprints.

Everything pointed to Huckleby. Nothing showed police where he might be.

Rosen got off the helicopter first, standing back to film the disembarkation of the manacled terrorists, followed by a squad of police officers. Fifty yards away, a Pan Am 747SP stood alone on the apron, a ring of police cars surrounding it. Rosen thought he could see a wall of faces staring out from the terminal windows, but he was uncertain because of the patchy sunlight reflecting off the glass.

The camera continued rolling as the terrorists were unchained and escorted aboard the waiting aircraft. They looked out the ports as the valuable cargo was loaded. Rosen wondered what was going through their minds. Pride that they had struck a blow for their respective causes? Or pride that they had pulled off the biggest heist of all time? Either way it did not matter. They were getting away with it, and the city of New York was a billion dollars poorer, not to mention a bridge or two and a few lives.

Denton had been back at police headquarters exactly seven minutes when the next telephone call for Mayor Scrivens was routed through. He saw Scrivens pick up the receiver and nod to the detective on the tracer line.

"This is the mayor. What do you want now?"

"How much longer is everything going to take?" Huckleby demanded. "I still think you're trying to trick me, and you know what's going to happen if you do."

Keep him calm, Scrivens advised himself. And keep him talking. "We wouldn't try to trick you. We haven't done it yet, and we won't do it now. We can't afford any more accidents."

"That's good. That's very good. Now how much money has been taken to the airport so far? How many of my men are there?"

"I don't have the exact figures," Scrivens said slowly. "About half your men are at Kennedy now; the others are on their way." Out of the corner of his eye, he saw Denton trying to attract his attention. He placed a hand over the mouthpiece. "What is it?"

"You know his name," the inspector whispered. "Use it."

"Are you sure?"

"Sure of what? That it's his name or that it's right to use it?"

"Both."

"Only one way to find out," Denton said. "Call him by it."

Scrivens removed his hand from the mouthpiece; at the other end of the line, Huckleby's voice was reaching fever pitch. "I know you're trying to trace this call! You're trying to trick me! But you won't win, damn it! You won't win!"

"Go on," Denton urged. "For Christ's sake, get on with it!"

Scrivens took a deep breath. "Take it easy, General Huckleby. We understand why you're doing this. Believe me, we even feel sorry for you about your wife." He looked glumly at Denton. "Forget it, he hung up as soon as I mentioned his name."

"Now what?"

"I'm going to appeal to him over the television," Scrivens decided. "Who's left?"

"The relief crew from MetroCity. They took over when Rosen and O'Neill went down to the heliport."

"Get it set up," Scrivens ordered. "Maybe if Huckleby thinks everyone knows his true identity, he'll pack it in. Turn over the keys and call it quits before anyone else gets blown off the face of the earth."

Denton mulled over the mayor's logic. "I hope you know what the hell you're doing, Mr. Mayor. One wrong word from you, and he'll flick every goddamned switch he's got."

"That's the chance I've got to take," Scrivens said.

The excitement, the anxiety, and the fury which he had been experiencing by increasing degrees were getting to Huckleby. His chest was bursting, his heart hammering through his rib cage. He had found the nitroglycerin tablets, but they no longer helped. As he looked over the Hudson at Manhattan, his vision blurred. The tall buildings on the other side of the water swam mistily in front of his eyes for a second, before he blinked them clear. Scrivens's voice over the television went unnoticed as Huckleby tried to control his body's faltering mechanism. Then he concentrated on the mayor's words.

"General Huckleby"—the soft, persuasive tones of the mayor purred silkily from the television speaker—"you are harming millions of innocent people. Your argument is not with the people of this city. I know I speak for all of them when I say how sorry we are about your wife and how indignant we are about the way"—Scrivens paused, not wanting to be seen laying blame on the police; their votes would also count in the next election—"the situation was so grossly mishandled. But nothing can be accomplished, nothing can be changed by what you are doing now. Please surrender yourself. Hand over the keys to those trucks. Hand them over before any more harm is done. We do not want to hurt you, General Huckleby. We want to help you. Make it easier on yourself by giving up now."

The last words had hardly died away before Huckleby was on the telephone, dialing frenziedly. "This is Huckleby! Give me Scrivens!" The mayor came on immediately, breathless from his ordeal in front of the camera.

"Scrivens here."

"I'll give you those keys when I'm damned good and ready, and not a moment before. You can't see it now, but you'll thank me in the future. Every American will thank me. I'm harming a few to save millions."

300

"You're what?"

"Saving millions of American lives. I couldn't give a damn about your city or who gets hurt there. I'm doing this to prove that our government has no defense policy. That we are powerless against any kind of invasion. I've proved it with this operation."

Scrivens was speechless. He stood gaping stupidly while Huckleby's words flooded over him, slowly understanding, remembering Huckleby's appearances before congressional panels on defense, before Senate subcommittees.

"You can't take those keys away from me," Huckleby carried on. "You can't capture me. Even if you knew where I was—and you won't until I'm ready to tell you—your men couldn't capture me. No matter what they tried—gas, sharpshooters, everything. I'd still have time to throw all the switches, and you know what that would mean. Now get off my back!"

The telephone slammed down in Scrivens's ear. He ran a hand across his wet forehead and looked at Denton for help. All the inspector could offer was a look of sympathy. There was nothing anyone could do until Huckleby was ready to end the drama by himself.

By eleven-thirty—half an hour before the deadline for the commandeered aircraft to take off for its undisclosed destination—all the terrorists and $485 million had been transported to Kennedy. None of the terrorists had shown the slightest interest in counting the money, although some had looked inside the bags to be certain they contained bills, not useless stacks of newspaper.

Inside the 747 the passengers strapped themselves into their seats, while the three Syrian pilots settled in on the flight deck, checking gauges, waiting for clearance to take off. On the captain's lap lay a bulky brown envelope containing the closing orders from the man who had organized the raid, the destination of the aircraft, and further, final instructions. Despite his curiosity, Mahmoud Assar did not let his fingers stray to the envelope, open the flap, and peer inside to learn the destination. His orders had been explicit—not to open the envelope until the 747 was airborne. He would obey those orders. The rough, summary justice handed out to Omar Baroudi had been enough to instill iron discipline in everyone. Nevertheless, he was certain the plane's destination was Libya.

In first class, Dieter Kirchmann sat next to Rolf Haller, with Magda Breitner and Horst Fischer directly behind. Conversation among the four was stilted, as if none of them could believe the attack had gone so successfully. No resistance. No fight. The city had just given in. Now they were on their way to a friendly nation with a planeload of money to be spent on furnishing a modern arsenal for every urban guerrilla group in the world. They would have no trouble finding arms sources. Russia was never curious where the money originated for the arms it supplied. Nor were the Czechs. With that kind of money, they could afford to buy the best. Perhaps even a small, easily concealed low-yield nuclear device; what power could be wielded with that!

Of the Irish, spread throughout the tourist cabin, only Kerrigan was talkative, regaling Coughlin with details of how he had left McGrath unconscious inside the Lincoln Tunnel truck. Coughlin grinned halfheartedly, knowing the story would be Kerrigan's main talking point for the next two years he spent in a Belfast pub, if any of them ever saw a Belfast pub again or had the courage to enter one.

On the tarmac outside the giant airliner, Babs O'Neill and Rosen stood listlessly. The newsmakers were inside the aircraft now. All that could be seen of them was the occasional glimpse of a face through one of the ports. Their part of the story was over. Rosen laid his camera on the ground and stretched himself. His mouth felt dry as he moved his tongue around, trying to find moisture. When he spoke, his voice was cracked.

"You know, Babs, when I was a kid, every time I'd see a plane or a train I always wanted to be on it. You ever get that kind of feeling?"

Babs smiled at him. "I know what you mean. You'd like to be

302

on any plane going any place . . . as long as it isn't this one."

"You've got it." He turned away to look at the hundred-plus police officers who ringed the aircraft. "Reckon we should ask some of New York's Finest how it feels to watch crooks fly off with the loot right under their noses?"

"We'd never be allowed to screen the replies." Nevertheless, Babs walked over to a police captain. "What happens now?" she asked. "When do the trucks get disarmed?"

"Soon as this thing gets into the air and reaches its destination. Which could be at least ten hours, depending on where it's headed. Huckleby will continue to hold the bridges and tunnel to ensure the aircraft's safety."

"Huckleby?" Babs asked, puzzled by the sudden appearance of the name. She had not yet heard of the results of the search team's work or of the use of the retired general's name on television. "General Harlan Stone Huckleby?"

"Yeah, he's the brains behind this whole thing," the captain said. "We identified him only a few minutes ago. He wanted to prove how right he was about the United States' being unable to repel an invasion. And he chose New York because he blamed the city for his wife's death." He brought Babs up to date quickly, using an economy of words to tell the story. When the captain had finished, Babs stood for fully a minute, unaware of what was going on around her, unconscious of the captain's concerned stare. Harlan Stone Huckleby? How did he fit into all this? Then she remembered her first interview with Inspector Denton concerning the Werner shooting, when Denton had shown her the pack of German cigarettes with the Howson Chemicals telephone number. Almost in a trance, she walked back to Rosen.

"Jerry, pick up your camera, and get us on the air. Something's just come up which is going to take a hell of a lot of explaining. If it can be explained at all."

Without asking questions, Rosen called the station to tell them to expect a feed. He picked up the camera and stepped away from Babs, catching her against the background of the waiting aircraft, moving around to bring in some of the policemen. As he waited for her to begin, he wondered what she could have learned.

"At Kennedy Airport, twenty-five minutes remain before the deadline runs out for the departure of the terrorists' aircraft," Babs said, dipping into her reservoir of memories as she tried to construct the story. "Police have learned the identity of the man behind the invasion of Manhattan, General Harlan Stone Huckleby, the multimillionaire president of Howson Chemicals in Newark, New Jersey. His motive? There were two of them. The first, to show by action what he had always preached, that this country is incapable of withstanding an invasion by enemy forces; secondly, he wanted revenge on New York City because his wife"—Babs struggled to remember the woman's name, finally coming up with it—"Alice, was killed during a bank robbery, when police, instead of bargaining with the robbers for the release of their hostages, decided to shoot it out.

"What nobody seems to have picked up yet is this. Alice Huckleby was killed by a member of the Puerto Rican FALN terrorist movement during the shoot-out. Yet General Huckleby has drafted an entire army composed of international terrorists for his attack on New York City. What baffles me—and I'm certain that a lot of police officers are now asking themselves the same question—is why General Huckleby should ally himself with the same kinds of thugs who were responsible for his wife's death. There is an old saying that politics make strange bedfellows. But this devil's alliance seems to beat everything. Babs O'Neill, MetroCity, Kennedy Airport."

With Inspector Denton for company, Mayor Scrivens kept a watch on the situation as it progressed, using both the reportage of Babs O'Neill and messages from police units reporting in. Scrivens's despair was lifted only by the knowledge that no more accidents had occurred. Huckleby was apparently keeping his word.

"Mr. Mayor, it's for you." A police sergeant appeared at Scrivens's elbow, holding out a telephone.

304

"Thanks. He put the receiver to his ear. "This is Scrivens."

"Mayor Scrivens?" A woman's voice, trembling, on the verge of tears.

"Yes," he said impatiently. "What do you want?"

"This is Linda Huckleby. I think I know where you can find my father."

20

SCRIVENS WAVED frantically at Denton to pick up an extension. "Did you say Linda Huckleby?"

"Yes." Linda hesitated, trying to choose her words carefully. "General Huckleby is my father. We had a big argument a few days ago—"

"What about?" Scrivens interrupted.

"It doesn't matter what caused it. But I moved out of the apartment Daddy bought for me. The fight was terrible, and I couldn't stay any longer in a home he'd bought for me. I think that's where he is now."

"Where is this apartment?"

"In Jersey. Fort Lee."

Scrivens clutched the receiver harder. When he looked across the room at Denton, the inspector was grinning in triumph. "Go on, Miss Huckleby. I'm listening."

"I've been watching this terrible thing on television—"

"Where from?" Scrivens cut in again, as Denton prompted him.

"From my hotel in Manhattan, the Americana. It's where I've been staying since I left the apartment. Now that the police say it's Daddy who's controlling the attack, I'm certain he's using my old apartment for it. He said he could see the bridge from where he was." The conversation broke down as the girl's voice wavered; then Scrivens could hear sobbing.

"Are you all right, Miss Huckleby?" He could think of nothing else to say.

Gradually the crying ceased. "The picture window of the living room looks out over the bridge," she said. "He can see both levels from there."

"What's the address?"

Linda gave it to him. Both Scrivens and Denton jotted it down. "Will anything happen to me?" she asked.

"That's difficult to say," Scrivens replied. He saw that Denton was off the extension, running to another telephone to alert the New Jersey authorities. "Why did you wait so long to call us?"

"Because I didn't know it was Daddy. I had no idea he would do anything like this. He's been acting very strangely for the past few months, as though he were leading up to something. He's very ill, you see, and I thought that might be affecting him. And he still hasn't got over Mother's death."

"So you had this argument?"

"Yes . . ." She began to sob again, and Scrivens strained to catch her words. "It was about a man I had been seeing. Daddy didn't like him very much. He said if I continued to see him, he'd cut me off without a penny. That was when I left. I couldn't stand to be around him anymore, not when he was stooping to blackmail."

"That was all?"

"What else should there be?" Linda asked.

"Don't leave the Americana." Scrivens felt like a police officer. Maybe he should have been, instead of going into law and then politics. Walking a beat—even in the South Bronx—must be a damned sight easier on the heart than being mayor. "We'll get back to you later on."

* * *

Backed up by local police, twenty federal agents surrounded the high-rise condominium building, taking cover behind cars as they awaited the next move. The agent in charge called for a bullhorn. He saw no point in evacuating the building. He just wanted to get Huckleby out of there as quickly as possible.

"General Huckleby! General Huckleby! Do you hear me?" The amplified words boomed back at him from the building's steep walls. Several tenants looked out their windows and moved back when police waved at them. "This is the FBI. The entire building is surrounded. We know you are there. You have no chance to escape. Give yourself up before anyone else is hurt."

Federal agents and police waited, all eyes on the window which the building manager had pointed out to them. Then the agent with the bullhorn tried again.

"General Huckleby! Do you hear me?"

"I can hear you!" The shout eddied down fourteen stories from the doorway which joined the apartment's living room to the balcony. "Go away! Before I blow up the trucks!"

"Huckleby!" The agent stopped whatever he was about to say. He looked to his right, where another man squatted, a twenty-two target rifle with a high-powered telescopic sight nestling into his shoulder.

"See if you can get him out on the balcony," the sharpshooter whispered. "One glimpse is all I need."

The agent nodded. "General Huckleby, we'd like to talk to you. We can hardly hear you from inside the apartment. Come out on the balcony, where we can hear you better."

The top of the balcony door was visible from the ground as it swung fully open. Beside him, the agent felt the sharpshooter tense up, finger curled around the trigger as his right eye sought the target which would appear any moment on the balcony.

"I'm holding the control panel!" Huckleby shouted down. "If you try to shoot me, I'll fall on it. Do you want that?" He came out onto the balcony, into full view. The agent pushed down the rifle. Huckleby had the control panel resting on the balcony ledge, hands poised above it, like a pianist at the keyboard.

"No, we don't want that," the agent said through the bullhorn. "That's the last thing we want." The sharpshooter quickly slid the rifle under a car, out of sight. "We just want you to come down here where we can help you. Give us the keys to those trucks."

From the balcony, his fingers covering as many switches as possible, Huckleby stared down at the police and federal agents. "Come and get them if you think you can. I told Scrivens that I'd turn them all over when I was good and ready. And not a moment before!" He leaned back as he finished speaking, his head light, the pounding in his chest reaching a point of excruciating agony. His left arm ached intolerably, and he wondered if he was having a heart attack right now. No, he couldn't be. God had promised to let him live long enough to see his dream come true, his revenge complete. Eyes watering, he checked his watch; another fifteen minutes to the scheduled takeoff. Surely he could last that long. Then it would not matter what happened.

He struggled to lift the heavy control panel and staggered back inside the apartment, kicking the door closed with his foot. The air conditioning made him feel better. He slumped down in the chair by the window. The police could wait. They would still be on hand when he was ready to surrender.

Scrivens had never felt so totally helpless in his entire life. Even against the earlier catastrophes which had befallen his administration—battling with the municipal unions, ordering out plows to defeat the blizzards of February, drafting the unemployed to fix the roads—he had managed to fight back. Now he could do nothing but watch the television screen as preparations were made for the Pan Am 747SP to take off with its cargo of terrorists and money. The telephone call from Huckleby's daughter had not really helped. Although they now knew Huckleby's location, there was nothing they could do. Scrivens was certain that Linda Huckleby was in the clear. Her father had used her, precipitated the row to drive her out of the apartment and give himself access to it. Detectives were on their way to the Americana now, to take the girl's statement, to try to learn if she fitted in anywhere. Scrivens doubted that she would. Nobody in his right mind would be a part of this holocaust.

Exhausted, he dropped down behind a desk, eyes riveted on the screen. The aircraft was moving slowly. The ring of police and official cars broke up to let the 747 taxi to the runway. Good-bye, he thought bitterly. Good-bye, terrorists. Good-bye, money. Good-bye to all hopes of reelection. He wondered if there was any point in calling Huckleby. He had the telephone number now. He could call the army general turned lunatic just as Huckleby had called him. He dismissed the idea. It would serve no useful purpose. All he could do was hope Huckleby would keep his word and turn over the keys once the aircraft had reached its destination, wherever that was supposed to be.

Scrivens was surprised to find himself subconsciously praying that the three Syrian pilots knew how to handle the huge aircraft. The last thing he wanted was an accident. All air force planes had been ordered to give the 747 a wide berth, stay well clear of its flight path. There was to be no interference from any sector.

Come on, God, Scrivens whispered, digging his nails into the palms of his hands. Listen to me, hear my prayers. Don't let them crash, God. Please don't let them crash.

Show those Arab motherfuckers how to fly that goddamned plane!

The interior of the aircraft was silent except for the hum of the engines. All the passengers felt drained by what they had been through, a sudden, sweeping flushing of all emotions as the 747 trundled over concrete toward its takeoff point. It was over. They had achieved the impossible, taken an aircraft loaded with hundreds of bags of money from the United States, and brought the nerve center of the country to a complete halt.

On the flight deck, Mahmoud Assar sat in the captain's seat, chest puffed up with pride as he guided the 747 to its position.

310

He looked sideways at his first officer, Hassan Basri, and behind to Abdul Wasim. Their eyes reflected the joy Assar felt, the culmination of a dream. Assar pressed down on the brakes, holding the 747 steady at the top of the runway, its engines murmuring.

"Freedom Flight One to Kennedy Tower. Request permission to take off." His English was clipped, unnatural.

"Kennedy Tower to"—a pause while the air controller verified the flight nomenclature—"to Freedom Flight One. You are cleared for takeoff. No other aircraft is within a fifty-mile radius of your present position." Normal procedure went by the board as the controller read off weather reports to Assar; he just wanted this 747 out of his jurisdiction as soon as possible, so that the airport—not to mention the city—could get back to normal. "Go on," he muttered, holding his hand over the transmitter, "get the hell out of here. And I hope some Hebe shoots your nuts off, one at a fucking time."

Assar pushed forward on the throttles and held the plane with the brakes while the engines reached an eardrum-splitting crescendo. The aircraft shuddered from the force of the thrust. Checking the gauges a final time, he released the brakes. The 747 began to move, slowly at first, rolling forward gently, then faster, faster still. Assar kept one eye on the knots, holding down the nose until the aircraft reached takeoff speed. Then he lifted back, and the nose began to rise; the aircraft soared upward, turning onto an easterly heading.

"Open the envelope," he said to Hassan Basri. "Tell our passengers where we are bound."

Basri felt himself pressed back into the first officer's seat by the force of gravity as he pulled back the flap of the brown envelope. "This is your first officer speaking," he called in English over the public address system. "We are about to open our sealed orders. Soon we will know which country will receive us as heroes."

The top of the envelope came away. Basri shook the contents into his lap. He looked puzzled as he gazed at the sheets of blank

311

white typing paper. "I don't understand," he said softly, forgetting that his words were being relayed throughout the aircraft. "There must be some mistake."

"What is the matter?" Wasim asked from the second officer's seat.

"There is nothing here but blank paper. What does it mean?"

Stiehl stood deep in the shadow of the bedroom, a sheet of asbestos propped up against the wall behind him. The window was wide open, a gentle breeze blowing in to fan his face. He felt at ease, ready for action. The waiting was finally over.

He glanced at the television without hearing Babs O'Neill's commentary. The big plane rumbled along the runway and lifted into the air. Soon the roar of engines changed place, coming from behind and above him instead of from the television. He gave a last look at the screen, watching the 747 become nothing more tangible than a speck in the sky. Then the entire house began to shake as the plane passed low overhead. The sound of the television was drowned out; ornaments on the dressing table jumped and chattered with the vibration as Assar made no attempt to gain enough height to limit the discomfort of nearby residents, as qualified airline pilots did as a matter of course.

Almost leisurely, Stiehl lifted the Redeye surface-to-air missile launcher he had taken from the trunk of Huckleby's Cadillac. He rested the launcher on his shoulder, sighted in on the Pan Am airliner, and fired.

The explosion was lost in the roar of the jet. Flame ripped from the back of the launcher, splattering harmlessly onto the asbestos. The missile sliced through space and began to rise, homing in on the 747, slashing the distance toward its target.

Stiehl dropped the empty tube onto the bed and ran from the apartment. He pulled off the white cotton gloves as he vaulted down the stairs, confident that the sound of the missile's launch had been blotted out by the roar of the jet passing low overhead. He could still hear the thunder of the engines as he reached the street. Then a dramatic explosion filled the air. Shock waves danced across the sky, shaking houses like an earthquake.

Later that day he would be able to read about and hear what others in the neighborhood had seen. The sudden white-hot explosion, the aircraft turning into a gigantic fireball before breaking up and plunging into a screaming dive toward the water.

"The plane's down!"

The three words shouted by a police sergeant were enough to create five seconds of pure silence at police headquarters. Denton's mouth sagged open as the implications of the crash became immediately clear to him. Scrivens felt his blood turn to iced water, chilling his veins. What had happened? Pilot error? Or a grandstanding air force pilot determined not to let this planeload of terrorists get away? It had to be pilot error. Please, God, let it be so. The three Syrians had never flown a jumbo before. Everything had been done to accommodate their lack of experience. And still, they had made one fatal error. But how could you prove that to a lunatic like Huckleby?

Scrivens swallowed deeply. "See if you can get a lead on what went wrong," he said to Denton. "Before I call Huckleby and beg him not to blow up his trucks."

Denton moved away swiftly. He returned less than a minute later. "All air force planes and police helicopters were grounded. So were civilian flights in the area. The 747 had clear airspace. But"—he drew out the word, not for effect but because he was unsure he could believe what he had to say—"radar reports a blip on the screen. Very small. Very quick. Seemed to rise out of nowhere and home in on the 747 as it passed over the Howard Beach area."

"A blip?" asked Scrivens incredulously. "You mean a surface-to-air missile?"

"That's what it sounds like to me."

"Oh, my God." Scrivens breathed out the words. Another nut, a member of one of these ultrapatriotic, right-wing, lunatic associations, sitting on his own private arsenal, determined that he alone would avenge the country by sending these terrorists to a

313

fiery death. Scrivens knew some of the crazies had enough small arms to equip a moderately sized infantry company, but where the hell had they got hold of a guided missile?

"We've got men checking on it now," Denton said, his words intruding into Scrivens's blackest thoughts. "House to house across the entire neighborhood. But the roar of the plane was so great, flying so low, that maybe nobody heard the sound of a missile being fired. If there was a missile."

"Of course there was," Scrivens said. There had to be. The way his luck was running, it could be nothing else. He sighed with the air of a theatrical Caesar going out to meet his fate on the Ides of March. "May as well get hold of Huckleby and get it over with. We needed a few new bridges anyway."

He called for a police sergeant to connect him with the luxury high-rise apartment in Fort Lee, using the time he spent waiting to formulate what he would say. Should he plead ignorance, say he had no idea why the plane had crashed? That was closest to the truth. Or should he come on heavy, tell Huckleby that it had been done on purpose, try to shock him into surrendering with a show of strength?

A telephone was thrust into his hand. All his thoughts flew away, leaving him with a blank mind. "General Huckleby?"

"This is Huckleby." The voice seemed calmer than Scrivens had heard it before; the irrationality and madness were no longer there.

"Mayor Scrivens here. Your plane has crashed." He waited for the explosion of words, the sudden sound of a receiver being slammed down, the torrent of threats. None came; only silence. "We're trying to find out what happened, General. It may have been a case of pilot error. There were no other aircraft within a fifty-mile radius to interfere with the 747. We followed your instructions very carefully." Was he getting through to the madman? By now he had expected Huckleby to throw every switch on his control panel. Come on, for God's sake; say something.

"I know all about the plane," Huckleby said eventually. "I

314

know about its crashing. The news was given on television."

"You're not going to do anything, are you? You're not going to hold us responsible for it, are you?" Scrivens's voice quaked. Huckleby's quiet, relaxed voice worried him more than the hysterical threats had ever done. He was coming down to the final showdown now and fancied his chances less than ever. "It wasn't our fault, General Huckleby. We obeyed your instructions to the letter, did everything you wanted." Damn it; he was repeating himself. "Please don't detonate your trucks."

"I won't."

So wrapped up was Scrivens in his own thoughts of the devastation that could befall the city at any moment he did not hear Huckleby's words. "Whatever happened to that plane was not our fault. You've got to believe me."

"I said I wouldn't detonate the trucks. You have kept your part of the bargain."

"You what?"

"The aircraft reached its destination," Huckleby said hollowly. "In fifteen minutes I will be ready to surrender myself to the police officers stationed outside this building. You will then have the keys, and you will be able to disarm the trucks."

"What do you mean the plane reached its destination?" Scrivens was flabbergasted. Huckleby might have sounded the calmest he had sounded throughout the whole ordeal, but his words were making no sense at all. "Your plane's in a million pieces across Jamaica Bay!" he yelled. "And you're trying to tell me it reached its destination!"

"That's correct, Mr. Mayor. That's exactly where it was supposed to finish up. In a million pieces in Jamaica Bay. You will have your keys in fifteen minutes, when I surrender myself to the police. Good-bye."

Scrivens held the dead phone, gazing blankly at Denton, who had been listening on the extension. "What do you make of that?" he finally asked.

"Not too much," Denton admitted. "Just be thankful he's calling it a day. At least, it saves our government the trouble of

315

trying to extradite them. All we've got to do now is drag the bay." He even managed a slight, cynical grin. "And it's only paper money—doesn't mean a goddamned thing."

Tom and Juliet Brenner greeted Stiehl excitedly when he arrived back at their house in Howard Beach. "You missed all the action," Tom told him. "We saw that plane carrying the terrorists explode over the bay. You should have been here."

"Where's little Peter?" he asked, disregarding their words.

"In the yard," Juliet replied. "Something wrong?"

"There could be. Unless you both swear I was here the entire night. And get little Peter to tell the same story if anyone asks him."

Tom Brenner held out a hand, laying it on his brother-in-law's arm. "What is it, Peter? Were you mixed up in that business?"

Stiehl recognized the look of alarm which spread swiftly across his sister's face and knew the inner turmoil she was suffering. He could not lie to her, but at least he could bend the truth. "Only in the ending, nothing else."

"The Concorde," Brenner whispered. "Is that how you did it? When I asked you once about bringing down the Concorde, you told me about some missiles. Which one did you use?"

"Does it really matter?"

Brenner allowed a smile to creep across his face, the tedium of his accountancy profession relieved for an instant by his relationship with this South African. "I guess not. As long as it worked out fine."

"Where was I last night?" Stiehl asked.

"Here," Brenner answered immediately. "The whole night. You had dinner with us, and we all stayed up till two in the morning watching the excitement on television."

"That's right," Juliet added. "The three of us sat together on the couch in the living room, glued to the set. Couldn't tear our eyes away." She kissed her brother lightly on the cheek and headed for the yard. "Peter!" she called out to her son. "Come in here. Uncle Peter's got a game he wants to play with you."

316

The excitement at Kennedy Airport was over. The police units which had acted as both escorts for the terrorists and guards for the huge amount of money dispersed slowly. They seemed to be unwilling to leave the scene as if they were trying to extend for another minute, another second, their identification with the greatest crime in history.

From the other side of the Pan Am terminal, a helicopter clattered into the air, carrying Rosen and Babs O'Neill to Fort Lee to cover the final chapter of the night's events. They said little during the short flight, content to look down at the city. As they passed by the George Washington Bridge, Rosen asked the pilot to guide the craft alongside the lower level. Havlicek's truck was still there, gray, immobile, between the two support towers at the New York end. Two police officers sat in a yellow and blue Port Authority cruiser next to the truck, guarding it against further lunacy.

The high-rise apartment building from which Huckleby had controlled the operation was ringed with police cars. Uniformed local police and neatly dressed federal agents stood by idly as the fifteen minutes Huckleby had requested to put his affairs in order ticked away. Eyes lifted momentarily as the helicopter passed overhead before settling down gracefully in the parking lot. Babs was first out, followed by Rosen. He ran over to the station's other remote unit, which had been ordered to Fort Lee, and grabbed a camera for another live feed. Later, when he was good and ready, he would take off a couple of weeks, sit down with a few cases of beer, and edit the videotape into one beaut of an Emmy-winning program.

Babs sought out the FBI agent in charge, the man who had earlier called on Huckleby to surrender. "What's the situation?"

He began to answer, then held out his hand, palm facing her. "Ssshhh . . ." He pointed upward, and Babs raised her eyes to see what was so important.

High above them, on a fourteenth-floor balcony, a body leaned over the brickwork, a man with iron gray hair cut short.

317

A large brown envelope fluttered down, twisting this way and that as it fought against the air, finally landing with a jingling noise at Babs's feet. She stepped forward to look at it, but the federal agent swooped first. He tore at the flap, shaking the contents to the ground. Keys tumbled out, each with a tag attached. Babs caught a glimpse of the simple block lettering on one tag. "Queens Midtown Tunnel," it read.

"He's jumping!"

The yell came from somewhere behind Babs. One of the local police officers had recognized the intention as soon as Huckleby raised his right leg and propped his foot on the brick ledge of the balcony. Rosen raised the camera quickly, fumbling with the controls in his excitement, zooming in close. High on the balcony ledge, the rest of Huckleby's body appeared, straight out one moment, plummeting down the next, arms and legs spinning in a human cartwheel. The body loomed larger in Rosen's viewfinder; there was no expression on the face; the lips were pressed tight together, eyes wide open.

As the body filled Rosen's vision, an alert federal agent grabbed the cameraman by the shoulders and dragged him back. Huckleby smashed to the ground an instant later, his blood spattering the MetroCity cameraman.

Scrivens put down the telephone and closed his eyes in a silent prayer of gratitude. Huckleby was dead. The police had the keys. It was all over. The nightmare, by some miracle, had finished. God had tested the resolve of the city's first black mayor again, and he had not been found wanting. Soon the trucks would be rendered harmless, their deadly loads driven away. The explosives would be either put into storage for future, legal use or detonated harmlessly.

Mentally Scrivens began to count the cost. The destruction of the Triborough Bridge's Manhattan ramp. Police officers dead. The Harlem River bridges. The cost of the blackout to the Bronx. And the airliner in Jamaica Bay, with all the terrorists certainly dead. That, as far as Scrivens was concerned, was an entry in the profit column. Police launches were in Jamaica Bay now to keep away fortune hunters from the mass of sodden money which was beginning to surface, much burned, many more millions still serviceable. Divers would go down later in the day to salvage all the money so that it could be destroyed. And to learn why the aircraft had exploded in midair. It had to be a guided missile launched from the shoreline, Scrivens was certain. Long after Babs O'Neill had made the first connection between Huckleby's wife and the terrorists, Scrivens had been given the same facts. Another part of Huckleby's mad scheme of revenge, he thought: Use them; then destroy them.

He opened his eyes and saw Denton moving toward him, a grim expression on his face. "Don't relax too soon, Mr. Mayor, It's not over yet."

Scrivens felt a cold finger trace down his spine. "What do you mean? Huckleby's dead. We have the keys. What else is there?"

"Remember what that O'Neill woman said on television? One of the terrorists is still trapped in the Lincoln Tunnel truck. End of a vendetta, knocked unconscious and left there by his partner."

"So the police will pick him up," Scrivens said. "And we'll finally get a lead on this whole mess, a witness who might be able to tell us who fired that missile. Other than what Huckleby's daughter can tell us—if she can tell us anything, which I doubt—we haven't got a thing to go on."

"We're getting the keys over to the respective police units now," Denton told the mayor. "Helilifting them in to save time. I'm in contact with the unit at the New York end of the Lincoln Tunnel. I want to see that man as soon as he's brought out."

"Fine. Look after it. And get traffic moving as soon as possible after the bridges are cleared. We'll show the world that New York can take it and still come up swinging."

Danny McGrath checked his watch. Twelve-thirty-five in the afternoon. The aircraft carrying the others had taken off thirty-five minutes earlier if everything had gone according to schedule. It was well clear of the United States, heading east across the Atlantic with one billion dollars. And he was stuck here, a prisoner in the truck's cab until the police came to get him.

He saw the glimmer of headlights coming around the curve reflected on the shiny tiled wall of the tunnel. Seconds later a blue and yellow Port Authority patrol car came cruising into view, two men in the front, a third in the back. The car stopped five yards from the truck. All three officers got out and walked warily toward their objective. The lead patrolman held something shiny in his hand, with a cardboard tag attached to it.

McGrath moved uneasily on the seat, perspiration making him stick to the vinyl through the cloth of his trousers. So this was it. The end of the adventure. They would unlock the door and take him out. Get him into the police car and beat him half to death, save just enough of his life's energy so that he could stand trial. Then a lifetime in jail. A short lifetime, guaranteed.

The patrolman with the key stopped by the passenger door and looked in through the window, studying McGrath thoughtfully. Didn't look like much, the patrolman mused. Weedy, thick glasses, and greasy hair. Is this an example of what terrorized the city? Brought it to its knees and almost made off with a billion dollars? Just goes to show you, looks don't mean a damned thing.

He reached up with the key, aiming at the door handle, hand steady, brain implicitly believing what Huckleby had promised. The key would turn easily, and the circuit would be deactivated, the explosive filling the truck made harmless.

McGrath grabbed at the inside handle a split second before the patrolman could turn the key. He felt absolutely nothing, not even the slightest whisper of the awesome energy he had set into motion. All he knew was the heady exultation of being the master of his own destiny, being able to control his final moments. The feeling of triumph might have been even sweeter had he known he had outlived Patrick Kerrigan by almost half an hour.

The roar of the explosion blasted through the New York-bound tube of the tunnel. The roof crashed in, the sides blew out in one stupendous, booming eruption. Tongues of flame leaped out from the center of the explosion, doused seconds later when the filthy waters of the Hudson River found a new path. Atomized particles of the truck mixed with pieces of blue and yellow painted metal from the patrol car, swirling along in the eddying waters.

For five seconds the other two tubes remained aloof from the destruction, shaken but not mortally wounded by the shock waves. Then trickles of water began to appear, sliding down the tiled walls, dropping onto the roadway. The trickles became streams, then rivers. Bricks and cement collapsed in the path of nature's oldest sources of energy. Gaping holes appeared as water poured in, gaining strength, probing weaknesses, finding new breaches, enlarging them. Pressure increased until the remaining defenses could take no more. They crumbled inward, yielding the battle, allowing the Hudson to duplicate the invasion it had perpetrated on the first tube.

By the toll booths at the New Jersey end of the tunnel, curious state troopers and Port Authority patrolmen ventured into all three tubes. The explosion had sounded like a gigantic cough, a blast of hot air ripping out from beneath the ground. The silence which followed was unnerving. The officers came to the water, ripples breaking quietly at their feet. Slowly, almost unable to believe what they had seen, they retreated to their cars, radioing in the news. It was impossible. The Lincoln Tunnel was like Manhattan itself, there for all eternity. And now it was no longer there. It was just another part of the riverbed.

One trooper separated himself from his colleagues and went to the trunk of his car. He pulled out a sheet of white cardboard and a black Magic Marker. He scribbled something on the board, then took a stand from the car which he set up by the toll booths. As he stood back to admire his handiwork, other troopers joined him, gathering in a small semicircle to look at the sign.

"Lincoln Tunnel closed until further notice."

21

THE CITY BEGAN to buzz again, a giant awakening from a deep sleep which had been filled with numerous uninterpretable nightmares. Tunnels and bridges were open, blocked by traffic streaming in and out of Manhattan. The congestion was caused by the destruction of the Triborough Bridge, the Lincoln Tunnel, and the Harlem River bridges and exacerbated by the throngs of motorists who came only to look, as if being near the scene would make them a part of the drama. Breathing heavily from force-fed oxygen, subway repair crews strained to clear the wrecked trains. City engineers perused the damages and guessed more than estimated when work could begin on reconstruction. Money for the repairs would come from the federal government. The President had already assured Mayor Scrivens of that. New York was vital to him for the next presidential election. In Jamaica Bay, police launches maintained their vigil over the area of the wreck, keeping away fortune hunters. The temptation for police to pocket any of the waterlogged bills was pushed away by the knowledge that they, too, were being watched, by federal agents and by countless representatives from the international press. And everywhere, police and federal agents were hunting a man named Adcock.

Two police cars drew up outside the real estate office in Howard Beach where Stiehl had gone after returning from the recruiting trip to Europe and the Middle East. A sergeant went in to ask about the two-family house the company represented. The same girl who had attended to Stiehl came forward, to see what the trouble was.

"We had a report of an explosion," the sergeant replied, consulting his notes. A neighbor had heard a whooshing, roaring sound coming from the direction of the house's upper floor. "Do you have the name of the party you rented it to?"

"I'll just check." She returned with a file. "An Englishman called Peter Adcock. Correspondent for a South African newspaper, the Rand *Daily Mail*. Paid cash."

Adcock. The sergeant looked down again at his notes. Yes, that name was there, too. But he had the man down as a South African, not a limey. Same difference.

"Can you show us over the place, miss?"

"Is it dangerous?"

"Not anymore. He's long gone. We just want to see what he left."

The girl stayed in the police car while the sergeant used the spare key to let himself in to the upstairs apartment. He threw back the door and stepped aside as two patrolmen carrying riot guns charged past. As the sergeant had guessed, the apartment was empty. The only signs of a former tenant were the overflowing ashtray, two large wooden crates on the bedroom floor, the rocket launcher tube on the bed, and the sheet of asbestos against the wall. The sergeant began to examine the asbestos, rubbing his finger experimentally across the center of the scorch mark. "Considerate bastard," he said to the two patrolmen. "Maybe he wanted to get his month's security back." He returned to the car and called in, saying the girl from the real estate office was on her way to give a description of Peter Adcock to the police artist. Maybe that would be something to go on. The police would have nothing else. Stiehl had been far too thorough for them.

The sergeant left one of the patrolmen to guard the apartment till the forensic experts arrived. Let them make of the cigarettes what they could.

MetroCity station owner Charles Kohn was penning his signature on the second check when the door to his office opened. He completed the check and looked up, eyes blinking in shock as he recognized Babs O'Neill and Jerry Rosen. They looked terrible, as if they had been out on a weeklong bender without going home at all to clean up. Babs's normally immaculate hair was awry, ends tangled, greasy. Deep bags sagged underneath her eyes, and her deportment had gone completely; she didn't walk, she slouched into his office. Rosen, too, looked asleep on his feet, sandy hair unkempt, face lined, gray eyes tired.

"You can both take Sunday off," Kohn said grandly, feeling it an opportune time to demonstrate an infrequent flash of humor. "In repayment for the job you did."

Babs eyed him coldly, not even bothering to smile. "Blow it out your left nostril, Charlie. I'm taking the whole damned week off after we get this thing together. So's Jerry."

"Jerry?"

"Yeah, me," Rosen said. "The guy who's been *shlepping* a camera around for the past three hundred years without any sleep. Remember me? You woke me up sometime yesterday— maybe the day before—to go look at something in the South Bronx."

Kohn bent down and took the two checks from the top of his desk, holding out one in each hand. "See if this eases your disposition at all," he said gruffly. "It's a little token of thanks for all the work you did. A bonus."

Babs glanced down. "Twenty-five hundred." She whistled. "What's the matter, Charlie? Succumbing to an incurable attack of generosity in your old age?"

Kohn waved a self-deprecating hand. "You deserve it."

"Guess we do at that." She turned to Rosen. "How about it, Jerry?"

He was looking at his own check. "Some deserve it more than others," was all he said.

"What do you mean?" She snatched the check from his grasp and studied the figure. "You're a cheap shit, Charlie! You know that? How come Jerry's only getting a thousand?"

Kohn's eyes opened wide in surprise at Babs's defense of Rosen. "You're the star of the show, Babs. That's why. Jerry's only the cameraman."

"Without a good cameraman, you don't get a star of the show, you jerk!" she retorted angrily. "If Jerry doesn't get the same, we're both going somewhere else. After last night there won't be any shortage of offers."

Kohn knew when not to fight. Reaching out for Rosen's check, he tore it into pieces and let them flutter to the floor like confetti. He pulled out a fresh check and began to make it out, this time for twenty-five hundred dollars. He could not complain. The station would be in the black for a year to come with what it had made from Babs's and Rosen's coverage. Still, there was never any harm in trying. He blotted his signature carefully and passed the check across.

"Happy now?"

Babs looked at the check in Rosen's hands. "I guess you could say that. Thanks, Charlie. You're really a sweet guy to work for, even if you do your best to hide it."

Kohn's face turned beetroot red as she leaned forward and kissed him on the cheek.

Stiehl was telling his nephew about Australia when the doorbell rang twice, long, insistent buzzes that indicated authority had come to call. He heard his sister call out that she would get it, followed by Tom Brenner's voice saying he would. Stiehl cocked his head at the sound of voices as the front door was opened, wondering what was going to happen during the next few minutes. The Browning was upstairs, stripped down and hid-

325

den in the false bottom of the suitcase, the dummy round in position at the top of the magazine. He could not use the gun here, not without implicating his sister and her family by association. The passport in the name of Adcock was gone forever, burned beyond recognition, its ashes scattered. Even the South African government would never be able to connect him with the fake document since its issuance was never registered in its files.

The living-room door opened, and Tom Brenner ushered in two men wearing civilian clothes. Behind them, Juliet Brenner hovered nervously.

"Peter." Brenner directed the words to his brother-in-law, not his son. "These two men are detectives. They want to ask us about what happened today. About that plane crashing in the bay."

"Just routine, sir," the older detective said, a man in his early forties; he sounded almost apologetic. "Did you ever see this man before?" He held out a copy of the sketch made from the real estate girl's description. It was good, Stiehl had to admit it; damned good. The felt hat, the thick horn-rimmed glasses with the shaded lenses. Her memory must be acute. It was Adcock to a T. It also bore little resemblance to Peter Stiehl.

"Can't say I have," Stiehl replied. "How about you?" he asked Brenner and Juliet.

"Nothing here," Brenner answered. "What do you want him for?"

"This guy rented an apartment where a missile was fired from to bring down that terrorist plane. He was an Englishman, supposedly working for a South African newspaper, the Rand *Daily Mail*. Or so he said. The newspaper has no record of him. Name was Adcock. Peter Adcock."

Stiehl looked studious. "Adcock. Wait a minute, why does that name ring a bell?"

The two detectives looked hopeful. Brenner's face was aghast, while Juliet turned her eyes away.

"Can you tell us anything about him, sir?"

Stiehl continued to look puzzled, rubbing his chin with his fingers. "I've got it!" he exclaimed, snapping his fingers. "It's just come to me, what with you mentioning the Rand *Daily Mail* and all. A man named Adcock used to play cricket for South Africa, twenty years ago or more. Fast bowler. But I think his first name was Neil, not Peter." He looked at the two detectives to see if they had understood what he was talking about; he was sure they had not. "My sister"—he indicated Juliet—"and I are from South Africa. You gentlemen just brought up a couple of familiar names."

"Oh." As if controlled by the same set of muscles, the detectives' faces dropped. "Thanks anyway. Sorry to have bothered you folks."

"That's all right," Brenner said, recovering quickly, unable to understand how his brother-in-law could make jokes at such a time. "I'll see you to the door."

Stiehl waited till the detectives had left the room; then he turned back to his nephew. "Now, where were we?"

"You were telling me about koala bears."

"Yes, that's right. Koala bears with their funny little faces and sharp claws." He carried on with the story as if the intrusion by the two detectives had never taken place.

Accompanied by Inspector Denton, Linda Huckleby was allowed to return to the Fort Lee apartment long enough to pick up clothes and personal effects. The living room was a mess, with police technicians pulling up the carpet, ripping apart the furniture, and even probing the walls. Linda had no idea what they hoped to find, and when she asked Denton, he was unable to tell her.

When she was ready to leave, she stood by the picture window and looked out over the bridge, oblivious to the activity around her. Had so much really happened since the night her father had brought Peter Stiehl to the apartment to show him the same view? She felt a lump in her throat, a pressure behind her eyes, and knew that tears would soon come. She walked out onto the balcony and blew her nose. Whom was she crying for? she wondered. Her father? Or for herself? She had been resigned for a long time to her father's passing, ever since the doctor had imparted the news of his illness to her mother and her. Why should she cry now?

From the door to the balcony, Denton kept a watchful eye on the girl. He knew from his own investigation that she had undergone intensive therapy following her mother's violent death. What effect, now, would her father's even more spectacular demise have? He was worried about the balcony. Maybe it hadn't been such a good idea to let her visit the apartment. Even worse, to let her wander out onto the balcony. Her father had jumped from there. Almost involuntarily he stepped out of the door and said, "Miss Huckleby, we'd better get you back to the hotel now."

She turned around and saw the middle-aged police inspector framed in the doorway. "Don't worry, I wasn't about to jump."

"I never thought you were," he lied. He could see the tears nestling in her eyes; they seemed to soften the brilliant shade of violet. "Shall we go?"

Linda took a last look over the balcony, first the bridge, then the opposite shoreline. "I think so." She accepted his outstretched hand as he helped her back inside.

As far as Denton was concerned, Linda had taken no part in the operation. She had had an argument with her father—obviously planned on his part, as it now appeared—and had walked out of the apartment. Her answers fitted in with his own conclusions. He did not believe that she knew anything about the man Huckleby had hired, this Peter Adcock, who turned up at too many important junctions to be anything other than the mastermind responsible for putting Huckleby's mad dream together. Successive interrogations had failed to change her story.

"What do you plan on doing now?" Denton asked as he dropped her at the hotel.

"Go to the funeral tomorrow," she replied. "After that I think I'd like to go away for a long trip, wash some of the last year out of my mind."

"It's been rough, hasn't it?" he said sympathetically.

"You could call it that. Traumatic is closer to the truth."

When Linda attended the funeral the following day, at the

remote cemetery in northern New Jersey where her mother had been buried, no military personnel were present to bid Huckleby farewell. No flag was available. The army was having nothing to do with the man who had disgraced the rank he once held. Among the mourners were faces Linda had never seen. Journalists and federal agents, whose main concern was not the deceased but the possibility that the missing Peter Adcock might show up to pay his last respects. They were disappointed.

For the next four days she did not leave the hotel room. Her meals were sent in, and hotel security staff kept the reporters away. Then, at seven o'clock on Monday evening, six days after New York had been rescued, Linda took a suitcase down to the hotel lobby and waited while the doorman hailed a cab. The taxi took her to the southeast corner of First Avenue and Sixty-first Street, almost underneath the Queensborough Bridge. As she alighted and paid the fare, a rented dark blue Thunderbird slid away from the curb and pulled into the space left by the taxi. Linda got in, pushing her suitcase onto the back seat. Stiehl gunned the motor, and the big car gathered speed toward the northbound FDR Drive only two blocks away.

"How are you feeling?" he asked.

She passed a hand across her forehead. "Better. I think the worst is over. You knew all along he was going to kill himself, didn't you?"

"Yes. But not that way."

"How then?"

"He told me he was going to miss out on his pills when the pain began. Make it natural, a heart attack."

"Looks like he lied to a few of us," Linda said. "You know something, when I was at the apartment the other day to collect some belongings, I stood out on the balcony where he jumped from, and I realized something."

"Oh? What was that?"

"I don't think I ever knew my father. I knew a general, a career officer named Huckleby. And I knew a company president named Huckleby. I don't think either of them was my father."

Stiehl understood what she was trying to say. "I think your father was a very complex man. Too many different facets to his personality. In the end, the complexities became too much for him to handle. That's when he cracked up." He jerked a thumb toward the back of the car. "Is that all you're taking with you?"

"I can buy new."

"Once they sort your father's will out, you can. Only I think his estate is going to be tied up in the courts for a long time to come, with the city suing for damages."

"Can they do that?"

"I would think so."

"I'll have to live off your money then," she said.

He laughed. "I think we're tied together whether we like it or not. Only you can identify me to the police, and I can tie you into the operation as well. You knew about it beforehand; you're as guilty as I am."

"I like the idea of being tied together with you." She laid her hand gently on his thigh, feeling his muscles tense. "So where to now? You mentioned Switzerland, but I never thought we'd be starting the journey on the FDR Drive."

He changed lanes and crossed the small rise leading to the Harlem River Drive. On the right, he could see repair crews working on the first of the bridges which had been damaged. Ahead of him, a notice was pasted over the sign directing traffic to the Triborough Bridge and Queens. "Ramp closed," it read.

"You can't be seen leaving the country," Stiehl said.

"I told the police I was going away for a long time."

Stiehl nodded. "Nevertheless, we'll use the Canadian border. You're an American citizen, so they'll wave you right through." He concentrated again on driving, flicking his eyes right each time they passed one of the damaged Harlem River bridges, until at last they came to the George Washington Bridge leading into New Jersey. The Thunderbird raced across the span, turning onto the Palisades Parkway, from which they could pick up the New York Thruway. As he drove, Stiehl thought over his decision to move Linda to Switzerland, set her up in Geneva, where she could remain while he went off to the Horn of Africa to find another taker for his specialized services. Since the conclusion of Huckleby's operation Stiehl had searched his soul deeply, realizing he could never be happy living off accumulated wealth. He needed action to live, as other men needed oxygen. To him, it was lifeblood, the very essence of his being. Without it, he was empty. Perhaps that was why he had agreed to go along with Huckleby. Life was fast becoming too dull for his liking.

Linda had to go with him, that was obvious. She'd be all right in Switzerland, with her fluent French, German, and Italian. Her background in art would not go amiss either; she'd find an interesting position to occupy her mind. Stiehl realized Linda was in love with him, and he questioned his own feelings about the girl. Did he love her? Or was it as close to love as he would ever allow himself to get? He needed someone, a woman who would be waiting for him whenever he returned from one of his trips, till that final moment when he decided that he was getting too old or his reflexes were becoming too slow for the life he loved. The tension, the anxiety, the sudden snap of a battle won by better planning, superior preparation.

By five the following morning, with Linda fast asleep on the passenger seat, Stiehl drove the car into the airport parking lot at Buffalo. Linda woke up, and they walked into the airport terminal to wait for the early-morning flight to Toronto, one hundred miles away. Customs and immigration checks at Toronto were nothing more than a formality. As soon as they were through, they went directly to the Air Canada desk and booked two first-class reservations on the nine o'clock flight that evening to London. With twelve hours to wait, they took a taxi to one of the airport hotels, where they slept, too exhausted by the long drive even to think about making love. At six in the evening the switchboard rang through with their wake-up call.

Despite the hours they had slept during the day, neither Linda nor Stiehl had the slightest difficulty in falling asleep again. They woke just in time to see the sun rise over the Atlantic, only ninety minutes from their destination. At Heathrow, they took a shuttle bus from Terminal Three to Terminal Two, which handled inter-European flights, and booked on the next Swissair plane to Geneva. Stiehl had always liked Geneva, full enough of old-world charm to make him forget the steel and concrete jungle of New York. He was looking forward to arriving. Perhaps he would even stay there a month with Linda before continuing on to Africa. A rest would do him good, tune him up for the work he would surely find.

An hour before takeoff, passengers were called. Stiehl passed through the scanner and waited for Linda to join him. They sat for half an hour, watching other passengers flit in and out of the duty-free shop. Stiehl checked his pockets and decided he needed cigarettes. He picked up a carton of Dunhills and waited in line to pay. A Japanese youth with slicked-down black hair and gold-rimmed glasses was ahead of him. Stiehl amused himself by trying to guess the age of the youth. He could never tell; the Oriental facial structure seemed designed to disguise a man's age. Stiehl waited patiently while the youth fumbled with some change, obviously unused to British currency.

Back in the lounge, Stiehl watched the Japanese youth walk over to two friends who were waiting for him. As soon as he sat down, the small group began to talk excitedly, glancing around every few seconds to see if their conversation was being heard or understood in other quarters. Stiehl took his own seat, next to Linda, but paid no attention to what she was saying. There was something about the Japanese trio that intrigued him. Perhaps it was just because they were there, in the lounge, waiting for the flight to Geneva. What would they want in Geneva? Were they investing in a bank over there?

Deciding he was being fanciful, he pushed the doubts to the back of his mind and concentrated on Linda instead. She really was beautiful, he decided, looking into her clear blue eyes. Maybe he'd spend two months in Geneva with her, he thought.

"Swissair Flight Eight-sixty-one to Geneva is now boarding at gate eleven."

As one, the passengers rose and headed in the direction of the gate. Stiehl took Linda's arm and joined the throng. They would have to stay in a hotel for the first few nights; then he would look for an apartment. After that, work. He did not have any contacts in Switzerland. The country did not produce mercenaries. Only bankers. And cows with bells around their necks.

As he stepped into the aircraft, he spotted the Japanese youth who had been in the duty-free shop. Another of the group was six rows back; of the third there was no sign. Looking over his shoulder at the people still waiting to board, Stiehl thought he recognized him at the rear of the crowd. Again, that prickling, nagging doubt assailed him. Now they were split up, whereas they had been together before. Had they booked late and been forced to take what was available? He had booked late as well, and he had got two seats together. It was like the dream all over again. Always being chased but never being caught. Never escaping either. It didn't add up.

Ten minutes after the aircraft took off, a flight attendant came around, offering coffee or orange juice. Stiehl and Linda took coffee. He raised his cup in a mock salute.

"To our new country. Pretend we're drinking Dom Pérignon."

She was about to reply when her violet eyes opened wide in fright. Stiehl began to turn his head to see what had scared her, but he knew it could be only one thing. He put down the cup of coffee and sighed aloud.

Maybe he should have suggested to Huckleby that he include these lunatics in the operation as well, he decided. Then these three would be in Jamaica Bay with the rest of them; they would not be on this plane instead.

Geneva's Cointrin Airport was in a state of turmoil. Anxious relatives and friends of passengers aboard Flight 861 crowded around the Swissair desk, their eyes held by the useless piece of information that the incoming flight from London had been delayed indefinitely. "Interested parties," it read, "should contact the airline directly."

"We'll tell you whatever we know as soon as we learn something," a harassed airline official told the crowd in German,

French, and English. "At the moment, the aircraft is heading toward Africa. When we know anything else, we will let you know."

He felt sorry for the people. They had a right to know what was happening to their loved ones. But even he could not tell them much. All he knew was that three Japanese Red Army terrorists had somehow managed to smuggle guns on board the plane in London and take it over.

He could see it being a very long night.